Freda Lightfoot

Freda Lightfoot was born in Lancashire but lived in the
Lake District for many years where she was a teacher,
bookseller and smallholder. She is married with two
grown-up daughters and still visits the Lakes as often
as she can.

Luckpenny Land

Freda Lightfoot

CORONET BOOKS
Hodder and Stoughton

British Library Cataloguing in Publication Data

Lightfoot, Freda
Luckpenny Land
I. Title
823.914[F]

ISBN 0 340 63519 3

Printed and bound in Great Britain by
Mackays of Chatham plc, Chatham, Kent

Hodder and Stoughton
A division of Hodder Headline PLC
338 Euston Road
London NW1 3BH

TO DAVID
with my love

Although this story is set in the Eastern Fells of the Lake District, the farms and their immediate environs are entirely fictitious. Whilst trying to give a flavour of the Cumbrian dialect, for the sake of clarity I have not attempted to reproduce it exactly.

I would like to offer my sincere thanks to all the people who have given so freely of their memories, expertise and hospitality. In particular, Mr and Mrs Vic Gregg, Miss H. M. T. Frankland, Lena Hill, Dorothy Knowles, Harold Wright. And to Veronica Toft who first introduced me to the joys and tribulations of keeping sheep. Any mistakes, or liberties I have taken for the sake of the plot, are entirely my responsibility and not theirs.

1938

1

'Anyone would think I was asking to go on the streets.'

The stinging slap sent the honey gold hair swirling about her face, enveloping her burning cheeks in a wash of colour that for a brief moment lit up the shabby kitchen.

Any ordinary face would have been hardened and cheapened by the cold light of the single Tilly lamp, but not this one. The girl's face was arresting, alive with the urgency of her request. There was strength in the way she firmed the wide mouth, resolution in the sweeping arch of the brow, in the smoke grey of the eyes fringed by a crescent of dark lashes above cheek bones that would hold their beauty long after time had wrought its damage.

But there was no one to be captivated by Meg Turner's youthful beauty here, certainly not her uncompromising father. Even her two brothers had withdrawn from the scene to a safer distance the moment supper was over, Dan to check the flock for any new lambs, Charlie reluctantly to clean out the sheds.

The remnants of the kitchen fire fell together with a small hushing noise. There was no other sound in the room, save for that of the rain that beat against the window. Outside, great waves of it washed down the hillsides from the high mountain tops, gushed into the overfilled beck and pelted onwards to the River Kent and the distant sea. They were used to rain in Lakeland and paid little heed to it, and the glowering skies seemed eminently suited to her mood. Meg wished she was out in it, letting it wash over her face and limbs, cleansing the pain and frustration from her as it so often did. The wind was rising, she could hear it whining in the great ash trees that lined the track to the farm and gave the name Ashlea to the place that had been her home for all of her nineteen years.

Inconsequentially, she remembered leaving a blanket loose on the line. She'd have to search for it in the bottom field come morning. Nothing that wasn't battened down would survive the helm wind that scoured these high fells. Though the wind could not penetrate the walls of the farmhouse which were four feet thick, solid enough to withstand the worst mountain weather, and keep her within, like a prisoner, Meg thought with resentment.

She started to clear the table with jerky, angry movements, swallowing the bitter tears of disappointment that threatened to choke her. She supposed the slap was no more than she deserved. She shouldn't have dared to repeat the rebellious statement she had made to Dan earlier when he had caught her pulling pints at the Cock and Feathers.

'Get your coat on,' he'd bluntly told her. 'You're coming home with me.'

She hadn't been able to believe her bad luck, having deliberately chosen the inn because it was far from the market area of town where her father conducted his business. Not for one moment had she considered the possibility of her own brother choosing to drink there. But losing her temper, she knew from experience, would get her nowhere. Hadn't she discovered so a dozen times?

Nevertheless, since it had taken her weeks to find this job, she wasn't for giving in easily. 'I'll not,' she'd said, continuing to pull pints, feeling the excitement of defiance in the pit of her stomach.

When she'd tossed back a ragged abundance of honeyed curls from slender shoulders, an unconsciously sensuous act, not a man in the room would not have willingly championed her.

Only Dan Turner was not a man to take on lightly.

The elder of the two Turner brothers, his short stature belied the beefy power of him. In his tweed jacket and waistcoat, flat cap jauntily tilted to one side of his large bullet head, he looked even more intimidating than in his more usual working overalls. He had the typically round, handsome Turner face, broad nose and very slightly projecting ears. But unlike young Charlie, this brother seemed to wear a perpetual sneer, which drew up one corner of his mouth and flared the nostrils in a way that gave off a strong warning to leave well alone.

The farmers, recalling Dan Turner's expertise on the wrestling field, fascinated though they were by this little drama, had drawn back slightly, shuffling uncomfortably.

'You should be selling the eggs, not swanning around behind a bar.'

'The eggs are all sold. What's so terrible about a little job? You drink in enough of these places. Why shouldn't I work in one?'

'You know damn' well why, because you're a woman! God knows what Father will say.'

'It's only Saturday mornings, for pin money.' She had spoken with calm assurance, desperately wanting to disguise the unease that filled her at mention of her father's reaction. 'You're not going to tell on me, are you?' But he had.

Now the man at the head of the table glared at her with a cold fury in his eyes that made Dan's seem mild by comparison. 'How dare you speak like a loose woman at a Christian table? I'll wash thee mouth out wi' lye soap if I hear the like in my house again.'

Unrepentant, Meg returned her father's accusing gaze, a show of bravado she did not quite feel in her young, fiercely rebellious eyes. 'I was only trying to make the point that it is a perfectly respectable public-house.'

'Palace of sin, more like! You should be grateful for a good home and food on your plate, not always be prating on after summat different.'

'It's not that, you know it's not,' Meg cried.

She longed to reach out, to touch the rigid figure, to seek some sign of affection, but knew such a gesture would be considered a show of weakness. They had never been a family to display emotion.

Life was grinding hard on these Lakeland fells, governed by the changing seasons with little time for sentiment. The year began in October when the rams were put to the ewes. Through the harsh days and long nights of winter the hardy Herdwicks and Swaledales survived on scant grass where they could find it, eked out occasionally by croppings of ash and holly. In March and April the flock was brought down ready for lambing. Later there would be the sorting, marking, dosing, clipping and dipping that marked the farming year until the autumn sales came and it all started again.

But Meg felt she had no part in this routine. Her life was spent almost entirely within doors, even more so since the death of her mother six months ago. And after that Joe Turner had fashioned an even tougher shell about himself. If Meg had never managed to penetrate that shell, even as a young child, how could she hope to do so now?

And she no longer had her mother's protection. Without Annie's steady hand to calm him, who knew what her father might do? Joe Turner didn't like any show of independence from his women folk. He liked to know where they were at all times, and said as much, frequently.

As he was saying now.

'I'll not hev you wandering roond as if you had no home to go to and no proper work to do. If you're short o' summat to do you can scrub the hen arks out.'

'I've done them.'

Meg felt the hot rebellion drain from her, and her shoulders slumped. What was the use? She could never win. She stared at her father and despite all her best efforts, she hated him. She hated his round, pugnacious face, the skin below the eyes loose and flabby, dragging the lids down at each corner. She despised the too large nose seeming to overpower the thin upper lip, drawn under slightly, to show a pair of expensive false teeth that grinned at him each night from his bedside table.

Meg knew all about honouring one's father and mother. It had been drummed into her at hundreds of unwilling visits to chapel over the years. But though she had willingly and lovingly done the latter there were shaming moments when she wished that it was her father lying in the cold earth and not her lovely mum. She longed for Annie now with a passion that brought a physical pain to her young heart.

'Are ya gan tell me what it was all in aid of?'

Meg blinked the threat of tears impatiently away. 'Oh, for goodness' sake! I'm like stupid Cinderella in that daft fairy tale, and I won't stand for it any more. I want to have a life of me own. An *identity*.'

'Identity?' Her father's scathing tone made the word sound somehow not quite decent. 'Thoo's my daughter, that's who thoo are. What's wrong wi' that?'

Meg sighed, knowing he would never understand but unable to prevent herself from trying. 'I mean I've nothing that's just mine. No time to call my own, not a penny to spend that hasn't to be accounted for.'

'What do you need money for? Fol de rols, I suppose. Useless flibbertigibbets.'

Meg put her hand to her head which was starting to ache from the day's endless arguments. 'Don't talk daft.'

'Daft, am I? When hev you ever gone short? Tell me that. You only hev to ask.'

'That's just the point. Why should I have to ask? It's undignified, having to ask every time I need something.' She thought of her friend, Kath, who had a monthly allowance paid into her bank account and knew a twinge of uncharacteristic envy.

'I'm your father,' Joe said stolidly, as if that explained everything. 'I hope I can keep my family wi'out help from a slip of a girl.'

Twin spots of colour lit the high cheek bones. 'But I *want* to do it. Mrs Blamire gets run off her feet and says she can't cope with all the cooking and serving on busy days, as she did when she was younger.'

'Mrs Blamire may do as she thinks fit, but no daughter of mine will work in a taproom. If women'd stop at home where they belong we'd soon cure the unemployment problem, you mark my words. Wilful, that's what you are, and it's time you learnt your place.' Dark brows met with the ferocity of his anger. 'You hev the hen money. It was allus good enough for thee mother.'

But Meg wasn't for letting go too easy, not now she'd got this far. In truth she didn't rightly know what she wanted but her confused mind desperately searched for something. She couldn't even put a name to it. Freedom? A purpose to her mundane life? Something beyond bringing in the coal bucket. She didn't particularly like the idea of working in a pub but it had been a job she could do, with money of her own at the end of it. The feeling had been a good one. And now it was gone and her father would never permit her to find another.

But somewhere, somehow, there must be a place for her. A place beyond this kitchen.

On her feet now, her small pert bosom rising and falling on shallow breaths of anxiety, she met Joe Turner's gaze with commendable courage and battled on. 'I'm not me mother. I can't take her place for you. Things have changed a bit since her day. Women should have the same right to work as men do.'

'I can't believe I'm hearing this.'

The cold anger on his face was such that Meg quailed slightly and decided to take a different tack. Deliberately she softened her voice. 'Cock and Feathers is a respectable house and I'd get up early and see to your breakfast before I went. I've plenty of time to sell the eggs and vegetables at the market before I start, and after I finish I'd see you all had a hot dinner to come home to. You'd never notice I was gone.'

Not entirely unaware of his daughter's burgeoning womanhood, for the most part Joe chose to ignore it. But he certainly knew how to protect it.

'Thoo would be open to all manner o' lewd remarks from the scuff of the gutters that frequent such places. I hope I know my duty as a good Christian better than to let you. I'll hear no more aboot it. I hev my name to keep up at chapel. What would they think? That I couldn't afford to keep me own daughter at home? It don't bear thinking of. Working in a pub indeed, where folk spend money they can't afford on demon drink. It didn't tek long for someone to see you and tell our Dan noo, did it?'

Meg opened her mouth to protest that Dan had gone in the Cock and Feathers himself for the purpose of drinking, but thought better of it. It would only make matters worse.

'Finish the washing up and get to bed.'

Joe's tone was stark in its decisiveness and he turned away to pull on the old mackintosh that hung steaming before the fire. 'And there'll be nae dancing for you tonight. You'd best stop in for a bit, see if that'll get rid of your hysterics.'

Meg's heart plummeted and all her defiance fled. She could still recall the humiliation of being kept in for a whole month after she had dared visit the Roxy Picture House in Kendal.

It had been her sixteenth birthday and she and her best friend, Kath Ellis, had ridden in on their bikes to celebrate by drooling over Humphrey Bogart. They had dawdled on their way home, stopping for a hot meat pie at the corner shop and arriving home later than promised. Their giggling happiness had soon been squashed. Joe Turner had reached for his belt and only Annie's pleading had saved Meg from a very sound beating. Even so, the punishment of being kept in for four long weeks had seemed severe and still rankled, nearly three years later.

And now it was all happening again. Only worse. If she was kept in then she wouldn't be able to go with Kath to the supper dance. More important, she would miss seeing Jack. The thought made her shrivel up and die a little inside. She had loved Jack Lawson for as long as she could remember and lived in hope that he would notice her one day.

She'd made herself a new dress 'specially for tonight and now Jack would never see her in it. Hot tears stung the backs of her eyes as she fought for control.

'I'm not a child to be sent to my room.'

'You're behaving like one.'

6

'I'm trying to show you that I'm a grown woman who wants to start work instead of being skivvy to two idle numbskulls.' She dismissed her brothers with a flap of her hand. 'Why must everything be done for their convenience? Why have I no rights?'

'Because the farm will be theirs one day, not yours. Because they do all the work on it, not thee.'

Meg choked back the agony of unshed tears. 'That's not true. I work as hard as they do, harder. Our Dan only does what he has to and Charlie isn't interested in the land, you know he isn't.'

'He'll do what he's told. You all will. Noo have done. I've heard enough.' Joe started to walk away but beside herself with the anguish of not seeing Jack, Meg snatched at his arm and pulled him round to face her.

'I won't stay in, I won't! And I won't skivvy for them two any more. They could do a bit more for themselves for a change. Fetch coal in for a start.'

Joe Turner went white to the lips, the spurt of flame from the dying fire reflected in the charcoal of his eyes. 'My sons hev enough work of their own to do without taking on women's duties. Trouble with thee, young lady, is you don't know when you're well off. You've good clothes on thee back, food in thee belly. What more do you want?'

He set huge hands down upon the table top, hands that could bring a lamb from its mother as sweetly as butter, wring the life from a fat chicken or shoot a troublesome dog without flinching. He balled them now into threatening fists. A man who read his Bible nightly, he nevertheless considered it his duty to exercise discipline when it was needed. And this young madam was getting above herself.

'You let the lads do whatever they like, why not me?' She knew the answer so why did she torture herself by asking?

'I thowt I'd made that clear.'

'It's clear you'd have liked me a lot better if I'd been a lad too.' Tears were standing proud in her eyes but she would not let them fall.

'Happen you'd've been easier to manage if you were. Just tek a good look at yourself, madam. Eyes mad as fury. Hair all roond your neck like a wild woman.'

'Would you prefer it if I had it all cut off? Then I'd look like a boy too.' She tossed back the wayward locks with a defiant twist of her lovely head.

'I'd prefer thee to act wi' proper decency.'

'If that is the only way to make you see me as a real person, and not simply as your serving wench then so be it.'

7

Snatching up the shearing scissors from the dresser Meg pulled her tangled hair down over one shoulder and began to hack recklessly with the sharp blades. Glittering golden tresses rained upon the scrubbed table top, curling and bouncing about with a life of their own

Joe Turner reached for the shears but she danced away, evading him, and continued with her relentless massacre, forcing him to remain a helpless onlooker.

She might have continued on this self-desecration had he not slammed those same fists down upon the table, seeming to make the whole room quake.

'Enough. What would thy mother say if she saw thee acting so wantonly?'

Meg froze, tears brimming over at last from her clear grey eyes, making the room swim dizzily before her. *What had she done*? She stared at the bright curls falling away in her hand. He'd driven her to it. It was his fault. But she wouldn't let him see her distress. Against the greater tragedy of a desolate life, ruined hair seemed of little importance.

Meg gathered up the cut tendrils into her palm, and tossed them into the fire where they crackled and fired up. A lump came into her throat. She couldn't go to the supper looking like this, with half her hair cut off. What would Jack think of her now?

'Noo thy'll hev to stop in,' Joe said with satisfaction, clearly reading her thoughts and walked, spine rigid, from the room, his whole bearing making it clear that he'd had his say and won. As was only right and proper.

It took Meg the best part of an hour in her distress to finish the washing up, tidy the room and replenish the fire which had sulked itself black. When she had done, she refilled the big black kettle and set it back on the hob, so there'd be hot water for a mug of strong tea for her brothers when they got in. Then she took off her floral apron and hung it on the peg behind the pantry door before climbing dejectedly up the stairs to her room.

Hardly bigger than a cupboard tucked beneath the eaves right at the top of the house, it was at least her own. The only place where she could be sure of privacy.

Ashlea had been built some time during the early part of the eighteenth century. New by Lakeland standards, it was a typical, unprepossessing yeoman type building of grey stone with a slate roof and the traditional cylindrical chimneys. For all its plainness it had seemed warm and alive when her mother had lived in it, its homely rooms muddled and untidy with Annie's tapestry work, bottles for the lambs, and the usual boots and buckets of farming life.

Once the house had smelled of beeswax and lavender, overlaid by the strong tones of woodsmoke from the fire that burned constantly in the kitchen range. But Meg found she did not have the heart to reach these same standards. She could never rid her mouth of the taste of dust and unhappiness, as she coped with the cleaning of the five-bedroomed house all alone, and the endless washing, ironing and cooking for four people.

It wasn't that she didn't try. Meg longed to recapture the scents of those lovingly remembered days. Of home-baked bread, the sharpness of bilberry jam and the tangy aroma of her mother's blackberry and apple pie. But her own efforts seemed poor by comparison.

So she loved her tiny hideway high in the attic, the only place where no demands were made and she could be herself. From the window cut in the farmhouse roof she could see right over the stand of ash and rowan behind the farm to the heather-carpeted turf of the high fell, clotted with broom and juniper and punctuated with the grey rocks that resolutely burst out of the thin soil at every opportunity.

Now the rain and wind robbed her of the solace of this much loved view and she fell upon the bed and lay on her back, determined not to cry. But despite her best intentions great fat tears rolled out of the corners of her eyes and ran down into her ears. She had chosen the wrong moment. Why had she risked spoiling the dance for an impossible concession? What had possessed her to be so reckless?

The thought of dancing with Jack Lawson made her stomach quiver with excitement. Now she wouldn't see him at all and he'd chat up some other girl.

She got off the bed to stand in front of the speckled mirror and confront the horror of her hair. One side was long as ever, rippling in waves over her shoulder. The other side was short, sticking out in a madcap sort of way like a halo. The oddness of it suddenly appealed to her sense of humour and she felt a giggle start deep inside. What would everyone say if she left it like this? They'd think she'd gone mad. The shortness of it seemed to exaggerate the devilish gleam of hot rebellion that still burned in her grey eyes.

The laughter started then, bubbling up and spilling over in great spurts of glee. And suddenly it didn't matter what her father did. She was young, wasn't she? Soon the dull days of winter and a cold spring would lighten into summer.

There was still time to find some other way of escape. And she would, too. However much she might feel that she belonged here, at Ashlea, she wouldn't stay as anyone's skivvy.

What's more, if there was some way for her to go to the lambing supper, then she would find it. She must see Jack, she must. But first the hair. Meg opened a dressing-table drawer and took out a pair of scissors. Short hair, Kath said, was all the rage.

It was Charlie who championed her, as always. He came in on a bluster of cold wind, banging all the doors.

Dan and her father were upstairs getting washed and changed ready to go out and Meg was drying her hair in front of the fire. She had cut and washed it and now it sprang in short bouncy curls, a wild mass of golden colour about her head. She rather thought it suited her but was still self-conscious about it. Charlie sank wearily into a chair, telling her about the latest lambs to be born and put with their ewes in the barn for the night. It was a moment before he noticed her hair. When at last he did, an explanation had to be given and his young face darkened.

'He treats you as if it were still the dark ages instead of the twentieth century. Don't let him get away with it.'

Meg gave a rueful smile as she brewed tea and set a steaming mug in his hands. 'I think I already said more than I should. We had a real ding-dong.'

'He'll not keep me locked up. There's a war coming, you know. Hitler won't stop till he's got what he's after. All of Europe no less. While we fuss over the cost of building aeroplanes, German forces have taken over Austria. Where next? France? Poland?' His blue eyes came alight with fervour and he ran one grubby hand through hair only a shade paler than her own. 'I'll be one of the first to join up if war comes. You just see.'

'You're too young,' she laughed, rumpling his tangled curls affectionately, but he snatched himself away from her.

'Don't say that. You sound like Father.'

She was at once contrite. Charlie was not a natural farmer, being better with machines than the blood and gore that was an unavoidable part of country life. And Joe never let an opportunity pass to taunt his younger son about his squeamishness which hurt Meg as much as it did Charlie, for they were close.

10

'Come on, love, have a piece of gingerbread while I go and shut the hens up. It'll warm you. There might be more to lamb tonight and you'll need to cope alone with Father and Dan both going out.'

The hens were making those warm, contented chutterings as Meg slid down the door over the pop hole to keep them safe from unwelcome night visitors. She loved looking after the hens, sliding her hands under their soft bodies to capture warm eggs for breakfast, tickling them under their wings with powder to keep them free of mites. She loved talking to them as they scratched about, telling them her secrets, letting the peace of the night soak into her.

'Stay safe,' she warned them, hearing in the distance the bark of a lone dog fox.

The small animals were her province. Looking after the hens, and turkeys in season, feeding the pigs, milking the two cows that provided the family with milk, Meg enjoyed all of that. The animals made her life bearable. But she was not permitted to work with the sheep.

'Not women's work,' Joe said, when once she had asked if she might help. In such a way that she had not mentioned it again.

The desire for purposeful work, an identity of her own, was challenged only by the greater need now to see Jack Lawson.

Meg clasped her hands together and stared about her. The black mountains seemed to shield her, crouching closer as her eyes grew accustomed to the dark, attempting to pick out the familiar detail that scarred their smooth surface. 'Please help me to find the words to persuade Father to let me go to the dance.' She couldn't believe she had been so stupid as to risk missing it. 'I must see Jack, I must. And don't let there be a war.'

She'd heard talk of war a lot lately but never too seriously. 'Charlie's sixteen, young and headstrong. He thinks only of aeroplanes and adventure, do you see? Not the danger.'

Would Jack? If there was another war, then he too might be called up. Worry swamped her. Oh, she couldn't bear it if either of them went away. They might be wounded or killed. It made her go all sick and funny inside to think of it. And her own problems seem small by comparison.

Back in the kitchen she made a fresh pot of tea to warm herself, trying not to listen as Charlie chattered on about the latest aeroplane that would blast the enemy from the skies.

Her father came in, looking uncharacteristically smart in his

11

setting-off suit smelling faintly of mothballs, firmly buttoned over his best waistcoat. But then nothing looked more polished than a farmer dressed in his finest. A man's pride would see to that. The neb of his cap, which he wore for every occasion, whether a birthing or a chapel function, was curled downwards from long wear, following the line of his thinned lips.

'I hear you and Meg have been having a bit of a set-to,' said Charlie, somewhat recklessly in her opinion.

'Aye, you could say so.'

'If you don't let her go tonight, everyone will want to know why. There'll be gossip. This dale is famous for it.'

'Pity folks hev nowt better to do then,' he said tersely. But the point had been made. Joe Turner could not bear to lose face. There was a long pause while he considered, then he turned upon Meg. 'See you're quick aboot it then, if thoo's coming. We hev na got all night. And splash thy face with cold water.' He indicated Meg's cheeks, hot from the fire. 'We doan't want folks to know we've been heving a few words.'

The remnants of her pride in tatters, her life in ruins, but the façade of family unity must be kept up. A tearing row passed off as a 'few words'. But Meg didn't care. The only thing that mattered was that she was to be allowed to go. She could fight her battles another night.

2

The silence of the Lakeland night was profound as Meg followed her father and brother along the rutted lane to the school where the social was to be held. There was nothing to break the silence but the suck of moist earth at her heels, and the fast beating of her heart. Would Jack be there, as he had promised? Once she heard a rustling in the undergrowth and paused to watch the fleeting glimpse of the white rump of a roe deer, still clothed in its winter grey, as it blundered away from her.

'I'm so sorry to disturb you,' she whispered, moving more quietly still, afraid to disturb any other night creature.

There was no sign of Jack as she took one of the hard wooden chairs lined up around the walls of the main room in the school hall. A group of farmers' wives exchanged gossip at one end as they slapped margarine and potted meat on bread rolls, interrupted from time to time by the need to reprimand one of the younger children who were practising sliding on the candle-greased floor.

Her father and some of the other men had gone in to the meeting room next door to listen to a speaker, but in this hall a special licence had been obtained so there could be dancing.

Meg spotted 'Lanky' Lawson, Jack's father, so called because his stature was anything but. He was working the old wind-up gramophone and later, if pressed, she knew he would play his fiddle and they would all dance the old steps, the Cumberland Square Eight or the Ninepins Reel. Meg acknowledged his wave with a smile. He was a dear friend but this evening she was more interested in a modern waltz with his son. The kind of dance which meant Jack must hold her close.

Everyone seemed to be dancing. She looked about the room with a casual air, trying not to let it show that she felt conspicuous sitting all alone, or that she was looking for anyone in particular. Where was Kath? She had faithfully promised to come.

And then she saw them, dancing together, so carefree and good-looking.

They were dancing a quick step, a Tommy Dorsey number, and Kath seemed to be clinging just a little too closely to Jack's broad shoulders and he was laughing just a bit too much at something her friend had said. Then Kath looked across and saw Meg and at once abandoned her partner to come swooping across the polished floor on fashionable two-tone high heels.

She was wearing a little white embroidered jacket over a silk flared skirt in pillbox red. Nipped in at the waist with a narrow red belt, the jacket was trimmed with a row of tiny pearl buttons. She looked wonderful, a million dollars, and knew it.

'What *have* you done to your hair?' she cried, hugging Meg in delight. 'I love it. Oh, I shall have to cut mine too. Where did you get it done?'

'Where did you get those shoes?'

'Fun, aren't they?'

Kath swung her own sleek bob about as she talked and Meg had to laugh as her friend prattled on, happily recounting her own latest encounters with hairdressers, which were numerous. Kath was constantly changing her appearance. One week she was a redhead, the next a brunette. For the moment she was blonde and it suited her.

Meg felt herself relax, enjoying as she always did Kath's lively company. They chattered easily together with the familiarity of old friends, laughing at nothing in particular and understanding far more than was actually said.

'What happened about the job?' Kath asked, innocently recalling the tensions of the day.

Fortunately she was saved from answering this loaded question by the arrival of Jack himself who looked less enamoured of her new hair style. A frown drew two lines of displeasure above his straight nose.

'Don't you like it?'

'Not much,' he said bluntly.

14

'Thanks,' she said, disappointment blocking her throat with a rush of emotion. This was proving to be the most awful day of her life. 'Wouldn't you say that it makes me look more alluring and sophisticated?' she asked, daringly teasing, but he only shook his head.

'Personally I like long hair on a woman, more feminine.' He was shocked by the change the hairstyle had made to her. With her hair long, never tidy, often dragged together with a bit of baling twine, she'd seemed like a young girl still. Now she looked like a woman. A sensual, mature woman. Long aware of her fancy for him, but also of his easy success with women, he'd thought he had plenty of time to play the field before he did anything about his feelings for Meg Turner. Now he wasn't so sure. Something had changed in her today, and if he was any judge, it wasn't just because of the new hair style.

'Jack and I have been showing the old biddies how it's done. But you can have him now,' whispered Kath, winking outrageously, and to her horror, Meg blushed.

But when he asked her for a dance she accepted eagerly, melting against him, unable to disguise her pleasure at feeling his arms about her. Pulling her close, he tucked her hand into his chest where she could feel the fast beat of his heart. Was he excited by her as she was by him? Meg longed to look up into his face, lean and hungry with teasing violet eyes, but dared not.

She had known Jack Lawson ever since their early schooldays together and had wanted him almost as long. He'd always seemed to favour the more feminine sort of girl, the kind who wore broad satin ribbons and didn't spend all their time climbing trees and damming up becks. He had never shown any interest in Meg Turner with her scruffy pigtails and scraped knees.

She hadn't seen him for some time after they left school. She'd heard he'd gone off to work in Preston for a while, on the docks. And then last backend at a shepherds meet, there he was, more handsome than ever with the same old wickedly teasing smile.

Since then she had come across him surprisingly often on the lanes and fields about her home when she was out walking. Though his father's land adjoined theirs, the houses themselves were a good mile apart. For a long time she had struggled hard not to read anything into these accidental meetings. Now hope rose hot and piercingly sweet in her breast.

They swayed together to the rhythm of the music. It was a Bing Crosby number, 'When the blue of the Night', and Jack crooned it

15

softly against her ear, making little b-b-boom noises in imitation of the singer's style. The warmth of his breath tickled her lobes, making her shiver with a new awareness.

'Been on any interesting walks lately?' he asked, his voice no more than a velvet purr.

'Some. How about you?'

He grinned and pulled her away from him so he could look down into her face. 'Tend to leave the walking to the dogs, but maybe I should take it up again. Where do you go to get away from that lout of a brother of yours? Wouldn't care to cross him on a dark night.'

Meg giggled, knowing Jack was not the only one to be wary of Dan. 'He tries to be tough, like Father, but it's all show,' she said. 'If he bothers you, you'd best stay away.' And see if I care, her tone said. The music finished and she walked away from him, burningly aware he was watching the swing of her hips in the new blue chenille dress.

He danced with Kath again after that and Meg wondered if perhaps she'd been a touch too casual. She should have given him more encouragement, tried to get him to make a proper date. She'd die if he didn't, she was sure of it.

Then later he took her outside. For a breath of fresh air, he said. Meg went willingly, heart thumping, aware that this was the usual mode of behaviour when a boy wanted to get to know you better.

The small schoolroom, a low, stone building that might have grown out of the rocky soil it stood on, was home to a few dozen children during the day and often commissioned into action as a social meeting point during the evening for the scattered farming community. Standing as it did in the middle of nowhere it was black dark all around, proving a great attraction for those wishing to try out a few undisturbed kisses. She'd noticed Kath make two or three well-timed exits, one of them, to Meg's great astonishment, with her own brother, Dan.

Now that it was her turn she felt quite sick with anticipation and excitement. What if she did something wrong, said something stupid? Jack was so sophisticated, with vast amounts of experience she was sure, while Meg felt simply gauche and juvenile.

He leaned placidly against the wall and lit up a cigarette. He offered her one but she refused. Somewhere an owl hooted.

'Your father wouldn't approve, I suppose?'

Meg managed a smile. 'I don't suppose he would.' She was tempted to take one, to prove she was her own person, but decided it would be childish.

His eyes were moving over her face and she put up a defensive hand to her hair. 'I could always grow it again,' she said, and his eyebrows lifted.

'For me?'

She wanted to fall into his arms and tell him she would do anything if he would only ask, but she smiled instead. Was he never going to kiss her?

'My father can be a pain too,' he said, sounding vaguely sympathetic. 'Always comparing me with my well-organised sister or pestering me to "put down roots", whatever they are. And me with my whole life before me. What's the hurry? There's always tomorrow, I say.' Jack laughed then tossed the half-smoked cigarette away with a careless flick of his hand. Almost in the same movement he pulled her into his arms.

His lips were cold against hers. She could taste the cigarette ash, smell it on his breath along with a pint or two of beer he'd had earlier. But his skin was soft and warm and, oh, it was wonderful to feel herself pressed so close in his arms. She wanted to stay there for ever. His teeth grazed her lips and she felt a bolt of excitement so intense it shot right through her stomach.

'Hallo, everyone, having fun?'

Kath came bouncing alongside, one of the Jepson boys in tow, and Jack broke away with a laugh to light another cigarette. A cold wind from the fells brushed over her lips and with sinking heart Meg realised that the romantic interlude, if that was what it had been, was over. And he still hadn't made a date to see her again.

The rest of her evening passed, as usual, with perfect decorum and at ten o'clock precisely her father took her home. Everyone else stayed on for the Conga and the Hokey-Cokey.

Meg flung open the back door and called for her young brother. 'Charlie, how many times do I have to call you?'

There he was, as she'd expected, expertly flicking cigarette cards against a row of them propped against the yard wall. With a sound of exasperation she marched over and gathered up the cards, tossing them angrily into the dustbin. He let out a howl of protest.

'What did you do that for, Meg?' He stood frozen, the next card poised between finger and thumb, bright blue eyes so affronted it was almost comical, had she been in the mood for laughing.

'You're too old for boys' games.'

'One minute I'm too young, now I'm too old. Make your mind up.'

Too young for anything serious like marriage or war, and too old for games, she thought, feeling ancient as she remembered the awkwardness of being sixteen.

'Haven't I been calling you this last ten minutes?' She turned from him and started to snatch pegs off the washing line, the raw April wind whipping colour into her cheeks like a lash, turning her hands, still wet from a morning's scrubbing, all red and chapped. Washing always made Meg irritable and she'd not felt quite herself since the dance two weeks ago.

She'd got so touchy about not hearing a word from Jack Lawson that she'd even stopped taking her usual walk each afternoon, just in case she saw him and he thought she was chasing him. It was the silliest attitude to take, Meg well knew, but somehow she couldn't help herself. Unrealistically, she wanted Jack to seek her out, to court her. Though how he would dare venture on to Turner property without an invitation from the men of the household was a puzzle she hadn't yet solved.

Now, as if to chastise herself again for wanting something she couldn't have, she poured all her energy into work, unfairly taking her ill temper out on her young brother.

'Didn't you hear me shout that it'd started to rain and to bring in the washing before it got soaked? I think sometimes you've only sawdust between your ears. Just look at these sheets, all splattered with mud. You and your games.' Meg flung the spotted shirts and sheets back into the basket, hard put to keep the tears out of her eyes. It had taken hours to soak, scrub and starch them all. Now she'd have to start all over again.

'I didn't hear you.'

'You didn't listen. You only hear what you want to hear, you great lump.' She thrust the basket into his arms and pushed him towards the kitchen door. 'Did you fill the log basket like I asked?' She knew, of course, that he hadn't. It still stood in the middle of the slate floor where she had set it hours ago, waiting to trip up any unwary passerby.

She spent the next two hours scrubbing the mud spots off the washing and setting it to dry on the wooden rack that hung suspended from the ceiling in front of the fire. Steam filled the small kitchen in no time, making her short curls cling damply to her rosy cheeks. Then Dan came in, reminding her to take his boots to the menders and presenting her with a whole wad of socks to darn that had somehow got collected up in the bottom of his drawer. Meg bundled them in to her sewing basket, telling him tartly to take his own boots to the menders.

'You go to town more often than I do.'

'Well, it's not my job to darn socks.'

Meg bit back the desire to tell him just what he could do with his tatty socks.

She brought the logs in herself, Charlie having disappeared off the face of the earth, and by the time she had finished all the usual chores, and prepared liver and onions for the dinner, she was almost too exhausted to think straight. But she'd go out this afternoon, come what may. A breath of fresh air would do her good.

The wind had chased the rain away and a fickle sun had come out when Katherine Ellis saddled her pony to ride over to Broombank early that afternoon. There was an ethereal radiance to the light that turned droplets of water into sparkling diamonds on the newly sprouting fernheads, their tightly furled croziers like miniature shepherd's crooks. The air was rich with the resonance of damp earth and new grass, and that feeling of hope that is peculiarly discernible when spring comes to Lakeland, as if to celebrate having survived winter.

'Come on, Bonnie,' she urged, 'stop blowing, then I can pull this damn girth strap tight.' Bonnie, being a slightly overweight fell pony of mature years, was not really Katherine's idea of a good mount. She would have preferred an arab stallion or a fine roan. One who pranced and whinnied with excitement when she took her out, not stand on three legs with eyes closed, or drop her head to the grass verge at every opportunity, resisting any threat of exercise.

But Bonnie was an old friend and thus not easily discarded. And Kath revelled in the freedom the pony gave her, even managing to stir Bonnie to a gentle trot if she squeezed her thighs against the pony's plump sides hard enough, though it might make her back and leg muscles ache.

She leaned forward and let the wind skim through her hair, knowing she should have worn a hat. Mummy was for ever telling her so. Just as she told her to wear a coat on a damp evening, or to take a torch and a whistle if she went over Kentmere. But Kath rarely listened to these words of wisdom. Where was the fun in life if you always did what was safe and proper?

Her mother was holding open the gate for her now, quite unnecessarily, at the end of the long drive that wound between jutting rocks to Larkrigg Hall where Kath had been born and in which she had been cosseted ever since as the unexpectedly late child of elderly parents.

The fine old house had once belonged to her mother's quarry-owning forebears. Larkrigg Fell was pitted with the remains of a dozen old quarries, once worked for the blue-grey slate of the Silurian beds formed many thousands of years ago when Lakeland was young. The entire landmass had been pushed upwards by volcanic disturbance, fold upon fold of rock and earth with the most ancient rocks to the north. From these natural resources men had made fortunes, Rosemary Ellis's grandfather among them.

And she had largely spent it.

'You'll be back by tea time, won't you, darling? You know that Richard is coming over and particularly wishes to see you, not us old fogies.'

Kath flicked her crop against Bonnie's flanks, wishing the pony would speedily gallop away so that she could pretend that she hadn't heard the question. But Bonnie slowed down to nuzzle Mrs Ellis's hand, just in case she had a treat secreted in the pocket of her soft tweed skirt. Kath restrained a sigh and smiled sunnily.

'I'll do my best. But don't wait tea for me. You know how totally unpunctual I am.'

Rosemary Ellis watched her daughter until she was quite out of sight, a frown of concern upon her face. How difficult girls could be, particularly Katherine who had always shown a ruthless determination to have her own way. Perhaps it was because she was an only child and, as Rosemary was well aware, thoroughly spoiled by Jeffrey, that she seemed so wild and out of control. But she was young still, at eighteen, and there was plenty of time for her to mature. It was only that with Jeffrey being unwell and the future so uncertain, it would be lovely if she would settle down with some suitable young man. Richard Harper was ideal and from a good local family, his father likely to be Mayor of Kendal next year.

'We'll wait till five,' she called out in desperation, just as the pony's grey tail swished out of sight.

The whitewashed stone longhouse that was Broombank Farm came into sight as Kath rounded the last hill and Bonnie came to a halt without any prompting.

'Even the horse can read my mind,' Katherine said crossly, forgetting the countless occasions she'd ridden this way.

It was early yet for the blaze of gold which would soon surround the farm with an almost magical light but the first spears were attempting to thrust through the thick green leaves.

Built as an Elizabethan manor farm, Broombank occupied three sides of a quadrangle though many of its buildings were now little more than ruins. Only its tall cylindrical chimneys stood proud, the narrow curtainless windows looking blankly out from thick stone walls that seemed to have shrunk in upon themselves with the passing of the years as if ashamed of the air of neglect. Kath knew that the inside was in an even worse state. It was hard to imagine the fine ladies and gentlemen who had installed the oak panelling and doors and whose initials were carved over the stone lintel taking too kindly to its present state. It was certainly not a house she would care to own. But it wasn't the building she had come to see.

'Let's see if he's in, shall we? Walk on, Bonnie.' The mare ambled forward readily enough knowing there might well be a mint humbug at the farm, if the old man was in. There was little Bonnie would not do for a mint humbug.

Jack came to meet them himself, just as Kath had hoped, as soon as they entered the farmyard. She stayed on the pony's back, sitting very straight to display her breasts to full advantage, and slanted a smile down at him.

'You're looking as devilishly handsome as ever on this glorious afternoon,' she said.

Jack Lawson rested one hand on the bridle and smiled back at her. 'And yourself.'

Four years older than Meg and she, Jack Lawson, with his black curly hair and sleepy violet-blue eyes, was the nearest thing to a rake that Katherine knew. A bit brash perhaps, just a little too full of himself, but one twist of that sensual lower lip and she could forgive him anything. Well aware that he belonged to Meg, or would if her friend had any say in the matter, still Kath could not resist testing her own standing with him. 'Show me a man and I'll wind him in,' was her favourite catch phrase. And, generally speaking, a true one. Jack Lawson was certainly a man who interested her but he was not proving an easy fish to hook.

'I was just giving Bonnie some much needed exercise and realised I hadn't seen you since the lambing supper.'

For all there was a coolness to the April breeze, Jack stood with his shirt sleeves rolled above the elbow, hands thrust in his trouser pockets, allowing Katherine ample opportunity to admire his muscles. He worked hard, so they were worth seeing. 'I've been busy. Why, have you missed me?'

Now she was thrown into a quandary. If she said that she had, it might make her look cheap. But if she said no, he'd wonder why she'd bothered to mention it in the first place. She decided to play it cool. 'Don't flatter yourself, Jack Lawson. It was nothing more than idle curiosity. Who else is there around here that isn't already half dead?'

They both laughed at that, aware of Kath's frustration with rural life and oft-pronounced intention of leaving the quiet fells to head for the bright lights.

'What about Meg? I thought you and she were inseparable.'

'So we are. When I can get her away from that sanctimonious old father of hers,' Kath agreed, sobering instantly. 'They do worry me, the Turner family. How on earth they managed to produce such a sweetie as Meg is quite beyond me. They are really quite dreadful with her.'

'You seem to find her brother amenable enough.'

She glanced down at Jack, startled for a moment as she remembered allowing Dan to take her outside at the supper. Something she had almost instantly regretted. He had smelled of beer and cow dung. She shrugged slender shoulders, a gesture that managed to look elegant even in the old green sweater she wore. 'He has a fancy for me, that's all. Not to be taken seriously. I can handle him.'

'As you can most men,' came the soft reply, and Kath glanced swiftly at him again, to see if he was just the teeniest bit jealous, but his head was down, concentrating on the horse. She looked at his hand instead, large and tanned, the skin rough and calloused from hard work on the farm, held flat now under Bonnie's soft muzzle. 'Not too many sugar lumps, they'll make her fat,' and they both laughed again.

'Where are you off to?' he asked, as she gathered the reins ready to move on.

She walked the pony round in a circle, aware of his eyes upon her. 'Over Coppergill Pass. I often go there on a fine afternoon.' Hazel eyes regarded blue for a moment in silence.

'So long then,' he said, sounding very like a gangster in one of those new American movies she and Meg occasionally went to see in Kendal.

22

Kath urged Bonnie into action and with an airy wave of a hand trotted out through the gate Jack obediently held open for her.

He stood watching her go, eyes on the delightful up and down motion of her rear as rider and pony headed off up the lane. It was the neatest little bum he'd seen in a long time and he almost regretted not offering to go with her.

It was late-afternoon before Meg set out, striding away up the fields towards Brockbarrow Wood. More a copse than a wood, the stand of trees stood high on the fellside, flanking the sides of a small mountain tarn, dark and skeletal against the glistening water. It was her favourite place even when the wind cut through like a knife. But today spring was in the air and her heart felt uplifted by the freedom of an hour out alone where she could sit and think without fear of being disturbed.

No one saw her go, not that she'd have cared if they had. She was entitled to a break she told herself. Meg loved walking and was never afraid to be alone. She had often thought it would be good to have a dog at her heels, but the only dogs the farm owned were working animals that belonged to her father and her brother Dan. They were treated well as there was nothing more important to a good shepherd than his dog, but they were never allowed into the house and spent their time in the yard or barn when not working. Meg felt she would like to have a dog beside her at all times.

'One day I shall,' she announced to the empty landscape, mentally adding it to her list of requirements for a happy life. As soon as I have a job, whatever that might be, and a place of my own. And Jack, she added silently. How any of these dreams would be achieved she had not the faintest idea but the determination was strong in her.

Meg continued upwards, her rubber boots slipping sometimes on the sharp stones. Above her the track narrowed and split into a dozen such sheep-trails, named 'trods' years ago by the Vikings who first populated these fells. The Herdwicks would later lead their lambs up them to the summer grazing, allowing the youngsters not a moment's rest in their eagerness to reach the heights. Today the fells were bare and quiet and she loved the silence, feeling it heave into her heart and push away all the unpleasant thoughts and niggling worries. A skylark soared, tearing up into a blue-grey sky in a frenzy of song, a winter migrant from a colder land. Meg called up to the small brown bird, assuring it that she would watch where she put her feet and not disturb its eggs.

'I wouldn't expect anything else from you.'

She stopped dead in her tracks, looking all about her for the source of the deep, disembodied voice.

'Jack?' she said, half hoping, half fearing. He stepped out from behind a rowan on the fringes of the copse above her and, leaning against it, grinned down at her, turning her stomach to water.

'Come on, slow coach. About time, I'm bored sick with trekking up this path to wait for you.'

Her heart leaped into her throat, soaring as surely as the skylark's song.

It no longer mattered that she'd near worn herself out with the washing all morning or that at the end of this suddenly wonderful afternoon she must return to a dour, taciturn father and two selfish brothers. He had come at last. And here, on this fellside, she felt suddenly wanted and alive.

They sat together under an old ash tree, leaning against its silvery-grey bark. Meg was so overwhelmed at finding him waiting for her, she could think of nothing to say. But she relished the warmth of him beside her. He smelled of tangy soap and fresh damp earth; something she could only describe to herself as masculine.

'Have you really? Been wanting to see me, I mean,' she asked, unable to resist knowing the answer.

'What do you think?'

She turned to him, half accusing. 'You never said. How was I to know?'

'I would have thought it was obvious. Most girls would have guessed.'

'I'm not most girls.' Meg had no intention of having him think her easy. She knew all about such girls and she wasn't one of them. All the same she trembled inside when he shifted his position, moving his body closer.

'What do you expect me to do? Call on your dad?'

'No. I don't blame you for being wary of Joe. And Dan!' The words started to tumble out, covering the sudden shyness which was so ridiculous with a boy she had known all her life.

'Maybe Dan and I might have got on better if it hadn't been pumped into me from the moment we were old enough to toddle about that the farm was for the boys.'

'What would you want with a farm?'

'I'd like the chance to decide for myself,' she said. 'Can't you see what will happen? Dan will marry and I'll be the spare part around the place, the unmarried sister.' She shivered. 'It doesn't appeal, thank you very much.

Jack shrugged. 'So leave. Do something different.'

'How? My father won't even let me go to town on me bike,' she complained. 'It's archaic.'

Jack made sympathetic noises but he wasn't really listening. He was watching the rise and fall of her breast beneath the pale blue blouse she wore. It strained enticingly against the buttons. A girl turning into a woman and she didn't even seem to notice. Jack wasn't sure whether it was Meg's innocence or her unconscious sensuality that so appealed to him. Either way it had come as a surprise to him since he usually preferred more sophisticated meat.

But however Joe Turner might try to keep his daughter a child she was very much a woman, and the ache in Jack's loins told him that he wanted her. And what Jack wanted, he usually got.

3

'Keep you short of money, does he?' Jack considered putting his arm about Meg's shoulders but she looked so fierce suddenly, he decided against it. He would content himself this afternoon with letting her chatter. There was plenty of time, after all.

'Money? I've none at all. How can he be so loud against women working when he has me labouring like a slave from dawn to dusk? How can he pretend to be so pious when everyone knows he's the biggest shark of a moneylender around these parts?'

'He's a fearsome character right enough, your dad. I know Sally Ann Gilpin is scared sick of him.'

'Is she?'

'They've been having their troubles lately. Her dad has been ill. Left them a bit short, I reckon.' Jack's eyes fastened on Meg's mouth, small and moist, a pink tongue darting excitedly over her lower lip as she talked.

'I see.' Meg was sad about that; she liked the Gilpin family and strongly disliked an old friend being scared of her father. 'How did you hear?' What she really meant was, when did you see Sally Ann? She felt a spurt of hot jealousy that Jack had talked to a pretty girl, and hated herself for it.

Jack was too busy gazing at the white column of her throat to notice the sharpness of her tone. 'I don't remember exactly. Her mam is having a real hard time of it, though.'

'I can imagine.' The women who lived in the row of cottages up by the quarry and were forced to avail themselves of Joe's money lending service in order to survive the week, had every cause to fear him. Nobody got behind with their payments with Joe Turner, not if they wanted to avoid trouble.

'Why do women always get the rough end of the stick? I've been trained to keep house since I was three years old. Not so the boys, who were somehow excused anything that smacked of woman's work. But it's going to change, I tell you. I can only take so much and one of these days . . .'

Meg felt the anger drain out of her, becoming intensely aware of the warm weight of Jack's body beside hers. What was she doing wasting this precious time together talking about her father? Jack moved a little, his thigh brushing hers and it was as if she could scarcely breathe, as if her lungs were bursting, squeezing inwards, pushing a pain deep down into her groin.

She was aware too of Jack's breathing, of its strangely uneven quality, that it became less and less pronounced. She felt him turn towards her and knew instinctively that if she looked at him he would kiss her, but she could not move. Much as she longed to feel the warmth of his lips move over hers, her body was stuck fast to the tree, her hands curled tight into the clumps of grass at her side.

'Meg?'

That was all he said. Her name. So softly questioning it was like a caress. Then his hand came up to her neck and she turned her cheek into it, lifting her face to his as if to the warmth of the sun. She had waited for this moment for what seemed like a lifetime and Meg closed her eyes and gave herself up to the joy of it without hesitation.

The kiss roughened and deepened, and then moved on to explore the warm curve of her throat and the sensitive hollows below her earlobe. She rubbed her cheek against the roughness of his coat collar, loving the feel of it against her silky skin. Happiness burst inside her like the opening petals of a new flower.

Meg gasped when she felt his hand move to her breast. She wasn't ignorant. Brought up on a farm, she was well versed in the mechanics of life and had filled in the gaps with Kath long since, giggling behind the barn with one of those books in plain brown wrappers Kath had sent for. But theory was one thing, practice quite another.

His fingers were growing more adventurous since she'd done nothing to stop him and were now busily engaged in unbuttoning her blouse. Did she want him to carry on further? She felt flustered, not wanting to appear silly and naive.

28

He had found her nipple, pert and hard beneath her hand-stitched camisole, and she gasped with pain and pleasure as he took it between his lips. 'Jack,' she whimpered, half in protest, half drowning in sensation. Even as she spoke, her body arched, instinctively craving for more. Wanting him more than she could say.

He pulled her down so that she was lying on the grass and she could sense the excitement rising in him. Something hard and pulsing was pressing against her leg. It seemed to make the pain worse.

'Come on, Meg, come on,' he murmured, then eased open her mouth with his tongue so she couldn't have answered him anyway, even if she'd known what to say. His tongue flickered between her teeth and curled about her own, thrusting, dancing, teasing, demanding. Despite herself she was catching his excitement, felt it run through her like a glow of liquid fire. She thrilled to his kisses, revelled in new sensations she'd never known before, responding to his passion without restraint.

'You want me, don't you?' he asked, letting her breathe for a minute as he nuzzled into her neck.

'Oh, Jack', was all she could say, a tremble in her voice. She was confused, filled with a racing desire to find out what it was her young body craved, even as some small part of her preached caution and held her back. Yet how could it be wrong if she wanted him to do these things to her? She felt dazed and weak, the longing to surrender almost beyond endurance.

His hand was on her leg now, sliding softly beneath her skirt, over her bare thigh. Then with a shock of breath in her throat she felt his hand creep beneath the leg of her cami-knickers. Very quickly she caught his hand with her own.

'Please, Jack, no.' But he wasn't listening, she felt him shudder against her, press the hardness of his body ever closer, and she remembered reading in the brown paper book how you shouldn't lead a man on. Was that what she was doing? Being a tease. He was saying something, whispering in her ear.

'It's all right, Meg. I can use something. You'll be quite safe.'

A warm, melting sensation flowed through her veins, making her want to let him slide right inside her. The sigh of the wind through the old ash trees above seemed to shelter them, whispering secrets still to be understood; the slip-slap of water from the tarn beyond lulled her so that she could barely drag open eyelids heavy with love. Safe? *Use something*? What was he talking about? And then it came to her, why her inner voice cautioned, what it was she must be kept safe from, and she began to wriggle. 'Give over this instant,' she cried, pulling herself free. 'My dad'll kill me if I get in trouble.'

'I wouldn't hurt you, Meg, you can trust me,' he said, still busy at her breasts. Dammit, he thought, I went too fast.

'And how do I know that?' They broke apart to stare at each other, eyes glazed, cheeks flushed, breathing ragged, and for a brief moment she thought he was going to be angry with her for stopping him but then the mischievous smile came back to his face.

'What you do look like,' he said. And then Meg started to giggle because it was true, they must look a proper mess.

She pushed him gently away to sit up, smoothing down her skirt, fluffing out her hair, unaware just how enticing she looked with pink cheeks and lips bruised and softened by love making. 'We should have taken a bit more care.' Oh, but she didn't want to take care, she didn't!

'I will in future, Meg. I'm sorry if I scared you.' He kissed her nose, thinking if he could get this far the first time, a second chance should be even more interesting.

To Meg, the implication that there could be a future for herself and Jack Lawson made her gasp. She'd never known such joy in all her life: to feel so loved, so wanted. And he must love her, mustn't he? Not only because he obviously wanted her so badly, but because he hadn't minded at all when she'd stopped him.

'You do respect me, don't you, Jack?' she asked, a touch of uncertainty in her voice, in case she had lost that precious respect by such wanton behaviour, but he only chuckled.

'Course I do, Meg. I've told you. I wouldn't be here else.'

Her mother had told her long ago that a boy never respected you if you let him go 'all the way'. Yet if she stayed here much longer, gazing into his violet-blue eyes with their long curling lashes, she'd throw respect to the four winds and let him do what he would with her.

'I must go.' She got quickly to her feet, and was delighted when he did the same, putting his arms about her once more as if he couldn't bear to let her go.

'You're not angry with me, are you?' There'll be another time, he thought, plucking a piece of grass from her hair.

'No, of course not. Why should I be?' They kissed again, softly now, with no urgency in it, and she knew it was all right. Life was suddenly wonderful and her heart was racing with happiness. Meg's only experience of love and romance came from her rare visits to the cinema, or flea pit as Kath called it. A diet of glossy sentimentality and cultivated passion filled with vows of undying love lightened by jokey wisecracks, always with a happy ending in the final reel.

'Will I see you tomorrow?' he asked, and when she hesitated he persisted. 'I must see you, Meg. I'm not made of stone, love.'

He'd called her his love. The delight of being wanted as those screen goddesses were wanted, was so delicious that Meg, as many a woman before her, felt suddenly heady with a sense of her own power. Reaching up, she wrapped her arms about his neck and kissed him good and hard.

'Will that keep you happy till I can get away again?' she asked, and turning from him, started to run down the hill.

Her feet had flown over the coarse grass, slipping and sliding down the hillside. She had the wind in her hair and exhilaration in her heart. Her father had been waiting for her when she got home, of course, complaining that his tea wasn't ready. He said nothing more but his silence was heavy and accusing as he riddled the coals in the grate and then banked it up for the night. He sent her up early to bed just as if she were a child and not a grown woman, she thought. But Joe Turner's disapproval couldn't touch her now, and she was glad to escape.

Meg undressed slowly and running her hands over her breasts before pulling on the flannel nightgown, she wondered if she was beautiful.

That night, in the secret darkness of her bed, she relived those moments over and over in her mind and knew with a shaming weakness that she had not wanted Jack to stop, not at all. Would she have 'let him' if there'd been anywhere more suitable than a copse of ash trees by a small mountain tarn? She didn't know, but curiosity was strong in her and the thought did not go away that life with Jack Lawson would be a good deal more exciting than waiting on her crabby old father and brothers.

They met regularly after that. In the mornings Meg raced through her work, humming happily to herself. And most afternoons found her slipping out the back door and striding off up to Brockbarrow Wood, heart pumping as she waited for Jack.

She knew Joe watched her, often with dark brows drawn into a

31

dour frown, but he never spoke about her change of humour and she never enlightened him. In her view, it was none of his business who she went out with. Besides, it was too soon to have their growing friendship examined by her grasping father. Joe would be sure to put the very worst connotation on it and start asking what Jack could offer as a prospective son-in-law.

He considered her too young for marriage. Meg knew he wouldn't want to lose her from the farm, not yet. Her job was to look after him, he said, until he retired or Dan married. By which time she reckoned she would be well past thirty and quite grey with age.

But she couldn't help telling Kath about meeting Jack at the copse, though she said nothing of the hot kisses or the furtive fumblings in her blouse. These were secrets best kept to herself.

'You want to be careful,' Kath warned. 'Jack has had loads of girl friends.'

'Oh, I know he's experienced,' Meg said. 'But he wouldn't take advantage. I trust him.'

Kath looked disbelieving. 'So long as you don't get any silly ideas about him, Meg.'

She took Kath's warnings with a very large pinch of salt. What young man didn't sow wild oats when he was young? And Jack was older than herself, twenty-three, nearly twenty-four, so of course he'd had a few girl friends. But she meant to be his last.

The thought of marriage with Jack filled her with delight. Even so instinct told her there was more in store for her than that. Somewhere there had to be a greater purpose to her life. Meg understood this somehow, deep in her heart.

So although the two girls always shared their thoughts and dreams, Meg had no intention of letting even Kath into this one. Not until she'd sorted out her own thoughts on the subject.

'Heaven forbid,' she scoffed. 'And spend my life in a kitchen?' And both girls giggled, content with each other, as they had always been.

Meg resolved then that until she had discovered what that something was, and had achieved it, she would not allow Jack Lawson to get so far with her again. It wasn't proper. But she would go on seeing him, as often as she could manage.

There was a late snow the next day, blocking the lanes and filling the shady sides of the stone walls, burying the sheep who had sought shelter. Her father and two brothers were kept fully occupied bringing them in, often discovering the bedraggled, crow-picked bodies of newborn lambs, destroyed before they'd had time to taste life.

Meg too worked flat out as the snow created its usual chaos and extra work. Clothes to be dried, hot meals provided at all hours of day and night without a word of thanks. And on top everything else, the orphan lambs to be fed at frequent intervals throughout the day and night and kept warm by the kitchen range until they were strong enough to survive outside without a mother.

And, worse, the snow meant that she couldn't get out to see Jack.

Through the long claustrophobic days that followed, confined to the farm, she dreamed of the warmth of his lips against hers, the feel of Jack's fingers threading through her hair and the sigh of the wind in the ash trees as it washed over them, wrapping them in an almost mystical enchantment.

A week passed, and another. Was Broombank cut off too? she wondered, and began to worry about Lanky. She had known him all her life and loved him almost as a father. There had been times when she'd wished he was. Meg knew that he hadn't been well recently and would appreciate one of her home-made pies. And so, as soon as the lanes were passable, she decided not to wait for the thaw. She would go anyway.

There were fox prints deep in the snow as Meg trod steadily upwards, leaving a trail of her own beside them. The thorn bushes were shrouded with white, showering the lane with yet more pristine crystal flakes as she brushed by. In her hand she carried a basket in which reposed the pie, deep and rich with gravy. There was also a small cheese and a pot of her best raspberry jam. Lanky Lawson, being a widower with only Jack at home, had few comforts these days. So even if the food was not up to her mother's standards, it would be welcomed.

The mountains glittered brilliantly in the morning sun, fallen rocks like glass marbles at their feet. Great banks of snow were still piled high at each side of the lane, alternately melting and freezing as the weather changed. Progress was proving difficult with her booted feet skidding and skating on the frozen puddles one moment, and the next knee deep in a drift. But she meant to get through, no matter what.

Stomach churning with excitement, she wished she'd thought to bring some lipstick with her or a dab of Boots 711 Cologne to put behind her ears. In her old raincoat and wellington boots she looked a bit too plain and well scrubbed. But the anticipation of seeing Jack grew stronger with every step, making her hurry so that by the time she finally reached Broombank she was sticky and flushed with the effort.

The farmhouse, with its projecting wings and dilapidated barn, saddened her. Its once white walls, roughcast better to withstand the weather, looked grey and pockmarked. To think this had once been one of the biggest and best sheep farms in the district with its two hundred and fifty acres of intake land and six or seven hundred more on the fells above. With Jack away so long in Preston, old Lanky had lost heart.

Meg greeted him with a cheerful smile when he opened the door, trying to prevent her eyes from sliding past him to see if Jack was home.

'Eeh, noo then,' he said, looking pleased. 'There's a grand sight on a cold day.'

She hugged the old man, kissing his too-thin cheek. The scent of St Bruno flake tobacco, wood smoke, and something indefinable that might have been animal feed clung to his parchment skin, like old leather against the softness of her lips.

Horny hands gripped hers with a strength that always surprised her, coming from such a small man.

'Come in and warm theeself,' he said, pushing the door closed behind her. 'There's a bit of a fire going.'

Moments later she had her hands cupped about a hot mug of cocoa, toasting her toes in the great fireplace which was wide enough, Lanky said, to take a horse and cart should you have one handy. No doubt the ladies of Tudor England spun their wool within its embrace, and wove the hodden grey clothing Lakeland was famous for. They would bake their oatcakes, known as clapbread since it was clapped flat by the palm of a hand, on the huge griddle that hung from the ratten hook in the centre of the huge chimney. Another hook held the great black kettle that now steamed and spat hot water into the flames as Lanky moved it to one side so she could feel the heat. The andirons still stood in the hearth but they did not hold in place a huge log on this cold day as they might once have done. Instead, an insignificant wood fire burned in an old iron basket, giving off very little heat and a good deal of smoke. It was no wonder that Lanky still kept a scarf looped about his neck, tucked into the vee of his waistcoat.

Lanky Lawson, for all his name, was a small, slight man with trousers that hung on braces from armpit to glossy boots, making his legs look like a pair of brown liquorice sticks, a bit frayed at the bottom as if someone had chewed them. And over it all he wore an old saggy tweed jacket that he declared 'had an easy fit to give him room to grow'.

'I'm right glad you came,' he said. 'Always did like a pretty woman to gossip with.'

Meg was at once sorry that she hadn't called more often recently. Her mother had been a frequent visitor with home-made titbits, Meg often accompanying her. Annie had loved Broombank with its spacious old grandeur crouching low in the rolling hillside.

Through the low oak door that led into the back dairy Meg could see the stone sink filled with dirty pots and plates. What was Jack thinking of to let them pile up so? She'd see if she couldn't tactfully deal with a few of those before she left.

There was no sign of Jack himself anywhere, which was a blow. Perhaps he was out looking for lambs, she reasoned, an endless job in this weather. Stifling the disappointment of missing him, she set the pie to warm on the trivet.

'How's Connie keeping?' she asked. Much in evidence from the many photographs that stood on the wide oak dresser, Connie rarely visited Broombank these days. There she was as a schoolgirl in pigtails, looking plump and serious. And on her wedding day, stoutly pleased with herself as well she might be. A sour-faced spinster for years, she had surprised everyone by marrying in her mid-thirties only a year or two ago.

'Oh, as busy as ever with her new house in Grange-Over-Sands,' Lanky replied, equably enough. 'She's a grand lass, if a bit pernickety. Coming home to see me soon, she says.'

Meg had heard this promise many times so took little notice but it saddened her to see the old man alone so much in his neglected house. Untidy and unkempt, it offered little more warmth and comfort than an empty cow byre. The thought came to her how much she would love to see it reborn, a loving home and working farm once more. She could see herself at one side of this great hearth and Jack at the other. The thought made her heart race with excitement.

'We used to have great hams hanging from the rannel balk when my wife was alive,' Lanky told her, following her gaze and referring to the thick beam that ran the length of the kitchen ceiling. 'We'll not see the like again.'

'You might. If your family produces lots of grandchildren for you to feed.'

'Nay, I doubt it. Jack's not about to rush into marriage, so far as I'm aware.' And when she flushed, confused by the meaning of his words, he gave a little chuckle, but not to mock her. He was thinking how her sweet beauty lit up his dusty kitchen and recalling how his own pretty Mary had once done just the same. Mary might not have been his first choice but she'd been a good wife to him all the same and he was not sorry that it wouldn't be long now before he saw her again. Till then he'd enjoy what time he had left, no complaining, and try to put things in proper order, as he should. If he could just work out what sort of order would be best, he'd feel better, he knew he would.

Lanky insisted Meg stay and enjoy a bite of supper with him and how could she refuse? For once she had nothing particular to hurry home for. Father was out on some business or other. Dan had been asleep in the fireside chair snoring his head off when she left, and Charlie, as usual, was fully occupied with his aeroplane models, books, and cigarette card collection. Besides, there was always the hope that Jack might come home.

When they had finished the pie, she ventured to ask: 'Is Jack out with the lambs?'

'Nay. He's gone off down town for a day or two. Claims he gets claustrophobia if he doesn't get away for a bit every now and then.'

'Oh.'

Jack still hadn't appeared by the time Meg finally put on her coat to leave but she hid her disappointment with a smile.

'I'll come again, Lanky. And I'll bring an apple pie next time.'

'Just fetch theeself lass, that'll do. I'll walk part way with you. Give me chance to look over the sheep. There's still one or two left to lamb.'

The two walked companionably together along the boundaries of the top field, instinctively watching for any sign of a ewe going off on her own, or turning round and round as she sought a place to drop her lamb. The sheep's silent presence, jaws grinding, incurious eyes staring, always filled Meg with a quiet calm. There were the Swaledales, pale and square, and the Herdwicks with their dark, barrel-shaped bodies, faces dusted with the same hoar frost as the coarse grass at their feet. Only these sheep could best survive the bleak conditions on the Lakeland fells.

'Do you remember when I insisted on buying that pet lamb off you when I was about ten?'

'Aye, I do that. You could have had it for nowt but you wanted to play at doing business, all proper like. You fed it with a bottle and it followed you about like a dog for a year or more.'

'I remember you even gave me the Luckpenny to go with it. Just as if I'd bought it at the auction.'

'Aye, well, it's a custom that goes right back to the Norsemen. Brings bad fortune if you don't give something back. Always remember that, Meg. And that li'le lamb thrived, a good friend to you.'

She tucked her arm into his, feeling a flood of warmth for this old man who had made a small girl feel important and happy for a while.

'Till Father sold it.'

'Aye. He would.'

'I loved it, and cried buckets when one morning I found it had gone. Didn't speak to him for weeks afterwards.'

'I dare say. You were nobbut a lass.'

'No room for sentiment in farming,' he said. 'Sheep aren't pets and women shouldn't meddle with matters they don't understand.'

'A pet lamb is different,' Lanky said, with the kind of understanding that had always made her love him.

They reached the stile and started to climb over. Amber eyes glowed in the swinging light from the storm lantern and Meg smiled at the sheep, as if to reassure them.

'Sorry to disturb you, ladies.'

'They don't mind visitors. So long as they only have two legs.'

It was then that Meg noticed it. One of the Herdwicks in a far corner did not look at all right. She pointed it out to Lanky at once.

It didn't take an expert eye to guess the problem. Even as Meg watched, the ewe went down and lay grunting on the grass. From the hind quarters peeped a nose, no feet, just one small black nose.

Lanky knelt on the frozen earth beside the ewe to examine it, prodding and probing with expert fingers, then to her great surprise stood up again.

'What would you do then?'

Meg stared at him in consternation. Wasn't he going to help the sheep? Its distress now was most apparent. Was he waiting for Jack? She looked about her hopefully, but only the sheep stared back, a little restless now as if sensing trouble.

'Why are you asking me?' The chill of the night made her shiver as it seeped into her bones.

'You're a farmer's lass. You should know.'

The ewe was starting to strain in her attempt to rid herself of the lamb which was locked fast in the passage, tied up in its own straggling legs. It might well strangle itself, and its mother, at any moment.

Meg stared helplessly into Lanky's eyes and saw the challenge in them. Was he testing her? *Surely he didn't want her to deliver the lamb?* She became aware that he was speaking to her again.

'You see to this one whilst I check on the rest. There's another over there might well be in a similar state.' And he walked away, leaving her alone with the poor trembling ewe.

For a moment Meg was paralysed with fear.

Her father's words echoed in her head like a litany. 'Farming is not woman's work. Don't interfere in matters that don't concern you.' But Joe wasn't here now. No one was. Not even Lanky who was attending to one of the other ewes. He must trust her or he wouldn't have left her alone. Perhaps it was this that gave her the much needed confidence, or else she could not help but respond to the anguished appeal in the animal's eyes.

It came to her then in a moment of startling clarity that she did know what to do. She had heard enough talk, watched enough births, if only from a distance, to have a pretty good idea how to go about it.

Setting down the lamp some safe distance away, knowing there was no time to waste, Meg took off her coat and rolled up her sleeves. As she made her preparations a calmness came and the fear left her.

'There now, young lady, don't you worry, I'm here to help.' The ewe rolled its eyes, baring its teeth in a silent scream of despair. She wondered, that if she did something wrong, if she lost the lamb, or worse, the mother, how she would ever live with herself. And Joe would half kill her.

'All right, all right, hush now, hush.' Meg put all thoughts of her father from her head. She didn't think of Lanky, nor even of Jack. There was a job to be done and she was the one to do it. Her one concern was to help the distressed ewe.

It was almost as if she had been waiting for this moment all her life. The stillness of the night held and shielded her in its silent embrace. The rime of frost glistened but Meg no longer felt the cold.

Talking quietly all the time, she moved with a natural instinct. Holding the sheep firmly, but gently, she pushed the lamb back inside the mother, calming her as she did so. Meg found she needed to use more effort than she'd expected and anxiety gripped her, making her sweat despite the minus eight temperature. Sorting out the tangle of front feet from the small pointed head took longer than she'd hoped but at last she had them both tucked neatly beneath the chin in the

38

correct position ready for birth, and with a little more urging they came sweetly forward and the tiny body slithered out on to the ice-frosted grass on a sigh of relief from herself as much as the exhausted mother. The lamb shook its raggedy ears and almost at once tried to get up.

Moments later a second lamb followed. Twins were rare with hill sheep so it would have been particularly tragic to lose these. The ewe turned her head to nuzzle them, making pleased little grunting sounds in her throat, and started at once on the task of cleaning each one in turn with her long black tongue. Meg sat uncaring of the cold on the freezing snow and watched the lambs as they circled their mother, and finally start to suckle. Tears rolled down her cheeks.

'There now,' said a voice in her ear. 'I knew you had it in you.'

'Oh, Lanky. I can hardly believe I did that. It was so wonderful.'

The lanes held that empty silence of a snow-filled landscape on the walk home, with only the squeak and crunch of ice beneath her wellington boots. Meg was glad of the lantern that Lanky had lent her. Its glow lit her way but made the vastness of the scene seem infinite and unreal. But she was not afraid. The empty mountains, the whispering trees, held no threat for her. This was her country and she loved it. The birth had been the most moving experience of her life, and it had told her exactly what she wanted to do with it. She wanted to be a sheep farmer. The very best in the district.

4

Following that spring day Meg expected, in some way, for life to change, but it continued very much as before, only now she had a goal to work for, an aim in view. It made her feel good and warm inside.

And even more glorious, she was seeing Jack almost daily. Though she took great care not to let her feelings run away with her again.

He occasionally objected to the boundaries she set but kept to them nonetheless.

Meg hugged to herself the memory of that night in April, one she'd come to think of as an almost mystical experience that had firmed her decision on what she wanted to do with her life. It seemed so obvious now. As if the knowledge had been there all along but she hadn't recognised it. Just because her father wouldn't let her help with the sheep at Ashlea didn't mean she couldn't work on another farm. And the best of it was that Jack was a farmer already. She began to fantasise about what it would be like if they married. They would be equal partners in the running of Broombank. Jack wasn't old-fashioned like Joe, he was young and modern and would expect his wife to share everything, and if she were that wife, she'd be only too happy to do so.

Meg visited Broombank regularly and took great care with her appearance, for didn't she want Jack to love her?

She would dive behind the barn to tidy her hair or rub the smuts from her cheeks the moment she saw him approach, making Lanky chuckle. But she didn't care. It made it an extra special visit when

41

they could work together, as if they were man and wife already. These were good times for Meg but sometimes Jack complained she spent too much time with Lanky and not enough with him.

'I like you to myself,' he would say, stroking her hair which she was growing to please him. 'You are my special girl and I want you to stay that way.'

Jack's girl. Oh, it sounded so good.

'Then will you kiss me?' she would ask, and he was always ready to comply. Life was perfectly wonderful in Meg's estimation. Nothing could possibly spoil it.

When spring ripened into summer they might walk over to Patterdale by way of Angle Tarn. As wild and lonely as anywhere in the Lake District, there they would marvel at the sight of a golden eagle dipping in the wind, or hares quarrelling furiously for no apparent reason. Then they would plunge into the water together, ice cold after the warmth of the sun. But no amount of sweet talk would persuade Meg to swim without a costume.

'Prudish little miss, aren't you?' Jack teased and Meg could only admit to her shyness and hold fast to her ideals, however much she might wish otherwise.

'Don't you trust me?'

'Of course I trust you.'

'Then come here. Prove it.'

Slapping water at him, she would laugh and swim away as fast as she could, thinking that perhaps it was herself she didn't trust. Will he get bored with me, she worried, if I keep him to such firm boundaries?

It was easier when they swam in their very own Brockbarrow Tarn and Kath came with them. Though Meg regretted the loss of intimacy on these occasions, she felt safer in an odd sort of way, knowing that Jack wouldn't press her too much with company present. And the three of them always had plenty of fun together.

Sometimes they would walk for hours up Bannisdale or along part of the old Roman road of High Street then follow the ribbon of water that gushed down into Longsleddale where they would take off their shoes and paddle their tired feet in the fast-flowing river by the low bridge, squealing like children. A perfect end to a perfect day.

And Meg, who knew herself lost to Jack's charms, ached for the day when he would declare his love for her openly. He was a cautious man, as farmers often are. Oh, but she was lucky. Any number of girls would envy her having Jack. She could afford to wait.

* * *

Joe Turner, not having been born yesterday as he was fond of saying, was well aware that something had changed in his daughter. He had his suspicions what it might be too, though nothing had been said between them.

He tried to work out a way to winkle the truth out of her, but she kept things close to her chest did Meg. It annoyed him sometimes how like her mother she was, always singing and smiling to herself as if she knew something he didn't.

He'd never been entirely sure what went on in Annie's head either, for all she'd made herself out to be a good, obedient wife. There'd been many a time, particularly in the early days, when she'd managed to speak volumes without opening her mouth. Now this little madam was behaving in just the same way. Keeping secrets. And he wouldn't have it, not in a house where he was master.

Love, if that was what was ailing her, had caused enough trouble for the Royal family with the King running off and marrying that Mrs Simpson. Joe would have no such nonsense at Ashlea. Duty and the needs of the farm came first and last in the lives of his own family if he had any say, which of course he did.

When she wasn't wandering over the countryside, goodness knew where, Meg was forever giggling and chattering with that Ellis girl, telling secrets he shouldn't wonder, as silly young girls tended to do. Getting out of control. And Joe Turner liked, above all things, to keep control in his own hands.

So one day he followed her and was surprised to find her land up at Broombank.

Now what would she be doing up there day after day? he asked himself, and came up pretty quickly with the right answer. Jack Lawson. Plain as the nose on your face. Now there was a turn up for the book.

And something he might well be able to use to his advantage one day. When the time was right. Joe was so pleased with his discovery he almost sang himself but remembered in time to keep his usual taciturn expression. Always the safest.

Visitors to Ashlea were rare. Farmers, not having much time for socialising at home, tended to confine their gossiping, which they loved, to their gatherings, meets and markets. And the womenfolk had their own list of busy chores which kept them at home just as firmly. So Meg was surprised to have a visitor one day in early summer. She was alone in the house, her father having gone to make arrangements with Lanky for the coming clipping. Dan and Charlie were out in the fields.

The day was sunny, ideal for a bit of gardening, washing curtains and baking a fresh batch of scones. Feeling well pleased with her efforts Meg quickly fed the new fast-growing calves then awarded herself a well-earned rest in the sun. She was sitting with her feet propped on an upturned bucket when Sally Ann Gilpin, the seventeen-year-old eldest daughter of the Gilpin family of Quarry Row came knocking at the farmhouse door.

She was a plump girl with a round smiling face. Meg remembered her from school as always wearing hand-me-down clothes a size too small, and she had changed little over the years, as untidy now as she had been at twelve. Kath, who of course had gone to a private girls' school in Carlisle, had never been a particular friend of Sally Ann's but Meg liked her. Sally Ann had a good warm heart.

'Is your pa in?' she asked now, hugging a buttonlesss cardigan about an ample bosom.

Meg explained that he was away and she wasn't sure when he'd be back. 'Dan's in the top field. I could call him for you.'

'No, it's all right,' said Sally Ann, too quickly. 'I can call again.'

Meg smiled encouragingly at her. 'He'll be in shortly, for his tea. Stay and have a cuppa with me and a bit of a crack. It's not often I get a chance for a gossip with another female. Surrounded by great clods of menfolk I am, and I haven't been out for days.' Meg laughed and Sally Ann, eyeing the scones on the kitchen table, quickly agreed.

'That'd be grand, thanks.'

They went inside while Meg brewed a fresh pot of tea and buttered several scones. She carried the tray out so they could sit in the sun, Sally Ann trailing silently behind her. But the small tea party proved to be a disappointing failure. Her one-time friend, perched uncomfortably on the edge of her chair, seemed lost in thoughts of her own and all Meg's efforts at cheerful conversation fell flat. Finally she recalled how Jack had told her that Mr Gilpin had been unwell.

'How's your dad? I hope your ma's managing all right.'

The girl swallowed a mouthful of tea, seemed to choke upon it and quickly set the mug down as she broke into a fit of coughing. Meg waited patiently for the spasm to pass.

'Dad isn't too good as a matter of fact. His leg was smashed by a boulder that ran loose in the blasting and he's had to give up quarrying. He gets a bit of labouring here and there. Doctor doesn't think it'll ever properly mend, not that we've had him up recently. Doctors cost money.'

Meg looked shocked. 'But surely your dad was insured, with the quarry?'

'Oh, aye, at least he paid his penny a week for a while, only it don't last for ever.' Again she swallowed a mouthful of scalding tea as if wanting to soothe away unpleasant memories. 'And there's not been much spare cash about with Dad off sick for so long.'

'No, there wouldn't be.'

'That's why I'm here, if I'm honest,' Sally Ann admitted, her voice so low Meg could scarcely hear her.

'You're wanting to borrow some money off my father, is that it?'

Sally Ann looked up at her with haunted eyes. 'Well, your pa's already helped us out a time or two. I was wondering if he'd give us more time to pay.'

Meg regarded the girl for a moment in compassionate silence.

Unable either to read or write, Joe Turner was nevertheless frugal and adept at saving money. And if he could make that money work for him by lending it out at a good rate of interest, nothing pleased him more. He kept track of every penny owed him on tally sticks which he kept in a sacking bag hung behind the pantry door. One for every client. He never made a mistake and Meg had seen grown women weep as they begged for more time to pay, and him just turn and walk away. It sickened her sometimes but it was infinitely worse to see it happen to a friend.

'He never likes extending the loan period. I do know that. Is there no other way you can get the money?'

Sally Ann looked bleak. 'I earn what I can at the Co-op shop and we're very careful. But Mr Shaw says he has to cut me hours from next week so I won't be able to pay so much back. And the little ones are needing boots for their feet, not new ones you understand, but teacher says they can't go to school wi'out. And the house we've found, well, hovel more like since we had to leave Quarry Row . . .' Sally Ann rolled her eyes as if trying to make a joke of it . . . 'needs a coat of distemper if only to kill the bugs. We can't go on like this much longer.' Her voice broke, betraying her resolution to remain calm.

Hearing her friend's problems filled Meg with shame. She was in the depths of despair any day she missed seeing Jack, agonising over

45

where he was and who he might be with. Only when she was with him was she truly happy. And Jack was growing ever more ardent. Sometimes his hands seemed to be everywhere and she worried about how much longer she could control him and if it mattered. She loved him so much and she did want him, she did. Only she was afraid of what might go wrong if she gave in. Meg thrilled at the new excitement that had come into her dull life, delighted that at last someone cared, but it worried her all the same.

Yet really it shouldn't, she told herself, not in comparison with Sally Ann's lot.

'I'll call and see your ma. We've more vegetables here than we know what to do with. And I could spare a bit of milk and eggs, for the little ones.'

'Oh, she'd be that pleased to see you.'

'I wish it could be more.'

'Just tell your pa that I . . .' Footsteps sounded across the yard and Sally Ann stopped speaking, clamping her lips together as Dan swaggered towards them. Meg poured her brother a mug of tea, buttered a large scone and handed both to him without a word.

He settled himself with a sigh on a low stone wall and looked across at the two girls seated on kitchen chairs before him, brown eyes speculative while he consumed his tea.

They talked for a while of inconsequential matters, mutual friends they knew who had married or given birth recently and various members of Sally Ann's large family. At last Meg turned to Dan with an enquiring smile.

'Do you know what time Father will be home? Sal has come to see him on a matter of business.'

Dan gave a grunting laugh as if she'd said something amusing. 'Women don't know owt about business.'

'That's not true,' Meg refuted stoutly. 'Women aren't given the chance, that's all.'

Dan glowered at his sister, bristled brows twisted in scornful mockery. 'You think you're so smart.'

'Maybe I am.'

'Smarter than me, a humble farmer, I suppose?'

'Most people are that. I certainly work as hard as you, great lazy lump that you are, and I don't pour as much money down me throat. What Father would say if he found out that's what you do, I don't know.'

'And you're going to tell him, are you? Miss-Goody-Two-Shoes.'

'No, I'm not the tell-tale round here. Stop trying to pick a fight, Dan, and just tell me what time Father'll be home so Sally Ann knows whether it's worth her while waiting.'

Clearing her throat, Sally Ann spoke up, perhaps thinking to stop this argument before it got quite out of hand. 'It's only about the loan.'

'Well now, if it's to do with moneylending, I'm the one you want to see, not me father.'

'Oh, but it was Mr Turner that I dealt with last time.' Dan was setting down his mug as he got to his feet. He looked impressive at full stretch, a well-built man it was true, but handsome when he made the effort to adopt a more pleasant demeanour. And all too aware of his own power.

'Well, you can deal with me now. Father leaves much of that side of the business to me these days.'

'Since when?' Meg asked, startled.

Dan ignored her. 'He has enough to do with the farm, he says. These financial matters are often left in my hands.' He smiled at Sally Ann.

In fact a year or two younger than herself, Meg thought Sally Ann looked suddenly old and haggard, and she was filled with pity for her. Dan had never been known for his caring personality. Rather the reverse. He had been the kind of child who pulled wings off butterflies and hated anyone to best him. She reached out a hand instinctively to reassure the other girl as she faced her brother.

'What do you know about finance? You couldn't even learn your multiplication tables.'

'If you're so clever I dare say you think you could run this whole farm better'n me?'

'You don't run it. Father does.'

Dan's face went red. He hated the idea that he must wait till Joe died before he had any say in running Ashlea, and it showed. 'It'll be mine one day. Then you'll have to do what I say.'

Meg was so infuriated by this high-handed bullying the words were out before she had checked them. 'Maybe it'll be mine and not yours, who can tell?'

'Huh, that's a laugh. Father'd never leave it to you.'

'He might, and I could do it too,' she protested, then quailed at the grimace of pleasure that came to his face.

'You? Run this farm? A woman?'

'Yes, me, a woman.'

'Go on then, let's see you try.' Dan jerked his head towards the empty field and the smooth green fells beyond, where could be seen moving flecks of sheep grazing. 'If you're so wonderful, let's see you fetch some of the sheep down for the clipping. Go on, I dare you.'

She could tell him not to talk so daft. It took three men with dogs to walk the several hundred acres of open fell and bring down the hundreds of sheep that belonged to Ashlea.

Perhaps it was the mocking laughter on his face, or his heartless bullying of poor Sally Ann. Or the fact that he had ruined her one chance of earning a bit of extra money by getting her in trouble with her father.

Or Meg remembering all too vividly that night in the snow.

She had told no one, not even her family, of that night, and neither it seemed, had Lanky. Perhaps because of that experience Meg felt certain she was capable of so much more and had a sudden longing to prove it.

'All right,' she said. 'You're on.'

Dan was turning his back on her, a sneering laugh on his lips.

'Don't talk soft. There's only two places where women should be. At kitchen sink, or in bed.'

That did it. Meg tossed her bright head, curls bouncing with boundless energy, grey eyes meeting her brother's with a challenging glare. 'Right. I'll bring some of your damn' sheep in. See if I don't.'

And leaving them standing open mouthed, she recklessly set off alone, up the fells.

Drops of water sparkled in the sunshine on firm brown flesh. Two bodies, now entwined, now swimming and diving, ducking and leaping, girlish laughter mixed with the more gruff teasing tones of the man who pursued her carried upward on the still warm air.

Not for this girl any sense of shyness or undue modesty. Her body was carefully toasted to a coffee and milk colour and she held no inhibitions about showing it. She knew her breasts were firm and full, her waist narrow over the seductive swell of girlish hips. Her legs were long with slim ankles and highly arched, pretty feet. She buffed the skin at night till it was smooth as silk, nurtured it with creams and lotions, and now gasped with delight as the ice cold tarn water flowed upon it, swimming as briskly as she could to keep her blood flowing.

'Come here, damn you!' Jack was after her in a second. When he caught her she wrapped those long brown legs about his waist, shaking wet hair back from her face. He buried his face in it, capturing her breasts with his hands. 'God, you're beautiful. You're like a drug I can't leave alone.'

'Why should you leave me alone?' Slanting hazel eyes regarded him with open provocation. 'When it's so good.'

'Oh, it's good right enough.' It was so easy to penetrate her here in the lake. He grasped her hips and pulled them down hard, making her scream and shiver with ecstasy as he plunged upwards into the soft warmth of her. The experience was intoxicating, addictive.

Later, when they lay spent on the cropped grass, gazing up at speckled sunshine glistening amongst the green leaves of an old oak, he swore softly through gritted teeth and she laughed. 'Don't tell me you want it again, so soon?'

'No, witch, leave me alone. Why do I feel so damn' guilty?'

Kath raised a languorous hand to smoothe it over the broad chest and down the length of his flat stomach. 'I can't imagine. It's not as if you're engaged or anything, is it? You're still a free man.'

He pushed her hand away and sat up. When she was touching him like that he couldn't think clearly. 'Meg seems to be making plans.' He couldn't understand how it was matters were moving so fast between them. She'd have him buying a ring soon if he didn't watch out, and he hadn't yet decided if that was what he wanted. But nor could he quite bring himself to give her up.

Kath sighed deeply, closing her eyes against the sun and enjoying the heat of it on her bare skin. 'Nonsense. Tell her not to. Life is too short for plans.'

'She spends hours at the farm with my dad. Keeps talking about farming. I think she's more besotted with the sheep than me.'

'I wonder why.'

He gazed down at Kath's nakedness and felt himself start to rise. 'Meg would certainly never lie here with me like this.'

Kath's eyes sparkled with a taunting challenge as she watched his discomfiture worsen. She licked drops of water from her upper lip and saw him groan in fresh agony as his eyes followed the movement. 'Well, there you are then. Nothing to worry about. She's happy with her sheep and I'm happy with this. No plans. No ties. Come here. Let me make you a happy man.'

Trying to fetch the sheep down on her own was, Meg discovered, the craziest thing she had ever attempted in her life. And it was all Dan's fault for stirring her up into anger.

49

Some of the greedy ones followed her, hoping for extra feed, but if she attempted to herd them in one direction they quickly panicked and set off at a gallop the opposite way.

She had run and stalked and circled wide, blocked up gateways, called, begged and even cried, but had known all along that it was useless. And all the time she was aware of Dan watching her from the house, laughing fit to bust, she shouldn't wonder.

In the end she realised she was in danger of risking injury to the precious stock and sat on a boulder shaking with fatigue and anger, letting the tears of humiliation and ruined pride fall.

What a fool she was always to rise to Dan's jibes. Why couldn't they have an easy relationship, like she had with Charlie?

And just because she had helped one sheep bring a lamb into the world didn't make her a farmer. Because she knew how to give a dose of treacle and egg white to cure its ills, didn't mean she could catch the animal in order to issue it. Sheep were not half so stupid as they looked, she decided.

Meg gazed about her at the majesty of the mountains that rose above the lower slopes of the fells and felt humbled. Patches of shadow, like giant grey sheep, were being chased over the barren fell by brilliant swathes of light. And on the ridges beyond, the remains of last winter's snow formed skeletal faces, warning people to tread with care. It put her in awe of the task of caring for heedless animals in such a setting. She was mad. She must be to let a little knowledge go to her head in that way. Perhaps Dan was right when he said she was too sharp for her own good.

Alone here, on the mountainside, she made a private vow that whatever she needed to know, she would learn. Deep inside her was an ache Meg knew must be satisfied. Nothing to do with love or Jack or even her family, though they made her more aware of it.

This was something to do with that night in April, with the search she had been engaged on all her life. With the destiny that she had found on that night. She drew in the sparkling air, deep into her lungs, and felt better for knowing nothing could touch that secret part of her.

In the end she was forced to swallow her pride and return to the farm.

Dan crowed with pleasure at her embarrassment and her father mockingly reminded her he had said all along that shepherding was man's work.

'I could do it,' she told them both, shame and humiliation adding unusual beauty to her rosy cheekbones. 'If I had a dog to work with. Even you couldn't do it without a good dog, you know you couldn't.'

But neither would admit such a thing so Meg held her silence for the rest of the meal. Only Charlie seemed to be on her side.

'I think Meg had guts to try. I couldn't have brought the sheep in on my own.'

'We know that, you great clod,' said Joe, masticating slowly. 'Nor would you have thought to try. Shut your face and eat your food.'

It was when she was washing up and Joe was settling by the fire with his pipe that the subject of Sally Ann Gilpin came up.

'What do y'mean, she came to see me? Why has no one thought to tell me.'

'I'm telling you now.' Meg took off her apron and hung it behind the door. 'Dan sorted it out, ask him. I'm off for a walk.'

'No, you're not. I want to know by what right thoo put her on to our Dan without speaking to me first.' Joe started to tamp down the tobacco with a yellow-stained finger as if trying to dampen his rising temper along with it.

For once Meg was surprised to see her elder brother wriggling with discomfort. 'It was only a small matter,' Dan muttered. 'Sal Gilpin needs to reduce the weekly payments for a while, that's all.'

'That's *all*?' The voice was ominously soft. Joe Turner had learned that a quiet tone injected far more menace into simple words. He stared unblinkingly at his son. 'Under what conditions did you agree to her reducing the weekly sum?'

'Conditions?' This from Meg who was anxious to provide Sally Ann with a defence at least. 'What more can you ask for? If she pays less each week it'll just take longer to be paid off, but you'll get your money in the end, and no doubt extra interest.'

Dan nodded eagerly. 'She'll call here regular to pay it, every Friday.'

Joe stood up to face his son, his body quivering with unspent anger. 'Didn't she tell you that I called at her house each week along with my other regular clients? Thoo hev no right to change the arrangements behind my back.'

Meg looked from one to the other, dazed by the tension that had sprung up so quickly in the small kitchen. 'For goodness' sake, what does it matter how you get your money? She'll do her best. Calm down, Father.'

'Don't thoo tell me to calm down, madam. This is my farm, and I'n. in charge of it.'

51

'You're in charge of everything,' Dan said in a rare show of rebellion. 'When do I get some rights? And some wages?'

'Wages? I doan't charge thoo keep, do I?'

'I'm not your whipping boy. You keep saying you'll retire. But you won't, I know you won't, and how can I ever think of taking a wife with no money coming in to keep her?'

Such an unusually long speech from Dan silenced Joe for a whole half minute. He chewed on his pipe and considered. 'It's come to a pretty pass when a man's own son is after stepping into his shoes before he's teken 'em off. Thoo could allus go and work for someone else if tha's dissatisfied.'

Dan subsided into his chair, his rebellion spent.

'I'm the moneylender in these parts, not you, you daft ha'porth. I'm the one that feckless women come running to when they find themselves out of money by Tuesday morning and need my coin to get them through the week.'

Meg found she couldn't let that pass without defending her sex. 'Women run out of money because their husbands don't give them enough. They drink it.'

'Very likely, but where would those poor women and bairns be without me, I ask you?'

'It's not their gratitude you enjoy, it's the profit you make out of them. Where would you be without those same poor women paying interest through the nose every Friday when you collect your coin back at the quarry face?'

'I'm not a charity, miss,' Joe roared, losing his calm again. 'Is it my fault if some chaps can't hold on to what they earn?' He pushed his face close to his daughter. At fifty-nine the years of toil, of being out in all weathers, had left their mark, worsened by lines of bitterness set there by a sanctimonious determination to make life as difficult for himself as possible. As if by doing so he could be brought closer to his elusive God. And what he suffered, he felt duty bound to make his family suffer likewise.

'Times are hard, don't you forget that. A bit more gratitude wouldn't come amiss. Sally Ann Gilpin at least never complains about her lot – she does summat about it. You don't know what it is to be wi'out food to put on the table. When hev you ever gone hungry, tell me that?'

How could she dispute such logic? Meg knew she was fortunate. They may be short of cash, and not keep so fine a table as Kath's family, but they never went hungry like the Gilpins.

She felt diminished, as she always did when her father turned the attack upon her. 'I was only meaning to speak up for Sally Ann,' she said.

'Aye, well, happen she can speak up for herself.'

On top of her foolishness of the afternoon Meg felt she had failed to defend her friend. Perhaps her father was right and she was selfish, ungrateful and greedy, with, as Dan said, too high an opinion of herself.

But if that were so then why did she feel deep inside that the name of the emotion she experienced so strongly was not greed but ambition? Not selfishness but self-esteem. She wished with all her heart that she could work it out.

5

On the last day of September 1938 Chamberlain was boasting of
'Peace for our time'. Czechoslovakia and later Britain herself would
have cause to doubt this statement but for now appeasement was all.
It seemed to Meg that similar political efforts were being made in the
Turner household.

She was determined to have no more arguments with either her
brother or her father. Life was otherwise too perfect to let them spoil it.

Sally Ann called regularly at the farm every Friday to pay what she
could and there seemed to be no further trouble there. Meg wished
with a deep longing sometimes that Jack could be as easily welcomed.
If only she could pluck up the courage to tell her father about him, but
she never managed to.

Though Jack sometimes complained she spent too much time away
from him, she loved him all the more for that little show of jealousy.
Meg too preferred it when they were together but she also enjoyed
helping Lanky.

She wanted Jack to come with them all to the Merry Neet which
was a favourite social event. It took place in the backend of the year
so that any sheep who had strayed through bad weather, dogs, or a
gate left carelessly open could be checked against the Shepherd's
Guide and their rightful owners take them safely home. Meg loved
these traditional get-togethers.

In the old days horse racing would often follow the serious
business. Nowadays it might be hound trailing or Cumberland and
Westmorland wrestling, both of which were favourite pastimes of her
brother Dan's.

There was a great fire at the inn to toast toes and cheerful faces. It burned so fiercely that after a while caps were removed, brows mopped and chairs eased back. The trestle tables were as packed with plates of hot pot and tankards of ale as the floor was with dogs. And everyone was expected to do a 'turn' as they sat and smoked and drank and chatted into the small hours.

The chairman in charge tonight was Lanky, and he volunteered to 'get the ball rolling' with a rendition of 'The Bonnie Sheep' on his fiddle.

Several other people sang songs while the shepherds beat time with their sticks, the dogs with their tails, and Meg and Charlie sat laughing together on the wooden settle in the corner, not taking part but privileged to be allowed to join in with the merriment. Oh, but how she wished Jack were here. He'd sulked when she'd insisted on coming tonight, wanting her to go with him into town.

'You'd love it,' she'd urged, kissing him softly on the mouth. 'Why won't you come with me?'

'You'll be the only woman there,' he'd said. 'And what would your father say?'

'No, I won't. And we don't have to tell Father about us. You're entitled to come with Lanky.'

But he refused, so she'd come with Charlie instead, and was glad.

There were no women shepherds here tonight. How she would love to be the first. But several of the wives had come.

And then cries went up for the gurning to start. A popular local sport it might be, nonetheless she was astonished to hear Joe volunteer. She watched him stick his round head through the horse collar, known as a braffin, and start to pull and stretch his lips and cheeks into the most horrendous face. All the farmers stamped their feet and roared with laughter. Meg couldn't believe this was her own, stern-faced father who was performing so outrageously. How could he be so unfeeling towards her, yet the life and soul of the party with his friends?

'Nay, Joe,' cried one, as he let his face relax into a grin. 'Give over, that's worse.'

He was declared champion gurner of the night and was so well pleased with himself he told them a lively tale of losing two sheep from the back of his van and chasing them all round town, which had the farmers almost falling off their seats with delight.

'Why isn't he like this at home with us?' Meg asked Charlie, but her brother only shook his head, equally bewildered.

'Because he isn't happy there,' came Lanky's voice from behind her. 'Not since your mam died. Come up and see me tomorrow. I've got summat to show you.'

She stared thoughtfully at her father and wondered if she knew him at all.

Meg finished her chores at home and walked up to Broombank as promised. She took her time, enjoying the softness of the autumn breeze which failed to shift the phosphorous cloud that clung to the mountain tops. Dundale Knott rose up at her left as she walked, looking like a lop-sided cottage loaf with a knob on top and a large slice of it cut away, leaving a sheer drop to a bubbling beck below. She found Lanky mending broken walls.

'You look busy,' she said.

'Thoo'll not catch me laikin. I've summat to show you,' he said again. 'Hold on a minute.'

He laid all the stones out on the grass and then it was like watching him put a very complicated jigsaw puzzle together. And he never picked up the same stone twice.

'It's nowt much, just by way of saying thank you,' he said.

Meg was deeply touched. 'Thank you for what?'

'For helping an old man.' He grinned, showing gaps in his teeth. 'But mainly for your company. Why a young girl like you should waste her time up here, I don't know, but I'm right grateful for it.'

'Oh, Lanky.' Meg put her arms round him and gave him a big hug.

'Go on. It's in t'barn. See what you think.'

'We have to put the cam stones back on top of the wall yet. Can't it wait?'

'No, it can't. Our Jack'll help lift these big stones. They're too heavy for a young lass and an old man. Go on. Get away wi' you.'

He was clearly as eager with his surprise as a young boy and, laughing, Meg ran down the slope and pushed open the great door. The barn was packed from floor to ceiling with hay as it always was at this time of year. Nothing else that she could see. Except the dogs, of course, who slept in a corner. There was a gap in the bottom of the door so they could move in and out of the barn at will on the ends of their long ropes. There was Tess, Lanky's old collie, and her two sons, Ben and Rust. She stared at them now, a sudden wondering idea coming to her.

Meg turned to look questioningly at Lanky. 'Tess hasn't had more pups, has she?'

'Nay, she's past it now. But Rust is young enough to risk with a change of master – or mistress.'

'Oh, Lanky.' She was stunned for a moment by his generosity. 'You can't. He's your best young dog. You can't give him to me.'

'I can do what I like, I reckon, wi' me own dogs. He needs someone young to tackle him. And Charlie says you'd like one.'

Meg grey eyes were shining. 'Charlie would say that. He saw me make a proper clown of myself trying to do something clever without one.'

Meg looked at the dog. Most of him was black, the colour of all Border collies, but the rest was rust, as if he'd been left out in the rain too long. Hence his name. He was standing in front of her, feathered tail out straight, one brown ear erect, the other black and flopping over. Feet foursquare, eyes bright and alert with a question in them. 'He understands. He's weighing me up. Can you see it in his eyes?'

'Oh, aye, he's not daft is young Rust. Lie down, lad.'

The dog obeyed instantly, falling softly to his belly, velvet eyes fixed upon Lanky's face. 'He'll make up for the pet lamb, eh?'

'Oh, Lanky. He's much better.' She could feel tears in her throat.

'You'll have to keep him fastened to you for a while till he gets accustomed or he'll keep coming back home to me.'

'Oh, I will. I will.' Meg held out the back of her knuckles, talking softly to the dog as she knelt beside him. 'I'll take good care of you, boy. You and me can be friends. Would you like that, eh?'

Tongue lolling from the side of his grinning mouth, he gazed at her, then up at his master.

'Aye, lad. Go on. It's all right.'

Reassured, the dog nosed the hand, indicating he'd be happy to have it stroke him. Meg obliged. Then she remembered what Joe had done with the pet lamb, all those years ago. 'Can I leave him here for a while though, just till I've made it right at home?'

Lanky smiled. 'Not told Joe yet then about your efforts in the sheep department?'

Meg lifted anxious eyes to his. 'No. I will tell him. In me own good time. You won't...'

'Nowt to do wi' me. But that cur will need training. He's young yet, coming up to twelve month. I'll teach you to whistle.'

And so he did. Meg spent hours practising the signals in quiet corners, finding it far more difficult than she'd imagined, and twice as many hours encouraging Rust to round up the ducks and hens in Lanky's yard, without setting them off in a flurry. Only when he had served a long apprenticeship, and obeyed her every command, would he be permitted near sheep.

And all of this had to be done in complete secrecy from her father and brother so Rust stayed for the moment at Broombank. But Meg meant to have him with her as soon as she had spoken to her father. There was so much now that she had to talk to him about, the prospect was chilling and exciting all at the same time.

Meg's peace ended one day in October. It was one of those quiet, still days only found in autumn. The leaves of the Lakeland woodlands were a paint palette of russet, gold and terracotta. A fat yellow sun that never seemed evident in August now turned the cooling lakes to a blinding sparkle of light. Dew-spangled cobwebs knitted the thorn hedges and, high above, swallows and martins bossed and ordered each other into massive groups ready for their flight south.

The weather was unseasonably warm, almost balmy, and Meg and Jack had walked to their favourite place in Brockbarrow Wood. As usual she had responded eagerly to his kisses, but this time he objected to the set boundaries and there was a particularly undignified tussle. Meg was forced to slap his exploring hand away, cheeks flying flags of hot scarlet.

'What kind of girl do you think I am?' she demanded to know, feeling disappointed and somehow guilty all at the same time.

'You're turning into a prude.'

'I'm not. I've told you I'm . . .'

'Yeah. Keeping yourself on ice. Well, maybe I don't want a woman with ice in her veins. It's hot blood that warms a man, Meg.'

She flushed. 'You know how I feel about that. I don't want to take any unnecessary risks.'

'Oh, come on.' He stroked her leg, making her shiver with longing. 'What's so wonderful about settling down, I'd like to know? Make's a man boring and middle-aged before his time.'

'It needn't.'

'Don't expect too much from me, Meg. I am what I am.' And brows meeting over violet eyes, he got up, thrust his hands deep in his pockets and strode briskly away, leaving her alone on the cold grassy slope where a moment before she had been warmly clasped in his arms. 'Let me know when you decide to be a real woman,' he tossed casually over his shoulder, his frustration finally spilling over into temper.

Meg thought of running after him but his broad back looked so furious and unapproachable that she let him go. An action she later regretted.

Meg spent several miserable days hoping Jack would come round and ask forgiveness for his ill temper. But he didn't. Nor did he meet her in their usual place each afternoon in Brockbarrow Wood. Her despair deepened. Perhaps she was wrong to hold herself back. Should she take the risk? She did love him, oh, she did. But any talk of marriage had come from her, not Jack. Surely that only meant he was waiting till she was twenty-one?

In the end she decided to seek advice about her dilemma, and who else was there to ask but Kath? Although it didn't seem quite right to talk about such personal matters, even to a dear friend. What went on between herself and Jack was their affair after all. But Meg was desperate to know what she should do, for she was so afraid of losing him.

'We'll walk as far as Whinstone Gill,' Kath declared, determined to enjoy the warm sunshine. A deep cleft cut in the rock, the two girls loved to scramble along the gill, sometimes as far as Whinstone Force, a gushing waterfall that burst out of the rock face itself from a network of underground mountain streams.

Kath had been out riding and her cheeks were prettily flushed by the wind. She wore jodphurs of pale cream cord and a shirt that was very likely silk clinging to firm uptilted breasts. By comparison Meg felt frumpish in her old sandals and cotton frock, and foolishly naive.

Nevertheless she decided there wouldn't be a better opportunity and, screwing up her courage, she put her question.

'Can I ask you something?'

'Goodness, this sounds serious.'

'I suppose it is.'

'Then ask away.'

'Have you ever, you know, gone all the way?'

Meg's cheeks were firing up with embarrassment.

Kath stared at her, startled for a moment. 'What did you say?'

'I was only wondering what it was like, if it was as good as all the romantic stories say? And if there is a really safe way of doing it?' she rushed on, finishing in a fluster of heated confusion.

'Safe?'

'Yes. To stop – you know – babies.'

Kath was stunned. 'Didn't your mother tell you? I mean, haven't you and . . . Oh, my God.' This was the last thing she had expected to hear and she wondered for a moment how to cope with it. Meg's attitude to sex had always been less down to earth than Kath's own though they'd discussed it openly enough between them. But not this, she'd never expected this.

'You really don't know? But I thought you and Jack . . .'

'That's just it. He wants to.'

'But you don't?'

'No. Yes. Oh, I don't know. The thing is, will I lose him if I give in?'

'Or will you lose him if you don't?'

Meg stared at her friend in consternation. Trust Kath to spot the nub of the problem right away. 'Something like that.'

'Would it matter very much?'

Meg flushed. 'Yes, of course it would matter.' Jack wasn't the only one to suffer. No matter how hard Meg tried not to think about it, as her love for him grew so did her need to demonstrate that love. Completely. 'I daren't risk getting pregnant and it would be just my luck to catch on first time. Father would throw me out instantly, if only to save his face at the chapel.'

'Funny, isn't it?' Kath agreed. 'How it's always the girl who is blamed, when it takes two to make a baby?'

'And how do I know that Jack would do the decent thing by me? It has been known for the man to walk away and deny the child is his. Not that I think Jack would be so cruel but, oh, it doesn't bear thinking about!'

She wished they didn't have to wait till she was twenty-one to marry. She wished they could go right this minute and live at Broombank and she could help him run the farm. Then they'd live happily ever after. Meg did her best to explain all of this to a suddenly silent Kath.

'So do you think I should – let him, I mean? Would he still respect me, still marry me?'

Kath and Meg had always been close ever since childhood. With few other girls their age living in the area, they'd been almost like sisters. Kath certainly loved her as a sister, but that hadn't stopped them being rivals, not ever, just as real sisters were. Now she felt, not guilt exactly but as near to it as Kath's selfish, careless nature could get. It came together with a great wave of protectiveness towards her more innocent friend. Kath chose her next words with care.

'I didn't realise he was so important to you.'

'Of course he's important. I love him. I've always loved him. And he loves me, I know he does.'

Kath turned away quickly, unwilling to meet the certainty in Meg's clear grey eyes. She climbed up on to the top bar of a wooden gate to give herself time to think. She swung one elegant, smoothly jodhpured leg as if they were discussing nothing more important than whether it would rain tomorrow. 'I thought that was all schoolgirl stuff.'

Meg's eyes widened. 'No, it isn't. It might have been once, but not now.'

'Jack's a rolling stone. He won't stay, you know.'

'He will. He loves Broombank. He's settling nicely. He would have left long since otherwise, wouldn't he?'

'You know he's no good, don't you? Never has been. He's had any number of girls.' Kath gave a little laugh, sounding oddly uncertain in her resolution to say what she must. 'He would once have been termed a libertine and a rake. Can't you just see it in those come-to-bed eyes?'

Never in all their long friendship had they had a really serious row. But Meg could feel the hot anger stirring within her and knew that at any moment she was about to spoil that good record. She bit down hard on her lower lip. Kath was her best friend, only showing she cared about her as she had always done, but Kath didn't understand. She didn't understand at all. For the first time in their relationship, Meg felt superior to her more confident friend.

'He might have been once, when he was younger, but not any more,' she carefully explained.

Kath's heart was sinking as she looked at Meg's earnest expression. Why hadn't she seen what was happening, put a stop to it earlier? How could she have been so blind? But then why hadn't Meg seen that Jack would never settle down? Not in a million years. And certainly not with a quiet little mouse like Meg, however resolute she might pretend to be beneath that meek and mild expression.

'Jack is only kicking his heels,' Kath said gently. 'Waiting for the right opportunity to leave Broombank and the Lake District for the great wide world beyond. Can't you see that?' She could understand that need in him. Didn't she have it herself? There was genuine anxiety now in her plea. 'Don't get caught up with him, Meg. He'll only break your heart,' she added, months too late.

Meg was listening appalled to all of this. 'How can you be so cruel,

Kath Ellis? You don't know him, not as I do. You don't know what it's like to love him as I do.'

Kath swung down from the gate and started to walk away. Shielding her eyes from the direct glare of the sun so that it was impossible accurately to read her expression she looked back at Meg. It was a long moment before she spoke again. 'No,' she said, 'I don't suppose I do.'

'Nay, gentlemen – that price won't do. People are trying to make a living here. Put your hands in your pockets and dust off your money.'

Laughter rippled among the throng of farmers who crowded the auction ring viewing the crop of ewes on sale. Some sat on planks, others leaned on the railing set up to prevent sheep from straying, though what chance they would have in that crowd was hard to see. Joe Turner was amongst them, standing next to his old friend and arch rival, Lanky Lawson.

The auctioneer's little jokes lightened the tension among the sharp eyed, tweed-clad farmers. Sometimes one would thrust out a horny hand to feel the hind quarters of a sheep, checking her fitness, or examine her teeth for age.

Hill farmers, known for their steady gait on the fells, were not men for unnecessary movement so stood like a still life, enveloped in their own fug of acrid blue smoke, hands on sticks or crooks, weather-beaten faces unsmiling, eyes alert for any sign of a sick or lame animal, the chanting rhythm and miming gestures of the auctioneer like some sort of comic opera carried out for their entertainment.

'Hoo's thisself?' Joe remarked.

'Ah was better afoor I met thee,' replied Lanky, equally laconic.

They had commented upon the weather, the state of market prices, and then a silence had fallen between them as business began. Joe would not dream of asking Lanky what he was bidding for, or even how much stock he was hoping to sell himself. Nor would he give the small man any indication of his own bids. Only the auctioneer, from long experience of his clients, knew each farmer's sign. It might be a rub upon a bristly chin or the stem of a pipe, a twitch of a bushy eyebrow or tug of a cap. The slightest gesture could signify a sale, so each would conduct their private business with the wily auctioneer out of eyeshot of each other.

The tension, at times, was palpable. The great heads of Europe might agonise over world peace but nothing was more serious to these men than the price they got for their stock, for upon that depended their very survival.

The room was damp and cold and Lanky succumbed to a fit of coughing.

Joe, his expression inscrutable, leaned on his stick and waited. 'You want to get that cough seen to,' he said, when the bout seemed to be ended.

Lanky made no reply.

The auctioneer started a fresh lot of bidding and when it was done the conversation moved back to the price of stock, the favourite topic.

'If thee were ever to think of selling, I might be willing to take a piece of land off your hands,' Joe said, putting no particular emphasis upon the words.

'Now why would I want to do that?'

Joe was not put off by the difficulty in obtaining information. He expected it, it being all part of the game. 'Thoo has too much, happen, for you and Jack to manage on your own.'

'We get by.'

Joe decided he had gone far enough down this track. Unusually, Lanky owned his own land, and though he no longer put it to full use himself, would not contemplate letting it out to anyone else. Joe envied him since he still only rented Ashlea, despite his best efforts to buy. It was common knowledge that Lanky's family weren't interested in the farm, yet he persisted in saving it for them. A criminal waste in Joe's opinion, and here he was with money set aside just waiting for a bargain, if there was one going. And if Dan was getting restless, Joe could do with a bit more amenable land on which to increase the flock.

This wasn't by any means the first time the subject had been broached between them and both knew it would not be the last. Joe's only hope of success was entirely dependent upon Lanky's stubborn pride.

What he didn't know was that Lanky meant him to remain disappointed. Joe Turner wasn't a bad farmer, not by a long chalk, but in Lanky's opinion he was a mean-hearted man with no imagination or human feeling in him. He'd never give what the land was worth and Lanky would never take less.

The two men gave their full attention to the auction for a while, both pretending indifference.

When it was the turn of Broombank sheep to rush and jostle into the ring, seeking escape and companionship of their neighbours all at the same time. Lanky was in the ring with them. There was no question but that he needed a good price, this year more than ever if he was to keep his head above water. The ewes he didn't need and some he did but couldn't afford to keep were being sold off to lowland farms where they would have an easier time of it in their later years.

He knew each one of them individually. Their faces, voices, the shape of their horns, were as well known to him as his own family, better perhaps since he saw little enough of them these days.

'That didn't take long,' said Joe, as a sale was quickly made, far short of Lanky's expectations. And he still had the 'luck money' to find by way of discount to the new owner. But if he wanted the farmer's custom again he had no choice but to pay it. Besides, it was bad luck not to.

'Thoo's not thinking o' retiring then?' Joe continued and laughed, making a joke of it.

'I'll retire when you do.'

Ashlea stock came next and it was Joe's turn to give his full attention to business. Good stock, all of them, fetching a good price. The bidding went briskly and, satisfied with the result, Joe went so far as to offer to stand Lanky a brew of tea and an eccles cake. Installed in a corner at a nearby cafe, he moved in for the kill.

'You'll be seeing your way clear to settling that other little matter between us quite soon, I hope?'

The 'little matter' in question was a sum of nearly one hundred and fifty pounds, loaned to Lanky over the last year or two to buy stock and attend to running repairs to the barn, in danger of collapse at one time.

'I've not forgotten.' Lanky replied with careful patience as was his wont but for the first time that day some of his confidence evaporated. Joe noticed and smiled to himself.

'No hurry, mind. Some time this backend will do, and I'll not raise the interest yet awhile,' he continued, knowing that if the money couldn't be found now, after the sales, there wasn't a hope of it later.

Lanky only grunted.

'Don't see much o' your Jack. Not like when he was a nipper. What's he doing with hissel these days? Is he still set on leaving the farm or has he sown all his wild oats?'

Lanky had no intention of telling Joe what he ought to be able to discover himself, so he made no reply to this either.

'Time he was wed, don't you reckon?'

The swift change of subject unnerved Lanky who was busily trying to work out where Joe was leading while at the same time worrying over the huge sum of money that was no doubt mounting up in interest on top of the borrowed one hundred and fifty. He wished now that he'd let the barn fall down and not tried to keep his cows. 'He's only three and twenty. Plenty of time.'

Lanky's voice, Joe noted, sounded positively tetchy and he fetched him another pint pot of tea, strong enough to stand a spoon in it.

'Problem, aren't they? Family.'

'Aye,' said Lanky, looking doleful.

'I once thought summat might come o' your Jack and our Meg, but they don't seem to be shaping to it, do they?'

'If you say not,' came the careful reply. 'You'd have to ask them about that. He tells me nowt.' So that's it, Lanky thought. If he can't get my land one way, he'll have it by another.

'Pity. They'd make a good breeding pair. Happen they need a bit of a push like.'

In answer to this Lanky only smiled and said what a grand lass Meg was. 'She's got a good head on her shoulders, that one, for all she's a bit quiet and shy. Come into her own proper one of these days, you see if she doesn't.'

'She's nobbut a female. I hev to keep a close watch over her.'

'She's bright. Runs rings round most chaps. You too, I shouldn't wonder.'

At this attack on his authority, which was a mite too close to the truth for Joe's comfort, he got up to go. 'Right then, I'd best be on me way. Let me know if you change your mind about the land and find you can't keep it on.' When you finally admit you can't find the money to pay me, he thought.

Joe pulled on his cap and tugged at the neb to his colleagues as he walked out of the cafe, well pleased with the day's business. He'd made a good start. The idea was planted, now let it grow.

Dan Turner was likewise feeling pleased with himself as he strode out with his dogs. Sal Gilpin called regularly to pay the money her family owed, missing only twice in the last three months. Six shillings was a large sum to find each week, but then it wasn't his problem, was it? If women weren't capable of organising their lives better, was it his fault?

He'd just laid a trail of aniseed and paraffin over a short six-mile training run. Now he slipped the lead on Silver Lady and a new young bitch he'd bought at the last hound trailing day he'd attended. Both dogs, excited at not having run for a day or two, shot off across the field, their graceful bodies making light work of the distance, easily scaling walls, hills, ditches or whatever came in their path as they followed the scent.

'Aren't they lovely?' Sally Ann said and Dan puffed his chest out, pleased by the compliment, then set off after them at an easy pace.

'Come on, Sal, shape to. If we cut through Brockbarrow Wood we'll be at the finishing post about the same time as them.'

'Don't go so fast then, I can't keep up.' She began to run alongside, puffing slightly from the effort but soon falling behind as Dan strode off on his long legs.

'Aye, she'll make a good 'un,' he announced as he watched the tawny animal's loose-limbed rhythm. 'Bit of training up and she'll do well.'

He was pleased with her. Not that he would ever hold her in any great affection. Dogs were dogs, kept for work and naught else. He'd feed her with good protein, best shin beef and egg, no yolks mind, and other secret ingredients he kept to himself. Warm bedding and regular exercise, and like a good woman, all she had to do then was exactly as he told her. And breed of course. Which brought him back to Sally Ann Gilpin.

He stood and waited for her to catch up. Fine-looking woman she was. He liked a bit more flesh on his women than on his dogs. And game enough or she wouldn't be here, helping him like this.

It had been a considerable stretching of the truth to say that Joe had handed all his financial affairs over to his son. Joe kept things very much under his own control, too much so in Dan's opinion. But Dan was glad he'd been allowed to take on this customer, despite his father's initial objections and Meg's protests. Far too good an opinion of herself that one. Always too ready to criticise him, ever since she was a nipper.

One day he'd get his own back on her for treating him like he was a fool, just see if he didn't.

Sally Ann reached him and, pleased with this unexpected success with a woman, Dan grinned at her. 'You're all right, Sal,' he said, and she was. Friendly and comfortable, with a sense of humour. Always cheerful and ready for a bit of fun and a laugh. 'You're not always wanting to pick holes in what a chap says. Not like our Meg.'

'Where is she?' Sally Ann wanted to know. 'Haven't seen her in ages.'

'Off on one of her walks. Quite a fetish she's got for walking these days.' Not one to waste energy himself, not unless there was profit in it, like his dogs, he couldn't understand it in others. 'There's better ways to spend time and energy, eh, Sal?'

He clambered over a stone stile and strode off on his ambling gait along the stony track that led up to Brockbarrow and on to Whinstone Gill, Sally Ann tagging along behind.

The weather remained good for the time of year and there were no mists on the tops today. Dan could see for miles.

'Come on, lass, let's sit here for a bit, shall we?' He winked at her. 'While we wait for them animals to come.' He laid his coat on the ground and Sally Ann raised a questioning eyebrow before hiding her smile and making herself comfortable beside him.

When he first spotted the fleck of colour on the distant hillside, Dan didn't think anything of it. Besides, he had other matters on his mind.

But it took no time at all for him to pound out his frustration into Sally Ann Gilpin. The wind was too sharp up here to dally so he pulled up her frock and got on with it. And she, gasping for breath, didn't seem to object.

Afterwards he had time to look about him and Dan's long-sighted shepherd's eyes found no difficulty in picking out the figure. It was Meg, no doubt about it. Across the other side of the dale on the lower slopes of Dundale Knott. And what's more she wasn't alone. She had a dog with her. He could see it darting about and running wide in the way of all sheep dogs, rounding up a pair of ewes. He saw her stop and whistle to it and the dog change direction to obey the call.

'Now then, fancy that.' As he'd said earlier, you never knew when a piece of information would come in handy.

6

When Sally Ann called one day that autumn there was no sign of the scared, uncertain girl who had come begging for help months earlier. Meg was glad of the visit from a friend since she had seen little of Kath since the day they had had words over Jack. It was silly really, but Meg had walked away from her friend, refusing to listen to any more, and Kath had stood there and shouted after her, calling her a fool.

She poured out a cup of tea for Sal and herself, ready to enjoy a bit of a gossip as usual, then Sally Ann surprised her by wanting to talk about Dan.

'Has he always been this way, a bit touchy like?'

'Touchy? Testy more like. Not even his own mother could manage him, bless her heart. Said he was the most stubborn of her brood.'

'He seems to blame you for that.'

Meg frowned. 'It's true he's always been jealous of me. I don't know why but there it is. Even when we were small he was constantly pushing me out of the way, grabbing my things, doing his utmost to stop me having or doing anything. He got so destructive he made it impossible for anyone to love him. Wild, he was.'

'Mebbe that's just what he needs.'

'What?'

'Loving.'

'You're not volunteering for the job, are you?'

'I might.'

'*Sally Ann Gilpin*.'

Sal flushed scarlet. 'Well, what would be so terrible about that? It's all right for you, Meg Turner, food in your belly every day, wood for your fire, all your menfolk in work. My dad's been given the push again for not being fit enough to work hard and we're all living on the parish now.'

Meg was shocked by this news. Being hungry was far more dreadful than being dissatisfied with boring kitchen work. Meg noticed then that her old friend did not look half so plump as she once had. Her carrot hair was clean enough but the pale, freckled skin seemed somehow tired and grey. 'I'm sorry, I didn't know.'

'He's thick, your Dan, I know that. He's rough and lazy and quick to anger. And he has an inferiority complex on his shoulders as big as the boulders in that quarry. It's because you're always so good at everything you do, and Charlie being so clever with his fingers, well, it makes Dan feel the odd one out. A proper fool.'

Meg was gazing open-mouthed, surprised by this unexpected view of her lout of a brother. 'Are we talking about the same man?'

'Aye, we are. I've known him nearly as long as you, don't forget. And he's been a proper gent these last months over our bit of trouble. I don't know how we'd have managed without him.' The cheeks grew pink and she smiled shyly. 'Well, almost proper.'

'Sal Gilpin, I do believe . . .'

Sally Ann got up and went to stand at the window which overlooked the farmyard. 'Look at him, great soft lump, feeding those hounds of his. They eat better than we do.'

'I shouldn't wonder at it,' Meg agreed, unable to resist a smile, astonished to hear her hard-bitten brother described as soft. Perhaps she should try to see him in a better light.

Sally Ann turned quickly to Meg, eyes suddenly merry and alight with laughter. 'Don't be surprised if you find yourself with a new sister one of these days. Would you mind?'

Meg stared at her for a moment, then opened her arms and wrapped them around the girl's shoulders. 'Oh, I should welcome it. Sometimes I'm bored witless out here on me own. Another woman around would be marvellous. You do realise how isolated it is, don't you? Farm life is hard and not all that comfortable. And Dan isn't the most talkative person in the world.'

Sally Ann smiled, a lovely open smile that plumped out her cheeks. 'It'll be grand. We'll find some way to fill the lonely nights.' And the two girls burst into a fit of giggles.

70

Dan came in at that moment and Meg turned away, not wishing to watch as the two of them went straight into the parlour without a word. If she hadn't been so full of her own delight these last months, she might have noticed more what was going on before her eyes.

But how would all of this affect her?

The thought kept popping into Meg's mind all the next afternoon as she put Rust through his paces. She would enjoy having Sally Ann at Ashlea. Besides Sal's friendship, she'd have more help with the chores which would be bound to result in more free time. It was a good feeling. She'd be able to see much more of Jack, and go more often up to Broombank.

But then she became absorbed, as always, with the dog and forgot about everything else, even Jack, as she worked.

She was having great difficulty in making him stay. Getting Rust to lie down when she was by him was one thing; at a distance quite another. But it was essential in a good sheep dog out on the hills.

'Take him up to the threshing loft,' Lanky had suggested, and gave her a few tips. So here she was, with Rust on the upper hay floor that came halfway across the open building and she on the cobbled floor below, urging him to lie down.

Rust, not understanding at all what was required of him, stood and gazed down at her with as close to a puzzled expression on his face as a dog could get. Every now and then he would bark at her, half in annoyance, half to remind her to come back and fetch him.

Meg climbed up the wooden ladder to reassure him. 'Lie down, boy. Lie down.'

Rust obeyed instantly, panting up at her, and remained still.

She knew if she said 'Good boy' now, he would bounce up and lick her to death, so she held a hand out flat telling him firmly to *stay* as she backed carefully down the ladder. By the time she was down again he was up on his feet, worried that he had lost sight of her.

'Lie down, boy,' she told him. 'Lie down.' Up on the threshing floor of the barn he couldn't creep round her legs and roll over as he so loved to do. But he wasn't getting the message. It was all in the inflection of the voice with dogs, so the fault could be hers. Meg tried again.

She was still struggling when Jack called. She went to him at once and put her arms about his neck, lifting her face for a kiss.

71

He did not immediately oblige. 'Are you coming? I thought we were to go up Dundale Knott this afternoon.'

'Oh, goodness, I forgot,' she admitted.

'You'd forget anything once you start playing with that dog.'

'I'm not playing. Rust is working, learning his trade.'

'And when will you have chance to put him through his paces?'

'Jack, you're starting to sound like Father. Stop it. I've already tried him out if you want to know. And he's good.'

Jack glanced up at the dog, now lying obediently on the threshing floor, nose just over the edge, so he could have a better view of what was going on below. 'Looks dangerous to me. What if he were to fall off?'

Meg cuddled up against him and tweaked his nose. 'So you do care, you great bully. Of course he won't jump off. I've told him to stay. Besides, he's too intelligent.'

Jack ran his hands over her slender figure, warmly dressed in plain skirt and jumper. 'Why don't you put something pretty on for a change, and we'll go to the pictures? Then you could put me through my paces.' He kissed her then, making her head spin.

'Oh, I'd love to, Jack. Only I'm not sure Father would let me.'

He made an impatient sound in his throat. 'For goodness' sake. You're twenty years old now. When will you stand up to him?'

'I do stand up to him,' Meg protested, feeling this to be unfair. 'It never seems to make any difference, that's all.'

'I'll ask Kath then and make you jealous. At least she doesn't spend all her time with dogs and sheep.'

Meg giggled. 'Stop teasing me, Jack, and kiss me again. I like it. I'll be half an hour and then I could meet you by the gate, bottom of Coppergill Pass. How would that be?' And she kissed him, marvelling at the smoothness of his skin.

But she and Rust were having such a good time, it was more than an hour later when she reached the appointed spot. There was no sign of Jack, and the afternoon was fading to the dark of evening.

The mellow days of autumn were already drawing to a close and soon the bite of winter would be upon them. Out in the fields could be heard the crash of horns as tups battled for the right to mate. A strange way of courting but the necessary prelude to a good lambing season. She and Jack were always sparring. Perhaps that too was a necessary part of loving.

Mists lay thick on the valley floors and the bracken had long since turned brown and started to wither and die. It was a time of year that Meg loved. She hadn't seen Jack for a week since that day in the barn but meant to call today and put matters right between them. They would go for a walk and lie in the tickly bracken, kissing wantonly.

'Thoo's got time to sit aboot, I see,' said Joe, coming in on a blast of cold air that sent a fall of soot all over the pegged rug.

'Didn't Dan sweep the chimney this year? Lazy item,' she groaned, reaching for a brush.

'You could hev done it theeself. It'll happen do you good to hev another woman in the house. Sharpen your ideas up a bit, stop your complaining.'

Meg sighed. She wasn't in the mood for a battle with her father today. 'You make out as if I complain all the time. That can't be true. I want a life of my own, is that too much to ask? A bit of independence.' Flinging open the warming oven door she pulled out a dish of stew, rich with mutton, potatoes, onions and gravy, and set it on the table.

'I want you to go up and see Lanky Lawson. He's still not well, or so I understand.'

Meg frowned. Unusual as it was for her father to show compassion, he was a man of the chapel and Lanky an old friend. 'I see him two or three times a week,' she said, trying to remember how he'd looked the last time she'd been up to Broombank but was ashamed to realise she'd been so taken up with Jack she hadn't paid much attention. 'I'll go up tomorrow, take him a hot pot.'

'Aye, do that. He'll be grateful I shouldn't wonder. He gets no interest taken in him by that family of his.'

Now was her opportunity. She'd never get a better. 'Jack's still there. He works hard on that farm.' She was trembling slightly as she doled out a portion of stew on to a hot plate. What exactly could she say? How to describe their relationship? She wished she could confront her father with a definite proposal from Jack. That would show him. That would be her escape, her revenge for his continued contempt of her. But it was too soon. Jack did love her, she was sure of it. He was only waiting until they had some money saved and she was twenty-one before he declared himself.

Less than a year but it seemed light years away to Meg. She was still trying to find the right words when Joe started speaking again.

'Has that lad o' yourn not popped the question yet? You'll be left an old maid if you don't watch out.' The look upon his grizzled face was triumphant. It said, quite clearly, I know it all.

Meg almost dropped the plate she was handing him, very nearly tipping it down his waistcoat.

As he chewed happily on his mutton stew, she put the question that burned in her brain. 'How did you know?' She asked it quietly but he only shrugged his shoulders and carried on eating. Meg turned away, not wanting to watch.

They'd been so careful. All those clandestine meetings, the careful planning, Kath coming along to give an excuse for Meg to be out of the house. And it had all been for nothing. Now, Meg guessed, he would take pleasure in putting a stop to the burgeoning relationship by making life as difficult for her as he possibly could. She felt sick at the thought. But she wouldn't let him win, she wouldn't.

At last he spoke again, his mouth full of hot potato. 'There's not much I don't know. You have to get up early to put one past me.'

'I wasn't trying to put one past you. We just wanted a bit of privacy, that's all.' The thought that her father might have been following them, even spying on them, made Meg feel quite suddenly ill. Her head spun giddily at the thought of Joe silently viewing those sweet, intensely intimate moments in their life together.

'Did someone tell you?' Surely not Kath, or Charlie? Dan perhaps? The prospect of her brother lurking behind trees and watching them made her feel even worse.

'I'm not daft. I can work things out for myself. He's not a bad lad. A bit of a rogue in his time, but he'll quieten. It wouldn't be so bad a match, I reckon. Like him, do you?'

Meg stared at her father, hope rising swiftly in her breast, blotting out the doubts in her anxiety to find what she sought in his expression. Could he really mean it? Perhaps he wouldn't disapprove at all, perhaps he really did care for her and want her to be happy. 'Oh, Pa,' she said, on a rush of affection. 'I do, oh, I do. I like him very much.'

She wanted to run to him then, to put her head upon his lap and have him stroke her hair and tell her that she was his own dear daughter and that anything she wanted she could have. She had seen Mr Ellis do that with Kath, but her own father had never shown affection, not when she was small, not ever. But that didn't stop her hoping for it. She held her place upon the chair and waited, her breath in check in her throat.

Joe spooned the last of the stew into his mouth, masticating noisily. 'Aye, well. It wouldn't be a bad match, as I see it. The Lawson land has its faults, parts of the valley bottom being a bit damp like, but it runs to a fair size and right alongside our own.'

It was as if he had hit her. It wasn't her feelings he cared about at all, nor Jack's. It was nothing more or less than profit. Meg managed, after a long moment, to get shakily to her feet and for the first time in her life did nothing to hide the contempt in her tone. 'You don't give a toss about me, do you? You don't care whether I love Jack or not, or whether he loves me. All you care about is the land, the damn' land.'

'I thought you loved the land too? Thee has said so oft enough.'

'I do. I love the land, the farm, and the animals with a passion you will never understand. But never, never, as long as I live will I put it before those I love, or my own flesh and blood.'

'That's what you say noo,' said Joe, chortling merrily as if she had made some joke.

There must be something wrong with me, Kath thought. She was sitting touching up the flawless beauty of her face in preparation for dinner, taking infinite care with the line of scarlet lipstick on her wide mouth. The dull November mists had turned to rain which battered against the window pane. Downstairs, in her view, was an equally dull crowd of people. Life, Kath decided, was boring and most confusing.

She stood up and swirled the skirts of her scarlet silk dress. They swished seductively against her bare legs. Delighted with the effect, she reached for her stockings and sat on the edge of the bed to pull them on, letting her thoughts turn back to her problem.

There was Sally Ann, a year younger than herself, and plump and homely to boot, walking out with the stolid Dan. And Meg, whom she'd thought was on her side in seeking independence, eagerly hoping for wedded bliss with Jack on Broombank Farm. Though whether he was quite so eager for a starring part in this production was another matter. Kath had tried not to see Jack recently, in deference to her friend, but it was not easy. The prospect of enjoying the devilish rogue while she could was too tempting. There was a war coming. Everyone said so. Then they might all be dead.

In any case, nothing had been settled between him and Meg. It might fizzle out. But that wouldn't solve her own puzzle, would it?

It was not simply a question of whether she wanted Jack Lawson, but whether she wanted any man, as a permanent fixture, that is. Why didn't she want the same sort of life that other girls craved? Marriage. Children. All of that stuff.

There had been several offers. From 'darling Richard' for a start. He would repeat it tonight and Mummy would send silent messages across the room urging her to accept.

Richard was eligible. His father was in local politics, had loads of land and was considered comfortably rich. But Kath wasn't interested in land or politics though money held a certain fascination. It was a commodity she had never been short of and she could hardly envisage life without it. But marriage was a high price to pay for an endless supply of it.

Sex was much more fun than suburban fidelity, a crusty-faced nanny and endless coffee mornings with flat-chested, bored housewives.

The dinner gong sounded and Kath sighed. She really would have to make up her mind soon on what she meant to do with her life, she supposed. She fastened her last suspender and swished the skirt again, smiling at her image in the mirror. 'Far too good not to share,' she told the reflection.

Later in the evening when it was carefully contrived for the young couple to be alone together, Kath had to admit that she was no nearer a decision.

They sat on the sofa in the drawing room in the prescribed manner and Kath allowed Richard to kiss her. His kisses were polite, guarded even, as if he were afraid of startling her. They bore scant resemblance to the impatient demands of Jack's thrusting tongue. But she could never marry Jack. He had no money, and no prospects of getting any. He hated farming and had nothing else lined up. But he was delicious fun. His sunburned skin all smooth and rimed with sweat . . .

'Do you think you can have good sex and a good marriage all in one neat package?' she asked Richard, quite out of the blue, so it was no wonder that he looked startled.

'Is that important?'

Kath pouted. 'Surely you're not going to pretend that sex is only for men? Oh God, how old-fashioned.'

'I didn't say that.'

'Good.'

'I think you come out with these things just to shock me.'

'Perhaps I do.'

'Have you thought about what I asked you the other day?' Richard had placed one hand tentatively over the curve of her breast. Kath let it lie there.

'Of course I have, darling.' She wondered if he would jump a mile if she placed a hand upon him.

'And your answer? Do you have an answer?'

If there was one thing she hated it was uncertainty in a man. Katherine Ellis always intended to be in charge of any relationship, but she liked the fiction of pretending it to be otherwise. 'I hate it when people try to pressure me into something.'

Richard at once demurred. 'No pressure, Katherine darling, but I would like to know where we stand.' He was such a very polite, well-meaning young man, medium brown hair, brown eyes, medium height. Everything about him, Kath thought, was medium. And profoundly sensible.

'Daddy once wanted me to go to university,' she said, making a tiny moue with her brilliant lips. 'His old one in Edinburgh for preference where I could learn the noble art of medicine. I might have done it too if he hadn't been so terribly pushy about it. Quite put me off.' She got up and went to refill her wine glass. She'd already had two and knew Richard wouldn't approve of her having a third so she filled the glass to the brim and offered him the small amount left in the bottle. He shook his head. *So* sensible.

'Just as well I didn't. Look what life as a boring doctor has done for him. He's a physical wreck, forced to take early retirement.'

'I was sorry to hear that,' Richard muttered.

'Yes, darling. I'm sure you were.' She sat on the chair opposite and drew up her skirt as she crossed her legs. The silk of her stockings squeaked and Richard's eyes were riveted upon them. So he was human after all, she thought, smiling to herself. 'I told him, no thank you, Daddy dear.'

'If you married me,' Richard urged, almost on one knee as he leaned closer, 'you would never have to worry about working. I don't think it proper for a woman.'

Kath rewarded him with a delighted smile. 'How very tempting you make it sound. But don't you think I should discover something of myself first, and something of the world? Try for a career or job?'

'What sort of job?'

Kath gazed into space, quite lost for an answer. Unlike Meg, she had never given work any serious consideration. She changed tack. 'Wouldn't marrying too quickly make Daddy even more disappointed in me?'

'I don't see why. You could have lots of babies.'

The smile faded. 'So I could.' She stood up. 'Perhaps we'll think about it at Christmas, darling. If there's still no war, of course. Would that do?'

Richard reluctantly conceded that it would do very well.

By then, Kath thought, she'd have found some way out of the cage, some place she could spread her wings and fly.

As if deciding on self-protection, Kath invited Meg and Jack to spend Christmas Day at Larkrigg.

'I feel the need for moral support.'

Meg, thrilled and flattered by Kath's invitation, broke into gales of laughter at the very idea of her sophisticated friend needing support from anyone. 'Of course I'll come. After lunch, when the menfolk are snoring their meal off.'

There was every sign of a white Christmas. The clusters of larch groves on the lower slopes stood out darkly against the winter pale grass. A time of year that Meg loved and a merrier party than usual to celebrate the festive season at Ashlea. She had taken her father at his word and invited Jack, but couldn't help wondering if the two would get on. Her regular visits to Broombank had been curtailed somewhat by the colder weather so it was important that Jack felt he could call on her at home, which so far he hadn't done.

At least their relationship seemed more settled. Following their tussle in the wood there had been many sweet apologies and lingering kisses, and Jack hadn't asked her to go too far again. Today being Christmas, Meg nursed a secret hope for more tangible evidence of his love. A ring perhaps?

'It's just like old times, when Mum was alive,' she said, on a rush of goodwill and emotion.

'Dinner was a bit late. Your mother was an expert cook. She'd never have been late,' complained Joe. 'You'll hev to shape better if you want to catch theeself an husband.'

'Thanks for those few kind words.' Hot and flustered from her long stint in the kitchen, Meg nevertheless managed to laugh at her father's put down.

'Your Connie not come home for Christmas then, I see?' Joe addressed Lanky, seemingly determined to spoil the mellow atmosphere by bringing a frown to the old man's brow.

'She has to think of her husband's family now. Said she might pop over at New Year,' said Lanky, smothering a sudden tickle in his throat.

'Aye. Happen.'

Lanky rubbed his horn hard palms together, clearly agitated by the questioning.

'Anyone for more plum pudding?' offered Meg quickly, sending a glance of displeasure in her father's direction.

'What? What have I done?' Everyone laughed and the tension lifted again.

It was a lovely day, crisp and bright as Christmas should be, a rose pink sky against cool blue mountain tops. High above a peregrine falcon circled, perhaps seeking its own Christmas feast. The two families took a long walk together, to shake down the rich food, as Lanky said. And perhaps replete after his good meal, Joe was as good as gold and made no more ill-tempered remarks. Even Dan congratulated Meg on the excellent meal. 'You know Father only wants what's best for you,' he added.

'He has a funny way of showing it!'

Meg suspected that Sally Ann had deliberately engineered for them to be walking side by side and she could see that her brother looked suddenly nervous as he cleared his throat. 'Sal and me are thinking of getting wed in the spring.'

Meg turned to him in a burst of genuine pleasure that passed for affection between them. 'Oh, I'm so glad. I like Sally Ann a lot.'

Dan flushed like a pleased schoolboy. 'Aye, well, we thought we might as well. If war really comes then it might get more difficult.'

'It'll come,' said Charlie. 'Congrats, old boy.'

Meg usually turned her mind obstinately away from all thought of war. She knew the threat was there but far away, in Germany and Austria and Spain. How could it affect them here on the Westmorland fells? Even so it was hard to be completely oblivious as a general feeling of unease was beginning to spread.

Even the Ellises could talk of little else as Meg and Jack sat politely sipping tea and eating tiny slivers of Christmas cake later that afternoon. There were several friends and neighbours present. The Jepsons, Mr and Mrs Parker from Swillhead, Hetty and Will Davies in their best clothes, looking faintly uncomfortable. And of course the vicar. Mrs Ellis was highly regarded at the church.

'They've given the schoolchildren gasmasks, can you believe that?' Rosemary Ellis said. 'Where in heaven's name would the gas come from up here?'

'It's only a precaution,' explained her husband, in his rather slow, kindly manner.

'Lanky says they were talking on the wireless the other day of evacuating children from the cities,' Meg put in.

Mr Ellis nodded sagely. 'Cities will be the worst places if war does start. We will be fortunate here. The war will not affect us at all.'

Kath, who had been feeding scraps of icing to the adoring Richard and taking little interest in the conversation, now turned abruptly to her father.

'That's the kind of talk that makes me wild. Of course the war will affect us. We could be bombed, you know. Even here. And there's talk of conscription soon. Some of us might be called up. Maybe even me.'

Rosemary Ellis laughed politely as if her daughter had made a lovely joke. 'Don't talk so foolishly, darling. Let's not spoil Christmas with all this morbid talk. More tea anyone?'

Meg was happy for the subject to change, for the thought of losing Jack in a war was too painful to contemplate. She slipped her hand into his when no one was looking and he squeezed it softly, as if to reassure her.

'Come on, everyone,' Kath cried, leaping up. 'Charades.' There was a general groan all round but she was adamant. 'You can't have Christmas without charades. I'll start. Come on, Jack. I've got a grand idea but I shall need you to play a part. Richard, you too.' Grabbing both men's hands she pulled them into the kitchen and everyone was laughing again, the black mood gone.

Meg sat feeling suddenly left out. She'd been quite happy in her mustard and tan suit until she'd seen Kath, lovely as ever in a new turquoise dress with gold buttons. And she didn't mean to be jealous, not really. It was an insecurity in her, a lack of confidence, that was all. One she usually accepted with equanimity. Not recognising her own fresh beauty, sometimes Meg longed for a touch of Kath's more exotic variety. Perhaps then Jack would declare his love more openly.

What she wanted most of all right now was for them to exchange their personal gifts in perfect privacy. She didn't want anyone to see her face when she opened Jack's. Meg was almost certain she would be engaged before the day was out. But privacy was denied them, though Jack did manage to sneak her a kiss when no one was looking as Kath handed out presents from the tree.

Sweetly sensual, his fingers slipped swiftly into the neck of her blouse to caress the swell of her breasts. Meg started, giving an embarrassed giggle, but a warm glow illuminated her face.

'I've knitted you some socks,' she said, and Jack took the carefully wrapped parcel in all seriousness, then they both laughed and hugged each other.

He held out his present to her, and her heart plummeted. Too big for a ring, and quite the wrong shape. Meg smiled up at him, swallowing her disappointment, not wanting him to see that it mattered.

She carefully unfolded the gold paper. 'A scarf. What a lovely blue. Just my colour. How did you guess?'

'Not good at shopping. I had some help.'

Some of the pleasure went out of the gift but Meg shook the feeling away. It was the thought that counted, wasn't it? He was saving the ring to give her later, when they were alone. This was the best Christmas ever. By next, who could tell? They might well be man and wife.

7

Later they all had a mad game of snowballs in the garden, stuffing them down necks like silly children with not a care in the world. And then Jack kissed Meg, making her head spin. Out of the corner of her eye she could see Richard doing the same with Kath but her friend didn't seem to be responding quite so enthusiastically.

Then Kath sent Richard inside to fetch mince pies and sherry for a special toast to Christmas beneath the stars.

'The way you bully that young man is quite wicked,' Meg said, but Kath only shrugged.

'The choice is his. Anyway, I wanted him to go away so that we three can have a precious moment alone together to toast a very special friendship.' She linked arms, hugging them close, one on each side of her. 'I want us always to be friends.'

'Of course we will,' said Meg, leaning her head against Jack's shoulder. 'For ever and ever.' She shivered, drawing her coat closer.

'Are you cold?' asked Kath, concerned. 'I thought it was warmer now the snow has come.'

'I'm fine.'

'Things can go wrong sometimes, even between friends,' Jack warned. 'If there is a war we might be separated. I for one will have to join up.'

'We'll all join up!' cried Kath, reckless as ever.

'Don't joke about it. It's too terrible,' Meg said, grey eyes alight with all the love and happiness she felt on this special day. 'You are my best friends. Who else do I have but you two?'

There was a moment's silence as both acknowledged the truth of this bleak statement. It was the penalty of living in such a remote spot.

Then Kath wriggled free to stand before them, one hand held out. 'Let's make a vow. A promise that whatever happens, we'll always be friends, deep deep down.'

Meg, knowing she'd drunk far too much wine, started to giggle. 'You make it sound like the Three Musketeers.'

'It is in a way,' Kath agreed. 'Come on, promise. Friends for ever.'

Meg clasped Kath's hand and covered both with Jack's. 'All right. A solemn vow. Friends for ever.'

'Promise?'

'Promise.'

They both looked up at Jack and he grinned. 'Promise.'

It was after eleven when they walked down the lane, arms wrapped about each other in the starry darkness, and Meg was glowing with love. The lack of a ring didn't trouble her at all. She knew they loved each other, that was the important thing.

But then in the contented silence, as so often happened, her thoughts moved on to her secret dreams. Of being at Broombank with Jack, as man and wife. She traced the picture of the great inglenook in her head and she and Jack seated within it, talking about their flock, as generations of Lakelanders had done.

'Lanky isn't well, is he?'

'Doesn't seem to be.'

'He should see a doctor.'

'He won't even bring a vet to the animals. He's too set in his ways. If it can't be cured with treacle or embrocation, he doesn't want to know.'

'Is he going to let you take over the farm?'

Jack looked surprised. 'Why should he?'

'Because he's ill and it needs attention.'

'Stuff the farm.' Jack pulled her into his arms and kissed her and Meg melted against him, happily relinquishing all thought but that of desire. When it was over she curled against him, cheeks flushed, eyes star bright. Jack's hands tightened upon her buttocks, rubbing her against him.

'Sometimes I think you fancy my dad more than you do me.'

Meg smiled mischievously up at him. 'Maybe I do.'

Jack bit her ear, making her squeal. 'It's not often I get you to myself these days. You always seem to have dogs around, or sheep.'

His lips were finding the curve below her ear, his tongue tickling enticingly. 'I reckon it's starting to snow again.'

Meg glanced in surprise at the clear night sky sparkling with a network of bright stars. 'Why do you think . . .?'

'Or maybe rain.' He started to unbutton her coat. 'Better take shelter, wouldn't you say? And how fortunate, here we are by our barn.' Jack was walking her backwards and with his arms still clamped tight about her she had no option but to go where he led her.

'Where are you taking me?' she asked in a breathless voice, not really caring. Violet-blue eyes, dark and teasing, ran over her face with a need that set a sharp and piercing ache somewhere deep in her belly. She knew what he wanted, what he had always wanted.

And Meg also knew that she wanted to go with him. Anywhere he asked.

It was warmer in the barn, amongst the hay. Rust welcomed her with thumping tail and wet tongue. But Meg had no time for dogs just now.

'Lie down, boy. Stay.'

Jack was leading her deep into the darkness, only a shaft of moonlight lighting the dustmotes in the musty air.

Meg reached for him, taking his beloved face between her hands, smoothing the dark hair. How she loved the way it curled into a point at his nape.

There was an impatience in him, like a fever. She could feel him tremble as he laid her down, lengthening himself beside her so that he could smoothe one hand over the curve of her breast and the flatness of her stomach. Very quickly it seemed to Meg, he had removed her blouse and camisole and her young, rosy-tipped breasts were exposed to his eager gaze. But she didn't mind, she welcomed it. She could feel the impatience rising in herself just as fiercely. When he caught her nipples between his sharp white teeth this time she did not protest, only arched her back and pushed herself into him, making him moan with agony.

This time she meant to show him how much she loved him. This time she would prove that she wasn't frigid. It would be her Christmas gift to him.

She wondered if it would hurt, the first time. As schoolgirls they had made wild guesses and there had been much talk once of blood and piercing pain. Would it be like that? Meg hoped not. She wanted to feel only pleasure and the proof of his love. Would he tell her that he loved her afterwards, when they were one? Perhaps it was these

confused thoughts that made the words she had so longed to say come
out in a muddle.

Jack's fingers were fumbling with her skirt buttons and she was
finding it hard to catch her breath. 'It's going to be all right. Father
doesn't mind. About us. He thinks it's a good idea,' she said, meaning
to encourage him, but at once felt him freeze.

'What did you say?'

Quietly, almost fearfully, she repeated the fateful words.

He pulled away from her to sit back on his heels and survey her.
Meg drew her hands over her suddenly chilled breasts, feeling
cheapened by the anger in his face. 'What is it? What have I done? I
only said . . .'

'I know what you said. Did your father tell you to come here, with
me, should you ever get the chance?'

'Don't be silly.' She reached for him again but he evaded her grasp.
'He tells me nothing, except to fetch home-made dishes for Lanky
now and then, but . . .' It was the wrong thing to say, she could sense it
the minute the words were out.

'To soften him up? And did he tell you to offer yourself to Lanky's
son for afters. Did he?'

Meg couldn't believe what she was hearing. How had it all gone so
badly wrong? What had she *done*?

'It's not like that,' she protested. 'I don't care about my father
any more than you do. It wasn't me who told him. He'd guessed. I
thought it would make it easier for you to call and see me.' But she
could tell Jack wasn't listening.

'Joe Turner has been wanting Broombank for years. And having
failed by the usual methods, he's trying bribery and corruption now,
is that it? Offering delicious home-made titbits, even his own
daughter in exchange. Or is it wedding bells he's after, to get
Broombank in the family, eh?'

Tears sprang to her eyes, filling her nose and mouth and seeming to
run all over her face. This couldn't be happening. What Jack was
saying was awful, terrible, *and simply not true*.

'I thought you loved me?' she said, trying to scramble free of him
and hiccuping like a child on her tears. 'I love you.' For so long she'd
tried not to be the first to say those words and now she had spoiled it
all by letting them come. Jack would never love her now. He blamed
her for everything, she could see it in the mutinous set of his
handsome face. Her heart ached to see it turn against her, to see the
sensual lips curl.

'Love? *Love*? Who are you to talk of love? For months you've hardly let me touch you. What do you think I'm made of? Stone.' He'd got her skirt unfastened and tugged it from her in a frenzy of frustration. Not listening to the voice of reason in the back of his head, he could feel only the pulsing heat of his loins.

'No, Jack.' Her voice sounded oddly cracked and surprisingly calm. 'Not like this. I don't want it to happen like this, in anger. You know you'll only regret it.'

'Damn you,' he said, flinging himself down upon her and starting to knead her breasts. She'd planned it all, he could see that now. Making him mad for her all these months, then when Joe Turner had had yet another refusal on his latest offer for Broombank, it was suddenly all right. She was begging for it. 'All this time I've wanted you and all you've given me is the prissy miss act, but Daddy says it's all right so here you are, the virginal sacrifice. Why do you want it? It's worth nowt anyway.'

'*No*. It's not like that.' Meg knew her words were lost on him. His legs straddled her and his mouth was grasping her nipple, suckling her, driving her mad with need. But this was all wrong. It wasn't meant to be this way. With shock she felt his fingers move deep inside her, thrusting and probing, and pain and pleasure swamped her. Dear God, how I love him, she thought. Let his anger go. Oh, please let him be kind. He must want us to be one, our love perfect, as she did.

'Kiss me,' she begged, but he ignored her as his fingers explored her with outrageous boldness, making the need worse not better, making her want him beyond anything she had ever imagined.

'Love me, Jack. I do love you so.'

She could hear her own voice begging for him as he'd said she would one day, feel her body arching against him, the wetness of herself a startling revelation. What was it he wanted of her? Not just to lie here, surely?

He was fumbling with something, talking of how much something or other cost and would she keep still or he'd tear it?

Then he was lifting her thighs, his fingers bruising her flesh as he pulled her against him. When he drove into her it took her by surprise and she cried out with the unexpected pain of it. Then he was pounding into her with such force her head was pushed uncomfortably against the wall of the barn. She lifted herself to him, wanting to be as close as she could get, to make the loving come right. Meg tried to match his energy and need with her own, but somehow all desire seemed to drain from her and she found herself wanting it all to be over as quickly as possible. When he finally withdrew, shuddering on the hay beside her, an aching disappointment left her spent and drained of emotion. And feeling very faintly foolish.

Afterwards, they lay in the hay side by side, not speaking. Meg became aware of a strange soreness in parts of her body she had never considered before.

'Feel better now?' Jack asked and she smiled shyly, not sure how to answer. It hadn't been exactly as she'd imagined. But perhaps that was because it was her first time, and she'd feel more involved when she'd had a bit more practice. Guilt washed over her. What was she saying? It'd been Christmas and the unaccustomed wine that had gone to her head. It mustn't happen again. Not till they were wed.

'We shouldn't have done that,' she said.

Jack was sitting up, lighting a cigarette. 'Why not? It's made me feel better anyway.'

'I wouldn't like to make a habit of it,' she said worriedly.

Jack chuckled, his eyes scanning her pale body in the shaft of moonlight. 'I wouldn't mind.'

She stroked one finger over the bow of his lips, giggling when his teeth nipped her fingertips. 'Why should I want Lanky's farm when I can have you? Land is easy to rent anywhere for a pound an acre. Love comes much more expensive.' And as his eyelids flickered slightly, eyes glinting, she kissed him softly.

'We'll marry in the spring,' she said. 'Then we can make love all the time. There. Will that make you happy?'

1939

8

Everyone in the farming community was glad that 1938 was over. What with the slump in prices and shortage of labour, things had been difficult and profits few. But with talk of a coming war it looked as if next year might be even worse.

Only Meg was happy. Meg positively glowed. Her life had changed beyond all expectation and she revelled in the joy of it.

She spent New Year's Day quietly at Broombank and it wasn't till a week after that the worrying started. Every morning when she got up, every night when she went to bed, she looked for the sign that would tell her all was as it should be.

But there was nothing.

Oh lordy, what if she were pregnant? Meg felt sick with fear. She imagined facing her father with the terrible news, for that's how he would view it. He'd do more than slap her face then, much more. She must have been mad to allow her feelings to run away with her like that, just because it was Christmas.

As each day passed she could hardly eat with the worry of it. She couldn't concentrate on any topic of conversation above a minute, and her stomach churned with anxiety so much it almost felt as if there must be a baby in there already.

When at last one night she woke to the familiar stickiness between her legs she actually wept with relief. Never, never, she decided, would she put herself through such agony again.

'The wine went to my head,' she explained to Jack as they sat by

Broombank fire taking supper together one evening. 'It mustn't happen again.'

'Why not, for God's sake? You don't seriously expect me to go back to sweet kisses and holding hands after that, do you?'

'It's only for a little while. Till we get married in the spring.'

'And what if your dad won't let us? You're not twenty-one until August.'

'Then it'll have to be August or September. He can't stop us then.'

The anxiety on Jack's face made her laugh. 'I've told you, he doesn't mind. But even if he does, this is just between you and me and nothing to do with anyone else.' She kissed him teasingly on the nose. 'Tell me you love me, go on, I want to hear you say it.'

'You know I do,' he said gruffly, and she laughed again at his embarrassment.

'Oh, I'm so happy. Isn't life lovely? Have you spoken to Lanky yet?'

'About what?' Jack's attention seemed to be far away. Tired, she didn't wonder, from his long hours working. He had probably been up at dawn to feed the animals and do the milking.

A great wave of love for him washed over her. When they were married she'd be able to help him by sharing the load. She'd get a girl in to do the rough work in the house so that she'd have the time to spend with Jack out on the farm. How she would love to make a warm home for him, sit with him here every evening, as his wife. Then he would turn out the lamp and take her upstairs to the big wide bed where they would make love. Meg went hot all over just to think of it. Best to keep to safer topics.

'I was talking to Lanky about him increasing the flock. Unless he wants to go in for more dairy? Has he decided yet?'

The violet eyes darkened and he kicked a log that had slipped a little back into the grate. A shower of sparks scattered like fireflies. 'You shouldn't bother him with such ideas. He's not up to it.'

'I thought you were dissatisfied with the farm and wanted to improve it. Perhaps he'll let you take over when we marry, let you do things your own way.' Meg knelt before him and leaned her cheek against his knee, eyes troubled. 'The farm needs proper attention from someone.'

'Don't blame me,' he said sharply. 'It's not my fault.'

She'd made him angry and dipped her head for a moment, blinking furiously as the colours in the rag rug blurred giddily before her eyes. Desperate to make it right, she plunged blindly on. 'It's only that this Christmas he's looked so gaunt, and that tweed jacket seems bigger than ever. The weight is dropping off him and he's coughing more. What is it? What's wrong? Can't you do anything?'

'You know I can't. I already told you.' There was bitterness in Jack's tone and he pulled her roughly into his arms. 'Now for God's sake stop going on about the farm. Give me some attention for a change.'

Spring came and the alder and hazel catkins clustered thick as clotted cream on the spindly branches. A blackbird sang his heart out, showing off to his intended, and Dan and Sally Ann married, as planned. Meg and Jack postponed their own plans to the autumn because she still hadn't plucked up courage to ask her father, and neither had Jack.

She was afraid Joe might put conditions on her, as if she were a cow at market and prove Jack right in his suspicions.

It wasn't long till she was twenty-one then she could please herself.

Sally Ann looked a picture in a dove grey dress and matching loose-fitting coat, despite the freckled paleness of her cheeks. Grey suede shoes with pretty leather bows and a tiny pink hat with a veil completed the ensemble.

She'd intended to be married in white and had spent hours with Meg poring over newspapers to see what 'This Year's Bride was wearing'. But somehow none of the designs had quite suited or been within her means and they'd always ended up reading depressing advertisements for black-out curtains or gramophones at six shillings a week that they couldn't afford.

'Look at this, sixpence to wash a bundle of clothes for an evacuated child. Well, I could always do that, couldn't I, as my war effort?' Sally Ann read, and Meg shivered, as if a goose had stalked over her grave.

'Don't talk about the war. I hate it.'

They told the postman, who delivered their morning paper, to stop bringing it if all it contained was bad news.

'I'll speak to the newspaper people about it,' he said laughing, and carried on bringing it, if only because he enjoyed the chat with Meg and Sal and the cups of tea they gave him.

They had gone into Kendal in the end to buy something pretty but serviceable. Meg too had bought a new dress, a deep cobalt blue that set off the burnished honey of her curls, now grown fairly long again as a concession to Jack. The dress hung in her wardrobe upstairs and she wondered when she would ever wear it again. On her honeymoon perhaps?

Sometimes, in the quiet of the night, Meg worried about the fact that she'd put a stop to their love making. She guessed it had something to do with her Methodist upbringing as much as her fear of her father that she couldn't think it right to give yourself to a man before you were wed. Yet she had done so, hadn't she? Not that she'd been very good at it, mind. No bells had rung or fireworks exploded and she had felt, in the end, as if it was all a bit messy and embarrassing. That was probably the worry, she decided. It wasn't Jack's fault, or hers. Everything would be all right once they were married.

She didn't regret it though. At least now Jack knew how much she loved him.

The installing of Sal in the kitchen at Ashlea meant that Meg had more time for herself as well as more time to spend with Jack.

She brought Rust home at last and was glad of his company for the dog had already proved to be a great friend.

'What are you going to do with the cur then?' asked Dan, watching her knock together a kennel for him out of some odd bits of wood.

'This is my dog. Leave him alone, right?'

Dan advanced a pace and Rust half rose from his lying position, giving a low growl in his throat. Dan stopped. 'You think I'd be interested in a puny creature like that?'

'He may be small but he's strong and a good sheep dog. He needs time to settle, so don't bother him.'

'You know nowt about sheep dogs, nor sheep for that matter.' He made no mention of having seen her once, working the dog. Never give away all your secrets, that was Dan's motto.

'Maybe I know more than you think.' Meg tied Rust to a post and rubbed his ear affectionately, much to Dan's amusement. But she took care to wait until her brother had left the yard before feeding the dog some titbits.

'There you are, boy. This is home now.' Rust gazed up at her with adoring brown eyes in which she could see her own image reflected.

Every day she took him for long walks over the fells, or more often up to Brockbarrow Wood where they would sit in the shade for a while and Rust would drink from the small tarn. Then on sometimes as far as Whinstone Gill. The stream wasn't gushing with quite its usual force through the rock because May had been so uncommonly dry but it was a peaceful, secret sort of place where you could be certain of being alone.

It was a pleasant surprise to find Kath there one warm afternoon in early June.

'What's this? Lady of leisure now Sally Ann is resident cook, eh?' Kath pulled a towel around her bare shoulders. Her hair wasn't wet but she was dressed for swimming in a pink cotton swimsuit. She started to pull on a swirling floral skirt.

'Taking a leaf out of your book.' Meg dropped on the grass beside her. A dipper was doing its clever underwater walk, forging its way against the current as it searched for tadpoles, worms and other treats. Meg watched it for a while, laughing, then rolled over on to her stomach. 'Have you been swimming? Why didn't you tell me? I would have brought my cossy and joined you.'

'I wasn't. I mean, this is hardly the place, is it? And the water's a bit too cold yet. It was just a walk, and a sunbathe. You're usually too busy working at this time of day.'

Meg wrinkled her nose. 'I feel lazy today. It's too hot to think, let alone work. I've been putting Rust through his paces and relaxing. Isn't that wicked? Oh, what's that?' She sat up quickly, staring into the bushes behind them. 'Did you hear something?'

'No. Didn't hear a thing.'

'Rust, what are you doing?' The dog was nosing about excitedly in the undergrowth that grew out of the cracks at the bottom of the crag, tail waving like a flag. 'What have you found?'

'Probably rabbits. There are loads about. Come on, let's go. I'm suddenly desperately hungry. You can take me home and feed me some of Sally Ann's wonderful scones.'

Meg laughed, enjoying the rare warmth of the sun too much to want to move. 'What about your diet?'

'Blow to that. Come *on*.' Kath tugged at her arm.

'I can take a hint. You should have brought a picnic if you were so ravenous.'

'We will have a picnic. Soon. A great big one.'

'No time. There'll be the clipping soon and Sally Ann and I will have to do the great bake-in for all the shearers who come to help.' Meg rolled her eyes. 'What a job. I think I'd much rather clip sheep than roll pastry any day.'

'You are a funny old thing. Personally, I'd rather do neither.' Kath linked her arm into Meg's and began to walk her along the path. 'Come on, let's go and be greedy piggies.'

'We're all very aware of your philosophy of life, Kath. Why do anything if you can get away with less? I don't know why I bother with such a wastrel.' It was said in a good-natured fashion as it was an old joke between them but Kath appeared to be taking it more seriously for once.

'Maybe I'll change one day and surprise you all.'

'Now that I would love to see. I shall look forward to it.'

'One thing's for certain, it won't be here, in this Godforsaken place.'

Meg stopped. 'How can you say such a thing? This is the most beautiful country on God's earth.' She looked about her at the mountains she regarded almost as friends. She knew every fissure of rock, every footpath. She recognised the light and shade of their moods which changed as quickly as the weather, and could not imagine a life where she would not walk upon them, or simply feast her eyes upon their mystical beauty.

'For you, yes.' Kath met Meg's shocked expression with a wry smile. 'This is your special place. You have your plans, something to look forward to. Marriage, motherhood. Who'd have thought it? You with your constant cries for independence.'

'Things change. You could have the same if you married Richard Harper.'

Kath rolled her eyes. 'And make Mummy happy that she has a conventional daughter, I know. But it wouldn't be right. I don't love him. I don't love anyone, I suppose. And I don't know what I want to do with my life. It is all very silly, don't you think?' There was an extra brightness to the hazel eyes and Meg felt a rush of affection for her friend.

'I used to feel just the same way, as if I had no purpose to life.'

'And now you've found it, like a mission. Wife and mother, just as Sally Ann wants to be, as all normal women want to be apparently. An essential part of life.' There was a tartness in the tone, unlike Kath's usual carefree self, that made Meg flinch.

'I don't see why a woman has to give up her independence just because she's married. I'll still be me inside. There are so many things I want to do. Life is so exciting.'

She wanted to be with Jack desperately. But the need to prove herself in other ways was growing almost as strong.

'So when's the happy day?'

'Nothing fixed yet.'

'Ah, yes, of course. Difficult to pin Jack down, I should imagine.' Kath glanced back over her shoulder. 'Hadn't you best call that dog of yours? Not too obedient, is he?'

'What did you mean by that?'

'By what?'

'Being difficult to pin Jack down? It's not that at all, as a matter of fact. We're waiting till I'm of age.'

Kath shrugged, still looking oddly strained as she smiled at Meg. 'You know my opinion of Jack Lawson. I haven't changed my mind. If you were to ask me, I'd advise you to stop seeing him for a while. Test him. See how long it takes for him to come running.'

Meg went very still. 'You're suggesting he wouldn't?'

'I'm not suggesting anything, except that you should tread warily, think carefully. Marriage is an awfully serious business. Try out a few more chaps first before you pick one.' The sensual scarlet lips pouted seductively. 'Spread a little happiness, that's what I say.'

Meg turned her head away to hide the quick flush of annoyance she felt at Kath's words and called to Rust. He was half inside the bramble bush by this time and she couldn't help but chuckle at the sight of his wriggling rump. Kath laughed too and it relieved the unexpected tension that had sprung up between them. 'Seems almost a shame to rob him of the pleasure. Rust! Here, boy!'

The small dog, who was having the time of his life, was most reluctant to abandon this much loved, familiar scent but bellied backwards out of the bush and looked after Meg's retreating figure. He waited for a fraction of a second, tongue lolling, just to make sure that she meant what she said. But as she continued to walk away he put down his head and streaked after her. It was hard, sometimes, for a dog to learn to change his allegiance but he was getting the idea.

'Where's Rust?' Meg faced her father and brothers as they sat at the breakfast table, cold fury on her face. 'Someone has cut his rope and let him free.' Her eyes went straight to Dan but he did not look up from spooning his porridge.

'If the cur had any sense it would stay here without a rope round its neck,' said Joe.

'I was frightened of him wandering off.' She meant being driven away, by her jealous brother.

Charlie set down his spoon. 'I'll help you look for him.'

'No need for that. Anyway you've got work to do,' Joe

complained. 'If it's gone anywhere it'll be back at Broombank where it belongs.'

Meg stormed up to the table and glared down at Dan. 'He was settling so well and you've just ruined it. I expect you booted him out. He wouldn't go willingly, not now.' She felt helplessness overwhelm her. It was always the same. Anything that was hers, Dan would try to take from her and Joe would not lift a finger to chastise him for his peevishness.

She blazed out the door and across the field on swinging, angry strides. She found the dog, as expected, comfortably ensconced in the old cruck barn at Broombank, looking pitifully guilty.

'No harm done,' said Lanky.

'Not this time, no, but what right has Dan to let Rust go? How dare he?' Meg's temper was firing on all cylinders so she didn't see Lanky put a hand to his brow and rub it with the heel of his palm.

'I shouldn't worry over it,' he said. 'One mistake won't spoil him. He's a quick learner.' He couldn't bring himself to get too excited about a dog that had come safely home even if it had been deliberately forced out. He had more pressing concerns.

1939 was proving to be the hottest summer that anyone could remember. The Herdwicks, in their newly clipped shorter coats, had climbed as high up the fells as they could get, to the benefit of the grass on the lower slopes, and lay gasping for breath in any shade they could find. Even the curlews were absent, spending their days seeking moisture in the swampy areas of Arnside and Leighton Moss. The air seemed uncannily still and languorous, the kind of day it was hard to contemplate work.

But Meg had been up since dawn, preparing the haytiming feast. 'Am I glad to have you to help me, Sally Ann!' she said with feeling, and her sister-in-law chuckled.

'I see, that's all you want me for, is it? A slave.'

'Sorry. I didn't mean it like it sounded.'

Sally Ann cast her a shrewd glance and jerked her head in the direction of the hayfield where the Turners and Lawsons were busy bringing in the crop.

'You'd rather be out there, wouldn't you, getting your hands mucky? Well, why don't you go? I can manage here.'

'No, no, it's all right. I'll finish slicing this ham.'

'You've been quiet lately. It's Jack, isn't it? Has he popped the question yet?'

'Oh, don't you start. I've enough with Father asking me day after day if young Lawson's intentions are honourable.' Both girls giggled.

'Well, are they?'

Meg flushed bright pink and followed Sally Ann's gaze to where Jack toiled along with the rest. He looked so handsome it made her heart ache just to look at him.

Every neighbour had come along to help, including the women and children. That was the best thing about the farming community in these parts, the way they helped one another. No family turned enough acreage over to growing crops to make the buying or hiring of a tractor pay, so the work had to be done mainly by hand. A lumbering fell pony pulled the Bamford mower over the smoother parts, with the men scything the corners and steeper areas in the old way.

They'd gathered the cut hay into small cocks, and then as it dried into bigger and bigger cocks to stand like a regiment of expanding soldiers' hats in the stubble for two weeks, or until the church bells had rung thrice, as the old adage said. And if the weather looked like breaking everyone would rush to load the hay on to the shelved carts and pack it into the high barns as quickly as possible.

Later, the great steaming, clanking threshing machine that travelled from farm to farm would come and do its work, much to the great excitement of the children. And the barns would be filled to capacity, ready for the winter. It was a good feeling, Meg thought.

'It looks very picturesque, doesn't it?' she remarked. 'But you'd think we could have worked out a quicker way of doing it by now.' Then glancing at Sally Ann's face, she smiled. 'All right. I'll answer your question. Nothing at all has been decided about marriage. But, yes, Jack is honourable. At least he doesn't push me to – you know. He respects the fact that I don't want to.'

'I suppose you've been brought up a bit more proper than me.' Sally Ann shrugged. 'Nobody would have cared if I'd got into trouble. Whereas with you . . .'

It wasn't necessary to finish the sentence.

'But now you're a respectable married woman. Oh, and, Sally Ann, I do so enjoy having you as a sister.'

Sally Ann reached for another loaf she had made only that morning, looking flushed and pleased. 'I confess I was a touch anxious about it at first. But we've got on all right, haven't we? And I'm getting used to this farming lark.'

Jack's muscled shoulders were burnt brown by the sun with scarcely any feeling left in them, having long since passed the pain barrier. He had been scything, mowing, raking and turning hay for weeks now, and he was bone weary. Long days working well into the night, able to snatch only a few hours' sleep before rising at dawn to start lifting and shaking the hay all over again. His legs felt hard as iron and his blistered hands burned as if they were on fire. All his hatred for the life he was leading was encapsulated in that pain.

The sun was starting to drop from the aching blue sky now, bringing a welcome relief, and he stopped to wipe the sweat from his brow.

As he stretched his aching back Jack wondered why he'd come back. Guilt and concern over Lanky, he supposed.

Connie had always been the clever one and he'd been glad to get away from the constant comparisons made between the two of them. What he'd discovered was a whole new world out there, a life in the cities and big towns that he hadn't even known existed. He'd been tempted to return home when his sister married, but his feet still itched to be off again.

This being the case, why was he committing himself to Meg?

He could see her setting food on a long trestle table beneath the big old ash. She and Sal happily cooked and baked for the dozens of workers, now that the haytiming was almost over.

He had himself brought over an entire barrel of beer that waited to be supped. His mouth watered just to think of it.

'Is that food ready yet?' he called, and grinned as he saw Meg instantly turn her head towards him, her whole face lighting up as if from some inner glow.

'Ready when you are.'

'Right.' He flung aside the pitchfork with relief. 'Come on, Dan. I'm starving. Let's eat.'

'Aye, let Charlie finish it on his own.' And when his young brother objected, a good-natured tussle broke out and the two men chased the luckless Charlie right up the hill to Brockbarrow Tarn. They were all breathless when they reached the top of the hill but Dan still found the energy to fling his brother in the deep pool, shouting with laughter as Charlie came up spluttering and gasping with cold.

'This is great,' he yelled, determined not to be bested. 'Just what the doctor ordered.' Then tugging off his boots and clothes he tossed them to the bank and lay back, paddling ecstatically in the fresh cool water.

Dan and Jack exchanged glances, then they too were stripping off boots and trousers thick with dust and hayseed and leaping in after him, slapping each other with sprays of ice water.

The worst part was putting the hot dusty clothes back on again, but, thoroughly refreshed, the men tucked happily into pork pie and home-cured ham, apple turnovers and great hunks of home-produced cheese.

The food was delicious and Jack congratulated himself on his good fortune. A man liked to have his fling, right enough, but when it came to wife material there were other considerations. Marriage might not be such a bad thing after all, he decided.

He watched Meg as she sliced ham for Lanky and Joe, her rounded arms tanned by hours in the sun, breasts moving enticingly freely beneath the thin cotton of her dress, and felt warm life return to his nether regions. Yes, Meg had shaped up pretty good for all she still held some girlish inhibitions. Now if he could just persuade her to stop worrying about Lanky and Broombank, they'd be off over the blue horizon come the year end, no matter what.

His father could sell the farm to Joe Turner if he so wanted. What the hell did it matter so long as Jack could get away. He'd had enough of liver fluke, blowfly, sheep dung and daylong back-breaking labour to last him a lifetime. He had other plans for his life and Meg would have to accept it.

Then why hadn't he chosen Kath Ellis instead?

As restless as himself in some ways, she was the obvious choice. Yet Jack instinctively knew he could never hope to keep Katherine Ellis happy. Whatever good times they might have had, and they'd certainly had that, it was all in the past. To have Kath for a wife would be like trying to control a flock of sheep without a dog. She'd run rings round him, play every feminine trick in the book, spend all his money and more besides, then toss him to one side as easily as Dan tossed Charlie in the tarn.

Besides, she'd started getting a bit troublesome lately. Why, only last week they'd been in the barn, as usual, him lying on the dusty bales and Kath standing in a shaft of sunlight that came down through the rafters. Just like a spotlight in a theatre, it was. He hadn't been able to take his eyes off her.

Unlike Meg, Kath was always happy to take her clothes off. In one way he felt it a pity because it was always a pleasurable experience, part of the enjoyment as it were, to take them off himself. But he was not averse to a little strip show. And there was no doubt Kath looked gorgeous in her silk slip, those magnificent breasts of hers peaking wantonly. He'd felt an erection starting before she'd hardly got her blouse undone.

But when he'd reached out a hand to stroke their smooth beauty, Kath had slapped it away and not with her usual teasing touch either.

'What are you in such a temper about?'

'You, you great oaf. We can't go on like this. I've told you before, we have to stop.'

'Stop what?' he'd asked, surprised by her fervour. 'I can't think what you're talking about?'

'You've got to tell her.'

'Tell her? Tell who what?' Kath had sighed but he'd been impatient to be done with talking and get on with the business in hand, or what he would like to have in hand. He'd reached for her again only to be disappointed. Kath kept herself just enticingly out of reach.

'About us, you goon. Meg loves you, and she's my friend. We can't keep on hurting her in this way.'

Jack saw at once then that he had a problem. Kath had totally misunderstood the situation. He'd never intended getting seriously entangled with her. She was big fish, out of his price range, fun to play with but never to land. He set about correcting her mistake.

'We haven't hurt Meg. She doesn't know anything about this and she's not going to. Anyroad, I never promised you anything, Kath. It was just a bit of fun.'

'I know.' Her face looked odd somehow, sort of stiff and fierce, and Jack suddenly saw how she would look when she was old. It was the weirdest sensation.

She'd come to sit beside him then, her long tapering fingers starting to unbutton his shirt. Damn the woman! How could he argue with her when parts of him were standing to attention? 'The thing is,' she was saying, 'I know it started off that way, but what if I decided to apply for exclusive rights? We might make a good team, don't you think? We could go places, you and I. Let's face it, we're neither of us country bumpkin types. If it weren't for you, and Bonnie, of course, I'd be bored sick here.'

'I'm glad you at least put me before the damn' horse.' She was starting on the buckle at his waist and Jack could scarcely contain his excitement.

'You're wasted on that farm.' She kissed his bare chest. 'Daddy could always find you a good job. He has friends, you know, contacts in Lancaster or Manchester, or even London if you prefer.'

If there was one thing Jack hated it was being organised, particularly by a woman, and he'd never expected it from the effervescent, fun-loving Katherine Ellis. It didn't appeal one bit. The pity of it was that she had a marvellous body but Jack's taste for it had quite gone. His ardour had evaporated as quickly as it had come.

Some sixth sense told him it was time to end this bit of fun. If Katherine Ellis was starting to make demands then there must be a reason and he wanted no part of it. No, it was time to make changes. He didn't like a pushy woman.

Jack made love to her, as required, but more out of obligation than desire. It left a taste in his mouth as dry as ash.

And so, since he liked the idea of having a woman to look after him and needed to escape Kath, it had to be Meg. She was a worker, no doubt about that, and a damn' good cook. And Meg adored him, didn't she? It was important to a man, to be adored.

And she had other delightful attributes of which she was only just becoming aware. He slid a hand up her skirt now and over her bare leg as she moved close by him. His fingers had very nearly found her crotch when she gave a smothered squeal and cast him a fierce look, making him choke on his pie as he laughed. Oh, yes, Meg got better and better. Kath would see how it had to be.

It was August, and Meg's twenty-first birthday, so a holiday had been awarded. They were to climb to the top of Kidsty Pike for a picnic. Jack and Meg, Sally Ann and Dan, and Charlie. And Kath and Richard, of course.

'Where's Kath? She promised she'd be here.'

'Don't let's waste time waiting for her,' grumbled Dan, but Meg insisted and they all sat about in the August heat, kicking their heels and getting far too hot.

Three-quarters of an hour later, even Meg had very nearly run out of patience when Kath's little Ford came bumping up the farm track.

'Where have you been?'

She shrugged and apologised. 'Richard isn't coming. He's busy.' He'd refused her invitation. It was the first time he'd ever gone against Kath's wishes and she'd been puzzled, so had gone to his house to find out why. Then a young girl had called to him from the french windows and all had been made clear.

Kath shivered, feeling oddly cold inside despite the heat. It wasn't as if she loved him. It didn't really matter. Except that it left this problem, still unsolved. Oh, to hell with it.

Linking hands with both Meg and Jack, she tossed back a sleek swathe of hair and laughed. 'Come on, what are we waiting for? I'm starving.'

They walked for miles through lanes fringed with thick clusters of lady's bedstraw, speedwell, pink campion and great yellow patches of celandines. Then on over the tough, sheep-cropped grass where the only touch of colour was the pale mauve of sweet-scented heather, thick with bees. For the last part they had to scramble over craggy rocks and rough scree to make the ascent but it was worth it, Meg thought, just for the exhilaration alone, let alone the view.

Here in the mountains she felt in tune with her world, a part of the green and blue beauty of it, laid out like a map before her. Far below, further away than it actually looked as distances were deceptive at this height, was the strung out blue-grey of Ullswater with the majesty of Helvellyn, Fairfield and Scafell beyond. And in the other direction lay the humble simplicity of Broombank and Ashlea. They lay along the edge of a long dale with Broombank at the apex of the ridge and Ashlea below, as if a giant thumb had scoured out a place for them.

'How can anyone bear to leave this?' Meg sighed, resting her chin on her knees as she gazed, contented, upon her beloved land.

'I could,' said Charlie, with quiet firmness. 'If I could do what I most wanted.'

'Which is?' asked Kath, clearing stones and brushing the heather with her hands to make a comfy spot for herself so that everyone laughed at her. But she only pulled a face at her audience, spread a clean white handkerchief and laid her head upon it, fluffing her pageboy bob into place. 'Go on, Charlie. I'm listening. What is it you want to do?'

'Fly.'

'Oh, me too,' murmured Sally Ann softly. 'Like a great heron, soaring high in the sky.'

'More like a big fat buzzard if you keep on eating at that rate,' Dan said, and got a swipe for his pains. Sally Ann was heard to mutter something about greedy husbands. But they seemed to be grinning at each other so that was all right.

'You might well get your chance,' put in Jack quietly, when the laughter had died down. 'To fly, I mean. I listened to the news the other day. It wasn't good. People are putting out sand bags and building Anderson shelters in their back yards in the towns and cities. Maybe we should get one?'

'Where'd we put it and who would fly over here? Unless they'd taken a wrong turning and missed Barrow or Liverpool,' said Dan, carelessly. 'Can I have another cheese and pickle sandwich?'

Charlie stood up, his youthful idealism incensed by his brother's offhand attitude. 'Don't you care? There's plenty as say our bombers can win this war in a matter of months. It's not a joking matter. If we don't do something, Hitler could walk all over us. And all you can think of is food in your belly. There could be people dying out there, in Europe.' He waved a hand vaguely over the idyllic view and then brought it down to slap the hunk of bread and cheese from Dan's hand and send it rolling downhill, bouncing over the crags and scree into Riggingdale below.

There was a short, shocked silence. Charlie was the quiet one, not easily roused to anger.

'I've already registered as doing work of "national importance", if you want to know,' Dan told him, getting slowly to his feet. 'I'm a farmer, not a fighter. And I'll not be bossed about by a young whippersnapper like you.'

'All right, folks, that's enough,' said Kath, not moving an inch from her supine position on the heather but bringing all eyes upon her nonetheless by the authority in her tone. 'Today has been declared a holiday so the rules are, no squabbling and no talk of war. Have we any cider left, Sal?'

'Plenty.' Sally Ann reached for a flagon, relieved to see Dan and Charlie sit down again, some distance from each other, still looking faintly ashamed of themselves.

'I think Meg and I will take a short walk,' said Jack. 'If no one has any objection?'

It seemed nobody had, so hand in hand they strolled away, and kept walking until they'd put several hundred yards between themselves and the others.

Only Kath watched them go.

The roebucks were the only active creatures on this hot August day. As the rutting season progressed their sleek red bodies were constantly on the move, often breaking into wild love chases as they protected their territory and searched for a mate. Trees and bushes were often damaged by the thrusting antlers as an animal deposited its scent around the boundaries of its kingdom. But let a huntsman kill the guilty stag and a host of young predatory bucks would flow into the territory, worsening the problem. Landowning bucks respected boundaries. If only men would, Meg thought, recalling her father's constant greed for more land.

She and Jack lay on the crisp, parched grass, staring up into a sky ribbed by soft cloud as white as snowy paw prints across the blue heavens. It was so hot even the birds were silent.

'We must have taken in our best crop ever this year,' she said. 'I hope the kale and potatoes are as good.' She let her eyes close so that the sun shone hotly through the lids.

Jack rolled over and tweaked her nose. 'Why do we always have to talk about the farm? I'm sure there are better things we could be doing.' He started to lift her skirt.

'Be careful, someone will see.' Meg artfully removed herself from his probing hands.

'No, they're miles away, I made sure of that.' He started to kiss her and for a long while talk was unnecessary and unwanted.

She always felt so alive in Jack's arms, so needed. She felt as if their love had made her grow as a woman in some mysterious way and he was now so much a part of her she would have trusted him with her life. The harshness of Joe's taunts couldn't touch her. Even Dan treated her with more respect.

'What you were saying earlier, about not wanting to leave here. Did you mean it?'

Meg looked at him sharply but he kept his face turned away and a small kernel of fear ripened inside her. 'Why do you ask?'

'I know you've taken it into your head to help me farm at Broombank. But what if I didn't want to? Would it matter to you, if you had to give up the idea of living there?'

Meg stared at him for a long moment as a small pain started somewhere deep within and began, quite slowly, to grow and spread right across her chest. 'Are you serious?' She was amazed her voice could sound so steady.

'You know I've never been as keen as you on farming. Would you mind if we didn't?'

Meg had known well enough but had always hoped he would come round to it, so had pushed any reservations to the back of her mind. But if she had to give up her dream of being a sheep farmer, would it really matter, so long as she had Jack? There were other things in life besides sheep. He would surely be worth the sacrifice. But it was less easy to say so, out loud, than she could possibly have imagined. 'I-I don't know. To do what?'

Jack slipped his hands under his head and a faraway look came into his violet eyes as he stared up into the bright sky. 'I've always had a fancy to travel. America, Australia, somewhere far away and exciting.'

'Just because it's far away from Westmorland, doesn't make it exciting,' Meg retorted, so abruptly he turned to look at her in surprise.

'There's nothing so very wonderful happening here.'

Meg was silent again as she considered the matter, then a thought occurred to her. 'Australia might be all right. They have a lot of sheep there too.'

'Sheep again.' He pulled her close against him, making her squeal with delight, and when he kissed her he robbed her body of every vestige of breath, making her head fizz with emotion. 'Say you'll come with me to the ends of the earth, if I ask it. Go on, say it.'

The mellow atmosphere of the late-afternoon, with the sun slipping slowly down the sky, the soft breeze upon her flushed skin and the warmth of Jack's body beside hers, made her feel romantic and generous.

After the slightest pause she obeyed. 'I'll come with you to the ends of the earth, if you ask it.'

Jack was anxious to have the matter settled between them. The way Kath had been looking at him lately had made him increasingly nervous. He spoke next with a show of idle innocence. 'We could talk about your birthday instead, which is why we're here, if I'm not mistaken?'

Meg peeped at him from beneath her lids and her heart warmed to see his lazy smile. So he hadn't forgotten.

'Close your eyes again,' he ordered, and when she mildly protested, he got up and started to walk away from her in long loping strides down the hill. 'Okay, if you don't want it.' So she was forced to scramble to her feet and run after him.

'I'm sorry, I'm sorry. Please don't go. You can give it to me now.' She lunged for him, laughing, missed the first time then caught at his shirt with her hand and then they were both falling and rolling over and over through a tangle of tall bracken, locked together. His mouth clamped tight to hers and desire flooded through her as it always did at his touch.

Then with her eyes tightly closed he was putting something into her hands and her fingers moved wonderingly, almost reverently, over the small square box she held. Her heart leaped into her throat and for a moment she dare not open her eyes, dare not open the tiny leather box just in case it was not what she wanted it to be. For she knew she could never bear the disappointment if it was no more than an ordinary ring. He would see it in her face. She couldn't hide it this time, as she had at Christmas.

But she need not have worried. The tiny sapphire winked brightly in the summer sun and even as she hesitated, Jack lifted it out and slipped it on to the third finger of her left hand.

'It was my mother's.'

All she could do was look at him, aware of the tears rolling down her cheeks.

'Hey. I thought you'd be happy.'

'Oh, I am, I am.' Meg threw her arms about his neck, crying with delight, and then he was kissing away each tear.

It was the hardest thing she had ever done not to let him make love to her there and then but as she explained so carefully to him, it would be a pity to get carried away by the romance of the moment and make a mistake, when they'd come this far.

'Best to wait,' she insisted.

'Isn't the ring proof enough I mean to wed you?' Jack asked, frustration warring with his pride in catching such a lovely bride. 'If you loved me, you wouldn't wait.' He slipped a hand over her dress to caress her breast. Meg pushed it away and kissed him lingeringly.

'Bribery won't work, Jack Lawson. You know I love you. But I can't relax, I can't just – let it happen – not until we're married. Then it will seem right. Try to understand.'

'I don't understand at all. It didn't worry you in the barn that time. You're mine already, really, so what's the problem?' His arms came around her again and she wriggled out of them.

'You know why it happened then. It was a mistake. It being Christmas and me not being used to sherry. Be patient, sweetheart, and kiss me. We don't have to talk to Father now. We can just tell him, make the announcement that we are to be man and wife.'

'You're a cruel, hard woman, Meg Turner.' But Jack knew when he was beaten and had to content himself with kisses. Meg kept her dress buttons very firmly fastened.

Later, with the sun staining the edges of clouds magenta and rose, they ran hand in hand down the hillside. She couldn't wait to show her ring to Kath and tell her the joyous news, tell her how Jack had made her the happiest woman alive.

Kath's lovely face went very nearly white when Meg proudly showed her the ring. She seemed quite lost for words.

'You never thought he'd do it, did you?'

'No,' Kath agreed. 'I never thought he would. Congratulations.'

'It was a surprise, for my birthday,' Meg repeated proudly, holding up her hand to admire her precious ring.

'It's certainly that.'

'Isn't it lovely?'

'Oh, love,' said Sally Ann, hugging her. 'I'm so pleased for you. We could have had a double wedding if he hadn't been such a slow clod.'

'Steady but sure, that's me,' said Jack.

'As steady as a rogue fox,' retorted Kath dryly and flushed as she caught Meg's raised eyebrows, awash suddenly with unaccustomed guilt. Then she put her arms around her friend and hugged her, as Sally Ann had done. 'Make sure he treats you well, love. You deserve to be happy.'

'You're crying,' murmured Meg softly. 'Oh, Kath. It won't make any difference, to us I mean. We'll still be friends,' she said, misconstruing. 'For ever and ever, remember?'

Later that afternoon when they got back to Ashlea and Meg and Sal went inside to brew fresh tea, Kath turned eyes more stormy than tearful upon Jack.

'Why didn't you tell her, you lout?'

Never had he looked more handsome, more desirable, and she hated him for it. One corner of his wide mouth was lifting in that beguiling way he had. She saw a glint of sharp white teeth and the pit of her stomach swelled and ached with a need so strong it unnerved her. Deep blue eyes looked frankly into hers, understanding her absolutely.

'Don't be a poor loser, Katherine Ellis. You know it's only my body you covet.'

'*Damn you!* I'd like to . . .'

'That's better. I prefer the mad Ellis to the guilty one.'

'You've played us both for fools. She'll discover that one day, then what?'

'Are you going to tell her?' He was careful not to show his unease.

He didn't want his plans spoiled by a spurned female who was feeling a bit piqued.

'Do you think I would?'

'Who's played with whom, anyroad? I didn't see you protesting.'

'I didn't think you were interested in marriage, with anyone. And why Meg? She's good, she's sweet. Too good for you.'

'Meg's OK. She's got guts.'

'More than you deserve. Why marry her? You'll only make her miserable.'

'Perhaps I love her.'

Kath gave a scornful laugh. 'You love her *tits*.'

'Yours are pretty good too,' he said calmly, letting his eyes rove frankly over her body.

It was the last straw. Eyes blazing, Kath grasped the fabric of her lemon silk print frock that had cost her an arm and a leg at Kendal Milne's in Manchester, and ripped it apart. Her breasts gleamed with a pale beauty in the sparkling sun, dark nipples peaking with the hard fury of her need. 'Go on, check them out, just in case you've got them mixed up and chosen the wrong ones. I'd hate you to make a mistake at this late stage.'

For a long, terrible moment they glared at each other then Meg's voice called from the kitchen door, asking if they wanted the tea out there. Kath gave a little sob, pulled the wrecked fabric about herself and, turning swiftly, ran blindly away.

9

Poland had been invaded, Hitler had signed an agreement with the Soviet Union thus securing his eastern defences, and Britain was to fight for liberty and justice. King George VI told everyone as much on that fateful Sunday evening, 3 September. He said that by speaking to them on the wireless it was as if 'I were able to cross your threshold and speak to you myself'. Words of comfort and resolution, helping to ease the fear. Meg and Sally Ann, sitting listening alone at Ashlea, burst into tears and sang a patriotic song, all at the same time.

The tension that had been determinedly kept back all summer now expressed itself in action. Black-out curtains were made, windows taped, sandbags packed the walls of the local hospitals, beloved motor cars were offered to help move any wounded and people queued to volunteer for service or waited half fearful, half excited, for their call-up.

And everyone fearfully scanned the skies for sight of the first German bombers.

Having no cellar, nor access to a shelter of any kind, all Meg and Sally Ann could do was check that the window shutters worked and cut out black paper to stick round the edge of the glass to cover any possible chinks of light.

'What will it be like? War.'

Sally Ann shook her head, carrot hair sticking out at odd angles from being raked by anguished fingers. 'Heaven knows, but I'm glad I have you, Meg, and I'm not here all alone. Will Dan have to go?'

'Shouldn't think so. Farming is an important occupation in

wartime. People still have to have food. But what about us? What do
we women do? I feel we should have some purpose beyond making
black-out curtains.'

'I suppose we look after the men. As we always do.'

Meg looked suddenly fierce. 'There's got to be more to it than that.
Maybe I'll ride my bike into Kendal and ask around.'

'Joe won't like that.'

'Blow him.'

'Well, don't forget your gas mask.'

Meg put it on and they both burst into a fit of giggles. 'I think the
stink of the rubber would knock me out if I had to wear it for more
than a minute.'

But Joe wouldn't hear of her going into Kendal.

'We still have work to do, girl. War or no war.'

And so life at Ashlea continued as normal. And in a way, she
hoped that it would remain so. She couldn't bear to think of the
alternative.

But only days later, everything changed.

Charlie was the first. He came in and told her he had volunteered.

Meg's heart dropped like a stone as she stared into her young
brother's face, alive with idealistic fervour and suppressed excitement.

'How could you? You're only just turned eighteen. And you don't
have to enlist, not as a farmer.'

He came and sat opposite her, took her hands between his. 'I'm
not a farmer, Meg. Never was. Dad's the farmer, and our Dan.
They wouldn't necessarily let me stay here, anyway. But you
know, you've always known, that I want to fly. The RAF
recruitment officer says I'm just the sort of chap they're looking
for.'

'Yes, of course he does.' She snatched her hands away, too upset to
keep the bitterness from her voice. She knew only that Charlie was
going off into unknown danger and she was filled with a terrible fear.
'Silly young fools who haven't the first idea what they're letting
themselves in for, that's what they're looking for.'

A bright stain of scarlet ran beneath his pale skin. 'Don't call me a
fool, Meg, I'm not that. I'm doing my bit, in the only way I know.'

'But a flyer. Do you know how dangerous that would be?'

He stood up quickly and turned away, impatient with her inability
to understand. Picking up his jacket, he made one last attempt.
'Goering says he will blacken our skies with his bombers. And I say,

"Just you try, mate, and see what you get. We'll shoot every one of your damned planes down."'

'Oh, Charlie.' She knew they were naive words, bravely offered, and folded her arms about him as she had so often done when he was small and had fallen and hurt himself. Hugging him as tightly as she could, wanting to keep him safe, keep him with her as if he were still a child and she could protect him for always.

Tears were streaming down her cheeks and he was hugging her now, assuring her everything would be all right, when they both knew he could offer no such assurance. Then Meg was packing sandwiches and clean underwear, issuing foolish instructions about keeping warm and taking care, and he was climbing into the old Ford van and Dan was driving him away.

But there was worse in store.

It had started as a perfectly ordinary morning with the washing blowing on the line, Sal and she preparing vegetables for dinner and Joe taking a break with a mug of tea by the kitchen range. Then Jack stood in the kitchen doorway, the first time he had come voluntarily to her house. His dark hair brushed the door lintel where the lucky horse shoe was nailed to keep out evil spirits. He looked at Meg and she knew. He was leaving too.

'I'm going into the Navy.' His voice was quiet, unlike his usual confident self. And there, in the bag he dropped by the table, was the proof that she was about to lose him. Sally Ann put down the potato knife she was using and quietly left the kitchen, dragging a complaining Joe with her.

Meg lifted her chin and bravely faced the man she loved. She wouldn't cry, she wouldn't.

'Must you go right away? It's all happening too quickly. It's only yesterday that Charlie left.' She thought of the wedding dress upstairs in her closet but he was nodding, not quite meeting her eyes.

'I'm not waiting for them to put me into some Army unit. It's the sea for me. Always has been a fancy of mine.'

'This isn't a cruise you're going on,' she said, her voice breaking.

'I know that. We start our training in Liverpool, first thing in the morning.' There was an excitement about him, a kind of intensity of expectation, and Meg fell silent as a sudden awkwardness hung between them. 'I'll be home again before you've even missed me,' he consoled her.

'Yes, of course you will.' There was so much she wanted to say to him but no words would come. They seemed insignificant in comparison with what they now faced. But there was one thing she must ask. 'What about the wedding? Can't we marry before you go?'

Jack shook his head, very purposeful and decisive all of a sudden. 'No time. Have to wait till I get leave.' He thrust his hands in his pockets and walked to the window, looking out over the fells. 'Anyway, this is no time to think of marriage, with the war and everything.'

'I hear lots of people are rushing to get married before it's . . .' she stopped and hastily readjusted her words as she realised what she'd been about to say. 'Before their fiancé leaves.'

He turned to look at her, his eyes dark and unreadable, gone from her to some other place. 'I don't think that's a good idea, do you? Being rushed. Let's leave it, for the moment, till we see how things settle down.'

Meg lowered her head, blinked hard and managed to give a little nod. She thought her heart was breaking. 'You'll write?'

He came to her then, took her in his arms and held her close, his chin against her hair, drinking in the sweet fragrance of her. And for the first time in his life Jack Lawson wondered if perhaps he did love this sweet girl more than he realised. At least, as much as he was capable of loving anybody. 'Of course I'll write. And I shall expect loads of letters from you, every week at least. And a photo to make the other chaps jealous.'

She laughed, a small hiccuping sound, but dared say nothing, not just then. The pain in her breast was too much to bear.

'You'll look after yourself. Don't work too hard,' he teased. Then lifting her hands kissed each fingertip gently, sensually, with the warmth of his lips. 'Keep yourself pretty for me. No calluses on these lovely hands, eh?'

'You sound like Father. Women will have to work too, you know, if the men are all called up. I'll have to do my bit, Jack.'

'We're not going to quarrel, are we? Not when I'm leaving.'

She laid her head on his shoulder. He was so strong, so handsome, so brave. She felt ashamed of her outburst, wishing she could take back the words, spoken too fiercely because of her distress. 'No, of course not.'

'There'll be plenty of time, when it's all over, for marriage and all that. Don't offer to come to the station with me. No goodbyes, eh? Just promise me one thing.'

'Anything.' Meg was proud and astonished how normal her voice sounded.

'Take care of Lanky for me. He's a funny old soul but he is my dad.'

'As if you need to ask.'

There was nothing left to say. His kiss was deep and long and broke her heart, then he was gone and she was alone looking out on to a beautiful sunny September day and wondering how it was the larks could still be singing.

She had never felt so alone in her life before. Charlie gone, and Jack, even Kath absent. What a time to choose to go off on holiday. Perhaps she'd come back now that war had been declared. Oh, Meg did hope so.

More than anything, she felt the need of a friend right now.

Ruby Nelson's boarding house took pride of place on the corner of a row of tall Victorian villas. The wide, tree-lined avenue, its pavements broad enough for the crinolines of a more genteel age, had one end open to the sea, a determined walk away. The wind funnelled up its length and swirled through the rarely open front door of number six, to rustle the newspapers piled tidily upon the hall table for guests to share.

Kath gazed up at the house with sinking heart. This was not at all the escape she had once planned or dreamed of. Why hadn't she gone to London? It wasn't as if she was afraid of being bombed.

No, it all came down to money. For the first time in her life, Katherine Ellis was short of funds. She had her allowance of course, but had never troubled about sticking to it so was not good at budgeting. Daddy was always ready to stump up more whenever she needed it. Or had been, until recently. Lately he'd been complaining that his investments wouldn't last for ever and his pension wasn't going near as far as he'd hoped. He'd even cautioned her to acquire the art of thrift, which was perfectly ridiculous.

'We're surely not on Queer Street?' she had protested.

'No more are we are on Easy Street,' he had told her kindly, but with unusual firmness. 'This house costs a small fortune to maintain, not to mention Bonnie, whom you rarely ride nowadays anyway. All I'm asking for is a little more restraint. Times are hard.'

So the idea of her father financing a small flat in London, as she had hoped, was out of the question.

Kath had stormed and sulked, of course, refused to speak to him for a whole five days while she sat in her room and picked at the food brought to her on trays by a devoted maid, wondering where she could turn for help.

Rosemary had been the one to come up with the compromise of Aunt Ruby. Bitter at Richard's defection, she fondly hoped a spell in Southport would put her rebellious daughter into the company of more prepossessing company than the farming folk she spent far too much time with.

'Spend a few weeks by the sea,' she had suggested. 'You're looking decidedly peaky. And I'm sure Ruby will be glad of your company. You won't be troubled by her guests. She keeps a strictly genteel establishment.'

So Kath had abandoned her hopes for the moment of a more exciting getaway and here she was, learning to make the best of things for the first time in her life.

She walked up the path and lifted the polished brass knocker. It sounded loud and echoing along an empty passage beyond. She wondered if Rosemary had written. Not for a moment did she consider that Aunt Ruby might refuse to take her in, or have no vacancies. She was family. That surely counted for something.

The door was opened by the skinniest, shortest maid Kath had ever set eyes on. She wore a sacking apron that reached from a pert chin right down to her polished black boots. Her small face was almost obscured by a white hat pulled down low over her forehead. Not a trace of hair showed.

Kath adjusted her face into a pleasant smile and indicated the crocodile bags which the taxi driver had deposited upon the path.

'Would you have those brought inside and tell my aunt that Katherine, her niece, has arrived.'

'Miss?' The little maid looked terrified. 'Are you expected?'

'I'm sure she'll receive me.' And with grand assurance, Kath stepped over the shining white doorstep and strolled elegantly into the house, drawing off her kid gloves and looking about her with practised ease.

'You'd best wait in the parlour,' the maid said, looking flustered. 'Madam doesn't like to be disturbed when she's taking her afternoon nap. I'll fetch you a cup of tea directly.'

'Thank you. Lemon, no sugar.'

'Very good, miss.' The maid bobbed a curtsey and closed the door softly behind her.

Kath walked over to the most comfortable chair and disported herself upon it. 'Well,' she said, addressing a tall aspidistra plant that guarded the front bay window, 'perhaps things won't be so bad here after all.'

* * *

Thank goodness for Sally Ann. Left alone with her father and Dan, Meg might well have gone mad. The thought of the days, weeks, months stretching ahead without Jack or Charlie made her feel ill.

The hens' complaining racket told her she had woken late. It was a wonder Joe hadn't come to drag her from her bed, as he had done so often in the past. Pulling on her skirt and jumper she ran to let them out, then quickly milked Betsy and Daisy. She fed the calves with skimmed milk and linseed and went into breakfast just as if life were normal, though with less than her usual appetite.

But this was war and nothing would ever be normal again.

'It's as if they've disappeared off the face of the earth.'

'I know. All we can do is wait. The thing women are supposed to be good at.' Sally Ann was hurting too as three of her brothers had been called up.

'I'm not good at waiting. I prefer action.' Depression swamped Meg as she viewed the emptiness of life ahead.

'How will Lanky manage?' Sally Ann asked as they took their morning cup of coffee together.

Meg shook her head, fighting back tears. 'I shall go and see him this afternoon, try to help him work something out. He'll need extra labour now that Jack's gone.'

'Perhaps he'll decide to sell.'

'You think my father will start on him again?'

The two exchanged a long glance. 'Dan says he's set his heart on having that place. Says we need the extra land so's he can make more money now we're wed. But I thought there was free grazing land in plenty on the high fells.'

'Yes, but it's poor. Broombank owns good intake land as well as woods and water. And has easier access to the fells than Ashlea. It's a neglected farm but with good potential.'

'Well, I don't understand all the ins and outs of it. But I wouldn't put anything past your father, war or no war.'

'Perhaps Lanky will sell. Right now I don't even care, Sal. I feel as if someone has gone over me with a steamroller. How can I live without Jack?' Tears flooded the grey eyes despite her best efforts and Meg shook her head, angry with herself. 'If I don't pull meself together, I'll blubber right into me coffee cup.'

'Blubber away. I'll join you.'

The sound of a car drawing up in the yard surprised them both. Meg's first thought was that one of the men had returned and she flew eagerly to the door. Could Jack have changed his mind and decided to register for farmwork after all? She flung it excitedly open. A tall, thin man stood upon the step. He wore a grey overcoat and a trilby hat which he lifted politely at sight of Meg. In his hand he carried a sheaf of papers and a pencil. He looked disturbingly official.

'Mrs Turner?'

'Miss ' Meg half turned to reveal her sister-in-law, her heart in her mouth. Surely not bad news already? 'This is Mrs Turner.'

The man gave a tired smile. He had been working flat out driving about the countryside for so many long days he was growing short on politeness. Nevertheless he drew in a deep breath and prepared for the worst. 'I'm from the evacuation board. I have an evacuee for you.'

For a short, stunned moment, Meg didn't understand. She put a hand to her head, trying to think. Of course. She remembered hearing it on the wireless. They were moving children out of the urban and inner city areas into the country for safety. Everyone was expected to find space for them. 'You mean from the city?'

The man licked his pencil and ticked something on his board. 'Manchester actually. Would you mind signing here, please?'

Meg looked all around him. 'Where? Who is this evacuee?'

'She's in the car.'

'Oh dear,' said Sally Ann. 'Joe won't want a girl.'

'You have no choice what you get. If you'd been at Oxenholme Station when they arrived you might have been able to choose. It's too late now.' He didn't go on to explain that this child had been rejected by everyone who had visited the station. It wasn't his place to say, nor theirs to complain. This was war after all.

'That's all right,' put in Meg, anxious not to seem unwelcoming. 'It'll be nice to have some female company. It's only that my father thinks men are more useful on farms.'

But the man wasn't interested in the Turner family's problems. 'If you'd just sign here, I'll fetch her. It explains your rights and everything.' Meg did so eagerly, thinking that perhaps a young child would help to fill the lonely days ahead. She felt ridiculously buoyed up by the prospect.

'Can we see her now? How old is she?'

The man looked dubious. 'I couldn't say. But I should warn you that she's not too keen.'

Meg felt a rush of compassion. 'She must be missing her mother. How dreadful to be swept away from home to live with perfect

116

strangers. Poor child.' She put a hand upon the man's arm. 'Don't worry. We'll take good care of her.'

Edward Lipstock looked up into clear grey eyes and fell instantly in love. He wished, with all the fervour of his forty-two years, that he could change places with the waif in his car and live day by day with this entrancing girl. 'I shall have to call from time to time,' he said, heart lifting a fraction at the thought.

'Of course you will. Sal, get Mr ... I'm sorry, what did you say your name was?'

Mr Lipstock told her, the smile warming as Meg shook his hand. 'Make Mr Lipstock a cup of tea. You don't know how you've cheered me today. I just needed to think of someone beside myself.' Then she was off across the yard before he could warn her, wishing now that he'd done so right at the start.

The child sat on the back seat, hunched up like some wizened little gnome. It was difficult in this position to guess her age and when Meg opened the car door she reeled back as if she expected to be attacked.

'It's all right. You can get out. We won't hurt you.'

She was filthy. The stench of urine and stale dirt almost choked Meg as she leaned into the car but she gave no sign of it. It wasn't the girl's fault if no one had taught her how to wash. The only clean part of her face were the whites of her eyes. A dewdrop hung from each nostril and she was dressed in an odd assortment of indescribable clothing with a large luggage label pinned to her flat chest, rather like a discarded parcel. Someone had obviously tried to clean up the skinny legs, as two white circles of flesh showed upon the bony knees. Clearly the effort had been too overwhelming for the rest of the legs were ingrained with a lifetime's dirt. The child did not move.

'I bet you're hungry.'

Dark brown eyes stared silently up at Meg. Beside her on the seat was a square box, obviously a gas mask, and a small brown paper carrier bag which the child clutched tightly to her side. Meg tried again.

'Mr Lipstock says you come from Manchester. I've never been to Manchester. Why don't you come inside and tell us all about it? We're having dinner in a minute. Beef stew and dumplings. Perhaps you'd like some?'

She was getting no response. If it were possible, the silence appeared to compound itself with increasing resolution the more persuasive she tried to be. Meg decided to try a different tack.

Turning away from the car, she carelessly shrugged her shoulders and started to walk away.

'All right, it's up to you. We'll see you later, after we've eaten.'

'I'm not bloody well stoppin' here!'

Meg stopped dead. She saw the shocked expression on Sal's face but her own, she felt, was very near to laughter. Without turning round, she said: 'Why not?'

'Them.'

Meg had to turn now to see what it was the child referred to. As she saw the direction of her terrified gaze she very nearly laughed out loud but managed to stop herself just in time. 'You mean the cows? Oh, you don't have to worry about Daisy and Betsy. They're soft as butter.' She chuckled at her own joke. 'Well, they would be, wouldn't they? Since they make it so well.'

But still the child did not move and Meg felt a twinge of disappointment. A few steps behind her she could hear Mr Lipstock whispering something to Sally Ann, saying how difficult the child had been. No doubt that was why he had brought her to this remote farmstead. None of the good ladies who had taken the trouble to visit the station to offer their clean homes to a poor evacuee would have been interested in this one.

Meg felt a cold nose touch her leg and instinctively put down her hand to fondle Rust's ears. Rust. Of course. Well, it was worth a try.

'I don't suppose you like dogs any better?' she said, with studied carelessness. 'This is Rust. He gets a bit bored up here on his own with no one to play with. I'm often too busy, you see. I don't suppose you'd consider . . .' Meg sighed and half turned away. 'No, as you said, you don't intend staying. I quite understand. Come on, Rust, let's go.'

'Aye, I do.'

Meg's heart leaped. 'Do what?'

The child was standing beside her now, having slipped silently from the car. Still clutching the brown paper bag and with her gas mask hanging on a string over a coat that very nearly reached her ankles now that she was standing, her scrawny figure looked an even more pathetic sight.

'Like dogs.'

'Oh.'

'I used to 'ave a dog once. Of me own.'

'Really.'

'It got died.'

'Ah, that's sad.'

'Me mam said it was rat poison what did it.'

Meg nodded wisely. 'You do have to be very careful with rat poison. We have to use it here sometimes, on the farm. Well, would Rust do instead, do you think? Just while you are here. I'm sure this silly war won't last long. You'll be back home again by Christmas, I shouldn't wonder.'

Dark eyes regarded Meg with uncanny intelligence and she tried again to guess the child's age. Nine? Ten? Yet the eyes looked older. 'I'll stop an' have dinner wi' yer. Then I'll see.'

'It's a deal.' Meg started to walk towards the kitchen door, Rust at her heel as usual. The child followed them right into the house. Mr Lipstock bade them goodbye and made a hasty departure, while the going was good.

'Would you like to wash your hands before you eat?'

'No.'

Meg decided this was not the moment to advocate the virtues of hygiene. Nor did she make any comment as the child squatted on her haunches beside Rust and start to stroke the dog's back with meticulous thoroughness. He lolled his tongue and turned gently patient eyes upon his new admirer. He was never one to object to attention and this was the first time he could remember ever being allowed inside this kitchen with all its good smells.

'You haven't told us your name.'

Never taking her eyes from the dog's face the child answered, 'Euphemia.'

Meg and Sally Ann exchanged rapid, amused glances. It seemed a very grand sort of name for such a small, scrawny child. 'How lovely.'

'Mam says it's Greek, an' it was all Greek to her how she come to 'ave me.'

Sally Ann spluttered and choked and had to give her attention to the pan of stew bubbling on the range to bring herself back under control.

'We won't wait for the menfolk today, since this is your first meal with us,' said Meg, and saw a pair of troubled eyes turn up to hers.

''Oo do yer mean? What menfolk?'

'Well,' said Meg, trying to sound encouraging as she set a chair at the table for Euphemia which the child ignored, 'there's my father, Joe, but you must call him Mr Turner. Then my brother Dan, who is married to Sal here. I have another brother, Charlie.' Meg swallowed. 'But he has gone to join the RAF.'

'Do they live here an' all?'

'Yes. But they're out in the fields most of the time,' she felt it necessary to add. 'You won't see much of them.'

Sally Ann placed a dish of succulent stew upon the table before Euphemia's empty chair. The steam from it rose enticingly and the girl's nostrils twitched.

She glanced at the stew, then quickly up at the two women before snatching the plate and running to a far corner of the room where she started to push fistfuls of the food into her mouth.

Meg was horrified. 'Be careful, you'll burn yourself.'

Sally Ann put a hand on Meg's shoulder, staying her as she would have gone to protest. 'Let her be. She's probably had to fight for every scrap, poor lamb, to survive.'

'Everyone calls me Effie,' the child mumbled at last through a mouthful of food, and held out the licked plate. 'Is there any more?'

10

Kath regarded her aunt with some trepidation. She sat like a matriarch in a wing-backed chair in her private sitting room, certain of her authority in the insular world she had created. Shrewd eyes lurked beneath a straight black fringe while fat ringed fingers were folded upon some knitting in her lap.

'You'll be looking for work, I take it?' The voice was well modulated, in a tone used to being obeyed.

Kath looked slightly startled. She had not thought any such thing. A few restful weeks was more what she'd had in mind, while she sorted matters out.

'It would only be temporary. I intend going to London in due course. But until I've made my plans I'd like to stay here.'

'At my expense, I suppose?'

'Indeed, no. I am perfectly able to pay my way.' Kath had rather assumed there would be no charge of any kind, since she was family.

'How old are you now?'

'Twenty, nearly twenty-one.'

'Hm. And Rosemary has kept you idle all your life, I shouldn't wonder. Always was an expert in idleness. Landed herself a rich husband and retired to cosseted domesticity. No doubt that is what you have in mind.'

'Not at the moment.'

Ruby Nelson sniffed. 'It wasn't the way my sister was brought up, I'll have you know, nor is it the way I have lived my life. You might as well understand that if you choose to stay here, you'll either pay your way or work. That's my creed in life, as you might say.'

'I understand perfectly.'

'Well, I hope you do. There'll be plenty of war work about, I shouldn't wonder.'

Heart sinking, Kath readjusted her plans yet again. Perhaps she could find quiet employment somewhere, driving the wounded to hospital, for instance. That sounded useful and not particularly onerous. On a sunny September day in Southport with only the sound of gulls in the air, it was difficult to imagine where the wounded would come from.

'Breakfast at eight precisely, luncheon at one and dinner at seven. Latecomers do not get fed. I prefer all rooms to be vacated each morning by ten. It only makes for more work if people stay in them. And the front door is locked at nine-thirty. My rules are strict but fair.' Ruby lifted the steel knitting needles and began to click away at some navy blue wool. The sound was almost as loud as the grandfather clock that stood in the corner and whose hands evidently governed the household routine to the second.

Kath said that she would make note of the times.

'No gentlemen callers, of course. I take only honourable single women or widows, and gentlemen with impeccable credentials. My charges are reasonable. You will find the tariff on your dressing table. Less, of course, if you intend to cook your own meals.'

'I would prefer full service, if you please.'

'I am correct in assuming you are unattached?'

A slight pause then Kath risked a smile. 'Yes, quite unattached.'

A nod of approval. 'Then I am sure we will get along splendidly.'

This was not quite the warm welcome Kath had hoped for. But what choice did she have? She couldn't go home and tell her parents the truth. If she had the courage, she'd go to some back street establishment and get the matter dealt with. But the idea of abortion revolted her. It wasn't the poor little mite's fault after all. She hadn't worked out all the details yet. How she would keep her pregnancy hidden for a start. But she hoped that here, in Southport, there would be good adoption agencies, or else in Liverpool not far away. Then she'd head south.

Her aunt's reaction to the news was another thing, best not thought about at this stage. Time enough to face that later.

The washing of Effie proved to be the greatest test of Meg's patience to date. The girl refused absolutely to remove a single garment. But she'd reckoned without Meg's own stubbornness.

'You are not sleeping in one of my beds dressed in those rags. Like it or not, you are taking a bath. Hold her down, Sal, while I unfasten her boots.'

'They ain't rags. Mam put me in me best to come 'ere.'

'Then God knows what your worst is like.'

'You can have hot cocoa if you take a bath like a good girl,' Sally Ann promised, using bribery in her desperation, but the offer resulted in only a momentary pause in the struggle.

It took all the strength of both women to peel the coat and dress, both stiff with dirt, from the child's emaciated body. When they had her naked on the rag hearthrug they both stopped and stared in awed horror. Great purple bruises covered her body.

'I fell down,' said Effie.

'Several times it would seem.' The lower lip was starting to tremble but the brown eyes blazed with hatred and fear. No wonder the child had clung so tenaciously to her rags. 'Come on,' Meg gently urged. 'The water will warm you and we'll be very careful, I promise.'

Effie had never taken a bath in her life, but testing the water with a tentative finger decided it might be worth the risk. She was curious to know what it might feel like to be clean. Mebbe the warm water would stop the continual itching that she suffered from. Very carefully, she lowered herself into the water and her small pixie face lit up at once with the pleasure of it.

Very gently Meg soaped the tender body while Sally Ann poured water from a large jug over the tangled hair. It took the best part of an hour and a half to bathe her and to clean and comb the walking masses from the hair, using copious amounts of lye soap and paraffin.

It was a shining little stranger who emerged. As the child sat wrapped in a towel by the fire, sipping the promised cocoa, Sally Ann and Meg smiled at each other.

'She's pretty,' Meg said.

'And smaller than ever. Have you realised? She's not got a stitch to wear.'

'I've still got me own bloody clothes!'

'I've put those in the outhouse to be burnt,' Sally Ann told her, so firmly that even Effie knew when she was beaten.

'You can have something of mine,' Meg offered. 'And I'm sure there must be some of Charlie's old shoes in the attic. Though if you are to stay, you'd do best to curb that sort of language here.'

'Joe would have a fit,' Sally Ann agreed.

'He will anyway when he sees her.'

'I dun't care what any old man thinks.'

'You will if he throws you out the door.'

'I'll go 'ome then.' But it was a chastened Effie who spoke, her voice already blurring with sleep from the depths of the warm towels.

She took no persuading at all to go to bed. Eyelids drooping as Meg led her upstairs, Effie opened them in wonder at sight of the small attic room.

'Is this where I 'ave to sleep?'

'You're to share it with me. Do you mind? I've made a bed up on cushions in the corner.'

Since Effie had never shared a room with anything less than her entire family before, and sometimes with perfect strangers, she merely shook her head.

'We can buy you a bed when you've decided if you're staying.'

'You mean of me own?'

Meg laughed. 'Of course. Come on, little Effie, you look all in.'

Now that the face was clean, purple bruises could be seen quite clearly beneath each dark eye. The child didn't look as if she'd slept for weeks, nor eaten. Meg felt a warm, protective glow inside that here, at least, she could do something to help another human being in this terrible time of war. Effie would eat well from now on, if Meg had to starve herself.

'You're not going?' Meg, halfway to the door, stopped at the sound of fear in the high-pitched child's voice.

'I could sit with you for a while, if you like?'

'Dun't matter.' The thin shoulders shrugged. But of course it mattered a great deal. Quite clearly the child had never been alone in her life before, Meg realised. In the tangle of bodies and human misery of the slums, privacy did not exist. She tucked the covers up to the child's chin and sat with her until the sound of even breathing heralded a deep sleep. Only then did she go back downstairs. And found herself thrust into the fury of a typical Turner row.

'Who said this young thug could come here?'

'She's a child, not a thug,' Sally Ann was saying, patient resignation on her flushed face while her father-in-law stood before the fire, blocking all heat from the room, waving a fist in the air.

'I'll not have strangers in my house without my permission.'

'The government doesn't need anyone's permission,' Meg quietly told him. 'Evacuees are being billeted on everyone.'

'If we have to have one, then it should be a lad. At least he'd be some use.'

'Effie is here for protection, not to work.'

'This is my house. I'll be the one to decide such things. If she's not going to work, she can leave first thing in't morning.'

'There's a war on, if you haven't noticed.' Meg reached for her coat.

'And where do you think you're going?'

'To see Lanky. I meant to go this afternoon but couldn't because we had Effie to see to.'

'It's too late.'

'It's no more than half-past seven. I won't be long.'

'I've not done talking to you yet.'

'Well I've done talking to you.' Meg closed the door on his fury. Halfway across the yard she thought she heard a scream and stopped. She decided it must have been a fox or some other wild creature and, pulling her bicycle from the shed, rode off up the lane.

Over the following week Meg did her best to keep Effie out of Joe's way. It wasn't easy. Sally Ann was nursing a black eye as a warning to them all of the risks they ran if they failed.

'Why didn't that lump of a brother of mine protect you?'

'You know Dan can't bring himself to contradict his father. They have a mutual adoration society going for them. Anyroad, nothing can stop Joe's temper.'

Naturally inquisitive, the child poked and pried in every corner, often wandering off and reacting strongly if Meg tried to curb her freedom.

'I goes where I wants to go. I'll happen go 'ome tomorrer.'

'I hope you won't. Don't you like it here?'

'Not much. It stinks.' Meg had trouble hiding her smile since this was an odd sort of accusation coming from a child who herself had been unapproachable until a few days ago.

She meant the animals, naturally, and nothing would induce her to go anywhere near them, coming almost to the point of hysterics at one point when Meg offered to introduce her to Daisy at close quarters.

'Not bloody likely,' she said, and set off down the hill at such a pace that Meg had to run to catch her and it took some persuading to bring her back.

'You mustn't run off on your own like that,' she warned. 'You might fall and hurt yourself, and how would we know where to look for you?'

It was only when Effie was fast asleep in her makeshift bed that Meg felt it was safe to leave her. She'd been so busy settling Effie in to life at Ashlea that she'd quite neglected Lanky and decided one evening that it was time to put that right. Sally Ann agreed to look after the child when Meg said she would walk up to Broombank for a change, since it was such a pleasant evening.

She was glad she had made the effort but regretted not bringing her bike when she found Lanky in bed, coughing blood and in obvious pain. There was no fire or heat of any kind in the cold house and no sign of his having eaten. The air was acrid with the tang of the old ash that lay untended in the grate, and a thin layer of yellow dust powdered everything.

'I'm fetching a doctor. Just as soon as I've got some hot soup down you.'

'No you're not. There's nowt he can do.'

'We'll see about that. And I shall light a fire in your bedroom, so don't argue.' With no telephone at Broombank and it being black dark outside by the time these essential tasks were done, Meg decided the doctor would have to wait until morning. There was no question of leaving Lanky alone, so she made up a bed for herself by the fire downstairs, and could only hope that little Effie would not wake and be frightened, all alone in a strange bedroom.

At first light Lanky seemed no better, though he took a little scrambled egg and a sip of tea. Meg quickly dealt with the milking, surprised and saddened to find Lanky had only four cows left out of a sizeable herd, then ran as fast as her legs would go to the doctor's house, more than two miles away. Her sides were near splitting when she got there but she leaned on the bell while she gasped for breath.

A large, well-set man, still with a marked north-east accent to his quiet voice even after more than thirty years in Westmorland, came in answer to the desperate ringing. But Dr MacClaren only gave a sad shake of his head when she told him the facts.

'I'll call in later this morning. Lanky has never been properly right since he got gassed in the First World War.'

'I didn't know. Why didn't he say?'

The doctor gave a wry smile. 'He's got his pride. Doesn't like to be a burden to anyone.'

'Oh, for goodness' sake.'

'That's the way he is, Meg. Your ma used to call on him quite a bit. It's good to see you taking over. He needs a bit of care.'

'I can see that. I'm very fond of him.' She might have said he was the nearest thing to a real father she had known, her own being very far from ideal, but it wouldn't have been proper, not to the doctor who'd delivered her.

'Keep him warm, well fed, and above all quiet. Rest is essential. The farm is too much for him but he'll never sell it. You look more and more like your mother.' The doctor grinned. 'No wonder he thinks you're special.'

She flushed with embarrassment, wanting to ask what he meant by that remark, but the doctor was on his way back indoors, eager for his breakfast before starting on the day's calls and surgeries.

She was back at Broombank before eight but Meg knew she had a problem. How could she return home to look after Effie when she didn't dare leave Lanky? He needed care too. Fortunately this was a quiet time in the farming year but there were the hens to be fed and a hundred and one other jobs at both houses.

'You get off home,' he said, reading her thoughts. 'I'll be all right.'

'Like heck you will.' Sal would have to look after Effie for once. She'd stop on, for a little while, and see to the old man.

It was early afternoon by the time Meg felt she could safely leave him. Loyalties to her old friend and to Effie still warred within. But first there had been the doctor to wait for and then she'd had to see that Lanky got a bit of dinner inside him. She'd spent a couple of hours hosing down the cow byre which really did stink, and had made some effort to clean up the house.

Then she had written a short letter to Jack, explaining that his father was ill. Would the Navy give him leave to come home and sort it all out? she wondered. Somehow she doubted it, but oh, what she wouldn't give for Jack to walk in the door this minute, smile that wonderful smile of his and place a sweet kiss on her lips.

Perhaps she could bring Effie back with her, then she could look after both at once. Meg brewed a pot of tea and took the tray upstairs to discuss the matter with Lanky.

'Aye, bring the lass here by all means. I'll be up and about in an hour.'

'Indeed you won't. I shan't move an inch from this chair unless you promise me you'll stay right where you are.'

Lanky's old eyes twinkled with pleasure. 'Just as stubborn as your mother.'

Meg kissed the wrinkled cheek. 'And as determined to get my own way.'

'Eeh, your mam rarely got that.'

'No, I don't suppose she did much, not with my father about.' Meg sat down on the edge of the bed. 'Tell me about her. You loved her, didn't you?'

His eyebrows lifted in astonishment. 'How did you guess?'

Meg gave a soft chuckle. 'I should have guessed long since if I'd had any sense, but it was something the doctor said. Go on, tell me.'

For the first time Meg could remember, Lanky flushed like a boy. 'It'll have to be our secret. It's not something to be talked of.'

'All right. I won't tell.'

'Aye, I did love her. I'd always loved her if you want to know, even when she was young Annie Follett. And I rather thought that she had a fancy for me. We'd certainly talked about getting wed one day. Nothing definite, you understand. Just youngsters we were, dreaming.' Silence fell and Meg thought the old man had fallen asleep but then he suddenly opened his eyes and continued. 'Then the war came and I went away. Joe didn't go. Flat feet or summat, I don't remember. Mebbe he just had to stay and look after the farm. When the war was over and I came back, she'd already wed him.'

'Why?' Meg was shocked by this apparent disloyalty on the part of her lovely mam.

'By rights you should ask her that, only she in't here any more so I don't suppose it'll matter. The truth is she thought I were a goner. It shook her when I come back. Not quite the man I was, admittedly, but with all me limbs in place which was more than some had. Anyway I met my Mary and wed her. We were right happy, but I never forgot Annie.' He started to cough again and Meg was all concern.

'I've made you talk too much. Rest for a while. Don't say any more. I've seen to the animals. Now I must pop home, check on Effie and fetch you some food.' She leaned close and laid her soft, warm cheek against the old man's rough one. 'I'm glad you loved Mam. It makes us seem more like family.'

Lanky gave a quiet chuckle and, lifting a shaky hand, stroked Meg's hair.

'You're a grand lass. You remind me of her in a lot of ways. I shall always be grateful for the joy you've brought to a foolish old man in his last years.'

'Oh, don't talk so daft.' She kissed him, trying not to let her tears

128

fall upon his cheek as his horny hand held hers, still with its startlingly strong grip.

'Don't hurry back. Do what you have to do. I'll be all right now.'

Unable to find her voice through the choking tears, Meg could only nod and stumble to the door. How different her life would have been if only her mother had waited and married Lanky.

Ten minutes later Joe walked into Broombank yard with a determined stride. He would have driven up in the old van but petrol was getting expensive and he didn't like to waste money. So he didn't see Meg running down the lane. He'd taken a short cut, telling no one where he was going.

It was more than twelve months since he'd last asked for his loan to be settled, the interest had accrued very nicely since then and he wasn't prepared to wait any longer. Now that war was a reality a man needed all his assets to hand. Particularly with a married son to keep.

He found Lanky by his fireside. He looked as though he had just got up. No wonder the place was going to rack and ruin.

'Never would have thought to find you indoors at this time of day.'

Lanky, having politely offered Joe refreshment and been refused, took a quick sip of his honey and lemon mixture, hoping to quieten the cough that he felt stirring. He wanted none of Joe Turner's pity.

'I suppose a chap can stop for a bite if he wants to.'

Joe sniffed his disbelief, as well he might for it was a time Lanky would normally have been out on the fells, working. But that had been in the days when he'd been fit. It was plain he was far from that now. 'Getting a bit slack, eh? You'll be missing your Jack.' Joe, as always, had the knack of pouring salt on a wound.

'He has to do his bit for King and Country.'

'I don't hold with wars.'

Lanky was feeling too ill for the roundabout question and answer game he and Joe usually indulged in. 'I've only stopped for a minute,' he lied. 'So if you've owt to say I'd be glad if you got on wi'it.'

Nothing could have suited Joe more. 'Aye, you can be blunt wi' me, lad. We've known each other long enough.'

'Then you understand that I'm a patient man but I have me limits.' The cough almost choked him as it burst forth and he quickly sipped the warmed honey mixture again. He preferred his own tinctures to the doctor's new fangled stuff.

'Thoo wants to get that cough seen to.'

When the spasm had passed, Lanky faced his rival with as placid an expression as he could muster. He felt so ill he wondered how he was managing to keep upright. 'I suppose you've come for your money?'

'Well, I'm not made of brass, tha knows.'

'I haven't got it.' There it was. The truth. Out in the open at last. Plain and simple. 'I can't pay you. Not now, nor in the foreseeable future, I don't know if I ever can.'

Joe clicked his false teeth for a bit, deep in thought. 'Weel noo, that's a shame. I was hoping we could have this matter settled today. Have you med up your mind what thoo is going to do about it?'

'No.'

The silence that now fell between the two men was filled with unspoken vengeance. A lifetime of resentments, one against the other. It was as if the veneer of friendship had finally been stripped away and the relationship shown up for what it truly was. A jealous, bitter rivalry with its seeds sown long ago in the distant past.

'So I'll hev to tek summat else then, in lieu.'

'You're not having my land, not now, not ever. Annie was right about you, Joe Turner. You're a cold-hearted son of the devil and no mistake.'

'And you're a stubborn old fool, that's what you are. And Annie a greater one for wasting so much time on you.'

The last vestige of colour drained from the parchment cheeks. 'Don't you besmirch Annie's name! There were nowt between her and me after you and she wed and you know it.'

'So you say.'

'It's true.'

'You could have had her, and gladly, in return for a hundred acres or so.'

Lanky half rose in his chair. Incensed by Joe's taunting he had a longing to smash the self-satisfied face to pulp but the exertion even of moving was too much and he fell back, the burning rasping cough starting up again, the phlegm in his throat near choking him. He knew he shouldn't let Joe's taunts provoke him. Joe was not a man to let his women wander. He always liked to be in control, bragging that Annie belonged to him and would do only as he directed.

When the honey and lemon had soothed the cough sufficiently for Lanky to speak again, his voice was low and resolute in its calm. 'So you'd take away a sick man's animals? You're a hard man, Joe Turner. With few morals.'

'Morals have nowt to do wi' business.'

'Do your worst then and see if I care. Only leave my land alone.'

The cough threatened again and Lanky calmed himself before continuing: 'You didn't deserve Annie. I can't think why she chose you. She should have known I would come back. I told her I would, even if I was poor at letters.'

A heat was closing over his head. It was like a fire that blotted everything out but the sight of Annie's pretty face. A face that had kept him sane when he was in the army hospital. So lovely she had been with her cloud of shining hair, just like Meg's. He could scarce think straight now but he was almost sure that she'd stood here, less than six months before she died, and told him that she had never stopped loving him through all those years. Words he'd stored in his heart with joy. So nothing Joe Turner could say would spoil that truth.

Joe, however, was determined to try. 'You should hev written to her more, told her where you were. She got fed up of worrying.'

Lanky, an intensely private man, best with his own company, and like Joe himself unable to read or write, still cringed at the embarrassment of having someone else write his feelings on paper. At first it hadn't mattered because he'd been given regular leave and their time together had been sweet. But then, without warning, he'd been sent to France and that was it. There'd been a third letter but that had never been posted as he'd been struck down by the gas and spent the rest of the war being moved from hospital to hospital.

He was glad she never saw him like that, so sick, spewing up blood and bile, half a man. He'd wanted to be well before he contacted her again.

But by then it was too late. She'd married Joe and his dreams had crumbled to dust. That was the one time in his life when he, a grown man, had cried.

'You're right though,' Joe said. 'She might have waited. Only when I told her you were probably dead, she agreed to marry me.'

'*You* told her what?' The faded eyes went blank with disbelief. 'You hadn't heard that I was dead, had you?'

'No, I hadn't.'

'You told Annie a deliberate lie?'

'I gave my opinion and she saw the sense in it.'

'Why?'

'I wanted her. Annie was a good woman, hard-working, salt o' the earth as you might say. Same as our Meg is, only Annie weren't nearly so rebellious.'

Lanky saw it all now. He saw that Joe had been prepared to lie to get his way, fooling himself that it might be the truth. He'd ruined Lanky's entire life, stolen the girl he had loved.

Oh, he'd come to love his own dear wife, Mary, and they'd been happy together. But it was true that Annie had remained special. Mary had understood and seen no threat in the sweet memory, for that's all it was in the end.

Whereas Joe had let the hatred and jealousy grow inside him like a canker. He had never forgiven Lanky for the fact that Annie still loved him, even to her dying day. He had won her in body, but never captured her heart. Getting Broombank land would have been revenge, as well as economically useful.

Lanky pulled himself upright in the chair and faced his old adversary with pride. 'Meg may be Annie's daughter, but she's also yours so not so easily squashed. She has a strength and a spirit that even you can't break, Joe Turner, try as you might. She'll follow her own plan in life, will Meg, not yours. Mark my words, she's a match for you any day.'

11

The moment Meg walked in her own front door she knew she'd delayed too long.

Sally Ann met her in the kitchen with the news that Effie had run off again. 'You'd best start looking for her. I've searched every corner of the house and barns and can find no sign. I tried to keep an eye on her but she's as smart as a ferret.'

'It's my fault, Sal. Don't blame yourself.' Meg called for Rust and with dog at heel set off down the cart track, calling Effie's name. Oh, why hadn't she come back for her sooner, taken her to Broombank last night? Yet she'd had no reason to know then that Lanky would be ill and need her to stay.

Effie should have waited. Why hadn't she?

Because Meg had promised not to leave her and she had broken that promise. Probably no one had ever kept a promise to her in the past so why should she be surprised if a perfect stranger let her down?

Meg trekked on, longing to find some sign of the once noisome Effie. Used to solitary walking, she never felt lonely as a rule. Now, for the first time, she did. The fells and dales, so named by the early Norse settlers, looked more empty and bleak than they ever had before. The cracks and fissures forming steps in the rocks, punctuated periodically with patches of green, offered a deceptively easy climb to the top. Try it and your shaking legs would be the first to spot the mistake. But Effie was ignorant of which parts of this remote landscape could be traversed and which should be left well alone.

Responsibility for these two people, one an old friend, the other a new, weighed down upon her heavily. Why couldn't she be more like Kath? Kath did not approve of responsibility. She said everyone thought only of themselves and that Meg should learn to do the same. It was not a belief Meg could ever subscribe to.

But supposing Effie were in trouble? One slip on those heights and you were done for. In her mind's eye, Meg saw the small child lying at the bottom of a crag like a broken doll.

'*Effie!*' she called out, her voice snatched and lost by the wind.

Oh, Jack. If only you were here, you could help me look. A lump came into her throat. Where was he? Was he in danger? Would they send him to France? Perhaps she shouldn't even be thinking of taking on an evacuee when all she wanted to do was pack her bags and go to him, wherever he was, so they could be married.

If only that were possible.

The old oaks and yews, their trunks twisted into grotesque shapes by the wind, whined and creaked, making her shiver. Meg searched till the October light was fading from the sky but could find no sign of the tiny figure. Her foot skidded on a stone and she pitched forward on to her knees. Tears stung her eyes as she picked the shale from her bloodied flesh. She was tired. Time to call it a day and go home. She'd go and see Mr Lipstock in the morning. 'Come on, Rust. Supper time.'

Sally Ann met her at the door. 'She's back.'

Pleasure and relief flooded through Meg and she grasped Sally Ann's hands with delight. 'Oh, that's wonderful. Then she trusts us after all.'

Her sister-in-law looked doubtful. 'Joe found her. I think she was lost, and very frightened. It's a big world out there.' Sal nodded in the direction of the stairs. 'He's with her now. Says we are not to disturb him while he teaches her the meaning of gratitude.'

Meg needed no further warning. Very swiftly and quietly, she flew up the stairs. Her hand was trembling as she lifted the sneck of the bedroom door. She had no wish to stir Joe's temper further but nor had he any right to chastise the little evacuee, if that was what he was about.

When she pushed open the door Meg did not immediately take in the scene before her. It fell upon her eyes bit by bit like a jig-saw puzzle.

Joe's arm raised. The silhouette of his lean body against the blue of the night sky framed in the window beyond. The flash of something long and leathery. The night-light by the bed shining upon a shivering white body and over it all a terrible silence broken only by a rhythmic, repetitive thwack.

'No.' Meg flew across the tiny bedroom, reaching for the belt that Joe held high above his head, ready to stroke its telling cruelty upon the torn flesh below. '*No!*'

She felt herself thrust fiercely aside so that she fell, knocking her head against the window frame. But she was up again as the belt met its target a second time. Not a sound came from Effie, lying curled up in her clean vest and knickers on the makeshift bed, arms about her head. Had she mercifully lost her senses? Meg grabbed for the raised arm again and this time grasped the belt firmly enough to twist it hard and wrench it from his grasp.

Joe Turner swung round upon his daughter and knocked her flying with the flat of one hand. It sent her into a crumpled heap in the corner of the small room, bringing the sharp sting of tears to her eyes as her head banged on the floor. Pain shot through her and the world tilted and turned black, fired by a kaleidoscope of colour in her head. But Meg did not care. She held tenaciously to the lethal belt beneath her.

'Stop that.' The force of the quiet voice from the door was electrifying. Joe, one hand on Meg's hair ready to drag her to her feet, stilled and half turned to face his daughter-in-law.

Sally Ann was standing in the doorway with a rifle in her hand. It was no more than an air gun used to pop rabbits but it could do considerable damage at this distance. Joe, one eye on the gun, attempted to brazen it out.

'There's no ammunition in that thing.'

'Try it and see.'

For a long moment everyone remained frozen. Joe felt a touch of admiration for Sally Ann. She was a fine figure of a woman standing there like some warrior queen with her red hair all about her head. It took guts to take up a gun against him. He gave no such consideration to his daughter whom he dismissed as a trouble-maker, beyond his control, but he released Meg's hair and she fell back upon the floorboards with a quiet sob. Before anyone could move, Joe had picked up Effie from the bed and shaken her like a limp white rabbit before tossing her back upon the thin mattress. 'Learn to do as you're told, brat. If I say you do summat, you jump to and do it. Have you got that?' He did not wait for any answer, which was just as well since the child could not have given one.

When he had gone Meg struggled to her feet and hurried to Effie's side. She found the child curled into a ball tighter than ever, eyes wide open, unblinking. Beads of blood showed on the white underclothing but she made no sound. No tears fell and not a muscle twitched. It was as if she did not feel any pain.

'Dear God, he's killed her!' Meg cried.

'No,' Sally Ann said. 'She's in deep shock, that's all. I'll fetch some salt water to clean her up. You stay by her. When she comes out of it she'll need a friend.'

It was perhaps to the child's advantage that she did not 'come out of it' until the next morning. Even then she did not cry and Meg found her acceptance of the chastisement almost more terrible to bear than the act itself.

Effie was sitting up in bed when Meg woke. Gently, she held a cup of water to the child's parched lips. 'Are you all right? Did he hurt you?' Inane remarks, but what else was there to say?

Effie gave a little shake of her head, denying the obvious truth. 'But I still won't milk his soddin' cows.'

Meg gasped, then reluctantly laughed. 'Are you saying you took a beating rather than milk cows?'

She would have to speak to Effie again about her language. It wasn't proper for so young a child to have so filthy a mouth. Oh, but it was wonderful to see that even in these terrible circumstances the girl's spirit was not broken. She was glad about that.

'I dun't like them monsters. I've had a beating afore.'

Something hardened deep inside Meg and a resolution was born. 'Well, you'll not be beaten again. You and I, Effie, are moving out of here.' Eager to put thought into action, she reached for her brown suitcase in the closet.

'Where we going?'

'You'll see. A place where there is only kindness and love, not anger and beatings.'

'Are there any cows?'

Meg looked at the resolute, pointed face and started to laugh. 'You might find, in time, that cows can be more appealing than your fellow men. Come on, can you get up, do you think? I'd like to be out of here before it gets light if possible. Can you walk?'

'Oh, aye.' She winced. 'I could dance a jig.'

They managed a steady pace up the path to Broombank, carrying the suitcase, Effie's brown paper bag and gasmask which she would not part with, and pushing Meg's bicycle between them. It was all they owned in the world. Padding along between them came Rust, where he meant always to stay.

Meg had left a note on the kitchen mantleshelf for Sally Ann, explaining where she'd gone. But she did not expect Joe to come after her. She knew that once she had left home, he would never allow her to return.

She was entirely dependent now upon Lanky's goodwill, but felt certain of a warm welcome.

Breakfast at number six, Southview Villas, was the most informal meal of the day. Alice, the little maid, would set out tureens on the long sideboard, rather as if for a grand country house-party, and everyone was permitted to help themselves. It was folly though to arrive more than a moment after the gong sounded for the number of sausages, kidneys or slivers of bacon was strictly limited and a latecomer ran the risk of going without. There was no question of the dishes being refilled.

Kath, however, found she could not face even the smell of food first thing in the morning so she made a point of waiting until her fellow guests had departed to their various shops and offices before slipping into the breakfast room to nibble on a slice of dry toast.

She was thus engaged, wondering if the nausea would ever pass and if she could face coffee this morning, when her aunt strode into the room.

Ruby Nelson never walked. She marched, strode or flounced, head thrust forward as if in a hurry to get where she was going. She was dressed this morning in a dark green spotted dress with a square neck and rows of beads reminiscent of the roaring twenties, in which period, apparently, she had bloomed.

'You'll be off out job hunting again today, my dear?'

Kath agreed that she would, though she had as yet, made not a single enquiry. She felt far too ill. Whoever had said pregnant women bloomed must have been mad. Or a man.

'I heard they might be wanting some kitchen help at the Kardomah.'

'I'll go and ask.' Kath finished her toast and decided against the coffee. Perhaps later.

She'd reached the dining-room door when Ruby asked her more pertinent question, very sweetly, as always. 'Was that you in the bathroom this morning, dear?'

'I always go to the bathroom in the morning.'

'You sounded dreadfully ill. Not sickening for anything, I trust?'
'Not that I know of.'

Ruby adopted her sympathetic expression. 'That's all right then. I do hope you cleaned the basin down when you'd finished.'

Kath's hand found the polished doorknob and got the door open somehow. She grabbed her coat from the hallstand and left the house as quickly as she could without turning to say goodbye. That way she could avoid the suspicion in her aunt's eyes.

The expression in Ruby Nelson's eyes was more that of shrewd speculation and frowning disapproval. She didn't trust that little hussy, not one bit, she thought. What Rosemary was thinking of to send her here in that condition she could not imagine. Did she imagine that her beloved sister had been born yesterday? Old maid she might be, but she could recognise a girl in trouble when she saw one. Something must be done about it, and right quick. Scandal was bad for business and Ruby had no intention of risking it.

'I'll not have her on my plate,' she announced, wagging a finger at the closed door. 'Oh dear me, no.'

And spinning on her heel she marched to the kitchen and flung open the door. 'Alice. Get this table cleared. I have some letters to write.'

Kath decided to walk all the way down to the water line this morning. It took a long time. The sea was far out on the wide flat sands, deserted at this time of year, but she needed to fill the day somehow, give herself time to think.

She checked off in her mind the tasks that lay ahead. She had to find a doctor who would tend her without asking too many questions. Not an easy task in itself. It had been a mistake to come to Southport, she realised now, for how could she pretend to be a widow or a married woman with her aunt to give the lie to the tale?

She needed to enquire about adoption agencies. Perhaps Liverpool would be a better place for that. And she still hadn't decided whether she should write and tell Jack about her problem. And what did she want him to do about it if she did? And then there was the vexing question of money. Dare she write home and ask for more?

So many decisions to be made when what she really wanted was a bit of fun to cheer her up. To go dancing and find some delicious young man. She was too young for all these problems. It wasn't fair.

Kath decided to put it out of her mind for a while. There was no rush after all, months and months before she need worry. And thinking too much was unsettling. She didn't yet feel ready to confront the reality of a baby growing inside her. A child that would one day be born and require looking after.

After her bracing walk she went in to the Kardomah.

'Coffee and a custard slice, please.'

'You'll be lucky, love. There's been that much panic buying and threat of restrictions we can't get half what we need. I can do you a nice toasted teacake and a pot of tea.'

'That'll do fine.'

Kath didn't ask about the chance of a job. The place seemed to be teeming with waitresses in their smart little aprons and caps. And the thought of working with food all day made her stomach heave.

It was raining when she got outside again but near enough to tea time to justify going back to Southview Villas.

'All the positions were filled,' she explained as her aunt sliced bread with lightning strokes. Kath crossed her fingers against the lie.

'I've been thinking about that, sweetheart. Since you're family I'd be prepared to forgo the cost of your board.'

'Thank you, Aunt Ruby. That's very decent of you.'

'Well, what's family for, that's what I say? And you look proper peaky. A bit of peace and quiet is what you want, not working in a noisy cafe.' The shrewd eyes turned upon Kath. 'Have to stick together in troubled times, eh?'

'Er, yes.'

'So you can forget the job hunting and give me a bit of a hand here. That would be lovely, wouldn't it? Us working together?' Ruby scraped off half of the margarine and butter mixture she had already spread upon the bread. 'Waste not, want not. Alice is set on going to work in a munitions factory in Liverpool. Sweated labour I call it but the money's good, or so she thinks, silly girl. So how about it then? You can work for your keep and that'll solve both our problems, won't it?'

'Yes,' Kath said slowly. 'I suppose it would.'

'That's a good girl. Now put an apron on and finish buttering this bread. Not too generous, mind.'

Thereafter, breakfast time was taken up with Kath cooking sausages and laying tables, or deep in suds up to her elbows. Her mornings were spent turning mattresses, making beds, sweeping floors, beating rugs, brewing coffee and peeling potatoes. It was a new, not altogether pleasant, experience.

'I thought you just wanted me as a waitress,' she said to Ruby one afternoon when her aunt presented her with a dustpan and brush.

'So I do, my dear, but there are plenty of other jobs involved in running a boarding house like mine. I have my standards and one of them is clean tablecloths. Naughty girl, you forgot to dust off all the crumbs after lunch before laying for the evening meal. I found several when I checked just now.'

Kath, in her best brown coat ready for off, stared in dismay at the implements. Her aunt must have scoured the cloths with a fine toothcomb to find one crumb, she thought angrily. 'But I'd have to clear all the tables and lay them all over again.'

Ruby wagged a chiding finger and smiled sweetly. 'Well then, that will teach you not to forget in future. It won't take a minute. Oh, and did you put the fresh counterpanes on everyone's beds this morning?'

Kath shook her head, feeling dazed. 'You didn't tell me to.'

'But we always put on clean counterpanes on a Wednesday. Now you know.'

'Don't go, Alice,' Kath groaned. 'Don't leave me to all of this.'

But Alice resolutely packed her bags and walked out, kicking the dust of number six from her feet with such joy in her step you could almost think she was glad about the war.

Kath tried not to grumble. Now that war had been declared she too could easily be forced to work in a factory. Southview Villas was surely better than that. Though sometimes she longed to take a proper part in the action. To do something crazy, or exciting, or dangerous.

In one of Rosemary's regular letters, Kath had learned that Jack had joined the Navy. She thought of him sailing across the seas to adventure and envied him. But the knowledge that he was on training in Liverpool, so close by, made her worry over whether she should go and see him.

But there was to be no escape. Reality came home to her each morning as she stuck her head in the sink as silently as possible, aware of her aunt's flapping ears.

Kath's only free time was in the afternoons. For two hours after lunch, always cold, and before afternoon tea and the evening meal had to be prepared, she was free to do as she pleased. Kath made the most of it. Whatever the weather, she went out.

Sometimes she wandered down Lord Street, in and out of the fashionable shops, spending money she could ill afford just to cheer herself up. At other times she would visit the Winter Gardens or take a ride on a tram. On very wet days she went to the pictures and had been known to sit through a film twice, one showing fast asleep.

Once she went to the bus station and very nearly caught a bus into Liverpool to find Jack. She stood there so long that the bus conductor called out to her.

'Are you getting on, love, or taking root?'

'N-no, thank you. I-I'm waiting for someone.' Pink-cheeked and embarrassed, she hurried away.

But her favourite place was the long beach that stretched right to the sand dunes at Ainsdale if she walked far enough. This, she had discovered, was a favourite place for a local stables to train racehorses. She loved to watch them gallop on the hard-packed sands, or spraying up the water on the edge of the tide. They needed no shoes on this surface as it was kind to their legs while strengthening the muscles essential to a good horse. Kath could understand this and sat for hours watching the training sessions thinking of her own much missed Bonnie, and of Meg, and home.

Oh, how I do miss you all. Why did I imagine I was bored at home? This is much, much worse. She ran her hand over her still flat stomach. When would she start to show? Something had to be done. Decisions could not be kept waiting for ever. Jack had to be told some time. Perhaps it would be better if he came here, to Southport. She'd ask him to meet her, far away from the house of course and Aunt Ruby's prying eyes. It would be good to see a friendly face. This decision made Kath more cheerful and she started to sing.

'Well, will you listen to that now? You've decided to smile at last, have you?'

Kath jumped and swivelled about. A figure rose from behind the dunes. Tall and dark, his face weathered and tanned from long hours in the open, he had a grin on him that would put a Cheshire cat to shame.

Kath was incensed. 'Have you been spying on me?'

'And would it be such a crime if I had? 'Tis one of the great pleasures in life for a man to peek at a girl. It's not an arrestable offence so far as I am aware.'

'It is in certain circumstances. Peeping Toms are not very pleasant.'

'Well now, and how did you guess that my name was Thomas?' He bowed low, with great exaggeration. 'Tam O'Cleary to be exact. At your service.'

A voice called from the direction of the race horses.

'Tam, get over here will you, and stop wasting time.'

'Sure and is there no peace for a poor working man?' And the stranger rolled his eyes in such a self-pitying way that Kath burst out laughing.

He started to stroll away from her, hands in pockets, whistling airily. He wasn't a big man, she couldn't help but notice, lean with a rangy long-legged walk, but well formed. Good to look at. He stopped and swivelled on his heel to meet her enquiring gaze.

'Have you had a good shufti then?'

She blinked and coughed, tugging her wind-flapped skirt down over bare knees. 'I wasn't staring.'

'You were too. So we're even. Except that you haven't told me your name.'

'Katherine Ellis.'

'Katherine, is it? Like my mother.'

'I thought all Irish mothers were called Kath*leen*.'

'And all Irishmen, Paddy, I suppose? And there's me forgetting to bring my shillelagh.'

Kath flushed. 'I didn't mean it the way it sounded.'

'Well, Katherine Ellis, I'll see you tomorrow mebbe, if I'm spared a minute for me own pleasure. And you've nothing better to be doing.'

And without waiting for her to agree or not, he swung on his heel and strode away.

'Of all the cheek. I won't come,' she called after him. And, shivering, returned to Southview Villas, putting him firmly from her mind.

Kath helped to prepare the evening meal and listened to the news on the wireless with her aunt which sounded far too grim for words, the BBC trying to say as little as possible about 'our boys in France' which made everyone worry all the more. Then at the earliest opportunity she went up to her room to write a note to Jack. She'd decided there was no reason why he shouldn't share the responsibility of deciding what was best to be done about the baby. It was his problem too, after all. She'd write and ask him to meet her.

The fire had long since died by the time they reached Broombank and Meg sat Effie by the empty grate, making her promise to stay put.

'As soon as I've seen to Lanky I'll get a fire going and make us some tea.'

'It stinks in 'ere.'

'It's mainly coming from outside, the animals and that, but the house could do with a good clean, I'll give you that. Lanky hasn't been well enough to see to things properly. But we're here now and just the ones to do it, I reckon.'

'I'm no good at cleanin'.'

'No,' smiled Meg. 'I don't suppose you are. But you can learn.'

She felt almost cheerful as she clattered up the stairs to Lanky's bedroom. Though she had been unable to return herself last night, as she had hoped, she'd left him the medicine and food by his bed. She hoped he would be feeling more himself as a result. She'd go and fetch the eggs in a minute and boil them each two for breakfast. Then she'd find some flour and make soda bread. You could face anything on a full stomach. Her mind was already stirring with wild, crazy ideas. Ideas that featured Lanky's son in important part.

The bed was empty, the covers neatly in place as if it had not been slept in, or Lanky had been up and about particularly early.

That must be a good sign, she thought.

The medicine bottle was on the bedside table with a spoon beside it. Very little had been drunk but some of the food had gone.

She'd give him a piece of her mind about that, gallivanting around this early without taking his proper medicine. Oh, but she'd watch him like a hawk in future. Make sure he didn't do too much. 'Stubborn old fool. I shall enjoy looking after you though.'

Back downstairs she found Effie shivering in the cold, huddled with Rust in Lanky's big chair. She'd taken the sheepskin that usually hung over the back of it and pulled it over them both. Child's and dog's small pointed faces peeped out above. And the delight in the dog's eyes showed that he thought he'd landed in heaven. He looked so comical that Meg started to laugh.

'What's so funny? I'm frozen.'

'Sorry. I'll light a fire.' She found some larch twigs and dead holly by the dry stone wall outside.

'Nature's firelight,' she told Effie as she broke them into small pieces. 'We'll soon have this fire going.' The last thing she wanted was for the poor child to take a chill after her shock. Meg laid an ash log across the back of the small pyramid of sticks and soon the room was filled with the fresh, clean scent of burning wood. She filled the smaller of the two kettles with enough water for tea for them all. Then she collected the eggs, surprised to find the hens still shut up, and put half a dozen in a small pan on the trivet over a small flame.

'We'll light the boiler after breakfast, then we can start getting this place clean. It'll be fun, you'll see. And you'll like Lanky.'

'We didn't bother with no cleanin' at home.'

Meg chuckled. 'I don't expect you did.'

When the old man hadn't appeared by the time the kettle was almost boiling, she decided to go and fetch him. 'You'd best stay here. I won't be a minute. He's probably doing the milking.'

The trouble was that now Jack had gone, Lanky needed more help about the place, more labour. Even Meg's help would not be enough and she knew that a solution to this problem would have to be found soon. But then she and Lanky had a lot to talk about.

The cow byre was empty and only two cows were in the field. There were four yesterday. Had two wandered off and got lost? Surely not. Perhaps Lanky had taken it into his head to move them to another field. She couldn't think where, or why, but she would see to the mystery first thing after breakfast.

Meg filled a jug with milk from the kit and cradled the heavy jug against her hip as she pushed open the barn door. If the dogs were gone then Lanky was already out on the fells.

They came to her at once, Tess and Ben, whimpering their pleasure at seeing her.

Lanky too was in the barn. He was hanging from a rope fastened very carefully to the rafters. His milking stool lay overturned on the ground beneath him.

The jug of milk slipped from Meg's hand and flowed into a pool as white as Lanky's face, all over the cold slate floor.

12

It was a perfect, crisp autumn day for the funeral. Overhead a buzzard circled in the clear air and in the hedgerow a pair of stoats played. Lanky would have loved it.

In her mind's eye, Meg could see his slight figure striding out over the fells, his familiar rolling gait making short work of the steep gradients as he checked on his beloved sheep. But Lanky was gone and would never breathe the clear, autumn air ever again.

Why had he done it? Dr MacClaren said that the sickness would never have got better, only worse, and that it was getting the old man down. But Meg felt she had failed him in some way. Why hadn't she been able to make him feel better, make him want to live?

'He knew I was coming back to him. Why didn't he wait?'

'Folks make their own mind up when they've had enough,' Effie said, with surprising wisdom.

Meg hated the air of awful sadness about the place. The work on the farm had ground to a halt and she supposed this was now the end for Broombank. Someone else would put the tups to the ewes and see to next year's crop of lambs. She couldn't bear to think it might be her own father.

A gate hung, creaking forlornly on a broken hinge. Stones from a wall that had tumbled down lay among long tufts of grass with no Lanky to put them back.

Meg got out her black hat and dusted it off. The last time she had worn it, for her mother's funeral, she had hoped never to wear it again. Now she placed it correctly upon her head, tucking up the honey gold curls as if it would be too frivolous for them to fly free.

145

She buttoned up her coat. 'There'll be a chill wind out, Effie, put your scarf on, there's a good girl.'

The child looked a sorry picture in a skirt that was too long, one of Meg's jackets cut down for a coat and tied in the middle with an old belt. It still came nowhere near her fragile size.

At least she was clean and the wounds upon her back, though still tender, were starting to heal. The bruises on her pinched face were purpling now and the fair skin had lost its perpetual greyness. There was even a hint of colour upon the too-flat cheeks. The country food and air was doing her good already, Meg thought with pleasure. She was looking forward to the day when the cheeks and tiny pixie-like body rounded and filled out to the childlike chubbiness they ought to be.

Effie was gazing up at Meg out of adoring eyes. Beside her sat Rust, his small black and tan body leaning against the skinny legs, his chin resting on Effie's knee.

How she would have managed without these two in the days since the discovery of Lanky's body, she couldn't imagine. They had all clung together for support and a bond had been forged between them.

It had been Effie who had made the watery porridge that dreadful morning and tried to force it between Meg's chattering teeth. Effie who had washed her face and undressed her with tender care, making her lie down between cold sheets while the doctor and the police went about their gruesome business.

Meg hadn't wanted to do anything, not even think. Her limbs had felt like jelly. And though she had been vaguely aware that people came and went, to and from the house, that voices spoke to her, they seemed to reach her from a long way off, as if through cotton wool.

She could only concentrate on the pain that had swelled about her heart, yet do nothing about its numbing effect. Great fat tears had rolled from the corners of her eyes, and her teeth kept chattering, out of her control. She had lost Lanky – a funny little old man it was true, but she had loved him. He was the only real father she had known, and the only friend in the world since Jack and Kath had left. How would she manage without him?

'I suppose I'll have to go now,' Effie had said, jerking her back to reality.

'No, of course you won't. Whatever gave you that idea?'

'Well, seems you 'ave no home neither now.'

146

The child would be sent back to Manchester and very likely bombed. Meg knew that whatever happened, she mustn't allow that.

But how were they going to manage? There was no food on the farm. She knew that for a fact. Except eggs, and they couldn't live on those indefinitely.

Joe would never allow them back in Ashlea. He would take his revenge for this latest show of spirit. Meg had flouted his authority once too often and he would gladly abandon her to her fate. 'Spare the rod and spoil the child.' How often she had heard that text. Had it not been for Annie's frequent intervention she too might have felt the lick of that strap. But Annie was gone now, and with the passing of her gentle protection had gone the last crumb of decency from her hard-hearted husband. Even if Joe had permitted it, Meg had no wish to return to Ashlea while he lived in it. She could never forgive him for beating a defenceless child.

She had pushed herself up into a sitting position and stared out through the window, a healing anger burning deep inside her. It wasn't right that Lanky had gone in this way. Whatever had driven him over that final edge would never be known. But life went on and he would be the first to say so. She couldn't neglect her responsibilities, to Effie and to Jack. Someone would have to take care of Broombank for him. Why not herself?

The thought had simply dropped into her head. Crazy, impossible, and wildly intoxicating.

She and Jack were to be married. She wore his ring, didn't she? So why not? Jack would not turn her out. Meg's heart swelled with love and thankfulness. She would be safe with Jack.

The rain started as the coffin was lowered into the dark ground, needles in the cold wind that made people hunch closer into their coat collars. They had sung 'Abide with Me', accompanied by the wheezing tones of the harmonium in the small dale church and now stood, black-suited, feet shuffling around the yawning grave in the tiny churchyard.

Everyone was here, all the neighbouring farmers in the good suits they always kept for funerals and weddings alike, paying their last respects to an old colleague they had known all their lives.

Meg watched them in silence. Joe looking suitably sanctimonious, Dan and Sally Ann trying to curb the smiles on their faces – news of a coming baby had been whispered into Meg's ear just as the service began. She had wanted to push her friend away, to shout: 'No, I don't want to hear about your happiness.' Instead she had managed a smile and a squeeze of Sal's hand.

There was Dr MacClaren, and Mr Capstick, the family solicitor. And a plump, matronly woman whom Meg assumed to be Connie Bradshaw, Lanky's married daughter. She wondered, fleetingly, why Mrs Bradshaw had not called at the house before the service but mostly her mind kept returning to the fact that there was still no sign of Jack. He had promised faithfully that he would be here, she had the letter in her pocket to prove it. But though they had delayed the little ceremony as long as was seemly, he had not arrived.

The statutory ham had been served, washed down by jugs of hot tea. In Lakeland the worth of a man was often judged by the size of his wake and Meg and Effie had slaved for hours to make Lanky's a proud one. Most of the ingredients had been supplied by Sally Ann from Ashlea's pantries, unknown to Joe. But Hetty Davies had likewise contributed a meat pie or two.

'Just to help out,' she had said kindly, and Meg had offered heartfelt gratitude.

The dalesfolk, having done their duty, felt they could relax a little in the warmth of Lanky's house. There was a log the size of a small tree sitting in the wide hearth 'specially cut by Dan for this day, filling the room with an acrid scent of pine and spitting larch. Everyone was enjoying exchanging gossip and indulging in a little quiet bargaining, respectfully like.

Joe was no exception.

'You'll hev seen them two cows is gone.'

For a moment Meg stared at him, uncomprehending. 'You took them?' Her voice grated in her throat.

'Aye, well, you should hev told your friend not to borrow money he couldn't repay.'

Red hot fury exploded in her head. 'You can't do this!'

'I've done it. Too old to be of any real value, but they rightly belong to me noo.'

'You took the others too, didn't you? Lanky used to have eight or nine at least.'

Joe ignored her and turned to help himself to a second piece of pork pie.

'Answer me. You took them all, didn't you?'

'Aye, I did. And he still owes me so I'll happen take the rest. Blame theeself. You should have persuaded that lad of his to stay and do his duty by the farm and his father.'

'There's a war on,' Meg said weakly, knowing it was no real excuse. Farming was a valid occupation during wartime and Lanky clearly couldn't manage Broombank on his own. 'He has more pressing duties to see to.'

'Lanky should have sold to me when he had chance. There's still a sizeable lump outstanding and dead or not, somebody has to pay it.' Joe started to walk away and then stopped and turned back to her as if on an afterthought. 'You can pack your bags and come home any time. But don't bring that brat with you. Send her back where she belongs.'

Meg could only stand speechless, impotent fury boiling inside her heart. How was it, she thought, that when good neighbours were treasured in this farming community, Lanky had to get saddled with Joe Turner?

Nothing would induce her to go back to live in her father's household. With or without Effie.

Though how they were going to manage if he took the last two cows, without milk or cheese, Meg dare not think. But manage they would. She straightened her back, unconsciously lifting her chin a fraction. If this was their own private war, her father was on the winning side. But only for now. Things could change quickly in a war, she told herself.

She went to the window and looked down the lane. The rain had stopped, thank goodness, and a thin sun was trying to break through. Jack would arrive soon and sort it all out.

Then she saw her father walk over to Connie Bradshaw and Meg's heart sank. What was he scheming now?

'Thy'll be wanting to clear the estate up quickly, I reckon.'

Connie Bradshaw was a woman who bore a grudge against life. Unmarried until the age of thirty-five, she still nurtured a feeling that life had passed her by. She had met her husband, a travelling salesman in farm machinery, when he had unsuccessfully tried to sell her father a tractor. Against all the odds, Peter Bradshaw had taken a fancy to Connie's robust plainness and called at the farm again. Within a matter of weeks they were 'walking out' and in six months they had married. Connie had gladly moved to a smart house in Grange-Over-Sands with her new husband. She had never relished the state of chaos that had always clung to life at Broombank. She disliked dirty boots, feeding buckets in the kitchen and nights constantly disturbed by the inconvenience of tending messy animals. Her well-scrubbed semi-detached was much more to her taste. Until she and Peter could change it for a new detached with a view of the estuary, that is.

While there would be no children from this late union, the two of them felt perfectly fulfilled, united by their ambition for a neat, ordered, comfortable life. The only problem lay in the paucity of Peter's salary. Hard as he worked, the monthly sum fell far short of their desires, if not their needs. It was unthinkable, naturally, for Connie to take employment. And now with the inconvenience of war to make matters worse, the death of her father had opened up to them the very real possibility of a useful windfall.

'Mr Capstick, our family solicitor, will be attending to the will shortly.'

Joe touched his forelock respectfully. 'I have no wish to intrude upon your grief, Mrs Bradshaw,' he said, with suitable deference in his tone. 'But I should point out that Lanky owed me a deal o' money. A sizeable sum in point of fact.' Joe handed her a sheet of paper which he had made Sally Ann write out for him the night before. It showed the sums Lanky had borrowed over the last several years during the slow decline of Broombank. The interest was also noted, and from the total he had deducted the value of eight cows, far below their true market value.

This was something of a shock to Connie and she stared at the paper, perplexed. 'I had no idea, Mr Turner, that my father was in debt.' The sum outstanding amounted to no more than a few hundred pounds. Not a fortune, but even so, hard to find just now. She had no illusions about the poor value of much of her father's land, and the business had as good as died with him. But she still hoped that the farm as a whole, with the house, buildings, implements and stock, would surely sell for a few thousand pounds. She smiled brightly at Joe.

'Your debt will be settled, naturally, when the farm is sold, Mr Turner.'

Joe returned her smile, the words music to his ears. 'Then I hope, if it is a sale you are considering, Mrs Bradshaw, you will give me first refusal on the land. It has little value to anyone, excepting meself, it being in close proximity to the high fell where I graze my sheep. Much of it is thin and don't grow grass well, and down in the dale, well . . .' Joe pulled a doleful face. 'Too damp, d'you see, for sheep.'

Connie Bradshaw's sparse powers of concentration were already wandering. She was anxious to see the back of these people and hear how much money her father had tucked away. Debt or no debt, he had always been thrifty so there must be something. She dismissed Joe Turner with a vague promise to talk again and moved across to Mr Capstick to instruct him to get a move on.

Jack arrived just as the family was sitting down with the solicitor around the kitchen table. Meg ran to him at once and hugged him. He looked so tanned and handsome in his sailor's uniform he quite took her breath away. She wanted to lean on him and drink in his warmth but he only kissed her briefly, his eyes going at once to Connie's disapproving glare.

'Sorry I'm late. The trains were all held up. Have I missed much?'

'Only your own father's funeral,' his sister said in frosty tones.

Mr Capstick cleared his throat. 'Perhaps we might get down to business.'

Meg sidled to the kitchen door, pushing Effie through it before her. 'We'll leave you to it then.'

'You'd better stay, Miss Turner,' said the solicitor. 'This concerns you too.'

If Connie's eyebrows had climbed any higher they would have taken off, thought Meg. Hiding her surprise, she instructed Effie to start clearing the living room and not to make any noise about it. Then she closed the door and sat at one of the kitchen chairs, opposite Jack. He smiled reassuringly at her and she took a deep breath. He still loved her, she could tell. The only worry was how long they would now have to wait before it was fitting for them to marry and she could become a real part of his life.

The solicitor was reading a lot of legal jargon about appointed trustees and executors from a piece of paper he held in his hand. Meg could see Connie frowning and fidgeting with her gloves.

'Can we cut all these unnecessary preliminaries, Mr Capstick, and get to the point. We are well aware my father has left the farm in a dreadful state. What we want to know is its value and how quickly we can sell it.'

Sell? Meg looked across at Connie Bradshaw with shock in her eyes. How could such a thing even be considered? Broombank Farm had been in the Lawson family since the seventeenth century. To sell it was unthinkable. Lanky had loved it. It was his whole life. She wanted to shout against the sin of such an action, point out the farm's great potential, the large amount of good intake land it owned, the tract of fell it owned outright, in addition to accessible free grazing on the higher fells not easily available to all farms. The woodlands and water. And then there was the house itself, a house that Meg already loved, neglected as it might be. She wanted to live here with Jack, and make it into a home. She wanted to farm Broombank land and make it good, more than she could bear to say. How dare Connie Bradshaw come along to Lanky's funeral after years of never bothering to call on him, and declare it must be sold?

Meg had been so busy with her rebellious thoughts that she had missed much of what was going on about her. But a loud squeak of anguished disbelief from Mrs Bradshaw brought her back to reality.

'*Option to purchase?* You cannot be serious. He must have gone mad. My father was senile, demented, that is quite clear. Or *she* has twisted him round her calculating little finger.'

And Meg realised that everyone, including Jack, was glaring accusingly at her.

'It is true that Mr Lawson left no money to settle his debts but neither did he wish the farm to be sold.' Mr Capstick tapped the parchment in his hand. 'The will states quite clearly that he directs his trustees, that is, myself and my partner, to...'

'I'm well aware who you are, and a right pickle you've made of it an' all,' protested Connie forgetting her usual resolution to speak 'proper'.

'If you will permit me to continue?' Mr Capstick, unflustered by the pent-up emotion that vibrated about the table, attempted to explain more fully.

'The will states that the farm business, including all the stock, farm implements and machinery, harvested and growing crops, be left to Meg Turner. Mr Lawson seemed to think that his son was not particularly interested in the farm.'

All eyes turned to Jack, who flushed with embarrassment but said nothing.

'He goes on to say, "I direct that my trustees shall not exercise their power of sale until they have offered to the said Meg Turner an option to purchase the said Farm and Land within five years of my death at the price of one thousand five hundred pounds..."'

'One thousand five hundred?' Connie's voice was little more than a squeak. 'You cannot be serious. It's worth two at least.'

Mr Capstick looked over his spectacles at her and understood perfectly, perhaps for the first time, why his client had arranged his affairs in just this way. 'The market is depressed at the present time, made worse by the war. And Mr Lawson was most anxious that Miss Turner have a chance, as he put it, to try her hand at farming. He seemed to think it was what she wanted.'

'I'm sure it is.'

'Is it, Meg?' This from Jack, his voice full of hurt pride, curt and strangely bitter. 'Is this what you wanted all along? Broombank?'

Meg, who had sat in a daze through all of this, tried to focus her eyes upon him. She tried to see him as he had looked when he had first smiled at her and kissed her outside the village hall, when he had made love to her in the barn. But that all seemed so far away now that she could scarcely reconcile it with the deep, hardening planes of his beloved face. 'I – no, of course it wasn't. That is, I mean . . . I do want to farm but . . .'

'There, you see!' Connie stood up and slapped her hands down upon the table. The sound was so loud that Meg actually jumped. 'She has planned this. Who knows what she persuaded my father to do, wheedling her way into his good graces, moving in to make herself at home by his fireside.'

Hot-cheeked, Meg faced her adversary with some spirit. 'He was ill. He needed looking after. Who else was there?'

The implication that Connie had neglected her own duties to her father stung, and she reacted badly to it. 'We're living in the twentieth century. You could have picked up a telephone, I suppose, and let me know how my father was.'

Subdued by this justifiable criticism, though it would have necessitated a walk of several miles to the Co-op where a phone was located, and knowing she'd been too busy looking for the lost Effie to think of it, Meg mumbled an apology. 'It all happened so quickly. I'd had the doctor to him and thought he was on the mend. How was I to know that he . . . that he . . .'

Mr Capstick cut in quickly, seeing the welling of tears in her grey eyes, and anxious to keep trouble to a minimum. He attempted to dampen the heat of the atmosphere with a smile.

'Ladies, ladies, there is little point in going over all this old ground. I am sure Miss Turner did as she thought best in what must have been very difficult circumstances. For whatever reason, Mr Lawson felt he could not go on. Painful as it is, we must accept that fact and as his trustee it is my duty to see that his wishes are carried out, to the letter.'

Silence fell, embarrassed and strained. Connie resumed her seat on persuasion, but with reluctance.

Meg whose mind was racing, trying to come to grips with all the implications, was the first to break the silence. 'May I please ask a question?'

'Of course.'

'This option to purchase within five years. Does that mean that I can stay here in the meantime?'

'But of course.' Mr Capstick picked up the document again. 'I'm sorry, perhaps I haven't made it properly clear. Until the five years expire, or until you find the purchase price earlier than that date, you are permitted to lease the farm from the trustees. Mr Lawson has stated in his will that the rent must be two hundred pounds a year, payable on the usual quarter days. Your first payment, since this is October, will be on Christmas Day, which is the first quarter day following the date of his death.' He smiled at Meg. 'Do you think you can manage that?'

The rent was reasonable, no one could deny it, less than the going rate. But a quarter of two hundred – fifty pounds – in how long? Less than three months. Not a chance. 'Yes,' she said, nodding briskly. 'I can manage that.'

'And he asked me to give you this.'

'What is it?'

The solicitor held out a coin. 'He said that you would understand.'

Meg took the coin and cradled it in her palm. 'It's a Luckpenny.' Her eyes filled with tears. 'He told me about the old Norse custom many times. It's to transfer one person's good fortune to another, and with it friendship. Always give something back, Lanky said.' She felt her heart swell with love and pride that he should have so much faith in her that he would leave her his beloved farm.

'Oh, I'll take good care of it, I will, I will,' she said.

'Good. Then everything is quite clear? You do understand the full responsibility facing you?'

Oh, yes, she understood perfectly. Taking in Jack's stunned expression and Connie's furious gaze, Meg understood that she had gained her longheld desire for a farm of her own, but very likely at the cost of something far more precious: Jack's trust.

'You shouldn't have done it. You didn't ought to have laid a finger on her.'

Sally Ann spoke the words quietly as she walked with Joe and Dan back down the lane towards Ashlea.

'The little brat is bone idle. And wick with fleas.'

'No, she wasn't. We cleaned her up. Anyway, that was hardly her fault, was it?'

'Then I don't know whose fault it was.'

'Joe.' Sally Ann laid a hand upon his arm. 'You do realise that Meg will never forgive you for hurting Effie in that way? You'll be lucky if your daughter ever speaks to you again.'

'She just has. I told her she could come home but all she cares about is Lanky's Shorthorns.'

'And all you seem to care about is getting your hands on Broombank land. Why? What does it matter?'

'Happen I think there should be only one head to a family, and that's me. Besides which, our Dan reckons he's underpaid.'

Dan took interest at this point. 'Does that mean I'm to get a rise?'

'Oh, shut your face, you daft ha'porth.'

Sally Ann hooked a hand into Joe's arm and gave it a gentle squeeze. 'All you have to do is say you got a bit carried away and you're sorry for hurting the child.'

'*Sorry?*'

'Yes. Sorry.'

'You want *me* to apologise?'

Sally Ann turned to her husband who was doing his best not to become involved. 'Tell him, Dan. He only has you and me now, with Charlie gone off to war. He shouldn't alienate his only daughter.'

'Charlie shouldn't have gone. He knows Dad didn't want him to.'

'Aye, that's right. What good did fighting a war ever do, that's what I say.'

Sally Ann swallowed her vexation. 'I despair of you both, I do really. I know you care about Meg really, deep down. Why in heaven's name won't you ever show it?' And because Joe had not shrugged off the closeness of her arm and she sensed an uncertainty in him, well disguised by bravado, she dared to voice her concern a touch more precisely. 'Well, I'll tell you this, Joe Turner. You'll not touch a child of mine in that manner, when it comes. Not while there's breath in my body.'

Keen dark eyes turned upon her. 'Are you saying it's likely there'll be a child?'

'I might be.'

A moment's considering pause. 'Aye, well, thee will hev a son. That's different.'

* * *

Meg could not deny that the news excited her. She nurtured the thrill of it in her heart and couldn't wait for the time when Connie and her long-faced husband had departed and she could plead her case with Jack, persuade him to start planning properly.

But Mr and Mrs Bradshaw were relishing their little holiday, at someone else's expense, and in no hurry to depart. The family passed a difficult weekend together, Connie taking every opportunity to make snide remarks, openly scathing that Meg could ever hope to find fifty pounds for the first payment at Christmas.

'So that will put paid to your fanciful notions.' There was grim satisfaction in the tone and Peter nodded in agreement, as he usually did.

Meg was hard pressed at times to bite her tongue but compelled herself to manage it, for Jack's sake. She was too busy in any case for argument, since the days were filled with putting on kettles for the endless washing up following the gargantuan meals she was expected to produce.

'My father always kept a good table,' Connie had a fondness for remarking, though where she imagined the food was coming from she never seemed to wonder and certainly never enquired. Nor did Meg enlighten her. If it ever got back to Joe that he was temporarily supporting two households, Judgement Day would surely dawn early for them all.

The atmosphere was so chilled at times with Connie either finding fault with Meg or at loggerheads with her brother that Meg felt dizzy with the worry of it.

If only she could speak with Jack, and see that he was happy for her. It affected them both, didn't it? The war wouldn't last for ever.

But all she could do was keep in the background as much as possible, even banishing little Effie to bed unreasonably early to avoid any danger of confrontation. And there was not a moment for Jack and Meg to have to themselves.

13

Monday morning at Broombank came in dank and cold. A mist clung to the upper reaches of Dundale Knott like wisps of hair round an old man's bald head. The mood in the farmhouse was equally grim. Though Connie and her husband were finally leaving, Jack too had announced he must be on his way and Meg volunteered to walk with him as far as the road, grabbing the first few precious moments for them to be together since the reading of the will.

'You don't believe I engineered all of this, do you?' she asked.

'I don't know what to think. One minute we're going to get married and start a new life together somewhere yet to be decided, the next you're setting yourself up as a farmer.'

She slipped her hand into his. It felt large and warm and strong, and she certainly had no intention of spoiling these last moments together in disagreement. 'Don't be cross with me, Jack. You know I always wanted to stay here. And you know you like it too, deep down. If you'd only give it a chance.'

He turned his face to hers and for a moment Meg looked into the eyes of a stranger. A cold shiver stroked the length of her spine but she shook it away, dismissing it as fancy. He was jealous, that was all, because there'd been nothing for his father to leave to him. 'You're just depressed, love, feeling left out of things because of the war. But can you blame Lanky for dealing with it in this way? You never said you wanted Broombank.'

'It doesn't greatly matter what I want at the moment, does it?' Jack said. 'There's talk of us going abroad soon.'

Meg stopped dead. 'Oh, Jack, why didn't you tell me? All this talk about me and Lanky and Broombank, and all the time you're going overseas, into the fighting. Oh, dear God.'

'Now don't start. I'll be all right.' Meg moved into his arms and Jack felt the warm pressure of her breasts against his chest. He slid his hands down over her small rump and pressed her closer. Drat Connie being there, they might have spent a much more pleasant night without his sister around with one ear cocked.

He nuzzled into Meg's neck, relishing the sweet scent of her. He'd forgotten how tantalisingly feminine she was, not at all like the rough types who frequented the bars around the Pool at Liverpool.

'One good thing about this, I'll get some leave before I go. Embarkation leave they call it. We can have a good time together then, eh?'

He moved his mouth to hers and teased open her lips, feeling her sigh against him. He didn't let the kiss go on too long though because he had a bus to catch.

Meg's eyes were shining up at him. 'Oh, that would be lovely. I wish we could get married before you go, but it wouldn't be proper, would it? So soon after the funeral.'

Panic came into his eyes but Meg was pressing her head against his chest so didn't notice. 'I don't know when we're going yet. It could be months. But anyway . . .'

'No, don't.' She pressed her fingertips to his lips when he might have said more. 'I understand you're going into danger. I know . . . that the worst might happen.' There was a catch in her throat. 'But I want to think that we at least had something, some time together, as man and wife. If they don't send you abroad for a few months, we could get married, couldn't we? Then we'd have known some happiness . . .' She stopped and swallowed carefully. 'I love you so much, Jack.'

He kissed her again and found himself sharing her rising excitement. It might not be such a bad idea. It might give him some hope for the future, to be married. Lots of his mates were doing it. Rushing in and marrying the first good-looking girl who crossed their path. Seemed to be all the rage. And Meg would never let him have her again otherwise. He'd given up all hope, knowing that her Methodist upbringing and fear of her father were too strong in her. Sometimes he wondered what it was about her that made him want her so badly when there were any number of girls only too glad to have him.

'Let's think about it for a bit,' he said. 'You still wear my ring?'

'Oh, yes.' Meg held it out so they could both admire the sparkle. 'I wear it all the time.'

'Well, see that you do. Some of the lads have been let down by their girls back home already, playing about the minute they'd gone.'

Meg looked shocked. 'Oh, but that's dreadful. To cheat on somebody when they've gone off to fight a war. I would never do that to you, Jack.'

He hugged her close, enjoying the feel of her small body against his. 'See that you don't, or I'll make you sorry.' He bent his head and kissed her lips, nipping them with his teeth so that fire shot through to her belly, shaming her.

She pulled away a little, feeling flustered. 'Have you heard from Kath?' She linked her arm safely in his as they sauntered on.

'Not for ages.' Then as an afterthought, 'Well, I did get a postcard from Southport.'

'Oh?'

'Staying with an aunt, she said.'

'I do wish she'd write to me. What have I done? Why doesn't she write? Or do you think she did and Father threw it away?'

'I wouldn't put it past him. Mean beggar.'

Meg considered. 'Southport isn't far from Liverpool, is it? I don't suppose you could call and see her? Find out what's wrong. Perhaps she's not well or something.' She held her breath as she waited for his reply. She missed Kath.

'What time do I get for going visiting?'

Meg sighed. 'I suppose not. Was there an address on this postcard?'

Jack shook his head. He didn't tell her what the message said, that Kath had asked him to call and see her. Made him feel a bit jumpy it had, though he couldn't rightly say why it should.

He pulled Meg into his arms. 'Stop worrying over Kath Ellis. She's probably married someone rich by now and forgotten all about us. Come here, let me show you what's really on my mind.'

Squealing with delight she let him chase her for a full hundred yards before she allowed him to catch her again. His kisses and the demanding hands upon her body more than quenched her worries over Kath. How silly she was. Jack was right. She always came up smiling.

'Maybe I do like the idea of your waiting here for me, making a home. Maybe one day starting a family.

Meg gasped. 'Oh, Jack. Really?'

The thought of going overseas thrilled and scared the hell out of him all at the same time. It would help to know Meg was here, a loving home to come back to. Who would buy the farm anyway, with a war on? It rankled a bit that his father had overlooked him in this way, yet it didn't surprise him.

But they didn't have to keep it for ever. Five years was a long time. The war would be over long before then and there was no possibility of Meg's finding the purchase price in any case. She'd be lucky to manage to pay the rent. After the war they could sell it at a good profit, give Connie her share and put all this nonsense of farming out of Meg's head. It would only take a baby or two to do the trick, and everything would be fine and dandy then. For now, he'd leave things just as they were.

It did not occur to him to ask if Meg was all right for money or if she needed anything. And Meg, being Meg, did not mention her need. He gave her one last lingering kiss.

'We'll give it twelve months, as we should in the circumstances, then see what we can do, eh?'

'Oh, Jack.' Meg squealed with delight and flung her arms about his neck while he spun her around, startling a flock of hedge sparrows into chaotic flight.

Meg was as near happy as she had been in a long while. And she was not unaware that she had Lanky as much as Jack to thank for it.

'I'll make you proud of me, you'll see,' she said into the darkness that night as she snuggled down in bed, dazzled by her good fortune and terrified by it, all at the same time.

She had no illusions about the amount of work involved but that didn't worry her. Meg had every faith that she could make a success of Broombank and restore it to its former glory. She certainly meant to try if only because it was something she could do on her own, to help Jack, while he was away fighting. It would be her contribution to the war effort.

She tucked the Luckpenny beneath her pillow and with a smile still upon her soft lips, fell quickly asleep.

But there was little time for dreaming now. Dawn found her out in the farmyard, paper in hand, making an inventory. If she was to make a success of this business she must first work out its assets. What exactly did she own? She knew the acreage but had no idea how many sheep there were. Though she saw, with sinking heart, Joe had kept his threat and taken the two remaining cows.

She studied the barns. Only one was sound, the hay barn filled with this year's harvest, so she ignored that and examined the others. They were in a worse state of repair than she had feared. Some of them were cluttered with old rusting handtools. She would need to check every item for its likely usefulness, clean every fork, rake, pail and sickle. Mend what was broken, if she could manage it. Fix the holes in the barn roofs, rebuild the miles of dry stone walls that lined the land. Count every bale of hay, and most important of all, check the well-being of every sheep.

And she had to talk to Effie. For a city child with a fear of animals this was hardly the best place to be. Life was going to be hard, no doubt about that. Effie had to be told what was involved and be allowed to make up her own mind about staying.

It was a subject Meg intended to raise over breakfast but the reality of their situation was brought sharply home to her before she got the chance.

'This is the last of the oats,' Effie announced. 'You'd best get some more.'

The last of the oats. Get more? How? She swallowed a sudden fear that constricted her throat and dipped her head so that Effie could not see the dawning horror in her face. 'Right,' she murmured, remembering her vow never to let the child go hungry again. But she had underestimated Effie.

'Mind you, there's plenty of cabbages round the back,' she said, pouring out a mug of black tea and passing it directly to Meg. 'The milk was sour.'

'Yes, I'll see about that,' said Meg vaguely, not quite sure how. 'Cabbages, you say?'

'Aye. A person can live on cabbages, if you have to. Surprising what you can do with a good cabbage if you set your mind to it, my mam ses.'

'We don't have to live on cabbages,' Meg protested, quickly rejecting the very idea. 'We have eggs, the chickens if necessary, though admittedly we can't kill too many as we need them to lay and improve the flock. And we have the sheep. But no lambs, of course, and we daren't slaughter any ewes right now, we need every one.'

Effie spooned porridge into her mouth and stared at her for a time in silence while she finished it, showing off her new table manners. 'So what do we eat fer our dinner?'

It was such a pertinent, commonsense question that it left Meg breathless. 'Is there nothing left from yesterday?' she asked, incredulous that so much food could disappear so quickly.

'Wi' that lot going at it night and day? Not a crumb.'

Then their situation was more dire than she had bargained for. Meg put down her spoon as her throat closed up, quite robbing her of appetite. How very silly she had been. Here she was starting on an inventory of farm implements and stock, excited at the prospect of running her own farm, and the reality was that she couldn't even feed the two of them for a day.

Most farms kept a pig. Lanky had been too sick to bother. Most kept ducks or turkeys to sell for Christmas; Lanky had sold his few ducks long since.

Meg had no money to buy fresh young birds, and it was probably too late in any case. Most farms had at least one, and preferably two cows who kept them in milk, butter and cheese. And Joe had taken all of Lanky's.

As if on cue, she heard a voice calling her name in the yard. Meg and Effie exchanged a long speaking glance.

'Keep my porridge warm. I shall need it later. I'll see what he wants.' But before she could move from the table, the door was flung open and Dan's bulky presence filled the frame.

'I'm not stoppin'. So no need to put the kettle on.' Meg hadn't thought to do so.

'I'm always glad to see you, Dan,' she said quietly. 'But I'd appreciate it if you'd knock in future.'

'Knock?'

'On the door. This is an all female establishment. I'd appreciate it.'

The sneer was back and his ears seemed to stick out further than usual as he grinned. 'Gettin' fussy, are you, now you 'ave a place of your own?'

'I just want our privacy respected, that's all.'

'Aye, well, that's as maybe. I only called to tell you that the debt's settled now, you'll be glad to hear. We've tekken what's due to us.'

Meg was across the room in a second. 'What? What have you taken?'

'What's due to us. You can get on wi' tryin' to make a do out of this ramshackle hole.' Laughing as if he had made a joke, Dan turned to go.

Meg struggled against the rising heat behind her eyes which seemed to stop her seeing properly. 'What exactly have you taken?'

'It's all legal and above board. Don't look so shocked. You know very well that lawyer chap said as how we could. Well, like I said, it's all done with.'

'Tell me.' She leapt forward and grabbed his arm, feeling the broad muscles ripple beneath her hand as he instinctively flinched from her. She dropped her hand and again he grinned at her.

'All right, all right, if tha wants to know. We've tekken a tup or two, and a portion of hay.' He looked beyond her to Effie who sat like stone at the great deal table. 'Is that your idea of a farm labourer? Well, I should say you'd be bound to make a fortune wi' that sort o' brawn to help.' And throwing back his great head, he laughed till he was forced to hold on to his aching sides.

The sound of his boots clomping across the farmyard cobbles echoed in Meg's ears long after he had gone. Only when the silence rushed back at her did she run across to the haybarn and fling back the doors. It was completely empty. While she had been busy feeding Connie and her husband all weekend, her father and Dan had brought a horse and cart and robbed her of her winter feed.

Weeping never did anyone any good, Meg told herself crossly, rubbing her eyes red raw with her efforts to make the tears stop. The Herdwicks didn't do well on hay anyway and she no longer had any cows. But it was upsetting all the same, for them just to come and take it. Every farmer likes to know he has a barn full of hay, just in case the weather turns bad and the grass is used up. But she'd manage. She wouldn't let this put her off. The farm could survive without a bit of hay.

The tups. Dan had said, '*We've tekken a tup or two.*'

Meg ran till her sides were splitting to the lower fell where she knew the rams had been enclosed. Her awful suspicions were correct. Lanky had kept at least half a dozen good strong rams. Now only two inexperienced young ones remained. Her shoulders slumped in despair. How could they survive now?

Though this was the quiet time of the year and the flock could largely tend to itself for a bit, within the next few weeks it would be time to gather the Herdwicks from the high fells and bring them down to be served by the tups. A portion of the lower fell was fenced off for this purpose since the good grass of the intake land must be protected for the weaker stock as winter progressed. Forty or fifty sheep would be put with each ram and Meg knew that it was a complicated task, necessitating careful markings of ram number and week served, so that it was clear which sheep would lamb in which week.

But without rams, there would be no tupping season. No seed would be sown for a crop of lambs next spring. She was finished before she had even started.

No rams, no money, no food, no cows, no small animals and no emergency feed for the sheep that she did have.

What had possessed her to think she could ever manage?

As she stood racked by the bitter wind and her own desolation on the bleak hillside, a small warm hand slipped quietly into hers.

'Yer not going to send me back, are yer?'

Meg looked down into the pinched features of little Effie. She had known this child for only a few short weeks and yet felt as if she had known her a lifetime. By Effie's side stood the devoted black and tan collie dog, loyally wanting always to be with them. If Rust ever left Meg's heels, which was rare, it was only because he felt it his duty to protect this small stranger he had taken to his big heart. Tongue lolling as usual, one brown ear erect while the black one lolled like his tongue, he gazed from one face to the other and waited patiently as if knowing a decision was about to be made.

'I dun't eat much,' Effie continued earnestly. 'I know as how I med a fuss when I fust come – first come. But I like it now and I promise to be good and learn to speak proper and everything.' She sought Rust's ear and nervously gave it a tug. The dog rubbed his face lovingly against her hand, eyes never leaving the child's face. 'And I can work hard. I'm strong.' She flexed a skinny arm so fiercely that Meg would have laughed out loud had it not been unkind to do so. She knelt down beside the child and gathered her into her arms.

'Effie, I would love you to stay, really I would. But it won't work, do you see? We have no food and I have scarcely any stock. I know very little about sheep and nothing at all about managing a farm all by myself.'

'You could learn.'

Meg sighed and stared up at the dark specks as they moved over the tawny ridges, wondering how Lanky had managed all on his own.

'You see those ewes standing guard on their favourite crag?'

Effie squinted in the direction she pointed. The size of these mountains made her feel smaller than ever, and she worried a bit that these same crags might drop down one of these days. But Meg said they'd been there since the ice age so why should they fall down now, on to her? And if Meg said they were safe, then they must be.

'You see they can easily become trapped on the narrow ledges in bad weather,' she was saying. 'Blown off in high winds or fall from simple panic. Lanky would climb down, agile as a monkey and rescue them with a rope and his own strength.'

'Can't you do that then?'

Meg gave an odd little laugh and shook her head. 'I thought I could but I don't have Lanky's agility, nor his strength. I don't have his knowledge or his expertise. I wish he was here now, Effie, to tell me what to do.' A sense of awful inadequacy swamped her. Following the old man about on his daily tasks had taught her nothing about sheep farming. Particularly since her mind had been too fully occupied with Jack at the time.

Her throat was growing tighter as she listed these very sensible reasons for giving up now, before she'd even started. 'And I'm a woman, nowhere near strong enough to do all the jobs that need to be done.'

''Oo ses so?'

Meg smiled sadly. 'I do. Oh, I'm strong inside, and proud with it. But it takes more than inner strength to be a good farmer. You need long legs to walk the hills, and broad shoulders to lift the sheep and heavy stones and sacks. I don't know how to gather the tups so I can put rud on them, how to catch and mark the sheep, how to keep them safe all winter . . .' Her voice tailed away as her eyes moved over the smooth rounded foothills, the blue and white crags that hazed the horizon beyond. Tranquil as it appeared it was a hard land, unbending, a remorseless taskmaster. But she loved it all the same. Meg swallowed and blinked.

'We'd best go and see Mr Lipstock this afternoon. I'm sure there are plenty of other people who would love to have you stay.'

Taking Effie's hand she started to walk down the hill but the child tugged her to a halt.

'Where will you go?' The dark brown eyes were burning into Meg's, beseeching, compelling her to find a better solution.

It was some moments before Meg could answer and the smile was more brave than convincing. 'Maybe I'll have to become an evacuee like you, and find someone to take me in.'

'Can't we leave it till tomorrer? Goin' to Mr Lipstock, I mean.' And then as if anxious to clinch the matter, she continued, 'I've found some tatties an' all. We could have bubble and squeak fer dinner.'

The small face, and the careful, rational appeal in the voice, so touched Meg that she burst into a peal of merry laughter. But only because if she hadn't laughed, she would have cried.

* * *

The next few days were the hardest Meg had ever spent in her life. She worked from first light to long past dark and still did not seem to get through half the amount of work needing to be done. She spent hours checking the sheep, mending walls, repairing the sheds, barns, fences and gates with odd bits of wood and rusty nails, pieces of netting or, when all else failed, bits of tatty string because when the sheep were brought down, she couldn't afford to lose any.

But she was only putting off the evil day. It was all a waste of time really.

As she worked, her mind gnawed away at her problems. If she had money she could hire tups. But she had no money. If she had no pride she could ask Joe for help. But she had far too much pride. There seemed to be no answer.

Effie proved herself surprisingly useful. If she had learned nothing of social graces and table manners in the slums of Manchester, she had certainly learned how to survive. And she never complained about the work. Her tiny, wiry body never stopped, the sound of her tuneless, high-pitched singing filling the dale.

She found and dug up quite a good store of potatoes and Meg taught her how to cover them with straw and soil in the darkness of an old shed, to keep them dark, dry and fresh.

'These'll last us all winter,' Effie said with pride and Meg tried to look happy about the prospect of living on cabbages and potatoes for months on end. Soon, too soon, the hens might stop laying. She would ask Sally Ann for some isinglass, then she could store some eggs in readiness for that dreaded day.

They picked blackberries from the hedgerows, filling their mouths till they were black, like young children out on a picnic. They even chopped down nettles and made soup. It tasted surprisingly good.

And each morning they would look at each other and Meg would say, 'We should go and see Mr Lipstock today.'

And Effie would shake her head. 'Tomorrer.'

Meg had the feeling that by taking the little evacuee back she'd be somehow admitting failure. Something she would much rather not do.

But for all Effie's hard work and inventiveness, it was a meagre diet, with too little protein and energy in it. How could a child grow strong on such fare? How could Meg do the work of a strong man?

If she did not solve her problems soon, they would not be able to pay the rent at Christmas and then they would be homeless. The end of her dream and Effie's peace.

But nothing got Effie down. To her, this was paradise. One day she brought Meg's lunch up to Dundale Knott where she was working, and drew in great gulps of fresh air as if she could eat it. 'It's bonnie here, in't it? We're all right now, aren't we? We're managing.'

Meg paused in her labours of slashing back the bracken which, if left, would choke the much needed grass that fought for light beneath. Thankfully she sat down to drink the milkless tea and eat the cold potatoes. 'We still need to find rams, by November, to provide next year's crop of lambs. And the rent by Christmas. But apart from that, yes, I suppose we are managing so long as my family don't decide to try any further funny business.'

'Why should they?'

'Because my father likes to be top dog, always in control. He doesn't care to be bested by a mere woman.'

Effie snorted her disgust. 'Sounds like my mam's sort of fella.'

'And he wants me to fail so that Connie can sell him this land. Then him and Dan can have it all to themselves and he can keep me in my place, by the kitchen sink.'

'Can't you talk to him, get him to leave you alone? He might lend you some money if you ask proper.'

'Over my dead body.'

'You'll have to talk to him some time or other. He's yer dad,' said the too-practical child, and Meg gazed at her in astonishment.

'Don't you hate him for what he did to you?' The physical scars on the child's back were healing well but surely there would be mental ones too, harder to cure. To have suffered bruising abuse in her own home was one thing, to find the same treatment in the place offered as sanctuary was inhuman in Meg's opinion and filled her with an odd kind of guilt, as if she were in some way responsible.

Effie shrugged. 'I've been belted afore. It dun't get to me, not the *real* me, d'yer see?' Fierce brown eyes looked up at Meg, dark as chocolate, like great melting pools in the white face. And Meg did see, she understood perfectly. The child was showing more courage than herself, and was wise beyond her years. What you were inside could remain untouched, private and special. Not even Joe could quench her spirit, if she didn't let him.

And Effie was right. She would have to make some sort of peace with her father, for Meg would need his help with the gather. The ewes needed to be brought down from the fells and given the autumn

167

dip whether or not she found any tups for them, and she couldn't do that by herself. And she couldn't risk not seeing Sally Ann or Charlie again.

But she still had to find solutions for all her other problems.

A voice shouted in the distance and they both looked up. Far below them, coming up the lane from Ashlea to Broombank, was a figure, waving an arm madly.

'Someone's coming,' said Effie.

Meg's heart leapt. Could it be Jack? Even as the hope came to her she rejected it. Hadn't he only just gone back? The figure had reached the farm door and was waving two arms and shouting up to them now.

Meg was on her feet, pulling Effie with her. 'Dear God, I think it's Charlie.' Then she was running down the hill with the wind behind her and joy in her heart.

14

Waiting in the farmyard was a young man dressed in RAF uniform, forage cap set at a killer angle just above his right ear, and a huge grin on his face.

Meg leapt at her brother to give him a big hug.

'I called at Ashlea first. They said you were up here. How? Why? Where's Lanky?'

'Weeks you've been gone and no more than a postcard,' Meg scolded.

Charlie had the grace to look sheepish. 'We've been drilling and square-bashing in Blackpool.'

'Landed on your feet there then, didn't yer?' chipped in Effie.

'Effie, stop it,' Meg protested but her eyes were merry with happy laughter. It was so good to have him home.

And while Meg told Charlie of Lanky's worsening illness which had driven the old man to take his own life, Effie went quietly into the house and put on the kettle. A sudden shaft of hot jealousy stabbed her young heart. It surprised her a bit how possessive she had come to feel about Meg and the farm but she didn't want their very private peace spoiled.

Privacy was a new phenomenon to Effie. She hadn't minded leaving the sewers of Salford, the squalor and overcrowding and the grunting of men and women doing unspeakable things to each other at all hours of day or night.

'There must be summat better in store for Euphemia Putman, that's what I've allus thought,' she told Rust now as he stood patiently beside her while she watched the kettle, just as if he were going to enjoy a cup of tea himself. 'Me having such a grand name an' all.'

But she'd been sorry to leave her mam. Mam was special. A bit short tempered mind, but then who wouldn't be, as she said herself, with six brats and a man to feed? It wasn't always the same man, but a man there usually was. And another family too often sharing the same room so that between them they might manage to find the rent from time to time. Enough anyroad to stop them being evicted.

Now Effie could have a whole room to herself if she wanted it, not that she did. This great farmhouse had been a bit overwhelming at first with its lobbies and two staircases, any number of pantries and six great empty bedrooms. Effie still didn't want to sleep on her own but she liked being here, with Meg. She liked it in the evenings when they banked the fire up with holly and juniper and the rich tang of old oak, and the flames would rise, straight and true, up the dry stone circular chimney. Then they would snuggle up in the sheepskin on the big carver chair and Meg would tell her stories, just as if she was Effie's real mother. She missed her mam a lot but Meg had made it all right.

No, she didn't want nobody else here. Particularly if this one was anything like the rest of Meg's family.

She was bringing him into the house and they looked so happy together Effie's heart softened and she decided to be generous. This brother was in the war, so he wouldn't be stopping long. And he looked pleasant enough. Quite good-looking in fact.

'I'll peel some more potatoes for the soup,' she offered.

'Oh, yes, you must be hungry, Charlie. Worn out,' Meg said, all concern. 'Have you been travelling long?'

'Hours. If a train runs on time it can stop for no reason at all. And you're stuck in the middle of nowhere with not the first idea where you are, even if you could see, which generally you can't because the journey has taken so long it's gone dark and there's only a daft blue light in the crowded carriage. I had to stand all the way. Don't know why I bothered making the effort.'

Meg pulled a face teasingly at him, filled with a surge of fresh optimism just seeing Charlie's cheery smile again. 'I'm glad you did.'

It would be just like old times, she thought, as she hurried to liven up the fire. With them having fun and not caring a jot about the world outside.

Effie held out a steaming mug of tea, small dark eyes measuring, assessing. She was starting to like this tall man, so like her lovely Meg.

170

'We've no sugar nor milk so there's no point in asking for any.' And she silently added there was precious little food either.

'Right,' said Charlie, and grinned, making Effie his slave for life. 'I've been having a great time, Meg.'

'I thought you were training?'

'We are. But we find time to go dancing.'

'Dancing?'

'In the Tower Ballroom.'

'Oh, you've time to dance then, if not send your sister postcards?'

He playfully punched her. 'All the dances were stopped at first, and the cinemas closed. But then they opened again and we all went along to celebrate. There's some pretty girls in Blackpool. I can tell you of one in particular . . .'

Meg hugged him again. 'You're growing up too quickly, Charlie lad. Come on, sit down and drink your tea. You must be dropping on your feet. You'll stay, won't you? I'll take your things upstairs. We're not short of room here, that's one good thing. We've more bedrooms than we know what to do with. You don't know how glad I am to see you.'

The three of them were sitting down to a much thinned potato and cabbage soup when there was a light tap on the door before it opened.

'Hallo. Anyone in?'

'Sally Ann!'

'Watch out. I'm carrying precious cargo here. One of my best steak and game pies.'

Whoops of joy came from behind and it was hard to tell who was the most welcome, Sally Ann or the pie. The table was swiftly cleared of its odious soup and it took no time at all to demolish the delicious pie, succulent with meat and running with gravy.

'Oh God, that was good,' groaned Charlie, staggering from the table on exaggeratedly bent knees. 'I shall never move again.'

Effie brought the tea and they all stared at the milkless fluid in the cups and then at each other.

'We could go out to a pub,' Charlie declared. 'Father won't know.'

'How wicked,' Sally Ann said, but Meg was forced to remind them of Effie.

'We can't leave her here alone while we go off enjoying ourselves.'

'There's the potato and beetroot wine I made,' Effie suggested, eager to be a part of this delightful party. 'It's not that bad,' she protested as faces were pulled and lips sucked.

And after two or three glasses, it wasn't.

'Or else it's scoured all the taste buds off my tongue,' murmured Charlie, half asleep in the chair. 'God, it's good to be home. No, I'll correct that. It's good to be here with you Meg.'

Brother and sister exchanged knowing smiles. 'It's good to have you here.'

'Has Dad been causing any trouble?'

'Nothing I can't cope with. More wine?'

'I've tried to talk to him,' said Sally Ann. 'But he just says you should come home and bring your head down from the clouds. He thinks I need help, which is ridiculous. I can manage perfectly well.'

Meg's heart fluttered. Looking at Sally Ann, she did seem a bit washed out. 'You mustn't let him work you too hard.'

'Don't worry, I won't. You're the one with your work cut out.'

'He was saying something of the sort to me. I told him you couldn't be in two places at once, and you had the right to pursue a dream if you'd a mind to,' Charlie blithely added.

'Bless you.'

'Mind you, Sal's right. How on earth are you going to manage here, on your own?'

Meg bounced to her feet, anxious not to go into it all now. It was so lovely to have Charlie here, and Sally Ann too, she had no intention of bothering them with any of her problems.

'Mrs Lawson's old piano is in the other room. Let's have a sing-song.'

'Can you play?' Sally Ann cried.

'Charlie can. Mum had one in the parlour for years at home. Come on, lad, give us a tune.'

'Right, you're on.'

That evening was the happiest that Meg could remember. Charlie thumped out song after song with more energy than accuracy but nobody minded. 'Kiss Me Goodnight', 'Little Brown Jug', 'Colonel Bogey', and a lively rendition of the 'Woodchopper's Ball', amongst others. They all sang their socks off, even young Effie who didn't know half the words. Later, Meg had them all in tears with a particularly moving rendition of 'Over the Rainbow'.

'Stand aside, Judy Garland,' murmured Charlie, grinning broadly. 'You've missed your vocation, Meg girl.'

Replete and happy, with Charlie tucked up in the best bedroom, Meg hugged him and gave him a kiss before turning out the lamp, just as she had always done when he was growing up. For all there was only two years between them, she was still his big sister, wasn't she?

'Go on, don't be so soft,' he laughed, pushing her away, but with the sort of expression on his face that told her he didn't mean it.

Meg knelt beside the bed, a patch of moonlight washing the bright colour from her face and hair. 'You will take care, won't you, Charlie? I couldn't bear . . .'

'Don't say it. It's bad luck to say it.' His face had gone white too with no help from the moon and she saw the extent of his bravery, covering up the raw fear beneath. She nodded, blinking away the tears.

'It's hard to think there's a war on out there. I forget sometimes.'

'You've got your own war to fight here. It'll take some doing.'

'I know. But I mean to try. Thanks for coming, anyway. You've been a real tonic for me, Charlie. Don't worry,' she quipped, 'only the good die young.' And ignoring his protests, planted another kiss on his cheek before going to her own bed.

Charlie left all too soon as he only had a forty-eight hour pass. Meg consoled herself that it had been good to see he was well, though it was hard getting back to normality. And potato and cabbage soup.

But a day or two later their luck seemed to have changed when Mrs Davies from Melgate called with a side of bacon.

'I hope you won't take offence by it, but your Charlie passed by our place the other day, on his way back, he said. Proper swank he looked in his new uniform, I must say. You'll be right proud of him, love.' She gave a soft smile. 'Anyroad, he happened to mention how you were a bit strapped for provisions like, Lanky not having kept any pigs this year. I should have thought of it myself. So I've fetched you a piece then you can take a shive off whenever you want.'

Meg gazed longingly at the huge, muslin-wrapped bacon that reposed behind the seat in Mrs Davies's old cart. 'It's very kind of you but I'm afraid we have no . . . I mean . . .' Meg swallowed her pride and met the older woman's kindly face with an embarrassed smile. 'I've no money to pay you for it.'

'Lord above, I don't want no money for it. I'm glad to be of use to you. We've more'n enough for our needs, Will and me. Even though we have a hired man and an evacuee to feed, we'll not go short.' She gazed sternly at Effie. 'You'll be sending her to school, I trust. How old is she? Nine? Ten?'

'About that,' said Meg, realising that until this moment she had never given a thought to school for Effie. But Mrs Davies was quite right. She should go.

'And church.'

It was not a question and Meg assured the good lady they would both be there, come Sunday. Well satisfied, Mrs Davies took tea, was shocked to find they had no milk and promised to look into the matter without delay.

Meg, worried that she meant to tackle Joe on the subject, urged her not to trouble. 'We can manage,' she assured her, but felt ashamed that she couldn't even offer the farmer's wife a scone or tea-cake by way of refreshment. As if divining the depth of the problem, Hetty Davies went on talking.

'You'd be doing me a service if you took some flour off me hands too. I don't know what William was thinking of to buy two sacks at once. Just because there's a war on there's no need to stock up for the duration already, I says to him.'

'Mrs Davies, you are an angel in sheep's clothing.' And they both laughed.

Meg's embarrassment washed away before the cheerfulness of her visitor. Mrs Davies had always been a kind neighbour and a stalwart of the local ladies' circle.

'Did Lanky keep a horse?' she wanted to know as she delicately sipped her tea.

'I'm afraid not.'

'Well, you're going to need one.'

'Why?'

'For the ploughing.' She looked into the blank face and sighed. 'Nay, don't tell me you haven't been taking in any news since you come up here?'

'I'm afraid we haven't seen a newspaper in weeks. Why, what's going on?'

'Only started a War Committee to tell us farmers what to do with our land, that's what. Got to plough up thousands of acres, and pretty quick too or you get in proper trouble.'

'Thousands of acres?'

Hetty Davies chuckled, making the flesh of her chin wobble alarmingly. 'Not you alone, Westmorland in general, I mean. I daresay someone will be calling to see you but in the meantime you'd best look out the likely land that'll take a plough. Not that there'll be much. We grow better stones up here than corn. I dare say Lanky has one rusting away somewhere. But if you don't want to have to do it by hand, you'd best find, beg or buy yourself a strong horse. And some labour to help you.'

'Labour?'

'Aye. You can't manage all this by yourself now, can you? Eeh, I remember the old hiring fair up at Ulverston. There'd be any number of farm girls and lads ready for tekking on. Some of 'em had never been away from home before. Don't know whether it's still going on though. And I recall a grand fair in Staveley too, when I were a girl. But that was for sheep. Shepherds came from miles around. They'd pay us children a penny to block off the gateways so's they could channel the sheep into the right field. We'd do it gladly for there were stalls and sideshows, swings and roundabouts to enjoy. And hot pot suppers. Grand it were. Nothing like that these days. All gone now.' Swamped by nostalgia, the farmer's wife shook her head and sipped sadly at her tea.

Meg attempted to direct Mrs Davies back to this new information she was giving them.

'Do you think Mr Davies would give me a bit of instruction? With the ploughing. I can't afford labour. Nor a horse.' But the prospect of ploughing even an acre by hand was too daunting to contemplate.

'Eeh, course he would, lass. Be glad to.' A plump lady in her fifties who, as she said, had never been blessed with children of her own, Hetty Davies looked with compassion upon Meg. 'I'll see if Will can lend you our Arlott for a day or two. He's an old fell pony, bit of a clodhopper but reliable, not one for easy panicking.'

Meg's heart swelled with relief and thankfulness. 'I'd be most appreciative. And there is just one more thing you could help me with.' The enquiring eyes were kind so she found the courage to continue. Clearing her throat, she began: 'I've found myself a bit short of rams this year. I wondered...'

Mrs Davies stood up. 'Say no more. I'll send our Will round first thing. He'll see what you need and put you right.'

Satisfied with her good neighbourliness, Mrs Davies said her farewells and climbed stiffly back into her cart. Instructing a very plump pony to walk on, she clicked the reins at it for some moments before it finally deigned to lift its head from the sweet grass verge and obey.

'I'll see you at church then, on Sunday. And you'll get that child into school.'

Meg said that she would and waved goodbye, sighed with relief then danced a little jig of delight with Effie all around the kitchen.

'Bacon for tea. I'll find some eggs and we'll have a real feast. Oh, things are looking up.'

'And flour too, did she say?' Effie's small face was alight with the promise of satisfying the rumblings of her continuous hunger.

'Flour, oh joy! I never thought to be so grateful for such a basic substance. We can have dumplings and potato cakes, soda bread . . . oh, all sorts of good things.'

Effie's cheeks burned with twin spots of colour. 'Do that mean that I dun't have to go and see Mr Lipstock? Do that mean I can stay?'

Meg sobered at once and regarded the young girl before her, very seriously. 'If I say that you can, Effie, you have to realise that the work will be hard. It won't always be warm. Winter will come and we might get hungry again. We have a lot to learn with the sheep and we mustn't risk losing any. We'll have to go out in all weathers to look after them. This is a farm so we will get more and more animals, I hope, as time goes by. Perhaps even cows again one day. You will have to learn to like them or at least get used to them.'

Effie chewed on her bottom lip. 'Will I 'ave to milk 'em? Hold their tits and things?'

Meg smothered a giggle. 'Not if you don't want to. But if you don't milk, you'll at least have to help sweep out the muck and clean the byre. I know you're getting pretty good with the cooking, but you will have to go to school, like Mrs Davies said. And church. If you live here, you have to become a proper part of the community.'

Effie would have agreed to stand on her head every morning if that was what it took to stay in this lovely place. 'I've never been to no school.'

Meg looked shocked. 'Then it's long past time you started. You'll also have to wash your face when I tell you to, instead of sneaking off and pretending that you've done it when you really haven't. You'll have to wear shoes instead of going barefoot. You'll have to learn to keep your clothes tidy and wash them regularly. And you'll have to get on with the village children, do your arithmetic and spelling and learn your scriptures, same as everyone else. Say please and thank you and no swearing. Do you think you can manage all of that?'

Effie gazed at Meg with her big dark eyes. She didn't quite know what half of these big names meant. But if Meg wanted her to do them, then she would find out how, and do it. Very solemnly, she nodded.

'I will, if you want me to.'

'That's settled then.'

They grinned at each other.

'It's going to be all right, Effie, you'll see. Hard work, painful, difficult, and no doubt loads of problems ahead, but we'll be all right. I know we will. Get slicing that bacon. I'm *starving*.'

The next day Effie came screaming into the kitchen as if the devil were on her tail.

'There's a man in the yard with two monsters.'

Meg glanced out the door then burst into laughter. 'You've a strange idea of what constitutes a monster.'

William Davies stood patiently waiting by the old yew chopping block. And two Shorthorn cows stood with equal patience by his side.

'Hetty said as how you were needing a couple,' he said by way of explanation. 'They're not me best by a long chalk but they still give good milk.'

And when Meg asked about payment he shook his head with its white grizzled beard. 'See me right some time. When you get on your feet like.'

'That's very kind of you.' A shy man, unused to company, Will brushed her thanks aside, anxious to be off.

'I've put the flour and rice in the lean-to. Let me know when you want to borrow our Arlott for t'ploughing and I'll give you a quick lesson. We can sort out the tups you need to borrow when the time comes. Owt else you want, give me a shout.' And touching the neb of his cap, he refused all refreshment and swiftly departed.

Buoyed up by the generous support of her neighbours, Meg rode into town on her bike that very afternoon to find out the details from the War Committee about ploughing and came back pink-cheeked with the thrill of discovery.

'They'll pay a grant of two pounds an acre, when the work's done. And there are more grants available for land draining.'

Effie looked blank. 'Is that good?'

'If we can do ten acres, that would be twenty pounds. Almost half the rent next quarter day.' Whether or not she had ten acres good enough to plough Meg had no idea, nor where the rest of the money was to come from. But her optimism was soaring.

Seth Barton from Cathra Crag stopped off later with five young goslings and half a dozen turkeys. 'I'm well stocked,' he said gruffly. 'They only need fattening up. And missus has sent a li'le bit o' smoked macon.' This last proved to be a piece of mutton, smoked like bacon, delicious, and sufficient to feed them three months or more. Their winter was secure.

'There's a bit more than a little bit here,' gasped Meg.

'Aye, well,' Seth explained. 'We were right fond of Lanky. And it's good to see the old place working again. Beggin' your pardon, but we know help won't be forthcoming from Joe. He won't like the idea of you getting one over him. You might do gay weel wi'out him poking around, and he won't like that noo, will he?' Seth went off chuckling, as if he'd made a new joke.

They celebrated that night with a thick slice of fried macon and potatoes, followed by creamy rice pudding with a touch of home-made raspberry jam that Sally Ann had brought. Meg, who had never gone short of food in her entire life before, thought a king could not have eaten better. Effie knew it for a fact.

They fell into an easy routine. Meg found she could cope with the work so much better now that she wasn't troubled by the nagging pangs of hunger.

Effie worked hard in the garden, digging and weeding. 'Next spring we could grow onions and turnips and carrots,' she said, getting carried away with this newfound enthusiasm.

But Monday was to be her first day at school and she was not looking forward to it.

'You'll love it, just you see,' Meg assured her as they sat beside the fire together, going over the day's events, as they so enjoyed doing. 'You'll make lots of new friends.'

'I dun't bloody want to go.'

'Effie! What have I told you about your language?'

She muttered a sulky apology. 'Who'll make the dinner while I'm gone?' she protested.

'We'll make it together, in the evening. It'll be all right, you'll see. You'll love school. I did. Miss Shaw taught me and you'll love her too, I promise.'

Effie looked astounded. 'Is she that old?'

'Go on, you cheeky tyke. For that, you can make the cocoa this evening.'

And without rancour, Effie obliged. Oh, yes, life was good. If only Jack were here, Meg thought, it would be perfect. A real family.

Later, when she tucked Effie up, she sat on the edge of the bed and smoothed the sheets beneath the child's chin with a tender hand. She was growing at last, her cheeks were plumping out a little and glowing with the good food and fresh air she was enjoying. The purple bruises on her body were almost gone, showing as no more than yellow stains on the pale flesh. Meg felt she had achieved wonders in such a short time but there was still room for improvement.

'Do you need me to come with you? Only I'm pretty busy and . . .'

Effie made a scornful sound in her throat. 'I'm not daft.'

'Well, you can find the school yourself, can't you? Now that I've shown you where it is. You won't get lost?' She meant, you won't run away, and they both knew it.

Effie shook her head very solemnly, then grinned her sudden, impish grin. 'And you won't let my half of the bed to someone else, while I'm gone?'

'No, I won't do that.' And they exchanged happy smiles.

Meg hoped that the discipline of school and regular contact with the other children would be good for Effie. She had succumbed to regular washing, agreed to sit up to the table and hardly ever resorted to her more colourful words and phrases these days. But Meg had so little time to spend teaching her that she hoped some of the other children's finer points would rub off.

'I think it's all a waste of time,' said Effie, as if reading her thoughts. 'They'll never manage to teach me owt.' But secretly the prospect excited her. Perhaps this was the start of her new life, her destiny. She might learn so much that one day she could get a job and earn real money of her own. Eeh, that would be grand. Then she could send some home to her mam.

Meg read her the *The Tales of Ivanhoe*, and Effie let her eyelids droop, enjoying the rhythm of Meg's voice while she played out her mother's joy and amazement in her mind.

Meg's mind too was elsewhere as she read. Oh, Jack, if only you could see how happy we are, here at Broombank. She would write to him in a minute and tell him of all the improvements she had made already, and about the generosity of her neighbours. She wondered when his embarkation leave would come. It seemed almost sinful to be so happy when he was waiting to be posted overseas.

The postman had brought her a postcard the other day. It showed a picture of the Liver building. It seemed so far away it might as well have been on the moon. The thought of Jack going even further away filled her with cold fear, when all she wanted him to do was write and say he was coming home and that they could be married.

When Effie was asleep Meg sat on by the fire, feeling alone. Effie was good company but still a child. Sometimes Meg ached for another adult about the place. For Kath. What was she doing? Why hadn't she written? Too busy enjoying her new life no doubt. Oh, but it would be lovely to see her. Kath always helped put things into perspective.

I wonder what you're up to, lass? Some mischief I'll be bound.

15

Kath was having a hard time too, though in a different way, and Tam O'Cleary was her only friend. Had she not felt so very unwell and unlike herself she might have been tempted to take it beyond friendship for he was a good-looking man. But this was not the moment, nor Southport the place.

Already preparations for war were encroaching upon life, making it less comfortable. The horses rarely galloped along the sands now and men in uniform shouted at her sometimes when she walked along it, as if they expected Hitler to arrive in a boat at any minute and kill them all. Kath ignored them and took no notice of the sandbagging that was starting in earnest along the front, the barbed wire that was being unrolled. She didn't want to think about the war.

She had plans. As soon as the baby was born she would move on. When, how and where were still undecided for she knew it was not going to be easy.

And Aunt Ruby continued to watch her like a hawk. Kath told Tam so one day as they sat in the sand dunes.

'You always think you're being watched.' His reply was, as usual, light-hearted. Nothing seemed to trouble him.

'You would too if you lived with that dragon. She sounds such a sweet dear, till you get to know her. Inside she's like a wire pan scrub just waiting to scratch you. Why my mother imagined it would be a restcure staying with her sister, I can't imagine.'

'And what would you be doing here then, might a fellow ask? Why should a fine healthy girl such as yourself be in need of a restcure?'

Kath met his shrewd, velvet gaze. 'Some folk ask too many questions.'

Tam merely quirked his brow and looked out to sea, pretending to have lost interest. Kath let the silence hang till she could bear it no more.

'All right then, I'll tell you. I have to tell someone or I'll burst. I'm pregnant. There. What do you think of that?'

'The thought had crossed my mind.'

'*What?*'

'No, I hadn't noticed the glow about you that pregnant women are supposed to have. More a sense of tension. I take it you have no husband and no intention of getting one?'

'You take it correctly. And I don't want to talk about it. All right?'

'All right by me.' Once more Tam O'Cleary addressed his full attention to the sea. It was miles out, no more than a thin line of silver on the horizon. They huddled deep in the sand dunes, trying to avoid the chill wind blowing through the marram grass. Kath shivered.

'Is that all you're going to say? Aren't you going to give me a lecture?'

'Nope.'

She fell into a thoughtful silence and after a while slanted a look at him. She hadn't known Thomas O'Cleary long but she had learned that he was an eminently unfussy person. Quiet, patient, usually keeping his opinions to himself. She liked that. Nor did he make any demands upon her. He hadn't even tried to hold her hand when they'd gone to the pictures the other night. She couldn't imagine that he didn't fancy her. He was simply a man a woman could trust. Not like Jack Lawson who had not bothered to turn up when she'd asked him to, nor written to say why.

'I can't stay at my aunt's for ever. I'll swear she's getting suspicious. I thought of moving into a flat, if I could find a job.'

'Difficult to keep a job on with a baby on the way, I would think. Unless you find someone sympathetic.' They both knew the impossibility of that.

Kath sighed. 'I suppose so.'

'What about your family? Can't they help?'

Silence again.

'I take it you haven't yet informed them of this joyous news?'

Kath was on her feet in a second. 'If you're just going to take the mickey . . .'

Tam grabbed her ankle to stop her running off. 'Don't fly off the handle. All right, it's got naught to do with me. But since you've told me the worst, I thought I might be allowed one or two questions.'

Kath sat down again but remained stubbornly mute.

'Well, I'll start by telling you about myself, shall I? You know me name. I'm what you might call rootless. I came from Ireland originally and America more recently. I'll work for the British even if I won't fight for them. I'll turn me hand to anything but I prefer working on the land. In the summer I did vegetable picking in Ormskirk, and now I'm working at a local yard. Though heaven knows what the war will do to racing. I muck out mainly, but they're starting to trust me with the horses every once in a while, if not as often as I would like. There now, that wasn't so difficult. Now it's your turn.'

'Some things can't be talked of,' Kath said at last, in a very small voice. 'I just thought, there's a war coming, we could all be dead next year, so what the hell?'

'Did you love him?'

Kath paused a moment. 'I don't think so. Not sure I could love anybody. Mummy says I'm too selfish.' She smiled, rather ruefully.

'Oh, I cannot believe that to be true.'

'You don't know me. As for my family ... Let's just say that they would not approve. Bringing home an illegitimate baby would result in the "don't darken my door" routine. Mummy could never take the scandal. It would ruin her reputation at the Ladies' Circle.'

'And what about your reputation?'

Kath laughed. 'That's ruined already. I'll tell you about my best friend, Meg, instead.'

And so she did. About Meg and her young brother, Charlie. About Ashlea and Broombank. Sally Ann and Dan. About swimming in Brockbarrow Tarn and picnics on Kidsty Pike. She made no mention of Jack.

'Katherine Ellis, these sheets have not been ironed.'

Kath lifted her eyes to the ceiling at sound of the shocked tones and whispered a silent oath. Caught out, she turned to face her aunt's fury with her most winning smile. 'I've smoothed them well enough. No one will notice.'

'Don't try cutting corners with me, girl, I always notice.'

You would, you sharp-eyed old cow. 'I'm sure Mr Wilson won't. He very rarely sleeps in these days. He spends more time at his fiancée's house.' There was light-hearted mischief in her tone but Ruby did not respond to it, putting on her shocked expression.

'I hope you are not judging my guests by your own standards?'

Kath became very still. 'What do you mean?'

Ruby sniffed and fingered the glass beads over her flat chest. 'You must know, my dear, that I have only your best interests at heart. Your mama would expect it of me. But I have to admit that I've seen you, walking along Lord Street with your young man.'

If Kath hadn't felt so annoyed at being very likely followed on her afternoon off, she might have laughed at her aunt's quaint way of speaking. She sounded very like a Victorian novel.

'He is not my young man.'

'Whatever he is, dear, you know nothing about him, now do you?' No man had ever looked twice at Ruby Nelson. Rosemary had been the pretty one with boys falling over themselves for her attention. It had rankled then and it still rankled now that some girls found it so easy to find a man. 'You have surely no wish to be accused of being . . .' Ruby coughed delicately. 'Loose is the word that springs to mind. That sort of behaviour does your reputation no good at all. Take my word for it.'

Kath's cheeks went pink. 'I'm not at all – loose, as you call it. And he isn't my young man. He's a friend. The only one I have here as a matter of fact.'

'You should find yourself a decent girl friend from a respectable family.' Ruby frowned. 'I'll speak to my neighbours. They may know of someone suitable.'

Kath stiffened. 'There's no need. I'm perfectly capable of choosing my own friends, thanks very much.'

'But are you?' Ruby wagged a finger at her niece, a chiding smile upon her face as if she were talking to a child with half a brain. 'Mark my words, such lewd behaviour will bring you to no good.'

Kath's cheeks burned with indignation. 'Lewd behaviour? Walking along a main shopping street?'

'People jump to conclusions.'

'Then they shouldn't.'

'All I am asking is that you behave with a little more discretion.'

What would the old cow say if she discovered Kath had already come to no good, or fallen, as she would no doubt call it? Having a child out of wedlock would be a sin beyond redemption in Ruby

Nelson's eyes. 'I'll bear your advice in mind,' Kath said coldly, and wondered why she'd ever agreed to come to Southport.

'Splendid. Now strip those sheets off, like a good girl, and iron them properly before you put them back. And don't think I won't notice. Nothing slips past Madam Ruby, mark my words.'

But if ironing sheets was a trial, washing them was worse. Kath had nightmares about the mangle. An old-fashioned, turn-the-handle-if-you-had-the-strength variety, Kath hated it.

Mummy had a new electric washing machine, a vaccuum cleaner and a maid to operate these modern delights. Aunt Ruby, for all she had more sheets to wash, stuck to a dolly tub and posser. And the mangle, with its vicious set of rollers, that either stuck fast and chewed the sheets to ribbons or took your fingers with them. Every time Kath operated this equipment she felt exhausted for hours afterwards, and anxious over whether the effort would harm the baby. She might not want to keep the little mite herself but she wished it no harm.

Kath eased her aching back and suggested, quite politely, that Ruby might care to enter the twentieth century and buy a washing machine of her own.

'It'd be much easier to manage than this old dolly tub.'

She saw at once that this small criticism of the way things were done at Southview Villas did not go down at all well.

'Electric washing machines are no substitute for good scrubbing, that's what I say.'

Since you don't have to do the scrubbing, Kath thought, but kept it to herself. 'Come to think of it, you could send all the linen to the laundry. That would save hours of work.' Particularly for me.

'And cost a small fortune into the bargain. Trouble with you young people today is you don't know when you're well off. I sometimes wonder why you stay, miss, since you seem to dislike it so much.'

There was a small silence, Kath for once at a loss for words. She couldn't tell the truth. Aunt Ruby would inform her mother, without delay. She had recognised a malevolent streak in her aunt during the weeks she'd been here. Ruby called it 'keeping up standards'. Kath recognised it as plain bloody-mindedness.

'I like the sea air. And there are things going on here, at the Winter Gardens and the pictures. And then there's Liverpool quite close by. Westmorland is too boring for words.'

'Hm.' Ruby gravely considered her niece. 'Feeling better, are you then?'

'Better?'

'Your tummy upset passed?'

'Oh, y-yes. I'm fine.' Kath decided it would be politic to make no further complaints at present and started to fold the next sheet ready for the mangle. But Ruby was not one for letting things pass.

'You'd tell me if there was something wrong, now wouldn't you, dear?'

'What could be wrong?' Hazel eyes opened wide with pretended innocence.

'I owe it your mother. To see that you are properly taken care of. You are young yet, Katherine, and could easily fall prey to all manner of unspeakable sins.'

Kath sucked in her cheeks. 'I'll do my best to manage not to.'

'I'm pleased to hear it. And should there be anything, anything at all, on your mind, you must feel perfectly free, to come and speak to me about it.'

Perhaps in view of this tricky conversation it was a touch reckless to allow herself to be lulled into saying what she did. But Kath had never been one to guard her tongue. She pushed back a damp lock of hair with a tired hand. 'If you want to know, I think it's time we had a bit more help around here. I don't see you doing much these days.'

'I *beg* your pardon? I am the proprietress.'

'I know, Aunt Ruby. But it's not fair to leave everything to me. The washing, the cleaning and bed making. Even most of the cooking. I can't cope. Perhaps a young girl? Strong. Willing. I won't be able to manage this job much longer, on my own.'

Glassy eyes surveyed her unblinkingly.

'I think we've had enough of willing girls around here.' And with this enigmatic statement, Aunt Ruby left the scullery.

It was a few days later that Kath and Tam came home, later than usual, having taken a bus into Liverpool to a dance. Tam had insisted on walking her home from the bus station.

'I don't want you accosted in the blackout, or falling down any big holes. I heard tell of one man who rode his bike straight into a tree. He thought he was on the road, d'you see, but the pavements are so wide here in Southport, he was riding on the pavement instead. He bounced up so high he landed on a branch and it was morning before anyone found him and brought him down.'

Kath was holding her sides with laughter. 'What whoppers you do tell. It's true about Irishmen and the blarneystone.'

And since it was pleasant to be mildly cosseted by a man, even one who hadn't laid a finger on you, Kath was happy to let him walk her right to the door.

They were still laughing, swinging along arm in arm as they rounded the corner, feeling young and happy, till Kath saw the lace curtain twitch in the front parlour window and the face of her aunt peering out.

Before she had time to lift the brass knocker the door was flung open.

'As I thought. This is what you get up to, is it, miss?'

Kath swallowed the first bitter retort that came to her lips and turned, smiling, to Tam. 'Thanks for seeing me safely back.' And just to prove that she was twenty years old, twenty-one on 3 December, and could do as she pleased, she rested her hands on Tam's wide shoulders and kissed him full upon the lips.

And with that kiss, sealed her fate.

The next morning Ruby was at her bedside a full twenty minutes before six-thirty, the usual time Kath was expected to rise and prepare breakfast.

'Get up and put on a decent frock. No lipstick or fancy combs in your hair. Plain and respectable, no more nor less.'

'Why? Is the king coming?'

'I'll take no lip, neither. I've had enough of your clever tongue, madam. Looking down your nose at me because I'm not so well placed as your darling mummy, and all the time walking the street with any Tom, Dick or Harry.' Gone was the smiling, social front her aunt usually adopted. Ruby reached down and stripped the covers from the bed while Kath still lay in it, gasping with shock.

'Here, what is this?'

'When you're dressed, finish stripping the bed and fold all the sheets. Then come straight to the kitchen. You can have a bit of breakfast before you go.'

'Go? Go where?'

'I've found you a job. And you are to leave right away.'

'A job? What kind of job?'

But Ruby, having reached the end of her tether so far as this little madam was concerned, had nothing more to say. She marched from the room, glass beads clinking with indignation, and Kath had no option but to do as she was bid, excitement and the smallest degree of disquiet beating a dull pulse deep in her stomach.

Greenlawns showed not a speck of grass to mark its name before an austere, grey-stoned exterior. A tall, gabled house, much larger than Kath had expected, it stood on the outskirts of Liverpool. It had taken a long bus ride to reach it but Aunt Ruby had said the place was prepared to offer her work, so here she was, dressed in her best blue suit with tan shoes and bag to match.

Kath had read in a magazine that a girl should look bandbox smart if applying for work in a city establishment. She carried only one small attaché case, Ruby having promised to send on her luggage later, on the railway.

'If you like Liverpool so much, you can go and work in it,' her aunt had said, and Kath had quickly agreed.

'But how did you find out they wanted someone?'

'Her next-door told me,' said Ruby vaguely. 'I've given them a ring and it's all fixed.'

It would certainly be an improvement on that dratted mangle and the constant changing of bed linen, Kath thought, not to mention all the vegetable peeling for the boarding house guests.

It was worth a try. A quiet clerical job would do fine. She saw herself sitting neatly at a typewriter. Not that she knew how to type, but she could soon learn. No need to mention her little 'difficulty', just wear a jacket all the time, or a loose blouse and a light corset. They wouldn't be too fussy anyway, with a war on. She could buy a cheap ring from Woolworths, in case it got to be a problem.

Then find herself good digs and enjoy city life. Just what the doctor ordered. She might even look up Jack. She should have come to Liverpool in the first place. She could see that now. And there'd be loads of adoption societies around here. Kath felt quite optimistic.

Pulling the bellpull by the great iron gates she waited patiently for a woman to cross the tarmacadamed forecourt and open it. She was grey-haired, about sixty, wearing a sour expression and a green wraparound overall. One of the workers, no doubt.

'Yes?'

'I have an appointment. To see Miss Blake.'

Green Paint would be a more appropriate name, Kath decided as she was shown in to a small office which seemed to be thickly coated from stem to stern with the stuff. But she meant not to be put off by the appearance of the place, or the stern thinness of the woman who sat behind the wide desk. At four and a half months gone she couldn't afford to be too fussy. Work must be found. It was time to get herself sorted out.

The woman seemed to be all spectacles, long nose and thin lips. Owning herself to be the Miss Blake Kath had been detailed to find, the woman started to speak, but Kath was so mesmerised by the fact the lips hardly seemed to move, that she missed most of what was said.

'. . . and such is the result of romance.'

'I beg your pardon?' It was that last word, romance, which had jolted Kath's wandering attention.

'It is our task to care for the feeble-minded.'

'Oh, is this a hospital?' Kath glanced about her. That explained the rather institutional, antiseptic feel to the place.

'No, not a hospital, more a kind of sanctuary.'

Kath smiled politely. 'I see.'

'It is our duty to protect people from themselves. Many are weak creatures, with little or no control. They fall by the wayside, overcome by their passions, used by merciless hands. It is our call in life to protect their physical and spiritual needs at all cost. We are not linked to any particular church but you will find that our aims are that of charity all the same.'

Kath was concentrating hard but still finding it difficult to follow where this long explanation was leading, being more anxious to learn about the job. 'I'm not sure that I . . .'

The woman had risen and was ringing a small tinkling handbell. 'You will be shown to your quarters and told of the daily routine and issued instructions on your work detail. You will find it in your own best interests to settle in as quickly as possible.'

'Of course. But – settle in? Am I expected to live here?' Kath too was on her feet, smoothing her gloves in her most ladylike manner. 'I'm not sure that I would wish to. I rather thought I'd find digs in town. Could you tell me a little about the work, so that I can judge whether it would suit? Is it clerical?'

The woman looked irritated, as if she were unused to being questioned. 'It might be. It might be anything. Whatever needs doing and you are instructed to do, you will do it. It is not your place to judge or make decisions.'

'I see.' Kath supposed that was the way of all employers, of whom she had no knowledge. 'And the pay?'

The woman's face went quite blank with shock. 'Pay?'

'My wages. What am I to be paid?'

'You are lucky, child, that we do not charge you for the privilege of staying here. Though it is true that we depend upon goodwill for much of our income. However, Greenlawns was started by the Misses Harris, now sadly departed, in the early part of this century, for those girls less fortunate than themselves. They left a large trust fund to go with the property so we are largely independent.'

'Trust fund? Less fortunate? I'm afraid I don't understand. What is this place? Where am I, for God's sake?' Kath was starting to feel a prickly heat all down her back.

Miss Blake looked slightly taken aback and then something very close to a smirk came over her glacial features. Ah, so that was the way of it. She had seen it so many times before. A family no longer able to cope with a rebellious girl, not even able to discuss the delicate matter with her. So tragic, that weakness of character could split whole families apart. In the end they were forced to call upon Greenlawns, where people of note and respectability could safely rely upon complete discretion. Greenlawns had learned such delicate skills, along with many others needed in its work, over the years.

'You are, my dear, at Greenlawns, Home for Wayward Girls.'

Effie sat huddled in the bushes. Rain was drizzling down but she paid no heed to it for her eyes were fixed upon the school. Square and squat, it was surrounded on three sides by a paved playground that seemed to teem with tiny bodies. All clean and well dressed.

Nobody had ever considered schooling necessary before. Certainly not Mam, nor any of her many 'lodgers'. There'd been no time for learning. It had been Effie's task to mind her younger brothers and sisters while Mam slept, so she was fit to go out at night, to work, she said. No wonder Effie was an expert at boiling spuds and cabbage, she thought.

Where they went or what they got up to she couldn't say. Nor, apart from Jessie, the youngest whom she had kept with her, did she rightly care. Effie only knew that if they stayed in the house and woke Mam and her boy friend there'd be one helluva row. And Effie was always the one who got belted, not them.

As for Effie herself, she used to stand on street corners and beg when she was smaller, often getting enough to buy a stale barm cake and stave off the constant hunger. But as she'd grown older it'd got more complicated. Men seemed to think she should pay them in kind for their coin, which was not at all what Effie had in mind. She was no fool.

And then the evacuee ladies had come round. None of her brothers and sisters was keen, but Effie had scented escape and jumped at the chance.

So here she was, staying in this lovely place with Meg and eating regular meals now they had a full pantry to go at. And if it meant putting up with queer monsters with things stuck under their bellies, and going to school, so be it. And she was sure the sickness in her stomach would go in a minute.

She heard a bell clang but didn't emerge from behind the bush until all the children had lined up and started to march through the school door.

'And who is this?' Miss Shaw smiled down at her. 'It's Effie Putnam, isn't it?'

Effie nodded. 'Yes, miss,' she said, remembering what Meg had told her.

'Come along inside and I'll introduce you to everyone.' Taking Effie's hand, she led her into a long room filled with wooden desks and laughing children. Above the teacher's high desk was a picture of Jesus. Effie guessed it was Him because he had a beard like in the Bible Meg had at Broombank. He had loads of children around his knee, too. The place seemed overrun with them.

There were other pictures around the panelled walls, of children picnicking or playing with dolls. Things Effie had never done in her life. There was a big round clock with cardboard hands and a fire burning brightly in a corner grate, surrounded by a mesh fireguard on which hung an assortment of the children's hats and scarves, steaming in the heat.

'Take off your coat, Effie.'

She did so but didn't rightly know what to do with it so she dropped it in a corner.

'There's a hook with your name on it in the cloakroom,' Miss Shaw told her.

Effie, her heart pounding, went to look at the gummed squares stuck on the panelled walls. They might have been Greek for all the sense they made to her. A group of children, hanging up their own coats, started to giggle. Effie began to feel quite hot around her middle.

'Go on. Don't be shy,' said Miss Shaw kindly. And, never one to allow herself to look a fool, Effie thrust her coat on the first hook she could find.

A great guffaw of laughter errupted from behind. 'She's put it on John Buxton's hook, miss.'

'That's all right,' said Miss Shaw, looking suddenly concerned. 'We can sort it out later. Come along, Effie. You can sit next to Susan and Jeffrey. Quiet, children. This is Effie, our new evacuee.'

A silence came upon the classroom and Effie was aware of all eyes drawn towards her, as if they'd never seen anyone like her in their lives before. In a way they hadn't. Poor as these rural children were, they were scrupulously clean, secure in their little world, and knew what was what. Here, to their delight, was someone who didn't seem to know anything.

Effie began to feel hot and uncomfortable, sure that at any moment she would disgrace herself and pee down her legs. She glared back at them, scowling ferociously.

All the girls were dressed in warm jerseys and neat wool skirts in blue, brown or check. They had socks and shoes, and ribbons in their hair. The boys had the same sort of jerseys which they wore over grey trousers that came to their knees. None of the clothes had holes in, as her own brothers and sisters had, though some sported patches on elbows, or neatly darned squares.

Embarrassment washed over her in a great hot wave. Meg had done her best from a limited range of garments. She had shortened a navy blue skirt for her. Even so, Effie was aware that it swamped her skinny figure, and was so big at the waist that it had to be gathered in with a belt from an old mackintosh. Over the skirt she wore one of Sally Ann's old cardigans that had shrunk and felted in the wash. It hung unevenly over a thin cotton blouse that had several buttons missing which meant that if Effie pulled back her arms you could see bits of liberty bodice over her flat chest.

And on her feet were a pair of clogs. Meg said they had once belonged to her brother, Charlie, when he was small. Effie had been proud of the clogs, for they made a grand clopping noise across the yard and she could make sparks with the iron bottoms on the stone cobs. Now she wriggled her bare toes within them and squirmed with agony.

Miss Shaw was staring at these items as if they offended her, and it was evident that her embarrassment was as deep as the child's. 'If we wear clogs to school, we usually leave them in the cloakroom.'

'I've got naught else to put on.'

'Haven't you brought any pumps, in a little bag, Effie? We'll be having country dance later and I'm sure you would like to join in.'

She shook her head. The only pumps she knew about stood in a back street, and you yanked the handle up and down to get water in your bucket.

She looked up into the teacher's kind, flushed face. Then at all the curious faces gathered about her. She could see the other girls in their smart jerseys, with their hands squeezed over their mouths to smother their laughter, the glee bright in their eyes. She hated them, instantly and intensely.

'I dun't like dancing. Anyroad, I'm not bloody stoppin' here.'

And satisfied by the sensation she had caused, she turned and ran out of the room, sparking her clogs all across the school yard just to show how little she cared.

16

The dull days of November were upon Lakeland. The birches and wild cherries, sycamore and oak, stood naked with their feet in a mire of dead leaves. Only the red-barked yew and the tall spires of Norway Spruce stood green against the cloud dark sky. The deer had withdrawn to their winter quarters, the red squirrels were hibernating and most birds had followed the north–south axis of the dale and headed for warmer climes.

At Broombank, rain ran from the roof into the barrel and overflowed to swill over the slate paving stones and wash down the lane, soaking anyone who ventured out even for a moment. On this day Joe chose to call.

'Right then. Let's be heving you. We've had enough of this nonsense.'

'What nonsense is that, Father?'

'Don't play games with me. Pack your bags and come home. Farming is a serious business, not for schoolgirls.'

Meg drew in a slow, deep breath. 'I'm not a schoolgirl. I'm twenty-one if you haven't noticed, and can please myself what I do.' Then, feeling a wash of compassion for him, standing on her doorstep stiff with pride, Meg reached out a hand. 'Why don't you let me show you round and tell you of my plans?'

'Plans!' Joe snorted. 'Selfish dreams more like. It's time you thought about someone else beside yourself for a change. Get your coat on. Sally Ann isn't well. We need you at home.'

'Oh, what's wrong with her?' Meg was upset, and filled with a sudden shaft of guilt to think Sally Ann might need her and she'd been too busy to notice.

'She's heving a bairn and can't do the work she normally does.'

Meg stiffened. 'That's all you want from your womenfolk isn't it? Work. Well, I'll call on Sal and see if there's anything I can do, but for her sake, not yours.'

He glared at her. 'Get along then.'

Meg did not move. 'I'll call tomorrow.'

Joe looked as if he might drag her from her own doorstep there and then so furious was he at her show of stubbornness. 'You've gone soft in the head if you think you can manage this place on your own. And that lad o' yourn won't thank you. Why don't you do yourself, and him, a favour and let Mrs Bradshaw sell it like she wants to.'

'So you can have it for Dan?'

'He's a man. He needs his own place.'

'Then give him Ashlea.'

Unusually, Joe looked uncomfortable. 'Ashlea needs to be bigger if it's to keep us all.' And on a sudden burst of anger he thrust a finger at her. 'And thoo hev it in your power to help us, your own family.'

'I'm sorry, I can't.' And she stood in wretched misery, watching him storm away.

Meg and Effie stood in the free market every Saturday morning selling eggs, butter, milk, bundles of kindling and any number of cabbages.

Will Davies harnessed the reliable Arlott and went through twelve acres as if it were butter and Meg duly collected the grant of two pounds an acre. It was her job, assisted by Effie, to take off the stones and pull up the rushes and thistles first, a task that left them both speechless with exhaustion.

Will also brought down her sheep with his own autumn gather so that she didn't need to call upon her family, which proved a relief in the circumstances. Not that she had many sheep to gather in, she discovered. Lanky's flock was in a very depleted state and building it up again would be her major concern.

She called on Sally Ann regularly every Wednesday afternoon and though her sister-in-law seemed a bit sickly, they supposed that was normal in this stage of the pregnancy. Meg could do little but offer moral support.

'You have enough on your plate, Meg, I'm all right. I'll get Dan to help a bit more.'

'See that he does.'

Hetty Davies showed them how to pluck the geese and turkeys ready for market.

'Don't scald them,' she warned, 'or you'll have pink meat. Best to dry pluck for pure white meat. Takes a bit longer but it's worth it and you get a better price.'

And indeed they did. The remainder of the rent was raised by selling three of the fat geese and all the turkeys at one shilling and threepence a pound on Christmas Eve. A good price which pleased her. Meg paid her first quarter's rent with a great sense of achievement.

One goose had been used as down payment to the Co-op shop on a new set of school clothes, boots, and the seemingly essential pumps for Effie. The outfit had so delighted her that she had returned to school, head high, mouth grimly set. And Meg had undertaken to give her extra reading lessons at home in the evenings.

The other goose was already in the bottom oven for their Christmas dinner which all her family were coming to share.

The fog on Christmas Day was so thick that visibility was down to thirty yards. Sally Ann was the first to arrive, feeling her way up the lane like a blind woman, bringing presents and the sad news that she had lost her baby.

'Broke Dan up it did. The baby would have been something of his own, you see, to love. But we'll try again, he says. We'll manage it next time.'

'Oh, Sally Ann, why didn't you let me know?' Meg hugged and kissed her sister-in-law and they wept together. 'Dan's right, for once. Sometimes it's nature's way if things aren't quite right. You're young and strong, there's no reason why you can't have a dozen babies if you've a mind to.'

'I know.' Sally Ann smiled bravely through her tears.

Then, because it was Christmas and they all needed cheering up, Meg insisted on bringing out some of Effie's potato and beetroot wine. 'It tastes awful but it's very potent, so who cares?'

She poured out three glasses and raised her own in a toast. 'Here's to the next time, and to an early peace.'

They all echoed the sentiment and drank.

'Lord, it gets worse,' gasped Meg, setting down her glass in a fit of coughing. 'What this girl will do to avoid milk.' And they all fell about laughing.

'What about Jack? Is he getting home for Christmas?'

Meg shook her head, eyes bright. 'I've had a lovely letter from him. But he says all leave has been cancelled while they take part in some special training exercise. He hopes to be home sometime in the New Year. Oh, I can't wait to see him. It seems ages since he was home.'

'And Kath?'

A shadow crossed Meg's face. 'Haven't heard. I saw Mr Ellis in town and he gave me the address of her aunt's house in Southport. I've written a couple of times, but no reply.'

'She might have moved on. Can't really see Kath staying too long in a place as quiet and genteel as Southport, can you?'

'No, probably moved on to London by now and has all the fellas eating out of her hand. Jack says she's probably married someone rich by now, so hasn't time to think of writing letters.'

'That's more like Kath.'

'Maybe I'll ask Mrs Ellis. She's bound to know, then I can write to her at her new place, wherever that might be. Meanwhile, come on, drink up, we've got work to do. You know how my dear father hates his dinner to be late. He will come, won't he?'

'He promised. I had a job persuading him, but he'll come, if only for the food.' Sally Ann glanced across at Effie who was whistling 'Jingle Bells' as she peeled potatoes, Rust by her side as usual. 'You've forgiven him, then, for what he did to Effie?'

A small thoughtful pause. How could anyone be forgiven for such a barbaric act? 'Let's say I've learned to live with it.'

Sally Ann nodded, understanding. 'She's looking well, little Effie, isn't she? But you'd best get that dog outside before the menfolk come or they'll think you've gone soft in the head.'

1940

17

The jollity of Christmas was quickly quenched with the start of food rationing in the New Year and the announcement that the Ministry of Food was to become the sole buyer at fixed prices of all produce and fatstock, including pigs and lambs that went for slaughter. Meg wasn't sure whether this would be a good thing or not, but at least it offered a guaranteed market.

Though things were running fairly smoothly, her problems were far from over. In the spring she would have to plant corn and barley, potatoes and kale, as ordered by the War Committee. She would need to find the money some time next year to pay for the two cows that Will Davies had given her, buy tups in readiness for next year, or at least have the money to hire. She couldn't depend upon good neighbours indefinitely.

She'd been forced to borrow hay for the cows but next year she must try for a good harvest of her own. Meg also wanted to buy pigs and young turkeys, for it was important that they be as self-sufficient as possible. And there was still the problem of labour to be solved. She didn't just want to take on anyone, not living here all alone as they did.

But that was all in the future. For now she was thankful to be well fed and happy in her work. Effie was settling into school, now that she looked the same as everybody else, and starting to learn her letters.

Then, best of all, Meg heard from Jack. He was staying for a few days at Connie's house in Grange. And would she come and spend a day there with him? Would she!

'What about the cows?'

'You can get Mr Davies to do them for once,' Effie said.

'Oh, but how can I leave you here, all alone?'

'I'll be all right. I can stay with Sal, I don't mind. Go on, go and see him, you know you want to.'

She'd been up hours before dawn to get all the necessary chores done, a lift to the bus stop in the Co-op van, a long cold bus ride, but it was all worth it. For now she was wrapped warmly in his arms, not noticing the bitter cold north wind that blew straight across the estuary into their shelter beneath the trees. Nothing would prise her from Jack's arms.

His kisses were everything she could remember, and Meg basked in her love and need of him. 'Oh, I wish I could stay for ever, here with you like this.'

Jack tickled her ear with the tip of his tongue. 'It would get a bit draughty at night.'

'Oh, stop it, you fool. You know what I mean.'

'I'm sorry Connie is so, well, you know, a bit funny with you. She'll come round, in time.'

'She's still mad about the farm, I suppose?'

'Mad as hell if you want to know. She thinks Dad should have left it to me, as his only son. And she does have a point.'

Meg tucked herself inside his greatcoat, her arms tight about him, and giggled. 'Yes, but he has in a way, hasn't he? Since we're going to be man and wife.'

'The farm would still be yours, whether we marry or not. Connie checked that out with Mr Capstick.'

'Oh.' Meg was silent for a moment. 'Does that bother you?'

'I can see why he did it. Never thought much of my efforts at farming. While with you, he thought the sun shone out of you. But I don't mean to be tied to farming all my life, whatever you say.'

Meg closed her mind to the warning in his words. She was too happy to be here, cuddled in his arms. 'Lanky was kind to me, and I loved him as if he were my own father.' She thought it politic to change the subject. 'Have you heard anything more about going abroad?'

Jack shook his head. 'I don't want to talk about the war. Or the farm. I get enough of all of that from Connie. Come here, let me warm my hands on you.' And he made her gasp in an agony of delight as he slid his cold hand beneath her jumper and over her breasts. When he put his mouth to hers, Meg forgot all about her worries about being accepted by his family, and about Jack's very natural jealousy over the ownership of Broombank. What did it matter? What did anything matter so long as they could be together, like this?

All too soon they went dutifully back to Connie's house for a cold tea of fish paste sandwiches and tinned peaches and then Jack walked her to the bus stop for her ride home.

This was to be Meg's last day out for some time as Broombank became locked into a hard, cold winter.

Snow filled the leaden skies for days and weeks on end. It piled four and five feet thick against the walls of the house and smothered the hen arks so thoroughly that digging them out and making space for the hens to peck about became a back-breaking morning chore. Wads of glistening white snow lay so heavily upon the oldest barn roof that it finally gave up the fight and fell in.

'Let's be thankful we have other barns,' said Meg, determined not be cast down by this expensive catastrophe.

So many of the local quarrymen were called up that only the old men were left and the quarry had to be closed. Those who were able worked instead on the roads, shovelling the snow out of the narrow lanes only to have the fierce winds blow it all back in again the next day.

For weeks they had seen not a living soul and even the little school had closed until the thaw. Their only source of contact with the outside world were the broadcasts on their battery wireless, listening to how the weather was creating nationwide misery, blocking roads, stopping trains, freezing lakes and rivers. It depressed everyone so much there was talk that there would be no end to the war, at least not until Hitler died.

Most of the time they sat in darkness, except for a wood fire, to save lamp fuel as the snow continued to fall relentlessly.

The sheep on the high fells would survive well enough but most of Meg's day was spent searching for those who had wandered lower, digging them out of the huge drifts that piled against the dry stone walls. Wet through and exhausted much of the time, never had she been more thankful for the help of her dogs, particularly the faithful Rust, as they spent almost every waking hour walking the snow-laden fells together. She would push her crook deep into the drifts, the collies would sniff and roam about then suddenly start to bark with excitement or claw at the snow with their paws, nose pointing to the spot where a sheep was buried.

'Good dog,' Meg would say, and she and Effie would start to dig, pulling another half-senseless animal out from the depths to drag it on the sledge back down to the intake field where it could recover. Then they would climb back up the fells and start the search all over again.

If Meg got depressed she only had to listen to Churchill, who always managed to raise spirits, once by announcing the rescue of 300 British seamen from a German prison ship, the *Altmark*, in a Norwegian fjord. But it didn't last long. By March, Finland fell and complacency vanished.

But the snow finally melted into a cool spring, the waters gushed in the becks, and life became a little easier.

Effie was a willing worker for all she was still a skinny child, wanting to take an active part in the running of the farm.

Once they spent an entire day building up the tops of one long wall over which the sheep kept jumping to reach the new green grass in the intake field.

'We must stop them getting in or we'll have none left for the new mothers and weaker lambs,' Meg said.

'Just look at that grey-faced one,' Effie pointed out. 'Hasn't missed a move we've made all morning. I wonder what she's thinking.'

'How she can reach this delectable meal.' Puffing for breath, Meg heaved yet another stone in place. The walls really were in a sorry state of repair.

At about three o'clock they stopped for a rest and a snack.

'Another two or three hours and we should be done,' Meg said, sighing with relief.

The words were no sooner out of her mouth than the grey-faced sheep Effie had pointed out earlier started to trot alongside the wall, seeming to sniff at it curiously.

'She's checking to see whether we've done a good job,' Effie chuckled, but the laughter faded as the sheep discovered the limits of their efforts, finding the next broken section they had still not mended and leaping through it with nonchalant ease. And where she went, her comrades quickly followed.

Meg leapt to her feet. 'Oh, no, now we have a dozen sheep to get out of the field before we can start the wall again. Oh, Effie, we shouldn't have stopped.'

But she was rolling on the ground with laughter, holding her aching sides, the tears sliding down her thin cheeks. 'You have to hand it to her, she's sharp that one. Who says sheep are stupid?'

Meg found herself laughing too. That was the good thing about Effie. She never let you take life too seriously.

* * *

'Will you bring me some supplies next time Dan takes you into Kendal?' Meg asked Sally Ann. 'I daren't leave the sheep just now, not with my first lambing about to start.'

'You're not going to try to do it by yourself?' Sally Ann said, half shocked and half resigned to Meg's foolhardiness.

'Do you have any other suggestions? I've no money to hire labour. The sheep have to be gathered and sorted, and I'll just have to manage on my own, except for Effie of course.'

'Oh, Meg.'

It had been arranged for Broombank and Ashlea sheep to be brought down from the fells together. The sheep from both farms would be compacted into one moving, seething mass, and following the whistled instructions of the shepherds, the dogs would drive them from the heaf, down the incline to be closer to the farm where they could more easily be sorted and supervised at lambing time.

Meg had arrived early at Ashlea, in good time for the gather, but Sally Ann seemed anxious to talk, for all it was scarcely four in the morning. The reason was soon made clear.

'I'm expecting again.'

'Oh, Sal, I'm so pleased.' Meg hugged her sister-in-law. 'You must take especial care this time. I hope that brother of mine is looking after you.'

'Oh, he is, he is.' Sally Ann's eyes grew soft. 'He'll hardly let me lift a finger. Always telling me to sit down and put me feet up. He even washed up for me the other day.'

Meg's eyes grew wide. 'Is the end of the world nigh?' And both girls laughed and hugged each other.

'Is Dan ready for the gather?'

Sally Ann let out a heavy sigh. 'Joe insisted they leave earlier than usual, in case the weather should worsen. They set off an hour ago.'

'But they said I was to be here at four.'

'You know what Joe's like when he gets an idea in his head.'

Meg uttered a silent oath. Now she would have to climb up the fells and find them all by herself. Trust her father to make things difficult. And she'd so wanted to be fully involved, show her worth, on this her first gather with Joe.

As she walked she gazed at the wilderness stretching ahead. At the lonely, empty fells where silence could be felt, like a presence. At the colours smudged together by a dampening morning drizzle, grey crags poking like dry bones through a green baize cloth. She loved this country, even when, like today, the sky was heavy with cloud and a thick swirl of mist was collecting on the tops. Only slightly paler than the rocky outcrops were the clusters of sheep compacted together by bright-eyed collies, without whose skill the task would be impossible.

It was not a good day for a gather.

'Will we call it off?' she asked her father when she finally achieved the top of Dundale Knott, leaning on a dry stone wall to catch her breath.

Joe and Dan had already made a start on collecting the ewes from the high fells.

'Not chickening out already, are we?'

Dan chuckled. 'She's happen wet and tired and didn't want to leave her bed.'

'Shepherds don't have time to sleep at lambing time, as she well knows,' Joe said, speaking about Meg as if she weren't standing right in front of him.

She clenched her hands and forced herself not to react. She had promised Sally Ann she wouldn't fall out with her father and brother today. Besides, she couldn't bring down the sheep on her own. Trouble was, Joe knew it.

'What would you like me to do then?'

'Keep out o' road, that's what. I've told thee afore, shepherding is not for women. It's hard work.'

Meg smiled, holding fast to her patience, wanting so much to get it right. 'I'm not afraid of hard work. I'm here now. Tell me what to do.'

Still Joe ignored her, his eyes intent on his sheep. 'Here, what's that young cur doin' noo?' He put a small flat whistle to his lips which he'd been forced to adopt since he got his false teeth. He gave two sharp blasts upon it. One dog shot smartly to the left and rounded up a few stragglers. 'Ga way by,' he shouted.

Meg watched, impressed, as Ashlea dogs went about their work with professional expertise. A fell dog needed to be strong and have considerable stamina as well as perfect obedience, for he could cover anything from thirty to forty miles in a day. He'd be soaked and muddied by the peat, snagged by the spikes of heather and bracken. The sheep would be quick to take advantage of any sign of weakness and it was not uncommon for a ewe to charge a dog and butt it if she thought she could get away with it, so a dog's personality too had to be strong.

Joe walked away and followed his sheep, leaving his daughter to the buffeting wind.

'I see you fetched yon dog,' said Dan, pointing his crook in the direction of Rust who was standing, legs foursquare beside her, eager to be off.

'I've brought three dogs, as you can see,' she said, closer to tears than she dared to admit.

'Aye. Is that the young daft one that Lanky gave you last year? Has he done a gather afore?'

'No, Will Davies brought the sheep down for me last backend, as you well know. But Rust is a good dog. He's ready for work. Strong, intelligent and quick-thinking, as he's supposed to be.' As I am, she wanted to add.

'Aye, well, I hope he doesn't tek it into his head to run off home when the going gets tough, as his mistress seems keen to do.'

'He won't. Nor will I. We're both ready. Let's get on with it, shall we?'

Then as they set off walking together, Dan seemed to consider. 'Did you see Sally Ann?'

'Yes. She told me about the baby. I'm so pleased for her, Dan, and for you.' She put a hand on her brother's arm. 'Take care of her. Don't let Father bully her as he does me and you. Stand up to him for a change.'

For once Dan didn't argue but seemed seriously to consider what Meg was saying.

'He's not an easy man to defy.'

'I know, but it has to be done if we're going to survive. He thinks he can dictate our lives to us and we mustn't let him. You're a married man now, Dan, with a wife and coming family to consider.'

'Aye. Try telling him that. It's all right for you, you have Broombank and can please yourself. I have only what he gives me.'

The resentment in his tone was hot and bitter.

'Let's get on with the job in hand, shall we?' Meg said, wishing to avoid an argument.

'Right, take your dogs round that knob. And remember, some of the ewes will be hiding in't bracken. So see your dogs don't just slink about. They should speak up and tell you if they find one.'

'They will,' Meg assured him, feeling her confidence strengthening bit by bit as Dan issued his instructions. Even so her gaze took in the enormity of the task. All the sheep seemed to have disappeared now, or were distant blobs on the horizon.

Tess and her son Ben were more used to Lanky's commands and were only reluctantly getting used to hers. And Meg only hoped that she could remember what the signals were that Lanky had taught her. She gave two quiet whistles and at once the dogs moved softly forward, eyes bright, ears alert. Meg's nervousness began to ease. She could do it. She *would* do it. She would show her father that a woman could make a good farmer.

It had been a long, hard, wet day and Meg was dropping on her feet. The weather, if anything, had worsened. Grey clouds were lying heavily over the peaks, rolling slowly down after them, gobbling up the heaf almost faster than the sheep could move across it. The whistles seemed to come from all directions as the dogs gathered the flock ready for the main drive down.

One sheep broke away and Meg gave a slow rounded whistle. Rust, who hardly needed to wait for the signals now, got there almost before she made a sound.

'Good boy.' She liked to praise him, show her appreciation. The sheep started to move forward with Rust at one side, Ben at the other and Tess behind, stalking them. Not too close, keeping wide.

The drive down was not as straightforward as she'd expected. Meg constantly had to urge the dogs to correct the wandering line as the sheep persistently sought any gap to dash through. Sometimes a whole bunch would break free then a dog would be sent off to run wide and round them up to bring them back, adding miles to the journey.

Up, down, right, left, forward, stop, forward again. Sometimes Meg wondered if they were making any progress at all. But the challenge was fascinating, engrossing her completely.

Ahead of them in the valley below was the enclosure. Getting the sheep through the open gate and into the field would be the easiest part of the manoeuvre. The sheep knew well that the grass beyond was always better and lusher. They had learned this when they were in-by at lambing time and never forgot it.

She stepped out purposefully, for she knew what needed to be done and was proud to be a part of it.

Afterwards there would be a soak in a hot tub and supper by a blazing fire. She felt exhilarated, alight with an inner glow at having accomplished so difficult a task. Her dogs had more than pulled their weight in gathering the ewes today. And Dan, perhaps even Joe, seemed to have accepted her as a useful part of the team which added to her sense of satisfaction. Of course Joe had shouted at her from time to time, and Dan had shown scant patience, but they hadn't packed her off home which she'd been half afraid they would do.

Then suddenly she saw it was all about to go wrong. She looked in dire danger of blotting her copy book good and proper.

Maybe she'd given the wrong signal, or perhaps Rust had been a touch over-enthusiastic. Whatever the reason, he had three sheep pinned out on a ledge and there seemed no way of getting round him to fetch them on to safe ground. They stood hesitant, poised to run if Rust came at them too fast or made one wrong move. And if they did fall, they would slide down the lethally slippery slope of a stony scree, bounce off jagged rocks and not stop till they reached the valley bottom, several hundred feet below.

Meg tried edging forward, but every time she moved the sheep panicked, compacted closer together and backed right to the lip of the precipice.

'Wait, boy. Steady, steady.' She chewed on her lower lip, agonising over how best to deal with them.

She could almost read the dog's thoughts, as frustrated as herself. And high above them on the fells, coming closer every minute, were her father and Dan, ready to see her mistake and judge her on it.

A buzzard swept past, the wind whistling through its outstretched feathers. Leave the sheep here too long and the crows and ravens would peck their eyes out where they stood.

Then suddenly Rust was away, running up the fellside away from the ledge. Meg watched him reach the top of the knob overlooking the crag where he stopped and lay down in the bracken. Following his advice, Meg moved quietly away too. Several achingly long moments later the sheep jostled each other, looked about them, then seeing the way was clear, darted forward, struggled through a narrow gap in the rocks and pelted off down the hillside to join their companions.

Meg laughed out loud. 'Well done, boy. You did it. You've taught me a lesson there.'

'Daft dog. Didn't I say you'd make nowt of him?' The figure of Dan loomed suddenly above them. 'Too eager. He could have killed them ewes.' And lashing out with his feet, he kicked at the dog. Rust yelped, desperate to try and avoid the toe of that great boot.

'*No!*' cried Meg and leapt forward just too late to stop Rust slithering right over the edge of the precipice.

Kath tugged at the sheet to drape it over the huge rollers, sweat pouring from her. Why had she ever complained about the old mangle at Southview Villas? The steaming hot rollers of this one were a thousand times worse.

Polly, who was the nearest she had to a friend at Greenlawns, urged caution, as always.

'Take your time. You can't hurry.'

Kath recklessly yanked at the wet sagging cloth which had wrapped itself into a proper tangle. 'Drat the thing.' But her efforts only made the situation worse.

There was the most terrible grinding sound as gears locked and then oil was spurting out, soaking a treacherous, sticky path over the white cloth.

Both girls struggled to free the fabric, glancing fearfully over their shoulders, anticipating trouble. They were not mistaken. Bearing down upon them came Miss Blake, her expression so sour you'd think she'd been sucking lemons.

'Don't say anything,' warned Polly. 'Leave it to me.'

Polly had been put in Greenlawns for stealing a loaf of bread. The fact that she had been starving at the time because her mother had abandoned her was not taken into account. She was fourteen years old and considered herself lucky that she hadn't been sent to prison. Kath had no such consolation. In her estimation she had done nothing wrong and it was perfectly ludicrous for her to be here at all. A Home for Wayward Girls indeed!

But then Polly was an exception. Most of the other girls were in Greenlawns for the same reason Kath was. Yet others, simply because they *might* become pregnant. Their crime, since that was how it was viewed, had been to 'entice' some young man into an 'immoral act', or even the threat of one.

At first she had protested vigorously at the very idea of Katherine Ellis, darling daughter of Larkrigg, being incarcerated in such a place.

'There must be some mistake,' she had said, over and over. 'There's no reason for my being here.' Not that anyone listened, and those that did only laughed.

'Does that mean that bump isn't a baby growing in your belly?' asked one particularly coarse warden, making even Kath blush.

'I don't see that that has anything to do with you. I'm leaving this very minute.' But all the doors were locked. And remained so, morning and night.

'There's no way out, once you're in,' one old hag told her. 'I came in as a girl for the same reason you've been sent here. By my loving, caring family. Ashamed of me they were, as yours are of you. That was so long ago now, I can scarcely remember when it was.'

Kath stared in horror at the grey bedraggled locks of hair and the wrinkled skin. 'I don't believe it. My family have no idea where I am. It's a mistake, I tell you. I thought I'd come here for a job.'

And the old hag had cackled with laughter as if Kath had made some joke.

The most humiliating part had been the shockingly intimate examination she had been subjected to on the day she was admitted. For venereal disease, the wardens had told her. If she'd been infected she wouldn't have been accepted. Kath had wondered since if that would have been so terrible.

Gradually her panic and temper were forced to subside, and the awful reality that dear Aunt Ruby had known exactly what was wrong with her niece and where she was sending her finally dawned. But Kath refused to believe that her mother knew of her fate. Let alone her lovely, kind, adoring daddy. She refused to believe that they would ever condone locking her in such a place.

'I'll write home and they'll come for me, you'll see.'

And she had written, countless times. Rules permitted one letter home per week, though they were all carefully vetted. Any sign of criticism and the letter was instantly destroyed. Kath made that mistake only once. The letter had been destroyed and she wasn't permitted to send any more for the next two weeks.

Nevertheless Christmas had come and gone, treated as any ordinary work day with no sign of a celebration. Up at six, work all day, watched the whole time by the sharp-eyed wardens. The midday meal taken at one. Stew, always stew. Half an hour was allowed for this followed by a walk around the cold yard then back to work. A similar walk was permitted in the evening but there was no hope of escape. The walls were high, the great iron gates kept permanently locked. Nobody outside knew what lay behind them, nor bothered to ask.

'This is as bad as a Victorian workhouse,' Kath protested, half in disbelief, half in fear.

'Aye, it is,' Polly agreed. 'Only worse, because you generally died quicker in them days.'

January had passed in an agony of bitter weather, getting colder as the snows filled the February skies. And there was still no sign of release, no reply to her letters. She was trapped, abandoned by those who claimed to love her, for the sin of carrying a child that would be born with the dreadful label of illegitimate, using one of the kinder words for it. The pregnancy grew daily into a heavier burden.

To think that not so long ago she had refused Richard Harper and turned her nose up at the very idea of marrying Jack Lawson. The thought made her ill.

Sometimes, on a Sunday after church, they were permitted to read books. Kath had fallen upon this small pleasure with relief at first, until she found that so many sentences were blacked out, even whole pages removed, that the story was rendered senseless. Or they might be shown a film only to find that that too had been given the same treatment. The wardens considered some passages inflammatory to a young girl's passions; be it only a simple kiss or word of affection, they were obliterated.

Knitting socks for servicemen, chopping and tying up bundles of firewood and endless mending were the only recreations considered safe.

The regime at Greenlawns must, in Kath's hotly held opinion, be far worse than any soldier's at the front.

'And what is it you've done this time, madam?' Miss Blake was eyeing the ruined fabric, glaring fiercely at Kath.

'Bit of an accident, Miss Blake,' explained the cheerful Polly. 'My fault, not hers.'

'Don't you argue with me, you little brat.'

'I didn't, I only said . . .'

'*Silence.*' And grabbing hold of the girl's arm, Blake twisted it painfully behind her back.

Polly gasped, sinking to her knees. Tears filled the girl's eyes as the arm, looking as if it would come off if it were moved another half inch, was held mercilessly by Miss Blake, the familiar smirk upon her face.

'Very well, if you wish to take the blame, you can spend your recreation time this evening scrubbing that sheet until it is as white as snow. See that you show it to me before you go to bed. Is that clear? I'll teach you to recklessly ruin perfectly good linen.' She gave the arm a final tweak before dropping it. Polly fell to the ground on a low moan.

Kath was incensed. 'For God's sake, we don't finish work till gone eight and we have to eat the loathsome stew you give us after that. How will she have time to wash your damn' sheet? It'll need to soak all night at least. It's stupid to expect otherwise.'

There was the most awful silence, the only sound that of the swish and grind of the rollers, the thump of wet fabric being scrubbed and beaten clean, scouring away the sins of the wicked, or so the girls were told.

Not a soul in the laundry glanced in their direction. No one moved to lift the sobbing Polly, whose arm hung at a dreadful angle. Kath understood everyone's desire not to get involved in case worse trouble should fall upon them, but it infuriated her all the same.

'*What did you say?*'

'I said, leave her alone, you great bully,' Kath said, and pushed at Miss Blake with the flat of her two hands. Perhaps she used more force than she intended, or the woman's heels caught on something, but she fell backwards on to the giant rollers.

The hem of her skirt got caught between the chewing rollers, winding her in like a rag doll. The breadth of her flat hips brought it to a halt but not before the flailing fingers of her right hand had been crushed to pulp.

The machine was switched off instantly by a quick-thinking girl but Miss Blake's screams echoed on and on.

Kath was marched off into solitary confinement, to allow her time to reflect on her outburst of temper. She went quietly enough, her moment of rebellion spent, frightened by the result of her temper. What was happening to her that she should let go like that? There she remained for seven days and seven nights on nothing but bread and water.

The fingers, except for the tip of one which had to be removed, were saved, though they would never grip a girl's arm quite so savagely again, nor knit another pair of socks. Kath couldn't help but hope that the disability would be a constant reminder to Miss Blake of her lack of charity.

Polly was 'removed' to another home. Friendships were not encouraged in Greenlawns and Kath's days seemed longer as a result.

By the end of March she was close to her time and exhausted. The callous treatment and the loss of Polly, the unrelieved treadmill of work, brought a grinding ache to her lower back which seemed never to leave her. The inadequate diet and the sense of hopelessness that permeated the place had quenched even Kath's rebelliousness. And still there had been no letter from home.

She longed for the day when her baby would be born. 'Then I can leave,' she insisted, refusing to heed the dour words of the old hag, that there were a hundred other girls in Greenlawns who had already given birth and remained, for their own 'safety', locked up. Their babies were sent for adoption or to the orphanage, name and identity quickly changed to avoid the lifetime's stigma that accompanied such a birth.

'That won't happen to me,' she said. 'My family will come for me any day. You'll see.'

She went into labour on a freezing morning at the end of March.

'I want Meg,' Kath cried as the full impact of the first pain seared its scorching path across her back. But nobody took any notice. Miss Blake's leering face grinned down at her. Her whining voice grated in Kath's ear.

'Don't waste any sympathy on this one. Hard-hearted little madam she is, and a troublemaker to boot.'

They put her in an empty room and left her to get on with it.

Tam O'Cleary was not normally one to make a fuss, let alone get involved with other people. He'd left a perfectly good home at the age of sixteen when he'd realised that America was not the land of milk and honey his family had hoped for. An Irishman living in the Bronx in New York did not have an easy time of it. Tam didn't want to struggle, as his father had done for years, trying to find work to feed his growing family. Besides, much as Tam loved his family, and there was no doubt that he did, every last one of them, he was young and could feel the blood pulsing through his veins, telling him to get out there and discover whatever there was to be discovered about life.

He had packed his bags and gone off to seek his own fortune, not wishing to be a burden to anyone.

Since then he'd had more jobs than he cared to count, spent years exploring Europe at a time when it was safe to do so. Considered himself, at twenty-seven, a man of reasonable intelligence, a raconteur and wit even, on his better days. He'd come to enjoy his footloose existence and considered possessions and people an unnecessary encumberance. Keep himself to himself, that was Tam O'Cleary's motto.

Hadn't he once tried to save a fellow traveller from certain death as he'd hung over the edge of a schooner? Only to have the man beat the living daylights out of him for his trouble. How was Tam to know the man had wanted to die anyway because of some broken love affair? People. You never knew where you were with them, not like horses.

He'd nursed two broken ribs and a sore jaw for weeks as a result of that good deed, and vowed never to be involved in other people's problems ever again.

Nor was wartime the moment to change that philosophy. He was Irish. His old country, and his new, were both neutral, and that was the way he liked to live his life, safe behind a screen of neutrality.

Yet here he was, breaking all those principles, over one young girl. Katherine Ellis was not even his type, and he'd known her only a few weeks. Yet he couldn't help thinking how his own mother would react if Mary or Jo or Sarah got into similar trouble. She'd open her heart and her home to them with no recriminations. And Tam couldn't help thinking that Kath's family had failed her when she needed them most.

So how could he, her only friend, fail her too?

He knocked again, louder this time.

It was the thought of that unwanted baby she carried. And the fact that she had disappeared, without warning, without even a goodbye. He'd thought nothing of it at first, but as the weeks passed it struck him as odd. He was not the melodramatic sort, never had been. But Katherine Ellis seemed to have vanished off the face of the earth.

For no reason he could justify to himself, he started hanging about outside Southview Villas. And now, quite against his better judgement, he'd walked up the scrubbed path and lifted the polished door knocker.

A plain-faced girl of about fifteen came to the door. He raised his cap.

'Good morning. I wonder if I could be speaking with Miss Ellis? The name is O'Cleary, would you tell her?'

'Miss Who?'

'Ellis.'

'I'll have to ask Madam. Wait here.' So saying, the girl closed the door in his face and Tam was forced to kick his heels and wait.

When the girl came back she was again alone. 'The mistress says as how Miss Ellis is no longer with us.'

'No longer with you? Lord above!'

The round cheeks flushed scarlet. 'Oh no, I don't mean ... Nothing like that. The mistress says she's gone, that's all.'

'Gone? Gone where? Home?'

'Ooh, I don't know.'

'Well, will you ask?'

'Ooh, I can't do that.' And she closed the door.

Freda Lightfoot

Tam touched his cap politely to the door and walked away.

He would try again mebbe, in a day or two. Or mebbe not. What a fool I am to be worrying over her. She'll have gone home to her mam and daddy, you great soft ejit. Hadn't she every right to go where she pleased, if she had a mind to, without consultation with him? He determined to put the matter out of his mind forthwith.

When the next pain came Kath was certain she was about to die. The world seemed to be swamped by it. It lashed itself around her back and plunged down into her groin as if a devil was dragging all the innards from her body that way. If she survived this ordeal, she thought, gasping for breath, she could survive anything.

When the wave had eased off for a moment, she tried to sit up. Maybe if she walked about a bit. She struggled from the bed and started to pace the room, but soon found the pain returning. A mile or more from the bed, Kath clung to a nearby washbasin. It was so loosely attached to the wall the thought flashed through her mind that she was not the first girl to cling to it as if it were a life support.

Back on the bed she vowed never to leave it again, but that didn't help either. In the end all her inhibitions deserted her and she screamed.

'Now we'll have none of that,' warned the stern-faced woman who bustled in, deputed to care for her in the last throes of labour. 'We don't want you frightening the other young girls.'

Those who have still to go through this terrible torture, Kath thought.

'Keep moving, and keep quiet.'

Walking, standing, sitting, lying. Now clinging to the bed rail, now kneeling on the floor, now desperately trying, and failing, to find the energy to will the pain away. Kath longed for darkness, for insensibility, for someone to tear this wicked blockage from her. She didn't care how, but it had to be done.

'Lie down, lie down now,' the voice urged. 'Time to push.'

You have to be joking, Kath thought, too exhausted to move a finger.

A white face floated above her as if in a mist. Every muscle and nerve in Kath's body strained against the pain. She would lose this battle, she would, if somebody didn't make it stop.

'I-I c-can't do it,' she tried to protest, shaking her head. Couldn't the woman see that she needed to rest for a while first? How could she summon up the arduous effort necessary for pushing a child out of a body that was already weak and exhausted from overwork. 'Let me rest. Let me alone.'

The woman, Dorothy Parkins, was not without compassion. She had seen too many girls in this situation to break her heart over them, but she cared nonetheless, and this one was well bred by the looks of her, beautiful probably at one time. Dorothy blamed society for its callous treatment of girls 'in trouble'. For all this was the twentieth century, the poor creatures were outcasts just as surely as if old Queen Victoria herself were still upon the throne. And where was the girl's family when she needed them? Hiding behind a veneer of respectability, no doubt, terrified a neighbour might discover that their precious darling had 'fallen'. And places like Greenlawns were left to pick up the pieces.

'Don't talk foolish, girl. Push. I can see its head. Come on, Katherine, *push!*'

Perhaps it was this use of her given name, the one her mother used for her, that gave Kath the energy needed for one last essential effort.

She shouted some obscenity as the world burst apart and a wet, slithering mass was sucked from her body, followed by a gush of warm liquid that ran over her legs and soaked the bed.

'I've wet myself,' she said, shamed. 'Like a child.'

Then she was crying and laughing all at the same time. The tiny blue-and-red-streaked object that was laid across her stomach was crying too.

'It's a girl. You have a fine, healthy daughter.' The woman was cutting the cord that attached the baby to her, paddling a flat palm into Kath's juddering belly to make the afterbirth come. Kath reached down and stroked the soft dark down of surprisingly glossy curls on the baby's head with one tentative finger. She could feel a pulse beating and the reality of this new life she had brought into the world suddenly astounded her.

'Is she all right?'

'Perfect,' said Dorothy.

The door opened and Miss Blake swooped in. 'Are we done yet?'

'Just about.'

'Good.' Wrapping the baby quickly in a towel, Miss Blake tucked the child under her arm.

'My baby!' Kath cried. 'I want my baby.'

Miss Blake looked down her thin nose and handed the child over to the other woman. 'Don't be foolish, girl. It would do no good to hold her.'

Kath leaned up on her elbow, trying to catch a glimpse of her baby. 'I suppose not.' The cries had stilled as the woman rocked her and Kath felt a sudden urge to be the one to soothe her own child. 'She's my daughter.'

'Not for long. Think of this as the end of a problem and the beginning of redemption. You will be washed and fed shortly,' said Miss Blake coldly. 'Then get a good night's sleep. I shall expect you back at work first thing in the morning.'

Kath gasped. 'So soon?' This was to be Miss Blake's revenge, was it? Treated worse than a cow that had calved.

'Can't I even feed her?'

As Miss Blake strode from the room, Dorothy smiled sympathetically at Kath, cuddling the baby close.

'It's best if you put her from your mind. Don't think about the baby. That's the only way. I'll give you something to make the milk go away.'

Not think about her. Kath sank back upon the bed. Perhaps it was the intense tiredness she felt that made the tears roll down her cheeks. It wasn't as if she'd ever wanted to keep the child. She had given no proper thought to the baby itself in these long painful months, only to her own survival. Now that it was born, Kath knew she should feel relief. Soon she would be free, out in the fresh bright spring morning.

'I'll be back in a minute to clean you up, then you can sleep,' Dorothy told her, bustling away.

The door was almost closed when Kath called out: 'Her name is Melissa.'

'I was wondering if you had a room to let?' Tam O'Cleary was standing on the doorstep of Southview Villas, smiling down into the dreaded Aunt Ruby's face with all the Celtic charm he could so easily muster, when he had a mind to. She was quite unmoved.

'I'm afraid I do not take in young men, particularly strangers.'

'I assure you I am perfectly respectable and can provide references.'

She remained unconvinced but Tam persisted. 'My employer will vouch for me. And I worked for a time on the Kilgerran Estate. You could ring there.' Once he knew that Kath and the baby were safe, he'd be content. Until then . . . He smiled at the look of keen interest that came into the watching eyes.

'Lord Kilgerran, you say?'

'In Southern Ireland.'

'You don't sound very Irish.'

'I've spent a good deal of time in America but I'm told we southerners have a softer lilt to our tongue.' He thought for a moment that he had won but then the eyes narrowed and she stepped closer.

'I've seen you before, haven't I?'

'Now I'm sure I'd be remembering if you had.' Tam took an instinctive step back, but it was too late. He saw the recognition dawn in her eyes.

'You're that friend of my niece's, aren't you? The one that's been hanging about week after week. Well, she's gone, so be off with you. I'll not be pestered by Irish scum here. Lord Kilgerran my eye!' She waved a fist at Tam. 'And if you come round here again, I'll set the police on you.' The echo of the door slamming sounded all along the street.

But if Ruby Nelson thought that would be the end of the matter, she had mistaken her man. Had she invited Tam in and chatted with him in a respectable fashion, told him some tale to satisfy his curiosity, he would have smiled and nodded politely and gone on his way. Instead, she had succeeded in annoying and insulting him, and Tam did not take kindly to either.

'So, you old dragon,' he said to the closed door. 'You think to ignore me, do you? Well, there's more ways than one of cracking a nut than stamping on it. I'll crack the mystery of this one, be sure if I don't.'

He spun on his heel and strode off in the direction of the sea and the stableyard where he worked. He'd collect the money that was owed him, pack his belongings, then he'd be off to Westmorland and see what he could discover there. He could remember the descriptions and details that Kath had given him. They would do for a start. Oh, yes, he'd find the answer to this puzzle, Aunt Ruby or no Aunt Ruby. For all he knew, she might have tipped the girl into the River Mersey.

So it was that when Meg pushed open the solid oak door and stumbled into her own kitchen, already calling out to Effie, she was confronted by the broad back of a man. Her heart leapt into her throat until she saw he was not Jack.

The stranger sitting at the table was laughing at something Effie had said. But where Jack's hair was near black, the dark mahogany of this man's glinted red in the light from the Tilly lamp and when he turned his face towards her at the sound of the opening door it wasn't

217

the violet of Jack's eyes that met hers, but the softest moss green. And to her shame, as he offered a smile, for some reason Meg was reminded that under all of her wet clothing, the mud and the grime, she was still a woman.

Effie was beside her in a moment. 'You're soaking wet through. Oh, Meg, let me take your coat.'

She tried to form her lips into the word, the one word that echoed in her head, but for some odd reason her lips wouldn't obey the command and her teeth were chattering as if they too had a will of their own.

The sound of Rust's body scraping and bouncing over the rough stones of the scree still rang in her ears.

She'd been shaking as she faced her brother, the rage in her running so hard and fast and furious that had she possessed the strength she would have kicked him off the crag too, right after her lovely dog.

'I never meant him to go over. He shouldn't have jumped away,' Dan had shouted at her.

Meg couldn't believe what she was hearing. 'You'd rather he'd stood still and let you kick him? Have you no brains in your head? Why must you always try to appear tough? Isn't one bully in the family enough?'

'He'll come home with his tail between his legs tomorrow.'

'If he comes home at all,' she had told him. No, she wouldn't even think that he was dead. He must be found, and quickly. A night out on the fells and he would be. 'I need a rope.'

Now, as her knees buckled beneath her, Meg had a vague impression of big rough hands, a lilting cry of concern, and the wonderful sensation of warm strength wrapped around her body as she was lifted and carried to the big chair by the fire.

Then a cup was rattling against her teeth and Effie's voice was urging her to drink. She turned her head away.

'There isn't t-time,' she murmured. 'I-I m-must get back.'

'You're going nowhere.'

'It's Rust.' She managed his name at last.

'I'll see to him,' said Effie. 'I've got all the dogs' dinners ready and waiting.' Meg pushed the cloying warmth away from her. They didn't understand. They weren't listening. Not even Effie was listening to her.

'He's g-gone,' she gasped. 'Over the edge.'

Someone swore softly but Meg couldn't find the strength to

chastise Effie for breaking her promise not to use bad language. She was too busy struggling to get into a dry raincoat, wrapping a scarf around her hair. 'It'll be dark soon. He fell off the knob on Dundale Knott. I think I can guess where'll he be.'

She started searching for the things she would need for the rescue.

'I've got everything we need.' The stranger's voice was firm, assured. In his hand he held a coil of rope, a sack and a torch. 'Let's get going.'

18

As they strode out together, back across the fells, Meg couldn't help but notice that the stranger moved easily, as if he were used to walking long distances, and in all weathers judging by his tanned face, weathered and creased by the sun and the wind. Glancing sideways at him, she decided the face held a certain arrogance, for all the bluntness of the jawline was softened by a lurking twist of what might be good humour at the corners of the wide mouth.

With a start she found he had turned his head to meet her curious gaze and there was downright mischief in the eyes half hidden beneath the lowered eyelids.

He's formed an opinion of me already, she thought, and wondered if there was any way she could find out what it was. She gave a half smile, embarrassed at being caught out in her scrutiny, and turned away.

The sheep were almost down now, and Meg waved to Dan, indicating that she had help already to find Rust. Dan acknowledged the wave but did not return it.

The stranger did not speak until they had climbed a hundred or so feet.

'You are Meg Turner?'

'I am.'

'Have you lived here long?'

'All my life in this area, less than a year at Broombank.'

He nodded, satisfied, as if she had solved a problem for him, and said no more.

A part of her was glad of the silence, worrying as it was over her lovely dog and if she would find him alive. But another, less disciplined part experienced an urge to learn more about this man who had so unexpectedly appeared in her home, starting with his name. But he did not offer and she would not ask.

After they had climbed to a good height, they edged their way along a rake, a diagonal groove that cut into the hill, and found Rust lying, as she had hoped, on a ledge halfway down the scree. It had undoubtedly saved his life and they approached with care, anxious not to slide down to the bottom themselves.

He lay on the ledge, much as he had learned to do on the threshing floor of the old barn, his obedience training and instinctive patience paying off in these dangerous conditions. He lifted his head at the first sound of her voice, thumped his tail on the rock and whimpered, telling Meg how glad he was to see her and how he had known all along that she would come.

She fell to her knees beside him and put her face against his. He was alive. Dear God, thank you for that. As the tears ran unchecked down her cheeks she could hear him breathing little gusts of his love into her ear. If he'd been a cat he would have purred.

'Let me look at him.' Tam ran knowledgeable hands over the dog's limbs. 'He's broken a leg, and probably his shoulder.'

Meg swallowed carefully. 'We have to get him down. Take him to the vet somehow.'

The stranger was tying birch sticks across the dog to hold his legs still. 'These will have to do as splints.' Then he tore open the sack to form a hammock. 'Help me lift him on to this, I can carry him on my back, across my shoulders.'

Meg winced and cringed as she lifted Rust into position, but if the movement hurt him he gave no sign. Velvet brown eyes gazed trustingly into hers the whole time. His brown ear was torn and a great patch of his coat had been grazed down to the flesh. He knew he had nothing to fear now. Meg would take care of him.

Miss Shaw kindly drove them to the veterinary in her little car since she'd called in to bring Effie some books. Rust was to stay at the surgery overnight to have plaster put on his fractures and be carefully checked over.

Now Meg and the stranger were sitting in Broombank kitchen, gratefully enjoying one of Effie's home-made soups.

'I owe you,' Meg announced, not looking at him. Whenever she did she was half afraid her cheeks would flush under his oddly probing gaze. 'And you haven't even told me your name.'

'Thomas O'Cleary. At your service.'

'Irish?'

'Irish-American-Liverpool you might say, and goodness knows what else besides.'

Meg smiled. 'Don't you know which?'

'I'm a mongrel. Like your dog.'

She was outraged. 'Rust isn't a mongrel, he has an excellent pedigree. I also own his mother and brother.'

The green eyes twinkled. ''Tis awful fond you are of that creature. Wouldn't a man give his eye-teeth to be so adored?'

A stillness came upon Meg and she heard Effie titter. She turned at once to the child.

'You ought to be in bed. You have school tomorrow.'

'Aw, Meg.'

'Go on. No messing.'

Dragging her heels, and taking as long as humanly possible without risk of inciting more stern words, Effie at last went to bed. When she had gone, Meg realised her mistake. She was alone with a stranger, and night coming on.

'Do you have a barn?'

Meg hid a smile at his uncanny ability to read her thoughts. She shook her head. 'We have several but none fit to sleep in, if that's what you're thinking.'

'Ah.' Tam glanced across at the window. The shutters were closed, but the rain could now be heard beating upon the glass. 'Now that's a pity, to be sure. 'Tis not a night for a lonely, unemployed male to be prowling about.'

Meg found her lips twitching upwards at the corners. 'If ever I heard a load of soft-soaping bunkum, that just about takes the biscuit!'

The strange, soft green eyes which reminded her so much of Kath, opened wide in false innocence. 'And what would you be meaning by that remark?'

Meg got up and removed the empty dishes to the sink. 'You can sleep here, on cushions by the fire.' And more sternly, 'Any prowling about in my house and you'll find I have other, more fierce dogs to protect me.' The thought of young Ben and quiet Tess setting upon this man almost made her laugh but she managed to keep her face perfectly serious. He didn't know how soft they were.

'I'll bear it in mind.' His gaze held hers for a moment, as if boldly challenging saying that he might try anyway.

Meg brought him a pillow and a blanket and placed them on the chair by the fire, hoping that she had made her point. As she started up the stairs he spoke in his quiet, lilting voice.

'I'm glad to have made your acquaintance, Meg Turner. I hope as how we are going to be friends and you'll call me Tam.'

For some foolish reason, Meg's heartbeat quickened as she looked down upon him. 'I think it's time you closed those Irish eyes of yours and got some sleep.'

Meg called at the surgery first thing the next morning. Rust had spent a comfortable night but was still drowsy from a minor operation he'd had to set his shoulder.

'He'll live. You can take him home later,' the vet said. 'When he wakes.'

'He will be all right?'

'He won't work again. A quiet life in future for this young man. If you decide to keep him, that is.'

'I'm not having him put down.'

The vet smiled. 'I didn't think for a minute you would. Nasty accident though. How did it happen?'

Meg hesitated. 'Just one of those things.'

She went straight from the surgery back on her bike up to Ashlea. She had it in mind to give a piece of her mind to Dan but found herself being interrogated by Sally Ann instead. Her sister-in-law was busy knitting khaki socks for her soldier brothers but was willing enough to put down her knitting for a minute and hear about the stranger who had helped to rescue Rust.

'And you let a man sleep all night in your house?' Sally Ann gazed at her in astonishment. 'Now I wonder what Jack would make of that?'

'Oh, don't. I daren't even think. He's Irish and behaved most properly.'

'He's good-looking then?'

Meg dropped the ball of wool she was winding for Sally Ann, so surprised was she by this remark, and had to chase it under the table. 'Why do you think so?'

'I can see it in the flush on your pretty cheeks,' Sally Ann said, making the rosy hue deepen as a result.

'What else could I do but offer him a night's accommodation? Him having helped with the rescue.'

Sally Ann's grin faded. 'How is the dog?'

'He'll live, the vet says.'

'That's grand news. He'll be out on the fells again before you know it.'

Meg swallowed. She wouldn't cry at the damage done to her good friend, she wouldn't. 'He'll never be up to working again, but maybe he won't mind so much. He always has had a fancy for the easy life.'

'Dan is real sorry about the accident. Could hardly sleep last night. He likes dogs.'

Meg was aware of her sister-in-law glancing anxiously at her and tried to smile but her skin felt all tight and stiff. 'I'm sure he is,' was all she managed.

'He didn't think. Oh, I know, that's Dan all over, you've said so a dozen times. But he is doing his best to change. He does try, if not often enough mind, to be his own man. But Joe goes on at him so much it's as if Dan has to prove how tough he is, even when he doesn't feel it.'

Meg reached out and squeezed Sal's hand. 'My father has a way of getting under anyone's skin and turning them into monsters. The dog will be fine. And it's true he did behave a bit stupidly. Rust has a nervous streak in him, as collies often have. Remember how he ran away that time? I don't think he likes Dan's booming voice.'

'I can sympathise with that,' laughed Sal. 'Here, have a piece of curd tart while I put on a brew of tea. It's freshly made.'

They sat companionably for some moments before Meg spoke again.

'I hope you don't mind my calling here so often. But I always enjoy our little chats, as well as your delicious cooking.' She grinned and took a bite out of the wedge of tart.

Shrewd eyes regarded her in silence for a moment. 'You miss someone to talk to up there, don't you?'

A flash of guilt crossed Meg's face before she could stop it. 'I do, yes. Effie's lovely but she is still a child. I forget that sometimes. I miss Kath, and oh, Jack of course, so very much. But that isn't the only reason I come here. I hope you and I would be friends anyway.'

'Course we would. But I know Kath is special to you. Sometimes, I used to think, a bit too special.'

Meg looked up at her sister-in-law in surprise. 'What do you mean by that?'

Now it was Sally Ann's turn to flush beetroot red. It clashed alarmingly with her hair. 'Trust me to put my big foot in it. I didn't mean anything, except, well, she did push in between you and Jack a bit much, didn't she?'

'Push in?'

'Yes. Going out with you on picnics and swims and such like. Wasn't natural, I thought, for a beautiful girl like her to want to be with you two. Just as if you were sisters and always had to be together.'

'I suppose we felt like sisters sometimes.'

'Why didn't she find a fella of her own?'

Meg sat and listened to the clock ticking out in the hall while she considered this. 'She was a friend. Still is. And therefore always welcome with Jack and me. We didn't mind.'

The sharpness in Meg's voice caused an awkwardness to fall between them, one that might have continued indefinitely had it not been broken by the arrival of Joe.

'Is that cur of yours still going strong then?'

'Yes, no thanks to your son.'

'Don't look at me so fierce. I didn't kick him down the scree.'

'No. But you put it into Dan's head to try and make it as difficult as possible for me to run Broombank.' Meg spoke quietly but her tone said she wasn't to be made a fool of. 'You've taken my hay, my tups, my cows, and now damaged my dog, but you'll not make me give up. I'll tell you that for nothing.'

Joe sat down in his chair, took off his cap and rubbed one hand over his thinning hair. He was quite calm, infuriatingly so in Meg's opinion. 'I've allus had a fancy for Broombank.'

'You can buy land as good anywhere.'

'Aye, but not cheek by jowl with me own place. Anyhow, it has more usable acres than I have and good access to the heaf.'

Meg steadied her breathing and sat down opposite her father. Sally Ann excused herself swiftly, and went off to find something that didn't need doing.

'This is about Mum and Lanky, isn't it?

The question was quietly asked but it was as if she had lit a match to touch paper. She watched his face turn red, then white as it drained of all colour, his mouth screwing into a tight knot of rage.

''Oo told you?'

'Does it matter? Isn't it all very old hat now? Does it really matter if Mum once loved Lanky? Who knows if anything would have come of it anyway? It mightn't have lasted, they were only young.' Like me and Jack, came the unbidden thought, and Meg quickly squashed it. Her love for Jack was absolute, not here today and gone tomorrow.

'Aye, she used to say that.' Joe reached for his pipe as he always did in times of stress and emotion. 'She spent half her life up there at Broombank, even when Mary was alive. After Mary was gone Annie still kept going. She was never away. How do I know what was goin' on?'

It hurt Meg more than she could bear to hear her mother's memory so defiled. 'You nasty old man! Mum, Mary and Lanky were good friends. That's all. They're all dead now, let them rest in peace. Why you always have to see the worst in people, I don't know.'

'Because it's generally the way things are. I don't trust women, never have, never will.'

For the first time she began to feel truly sorry for her father. He lied and cheated to get Annie to marry him but had never felt secure with her. Because of that he'd kept her close to the house, and her daughter too in the fullness of time. He'd bullied his two sons, each or different reasons, but he hadn't managed to make any of them love him either. It was really very sad.

Meg went to kneel by his chair and Joe looked directly into her eyes, surprise in his own at seeing her beside him thus.

'Why do you have to be pushing and shoving all the time, and ordering people about? Why can't you just let things be? Maybe, if you gave me the chance, you might find something in me that you like. Would that be so terrible? Would it really damage you, or Ashlea, if I managed to be as good a farmer as you?' She didn't say better, that wouldn't have done at all.

Joe made no reply.

When he made no move towards her, Meg got wearily to her feet and stood before him. 'I don't want to fight you, but I will if I have to. And every time it makes me a little bit stronger, gives me that little bit more confidence to cope. If Mum hadn't the courage to stand up to you, and escaped at every opportunity to a place where there was friendship and love, you've only yourself to blame. As I have escaped. And Charlie. And if you don't watch out, Dan will do the same.

'But I'm still your daughter, Joe Turner, and I'm certainly not going to deny that fact, nor give in to your bullying. Nor will I fail in this enterprise. In fact, I intend to be a great success. Have you ever considered that I might want to be like you, and not my mother?'

Then, bidden by some instinct she could not at that moment define, Meg leaned over and kissed her father on the cheek. She left the kitchen quickly before he had time to reply.

'Walk with me up the lane for a bit,' she said to Sally Ann.

'You haven't had another falling out?'

Meg shook her head, tears welling in the grey eyes. 'I don't want to talk about it, all right?'

Sally Ann nodded in silent misery and Meg could see her sister-in-law wishing life with the Turner family could be a lot less complicated. So did she.

'You've not taken the hump, have you? About what I said earlier, about Kath?'

Meg shook her head. 'Course not. It's always hard to understand other people's friendships. Forget it, I have.'

They stopped for a while and smiled at the hectic toing and froing of a pair of hedge sparrows, busily preparing their nests. 'I feel like that sometimes,' Sally Ann said. 'It's good to get a breath of fresh air after all this rain and mist.'

Meg glanced at her sister-in-law anxiously. 'You are all right? The baby and everything?'

Sally Ann smiled a contented smile. 'Oh, yes, never better.'

Meg relaxed again. 'I'll be getting more than enough fresh air now with the sheep to sort and the lambing about to start.'

'You enjoy it though.'

'I love it.'

'Will you keep him on?'

'Who?'

'The Irishman. Whatever he's called.'

Meg jerked up her head and looked at Sal, the idea new to her. 'I hadn't thought.'

'Well, it's worth thinking about. Things aren't always going to be this quiet, are they? I keep expecting the skies to be filled with aeroplanes and parachutes, but nothing's happening, is it? Except that everyone you see has faces as long as a wet fortnight, thinking of their loved ones going overseas.'

Meg too looked suddenly glum. 'Jack will be going soon. I can't bear to think of it. I don't see much of him but at least I know he's safe.'

'Do you think we'll be safe, up here?'

Meg tucked her arm into Sally Ann's. 'Of course we will. It's a bit shaming really, to feel so far away from the action. I intend to work extra hard on the farm. People are going to need food, it's an important job too.' She laughed, rather self-consciously. 'That's what I tell myself, anyway.'

'You're right. And all I seem to do is start babies.'

'Well, you're going to finish this one. A real beauty it will be, with a cheerful smile just like its mother. Take care now.'

And as Meg strolled away, Sal called after her: 'What was it he wanted, this Irishman?'

Meg stopped in her tracks. 'O'Cleary. His name is Thomas O'Cleary. Known as Tam.'

'Tam, is it?' Sally Ann's lips twitched with teasing good humour. 'Maybe you won't miss your Jack as much as you think.'

'*Sal!*'

'You said he was waiting in your kitchen. Well, what was he doing there?'

Meg blinked. 'Do you know, I haven't the first idea. But I mean to find out.'

Tam O'Cleary declared himself in no hurry to depart and seemed willing enough to help with the sorting. Meg picked out the ewes that appeared weakened by the hard winter and put them closest to the farm where she could keep a better eye on them. The rest were divided up into their likely lambing weeks and enclosed in-by accordingly.

'Have you worked with sheep before?'

Tam shook his head. 'Horses. Cows.'

'I need a sheep man.' She wasn't sure she wanted Tam O'Cleary about in any case, though Meg couldn't rightly say why. 'I've too much to learn myself to try to teach you. Green as they come, that's me.'

'Not quite,' said Tam softly. 'You were born and raised on a farm.'

'Yes, but not allowed to work with the sheep.' She lifted her chin a notch. 'But it's what I want to do, so don't you start telling me how hard it is and not women's work.'

He checked the mark on a sheep, shifted a hurdle and let it scamper through, then closed it again. 'But you need help, that much is certain. And where else would ye find a fine strong man like meself, with a war on?'

Meg couldn't help but smile at the deliberate use of the Irish accent, finding herself warming to this man though she really felt she shouldn't. 'How you can turn on the charm, Tam O'Cleary.' And they both laughed, eyes meeting, shifting, dancing away. She decided to be entirely businesslike.

'We don't dip the ewes in the spring. But the hoggs, they're the first-year lambs that have spent the winter at farms on lower ground to give them a good start, will be returning on the fifth of April. That's Hogg Day, and they will require dipping and marking up before we let them back on to the fell.'

'You'd want that done before the lambing starts?'

Meg agreed that would be for the best. 'Though it doesn't always work out that way, or so I'm told.' She screwed up her eyes as she gazed over her stock, wishing Lanky was here to pass judgement upon them, help with the weeks of lambing she now faced. 'When the hoggs have been dipped,' she continued, aware that Tam was watching her, 'they always go back to the part of the fell where they spent the first summer with their mothers. It's a wonderful homing instinct that keeps them safe on their own ground, which is vitally important on these vast areas of high fell.'

'And you are the same. Safe here, on your own ground.'

Meg smiled, unaware how it lit up her face, golden curls streaming in the wind. 'Something like that.' But she recognised the pensive expression in Tam O'Cleary's face and it confused her. He was a man, after all, and had a way of reminding her that she was a woman just by the look in his eye.

'No more talk. There's work to be done,' she said crisply, and tried not to watch his smile.

Later, when the work was over for the day and they'd all enjoyed one of Effie's cheese bake suppers, the question that had been teasing her for so long finally came out.

'Why did you come?'

Meg had meant to ease into the question politely, in a roundabout way, a method in which her father was an expert. But as ever she was too frank and straight, and the question came out boldly, tactlessly even, making her blush. 'I'm sorry, I didn't mean it to sound so blunt. Only, you never said, what you were doing in my kitchen that day?'

'I came because of Katherine.'

'What?' It was the last thing she had expected to hear. 'How do you know Kath?'

Tam told the tale of how he first met Kath and her subsequent disappearance. He showed not a trace of his usual teasing humour, nor made any mention of the pregnancy at this stage. He wanted to tread warily in that area, for no reason beyond instinct.

'Are you saying the old girl has done her in?' asked Effie, eyes like saucers.

Meg's glance quelled her into silence. 'Don't be silly. This reading is doing your imagination no good at all, Effie Putnam.' And turning back to Tam: 'Where could she be? And why do you think there is anything wrong at all? She might just have taken it into her head to leave. Kath has always maintained that she wanted to go to London. I can't think why she didn't go there in the first place.'

So here it was. 'She was short of money, her family not understanding her problem. And perhaps she was nervous there might be bombing, with the war about to start.'

Meg pooh-poohed this idea at once. 'Kath isn't a weak weed. She isn't afraid of anything, and certainly wouldn't let the rumour of bombing, that might or might not happen, stop her doing what she wanted.'

'Maybe not, in the normal course of events. But then there was the child to consider.'

'Child?' Meg frowned. 'What child? I don't understand.'

Tam glanced sideways at Effie's face, avid with interest. Meg took the message.

'Good heavens, it's past six. Effie, be a dear and feed the hens, will you? I forgot at lunchtime with being so busy.'

'Aw,' Effie groaned, realising she was about to miss some glorious tit-bit. As if there was anything they could say that would shock her? Not that she dare admit as much.

'Perhaps you'd rather do the milking? I have to do that too in a minute.'

Effie was convinced. When she had gone, on feet so rapid it was a wonder she didn't fall over them, Meg turned at once to Tam. 'Best make it quick, whatever you have to say. She'll be back before you can shake a lamb's tail.'

'Kath was pregnant when I last saw her. So far as I know she hadn't told anyone else besides me. Probably only told me because I was a stranger. I wondered if mebbe her aunt discovered it.'

'Kath? Pregnant? I don't believe it.'

'I'm afraid it's true. And no, she isn't married, if that's what you were wondering.'

An odd little pang of disappointment pinched at Meg. Why should

231

Kath tell this man, this stranger, about her problems and not herself, her one best friend? But she mustn't show that it mattered. It would be foolish. Only Kath's health and well being was important. 'Poor Kath, suffering this terrible ordeal all on her own. So that's why she went off abruptly to Southport, to hide from the disgrace. I wonder if she's told her parents?'

'She said not.'

Meg looked solemn. 'No, I can understand that. Mr and Mrs Ellis are very – proper. Doctor and magistrate Mr Ellis is, and Rosemary organises the flower rota at the church. Oh dear, how dreadful. Poor Kath. And you think that this Aunt Ruby threw her out?'

'Or took her somewhere. The point is, where?'

19

'I don't believe a word of it.' Twin spots of outraged colour burned high on Rosemary Ellis's cheekbones but Meg was more interested in the fingers pleating and unpleating the linen skirt to take too much notice. It was the sign of a nervous woman, rather than an angry one.

They sat politely at either side of the marble fireplace in the aquamarine and white drawing room and Meg had never felt so uncomfortable in all her life. Rosemary Ellis preferred not to associate herself with the common-or-garden dalesfolk, casting herself instead on the fringes of the upper echelons of Lakeland society. She used as her model such notables as the Bagots of Levens, the Hornyold-Stricklands of Sizergh and the Lonsdales.

'I'm sorry to have to be the one to break this news, Mrs Ellis, but there it is, these things happen in the best of families. Better you hear it from me than from anyone else.' The effect of these simple words, meant in a kindly way, was electric. Rosemary Ellis was on her feet in a second, though looking as if her knees might buckle under her at any moment.

'Anyone else? What do you mean? Who else could possibly know?'

Meg wondered whether she ought to involve Tam, but saw no help for it. She would have to offer some explanation for her learning the truth. Sighing softly, she told of Tam's arrival at Broombank and how he had been concerned for Kath. She even told the story about Rust, and how well he was doing now, the leg mending nicely, just to give Rosemary time to collect herself.

'He asked after me at the Co-op and they directed him up to Broombank.'

Rosemary was white to the lips. 'Is he the father? Because if he is ...'

That idea had not, until this moment, occurred to Meg. Oddly enough, she felt a pang of anguish at the thought, then realised it was impossible. 'No, no, he couldn't be. They've only just met. They are just good friends, Tam says. Both lonely people, away from home, I suppose. Look, would you like me to make you a fresh pot of tea?'

Rosemary dropped back on to her sofa with the movements of a woman twice her age. 'No, thank you. I'm perfectly all right.' The fact that she didn't at once offer to make a fresh pot for Meg proved the opposite to this brave declaraton. Rosemary Ellis, the hostess *par excellence*, would never have committed such a breach of good manners.

Meg cleared her throat. Sorry as she was for Mrs Ellis, she felt more compassion right now for Kath. 'You wouldn't have any idea then, where she might be?'

'Me? Why should *I* know where she is?'

Meg might have reminded Rosemary that she was the girl's mother but thought better of it. 'I don't know. I just thought that perhaps Kath might have written to you, told you where she was staying.'

'I have not the faintest idea what my daughter has chosen to get up to.' The sharp edge to the voice surprised Meg. Had she perhaps outstayed her welcome? She got up at once to go.

'I'm sorry to have caused you any distress.' Meg found herself being shown to the door with a speed quite unlike Rosemary's usual politeness. Meg gave the older woman a reassuring pat on the hand. 'I shouldn't let it bother you too much. Kath isn't the first, nor will she be the last, to find herself in this situation, particularly now, with a war on. She'll cope.'

'I'm sure she will,' said the icy voice. 'She always was wilful.'

The door was held open, Rosemary clearly anxious for her to depart, and Meg only too ready to obey, when stubbornness gripped her. 'I've written to Southview Villas so many times and got no answer but I won't give up. I want to see her, write to her at least. If you hear where she's moved to, you'll let me know? I worry she might be ill or something.'

'Katherine is perfectly well, I tell you,' snapped Rosemary, and Meg couldn't stop her eyebrows rising in surprise. Very quietly, she pushed the door closed again and stood facing Mrs Ellis.

'You do know where she is, don't you? I wish you'd tell me.'

Rosemary Ellis's eyes held sudden panic then a plea for understanding and all her confidence seemed to seep away. 'I had to do it. Her father would have been devastated if he'd found out. Once the baby is born Katherine may live where she chooses but no one, most of all Jeffrey, must find out about her condition.'

'Where is she?' Meg quietly persisted.

Rosemary ignored the question. 'He hasn't been at all well. And on top of everything he is recovering from a severe bout of influenza. It would quite ruin his health if word were to get out about – about Katherine. You must *promise* me that you will say nothing, not a word to a soul? Promise!'

Meg grasped the hands that Rosemary was wringing with such anguish and squeezed them gently. 'I will say nothing if that's what you want, but you must tell me where she is. I am her friend and surely have a right to know. I'm worried about her.'

Jeffrey Ellis chose this precise moment to walk into the sitting room. He was wearing a blue checked dressing gown though it was past eleven o'clock in the morning. He seemed pleased to see Meg.

'Hello. How is the farm doing?'

'Very well, thank you.'

Meg had always thought he was a man who carried a sort of quiet dignity about him, as all good medical men do. Now he seemed thinner, more tired, with an air of resignation or defeat about him. 'Have you heard from Katherine?' he asked and Meg shook her head, unable to trust herself to speak as she watched the light of hope die in faded eyes so like Kath's own. 'I was hoping you might have. She's adventuring somewhere. That's my daughter, never still for a minute.'

Meg caught the expression in Rosemary's eyes, begging her to leave. 'I must go. Work to do, I'm afraid.'

Mr Ellis grasped her hand as she reached for the door handle. The grip was surprisingly firm. 'You'd let me know if you did hear, wouldn't you?' It made her shiver to hear her own words of a moment ago echoed back to her. She smiled and nodded. Somehow she couldn't see this gentle man as the censorious creature Rosemary made him out to be.

'Of course.'

'If she writes to anyone it will be to you.' Which gave Meg pause for Kath had done no such thing. Why was that? Shame, she supposed. How very silly.

At the front door she tried one last time. 'I'll write to her aunt once more then, just in case. Miss Ruby Nelson, isn't it, Southview Villas? Perhaps she might have heard where Kath is by now.'

But Rosemary was pushing something into her hand, a scrap of paper, crisp and rustling, whispering feverishly as she glanced back over her shoulder, half an eye on her husband wandering like a lost soul into the drawing room: 'You can check if she's all right, if you like. Don't come again. And I don't want her here. Not till she's rid of it. Then she can come home as if nothing had happened.' And the door closed firmly in Meg's face.

Standing on the empty driveway Meg read the address: 'Greenlawns Home for Wayward Girls'.

'I can't go. Not yet, much as I'd like to. I'll write and tell her that I'll come as soon as the lambing is over.'

'She's your friend,' Effie pointed out.

'And the sheep are my livelihood. I can't neglect them. It would take days to go to Liverpool, find this place and come home again. I'd have to stay overnight, maybe longer with the trains the way they are. And she might refuse to come at first and it would take time to persuade her.' Meg wanted to drop everything that very moment and go and find Kath but how could she? She simply daren't risk leaving her flock at this important time.

'What can I offer anyway? Her own mother won't have her home.'

'You could let her come here,' Tam suggested.

'I will. Oh, I will. There's nothing I'd like better. I'll bring her to Broombank where she can have all the love and care she needs. But I must be sensible.' She looked from one to the other of them, begging them to understand. 'The next weeks are the busiest in the farming calender. I can't leave now.'

There was no one else to stand in for her. Effie certainly couldn't deal with the lambing, nor could Tam manage on his own, since he said himself that he was more used to horses. 'I'm sorry, but it has to be. Mrs Ellis says she is being taken care of. We'll just have to believe that.'

'She also said that she hadn't the first idea where Kath was,' Tam added, in his quiet, lilting voice.

Meg turned on him at once, upset by the implied criticism. 'You go then. You find her if you think I'm so wrong.'

'I didn't say that.' He sighed. 'I dare say you're right. This is your first lambing season. I don't suppose another week or two will make much difference and I rather think you're going to need all the help Effie and I can give.'

236

She puffed out her flat chest, pleased at being included. 'I'll keep you all fed, anyroad,' she volunteered, just to make sure they understood that she wasn't having anything to do with the underparts of sheep.

Tam grinned. 'And I'd like to see how it all pans out. So I'll stay on if you don't mind?'

Meg was surprised, alarmed by the offer, and strangely relieved all at the same time. 'I can't pay you. Not yet anyway. Not till I sell the lambs in the backend probably.'

'Did I ask for payment?'

'Nobody works for nothing these days.'

'I like to be different.'

'And you know nothing about sheep. What use would you be to me?'

'I don't think you can afford to be choosy. And I will work for my keep to begin with. Let's at least make sure you have some lambs to sell.'

He was far too sure of himself in Meg's opinion. Whenever he stood about watching her, she felt strangely inadequate and came over all ham fisted and clumsy. And Tam was too good-looking for his own good, certainly for hers. She daren't think what Jack would have to say about him staying here. Yet it was true that she needed help, very badly. Reluctantly she felt forced to give in.

'All right. You can stay till the autumn sales. See how we go on.'

Tam O'Cleary smiled, as if he had known all along that she would agree. Effie giggled.

'Now that's settled, perhaps we should work out a shift system. They'll need watching round the clock presumably,' he said.

And so will you, came the unbidden thought.

The first lamb died. The failure was such a devastating blow to Meg that she redoubled her efforts to shepherd the sheep more carefully. It was important that she had a good crop of lambs this year if she was to build up the flock. She set an alarm clock by her bed. Every two hours it woke her and she would pull on her boots and raincoat, usually with her eyes still closed, pick up her torch, and walk out into the bitter cold night to check her precious flock. Her successes were sweet but every time a lamb died she blamed herself, whether justifiably or not.

The ewes were not in their best condition. They'd had a hard time of it through the frost and snow, so mortality was bound to be high. Broombank did better than some places lower in the dales so she knew she shouldn't complain.

And then came the day when she had to skin a dead one and pull its skin over a live orphaned lamb so that the bereaved mother would accept it as her own. Meg performed the task but then went and vomited her breakfast into the hedge.

Could Joe have been right? Was farming too tough for a woman?

Determined to prove herself, she refused help from anyone. Out every morning before dawn, she spent all day amongst her flock, missing meals and far too much sleep.

'I have me pride, for God's sake,' Tam said. 'If I can birth a mare surely a ewe isn't all that different? You can trust me to do a shift on me own, ye know. You'll be no good to anyone if you collapse.'

Shame-faced, feeling oddly light-headed, Meg allowed Tam and Effie to chase her off to bed for a proper night's sleep for once.

It was Effie's task to feed the orphan lambs that the mother sheep rejected or had insufficient milk for.

Meg came down to the kitchen one morning to find them all gathered, bleating madly, about Effie's legs.

'They're driving me crackers,' she mourned. She was holding two bottles at once to a pair of fiercely sucking lambs while the others desperately nuzzled her hand wanting their own share. Meg watched as she got herself a mug of tea, a smile on her face.

'How do you know which ones you've fed?' she asked.

Effie gave her an anguished look. 'You might well ask.' The two bottles were now empty and Effie dabbed a blob of milk on the top of each head to identify the two fed lambs then went to refill the bottles with fresh mixture. The moment her back was turned the other lambs leapt upon the first two and quickly licked off the delicious fluid. Meg burst into laughter.

'I don't think your system is working,' she explained what she had seen.

Effie stared at the milling lambs in despair. 'Drat! No wonder some get fat while the others stay skinny.'

Effie met Meg's gaze, brimming with laughter, and burst into giggles herself. Then they were both laughing so much Meg was clutching her sides in agony. 'Oh, the thought of them licking up the milk as fast as you mark them with it . . .' And they were off again. It was some moments before the two of them could wipe away tears and bring themselves back under control. 'Well, come on, what do you suggest?' Effie asked.

'How about some sort of label?'

So luggage labels were found, one attached to each lamb and duly numbered.

'Now you start at one and keep going, in order, till they're all fed. Easy.'

'Let's hope they don't eat labels,' chuckled Effie. But the system seemed to work and the lambs started to thrive better after that.

It was the middle of May before Meg felt it safe to take time off from her duties. A familiar twittering warble told her that Broombank's swallows had returned to take up summer residence and there were five blue eggs in the dunnock's nest by the gate.

The lambing season had been long, and harder than Meg could ever have imagined. But her first crop of lambs were safely delivered; smaller than she would have liked, but it was a start.

Oh, and how she had loved watching her lambs grow, seeing them play 'I'm the King of the Castle' each evening as they gambolled and frolicked on the knolls of grass about the farm, as lambs are supposed to do. It filled her with such pride to watch them that it took her twice as long to get her chores done. She had survived her first winter, and the knowledge seemed to give her fresh courage, ready to face anything, even this sour-faced woman who was taking an age to answer a simple question.

She tried to imagine Kath sitting here in this green-painted room in exactly the same way. Though not quite the same, for Kath's mind would no doubt have been a turmoil of misery and confusion, worrying over her baby and her own future. How long had she been in this place? Six, seven months? Maybe longer.

Meg had disliked Miss Blake, who sat opposite her, on sight. And there was a smell about the place, rather like the paraffin and sand they used to spread over 'accidents' in infant school. It made her feel uneasy.

'She probably came at the end of last year,' Meg helpfully reminded her. 'A pretty girl she is, with fair hair worn in a bob.'

The woman sniffed. 'They're all pretty, or so they think.'

Meg watched the woman leaf painstakingly through a long slim book and wished she would hurry up. Meg wanted to get this mission done with and be back on the train before nightfall. This was not a time to linger in Liverpool.

The wisdom of her coming at all had been debated long and hard for some weeks. They'd listened to the news every night, horrified by what was happening. The phoney war had turned into a real one as

Hitler occupied Denmark, Norway, Holland, and swept on through Belgium to France. Mr Chamberlain had gone and Winston Churchill was now the Prime Minister, promising them nothing but 'blood, sweat, toil and tears'.

'What if you get bombed?' Effie had asked, panic in her voice.

Tam calmly told her that nothing of the sort had yet happened so why should they choose to drop one on Meg the moment she sets foot in the city. Tam O'Cleary was good at easing tension, Meg had discovered. He was good at a lot of things.

So she had first taken the train to Southport and been forced practically to bully the directions to Greenlawns out of Ruby Nelson. It was as well she had since nobody else in Liverpool seemed to have heard of the place when Meg finally arrived there.

Miss Blake paused at a page in her large blue book, peering through narrow-rimmed spectacles. 'Ah, here we are. Yes, we did take in a girl of that name. Katherine Margaret Ellis, aged twenty. She came to us in November last. Yes, I remember her now.'

Meg felt a flood of relief. 'Is she still here?'

The pale eyes regarded her in vaguely troubled surprise. 'She has not been a particularly good influence upon our other, er, residents. Something of a trouble-maker is our Miss Ellis.'

Meg's lips twitched. 'May I see her, please?'

'That is rather irregular. It can be most unsettling for our girls to have visitors from the outside.'

'From the outside?' Meg echoed the words in amazement.

Miss Blake leaned forward. 'Are her family ready to reclaim her?'

'Well, not exactly,' Meg admitted and Miss Blake sniffed, very nearly with pleased satisfaction.

'You must appreciate that most of our girls have been abandoned, by their family, by their friends, by society. There is nowhere for them to go. The charity of Greenlawns is all they have to depend on.'

'Kath – Katherine – has not been so abandoned. She still has friends. Me, for instance.' Meg smiled sweetly, grey eyes issuing a challenge.

'Are you wishing to take her with you today?'

'That is my intention.'

'If you do so, you must undertake to be completely responsible for her health and well-being. She has not been – well. And she may sin again.'

'I will gladly undertake to care for her.'

A long pause, then a small bell was lifted and rung, sounding loud in the still room. An even longer pause followed it. Finally, steps were heard hurrying along the corridor outside, a rapid knock and a figure appeared, slightly breathless.

'Sorry, Miss Blake, I'd just gone out for a moment.'

Instructions were given to bring Katherine Ellis to the office.

As the heels clacked away again, Meg cleared her throat. 'I understand that there was a child?'

Miss Blake adjusted her spectacles and returned her piercing gaze to the book, reading the reports written by each name, giving details of each girl's history and behaviour. Katherine Ellis had a long string of convictions for temper and the inciting of rebellion. If this young woman planned to take her away with her, Miss Blake would not object. 'A female child,' she read and Meg cringed at a baby being so described. 'Born 27 March, weighing six pounds, seven ounces,' She closed the book, as if the matter were dealt with and there was no more to be said.

'And?'

'I beg your pardon?'

'Where is it . . . she?'

'In the orphanage, awaiting adoption, of course. We are not a children's home, *Miss* Turner.' The emphasis on the 'Miss' caused Meg to squirm. 'We offer no provision for infants here.'

'I see. And have any adoptive parents been found for her?' Meg held her breath, wondering what answer she hoped for.

'Indeed it is difficult at present, with the war. People have enough to worry about without taking on other people's byblows.'

The word was so offensive to Meg that she had to bite her lip very hard to keep her good manners in check. Then came the familiar tap of heels, the rap upon the door, and the woman was there again.

'Katherine Ellis.' And Meg gazed upon a stranger.

'Kath?' Not a vestige of girlhood remained in the narrow planes of the sunken cheeks. The lovely swinging bob had been cut close to the finely shaped head. The porcelain skin was ashen, almost grey, the hazel eyes rimmed by the red of exhaustion. And the hands, those beautiful tapering white fingers with pearl-shaped nails that Meg had always envied, now picked restlessly at the cotton of her green overall. Workworn, blistered, the nails bitten down to the quick, they looked red raw, as if they had recently been bleeding. 'Dear God, what have you done to her?'

At the sound of Meg's voice the heavy lids lifted, revealing a blankness in the eyes, and a terrible despair. The sight brought such pain to Meg, she had to fight hard not to burst into tears as emotion thickened her throat.

'Meg?' There was wonder in the question. And disbelief.

Then Meg opened her arms and Kath stepped into them with a quiet sob.

Lime Street railway station was thronged with people, many of them in uniform, most crying. Meg felt like crying too, though not for the same reason. She wasn't seeing someone she loved off to the war. That had been done months ago and not a day had passed since when she hadn't thought of Jack. Now she thought of him for a different reason.

When Kath's baby had been put into her arms, Meg had gazed down upon the small bright face, the halo of glossy black curls, the violet-blue eyes, and had known instantly whose child she was. Everything seemed to come clear in that moment. It was all so obvious, so stupidly plain.

She wondered now how she had managed to remain so calm. There had been no doubt in her mind, and if there had been, one glance at Kath's face confirmed her worst fears.

'Jack?' Meg had whispered, and Kath had put her hands to her lips to stop the sob that escaped.

'I'm so sorry.'

That was all that had been said. All that needed to be said. They had signed the necessary papers, collected the child's documentation and walked out on to the bustling streets into the sunshine of a perfectly ordinary spring day. But Meg felt it would never be ordinary for her again. Life would never be the same again. She felt numb inside as if it were all over.

The stretching sensation around her heart must be pain, though it was difficult to describe it as such. Her body continued to function though she had no control over it. She could walk, count the money out of her purse to pay for a bus fare, hand in her ticket at the station. But for these things no thought was required. Her mind was not in any way engaged. It lived in another space, another time, a world of silence, and she had no wish to disturb it. Not yet. Let it rest there for a while, instinct told her. There would be time enough later to get it out, examine it, nurse it.

Doors were banging, there was the hiss of steam, the sound of quiet, desperate sobbing from the mass of people facing separation from their loved ones. Bags were flung into compartments, windows dropped open, hands reached out. Meg tried not to watch.

A whistle sounded.

'I can't come with you.'

Meg struggled to focus her eyes upon Kath. 'What did you say?'

'I c-can't come with you. I can't go home. Not now. Not like this.'

'Where will you go then? You have no money.'

'I have some, enough. I'll get a job, join up perhaps.' Kath opened a carriage door and pushed Meg inside, the child still in her arms. 'Can't you see? I'd be no good as a mother to her. I don't know her. I don't even love her.'

Meg was shocked, annoyed suddenly at Kath's lack of responsibility. 'How can you say that? She's your own child.'

A small sob sounded, quickly stifled. 'I've never held her. Not even when she was born. They wouldn't let me. Now I think it's too late.'

'Kath, this is madness. You must come home. We need you. You need us. Look at you, you're like a skeleton.' Again a whistle sounded and the guard was moving along the platform, slamming doors, telling people to stand back. 'You can't just abandon her like this.'

'I'm not. She's got you. And Jack. I'm sorry if we hurt you. We didn't mean to. Don't blame him. It was a game, that's all, a kind of madness in those lovely hot summers when we believed, hoped anyway, that war wouldn't come. Love her for me.' The tears were spilling over and then she turned abruptly and hurried away. The last sight Meg had of Kath was her little tan hat with the silly veil disappearing into the crowd.

The train gave a sudden lurch and as it started to move out of the station, Meg sat and held Jack's child on her lap and the tears ran unchecked down her cheeks and dripped on to the baby's shawl.

She took a taxi from Kendal Station to Broombank, extravagant but necessary, she decided, with the baby and her bag.

She had no recollection of the journey. Glad only that it was over and – and what? Where did she go from here? Without Jack. Without Kath. The shock was easing now and in its wake came pain. Pain so terrible it didn't seem possible to bear it.

'Meg?' Effie, dear Effie, standing in the doorway, her arms outstretched. 'Oh, Meg.'

She would keep her self-control, she would. Meg laid the baby in Effie's arms and watched as the girl, little more than a child herself, drew her close and whispered love into the baby's ear. Love. What was that? Not something to rely on, love, not if it brought this much hurt.

Meg walked into the farmhouse like a sleepwalker. She would go upstairs, lie down for a bit, think over this terrible thing that had happened to her and sort out how she felt about it. She only needed a rest and it would all come right in her head.

Tam, who had evidently been sitting at the table, taking supper, stood up, blocking her way. Big and patient, saying nothing, asking no questions. But something drove her to look up into his eyes. No sparkling, glinting green challenge in them today. Only a gentle wash of jade, like rain on glass.

'Kath is all right,' she said, and as he nodded he opened his arms and this time, unable to prevent herself, Meg walked into them. She laid her head against the broad strength of his chest, felt his arms wrap her in their warmth and let the tears come. Great wet globs that rolled down her cheek and into the neck of her best blue blouse. Not a sound came from her throat, only the silent anguish of a woman betrayed.

20

It was all around the close-knit community in no time at all that Meg Turner had a baby.

Even the thrill of Dunkirk failed to distract the gossips for long. In no time they were back to worrying over whose baby it was, and how it had appeared, out of the blue, in Meg Turner's house.

Effie was shocked to see how quick everyone was to condemn.

'Sanctimonious old biddies,' she muttered as she stood in a queue for new ration books and overheard a snippet of tittle-tattle she wouldn't repeat to her worst enemy, let alone her lovely Meg.

Though she supposed the long hard weeks of winter had something to do with it, what with keeping them all indoors so long, and then Meg being busy with the lambing and disappearing off to Liverpool so soon after that. There were plenty ready to think she'd emerged from the winter with a babe in her arms. Folk being folk would assume the worst. But if they stopped to think about it, they'd see it was a daft idea. Not unless they believed in immaculate conception.

This last phrase had been learned in the Scripture lessons at school, explained by a blushing Miss Shaw. Not that she need have worried where Effie was concerned. You'd have to get up early to make me blush, Effie thought, with some pride. But she enjoyed new words and struggled with the newspaper every morning in her efforts to improve her reading.

The voice rose and carried on the morning breeze and the people in the queue heaved forward so that they didn't miss a scrap.

'Indeed, who would have thought it of her? So well brought up an' all, and her father quite a big man in the chapel.'

'Indeed, I admit to being quite shocked myself, when I heard,' said Hetty Davies, quite put out that she had not been aware a baby was even expected, in all of her regular visits to Broombank. 'How she kept it hidden I cannot imagine.'

'We mustn't jump to conclusions,' warned the less excitable Miss Shaw, privately thinking with joy of yet another child for her school, in the fullness of time. 'It's true there has been no sign that, well, that a baby was on the way. And Meg is not at all the sort of girl...'

'No smoke without fire,' chimed in another voice.

'And she has been seen driving through town in a *taxi*. Had the baby somewhere away, to try to hide the fact no doubt, and then couldn't get it adopted because of the war, so had to fetch it home again.'

A third added the titillating information that Meg had a man staying in her house. 'Been living there for some time, he has. And not in the barn neither. Now what is that, if not blatant disregard for what is right and proper? Doesn't it just go to show?'

'Tch. You never do know about people, unless you live with them.'

'Oh, dear me, no.'

Effie had heard enough. 'You bad-mouthed old besoms,' she shouted, making them jump as no one had seen her small figure, hiding behind large bosoms and baskets. 'How dare you condemn her when you don't know nothing about it? A saint, that's what my Meg is, and if you knew the truth you'd chop your lying tongues off.' Then to her complete mortification, Effie burst into tears and had to turn and run from the queue and the shocked, questioning eyes. She had reached the Shambles before she realised she still hadn't got the new ration books after near an hour of queuing and would have to go back and start all over again.

But yet the rumours persisted. And in the end, as expected, Joe came.

'What's all this then?' he began, mildly enough. Meg lifted her chin a fraction and tightened her lips to something very like a button. 'Where's this child you're supposed to have? Or is it all daft talk?'

'No, it's not daft talk,' Meg admitted. 'But nor is there any truth in what you're thinking and everyone is saying.'

Joe took a seat by the fire and glared accusingly at his daughter, still far too wilful in his opinion. 'Where is she then?'

'She's upstairs asleep and I'll not have her disturbed.'

Meg was glad, for once, that they were alone. Effie was upstairs with Melissa, and Tam was out seeing to the cows. It would give her time to calm her father down, explain something of the truth. 'She isn't mine. I brought her from Liverpool. She's – she's an orphan.'

'Orphan my eye! What were you doing in Liverpool?'

Not for a moment did Meg consider telling him about Kath. 'She is. I'll not have anyone say different. How can she be mine anyway? Don't talk soft.'

'It's not that long since that lad o'yourn left. It could be.'

Meg swallowed carefully, painfully aware that he spoke the truth. She wasn't a virgin, after all. That one moment of madness in the barn with Jack could very easily have resulted in a child. But that had been more than a year ago and they'd never repeated it, not once since.

But Kath had.

Oh, but how different things would have been if Meg herself hadn't denied him the love he clearly wanted. Maybe he wouldn't have bothered with Kath then. Was it all her own fault? she couldn't help wondering.

Meg would have written to Jack with joy if the baby had been hers, eager to tell him he was to become a father. They would quickly have married and everyone would have counted a little on their fingers and smiled and sighed and said, 'Ah, yes, but they're young and there is a war on.' But that was not the way it had gone. Melissa was Kath's baby. Kath's and Jack's. And it was all too terrible to think of.

Meg was spared from answering Joe's direct accusation by the arrival of Tam. Joe took one look at the tall, well-set Irishman, got to his feet and stood glowering before him.

'So this is how the land lies. Mebbe you're the one who has caused this trouble.'

Tam's brows lifted very slightly in surprise. At any other time Meg might have laughed at the comical sight of her father trying to outface a man a good six inches taller than himself. But this wasn't the moment for humour.

'Dad, leave Tam alone. You're making a fool of yourself.'

'A fool am I? And there's me thinking it's my daughter who's the laughing stock aroond here. And I can see why. I think thee had best leave, son.'

'Leave?' Tam smiled down at Joe. 'Now why would I be doing that?'

'Pack your bags or whatever it is you roving Irish carry your chattels in and *go*.'

247

Tam lifted his eyes slowly to Meg and held them for a long moment before returning them to Joe. 'I'll go when I'm good and ready, and when Meg tells me to. I don't think you have any say around here.'

'Hev I not? We'll see aboot that.' Joe was beside himself with fury, almost spitting with rage. 'Naebody gainsays me without being sorry for it,' he roared. 'I'll not have my daughter preyed upon by strangers, and foreigners at that.'

Meg stepped up to Joe and laid a hand upon his shoulder 'Dad, stop it. Tam is right, This is my house, my farm, and you are the visitor here.'

'What?'

'So I'd be obliged if you left without any bother. Tam has nothing to do with any of this. He is my employee and, I hope, my friend. And I'll not have him tainted by your nastiness.'

'Thoo hes a funny way o' choosing thy friends.'

'The choice is mine.'

Joe glared ferociously at her. 'Well, don't expect me to come and bail you out when naebody will lift a finger to help thee, because of him and what he's done to you.'

Meg almost laughed. 'What have *you* ever done for me so far? Nothing. Everything I have here has been achieved in spite of you, not because of your help which has been non-existent. Now get out, before I forget I'm still your daughter and thump you one.'

So startled was Joe by this suggestion, he glowered once more at each of them then stormed out, slamming the door behind him just to show who was boss.

Meg walked into Melissa's bedroom and gazed down upon the sleeping child. Effie had made a bed for her in a large drawer and Meg knelt beside it. The sound of the baby's breathing was oddly calming and filled Meg with the fierce need to protect her. Protect her from the war, from unthinking gossip, from all the problems she might meet as she grew. Meg stroked the back of one finger over the soft down of the baby's cheek. So tiny. Such a frail scrap of humanity. A bubble of milk dribbled out upon the rosily pouted lips and Meg smiled.

'It's not your fault, little one. You didn't ask to be born, nor to be abandoned. Kath, your mum, didn't mean to be heartless. It's the way she is, a bit reckless and impulsive. Never gives a thought to anyone but herself, and look what a mess she's got herself into. Things are difficult for her right now, what with being thrown out by her ma and pa, and not having any job. And things aren't too good between her and me either. Not like they used to be, nor ever will be again, I don't suppose.' Meg smiled sadly down at the baby. 'Still, given the chance, she might have loved you.'

She bent over, about to gather the sleeping baby in her arms, so deliciously sweet did she look, then stopped as the thought entered her head: *As I might come to love you.*

It jolted her and Meg became very still. Aware, in that moment, of a new risk. The possibility of fresh pain in the future if she came to care too much for Kath's child.

She took a step back, away from the sleeping baby. No, that wouldn't do at all. She must think very carefully about this.

What would happen when the war ended, and Kath and Jack returned?

Melissa must be fed and given a home, as was only right and proper, until her mother came to claim her. But that was all. You're not mine, do you see, so I can't love you as a real mother would. Wouldn't be right. Or safe, for either of them.

Meg turned and left the room without another glance at the makeshift cot. No, she'd make the necessary arrangements for Melissa's welfare, but she herself would keep well away. She would concentrate on the farm. That was all that mattered now.

But being responsible for a baby on top of all her other chores caused endless complications for Meg. There never seemed to be a moment to herself. Admittedly it was pleasant sometimes simply to sit and watch the baby gurgling happily in the summer sunshine but Meg preferred not to allow herself such treats, and she didn't feel she could ask Sally Ann for any help since her sister-in-law gave birth to a baby herself in June. A boy, Nicholas David Turner, much to Joe's delight. Both mother and child were doing well and Dan walked about as if he had done the whole thing singlehanded.

So Meg was relieved when the school term ended and Effie took over, leaving her free to concentrate on the farm. During the long hot summer everyone feared the south of England was about to be invaded but September dawned and though the battles still raged over London, here in Westmorland the quietness of the coming autumn hung in the air, an almost guilty peace.

In the woodlands the red squirrels were busily burying their nuts, constantly chittering reminders to themselves not to forget. Even the youngest stags wore their hard antlers as they cleared the after grass following the hay harvest, and sleek young foxes learned to hunt alone.

In the first week of September, Effie handed Mrs Davies a basket of fruit and vegetables with a satisfied flourish. 'All home grown,' she said.

The scent of fresh fruit rose tantalisingly to Hetty Davies's nostrils, seeming to fill the small church. She looked at the girl before her and laid aside the bronze chrysanthemums she was arranging in a vase on the altar table. Chrysanths were always lovely at this time of year, and Will had quite a talent for growing them, something not everyone had, oh my word, no. 'You do realise we're not having a harvest festival as such this year?'

'I hear folk are bringing stuff, all the same.'

'Those who can afford it. But nothing like we usually have, not with the war and the shortages, oh dear me, no.' Mrs Davies offered a kindly, if slightly embarrassed, smile to Effie. She was sorry they'd got this trouble at Broombank. Hetty had always liked Meg and had felt a keen disappointment that she had turned out to be, well, just as silly-headed as all the rest, as you might say. She hadn't felt it right to call, since she'd heard.

But Effie was still talking. 'Sending the produce to a children's home, I heard. That right?'

'Perfectly correct.'

'Then I'll leave them, if it's all the same to you. And Mrs D, I'd just like to say as how I'm right sorry my tongue ran away wi' me in the queue that time. I were that mad, I dun't know what come over me. Only it didn't seem fair, what people were saying about Meg.'

Mrs Davies cleared her throat and a well of pity rose in her ample breast. Who was she to cast the first stone, even if it were all true? What she wouldn't give for a baby half so delightful as this one was said to be, from those who'd been lucky enough to catch a glimpse. And hadn't she and Will had their moments? Once upon a time.

'There's no need to apologise. No need at all. Perhaps I should be the one to apologise to you. Gossiping is a dreadful sin, and I should have known better than to think such things about our poor, dear Meg.'

Effie smiled. 'It dun't do her no good, no good at all, mind, to have everyone taking sides against her, when she's only doing her best to make a go of things. Hasn't she enough trouble, with Joe Turner on her back?'

'Oh, indeed, yes. A most dreadful man.' Appalled by what she had just said, Hetty cleared her throat. 'I mean...'

'It's all right. I know exactly what you mean. And I agree wi' yer. I wondered if happen you could let it get round like, about the baby coming from the home in Liverpool? Greenlawns, it were called.' So there, said the tone, as if adding a name gave truth to the tale of an orphan child plucked from the jaws of certain death and uncaring deprivation, as Effie understood only too well.

'I will indeed, Effie. I will indeed.' Mrs Davies's face became very still. Perhaps they might have other babies needing a home? No, she shook the idea away. She was far too old now for sleepless nights and she and Will were comfortable enough together. But she could at least help Meg, try to make up for her own unkind remarks.

Effie was anxious to go, but there was one other matter needing to be settled. 'Meg says as how you can call an' see our Lissa at any time. You might like to take her for a walk.'

Hetty's cheeks grew quite pink with pleasure. 'Oh, that would be lovely. I'll be round tomorrow. If that's all right?'

'I was wondering if you might feel able to do a bit more than that, Mrs Davies.'

Dark eyes, large and beseeching, gazed up into the woman's enquiring gaze.

'Oh?'

'Well, what with me having to be in school much of the day, and Meg busy about the farm, proper thrang she calls it, and Sally Ann up to her ears with her own bairn, not to mention looking after that lot at Ashlea, well, it crossed my mind like, you might be willing to have our Lissa for an hour or two each morning? Just to give Meg a chance to get on. She could manage her in the afternoons, till I got home.'

'Oh,' Mrs Davies breathed, too stunned to speak for a moment. 'Oh, yes. I would like that. I would like that very much.'

Effie beamed and stuck out a hand, rather grubby and stained red from the blackberry picking. 'It's a deal then?'

Mrs Davies regarded the hand for a second then shook it firmly. 'It's a deal. Oh, my word, yes, it is indeed. And thank you for the fruit,' she called as Effie departed, flourishing an airy wave.

Hetty Davies returned, quite flustered, to her flowers, but her mind was no longer on the beauty of the chrysanths.

'Now I wonder if Will ever threw that big old black pram away that we kept up in the loft all those years...' She'd look it out, the moment she got home.

* * *

In the days and weeks that followed, Meg buried her pain in work. She was glad of it, welcomed it. Up before dawn each day she laboured, blotting all thought from her mind. During the day she could concentrate entirely upon seeing to her flock, milking her two cows, seeking ways to make her farm pay. Come the evening she would eat one of Effie's suppers, though it might be sawdust for all she noticed half the time, and fall into bed praying for oblivion. Rarely did she find it. More often than not she found that was when the thoughts started, turning over and over, replaying the events that had led to this pain. Seeing Kath dancing in Jack's arms, laughing up at him with her lovely hazel eyes.

Why hadn't she realised what was going on? How blind and naive she must have been. So much in love she hadn't seen, because she hadn't wanted to see.

'Will you take the bairn for a walk?' Effie would ask her each day. Or: 'Will you give Lissa her bottle?'

Requests that became a constant thorn to stab into her heart.

'I don't think so. I have work to do.' And Meg would hurry from the kitchen, back to the peace and sanctuary of the heaf and her sheep, aware of Effie's troubled gaze upon her.

But the thorns kept on stabbing her.

What had she done to deserve such treatment?

Wasn't Kath her best friend, and Jack much more? The thoughts whirled and burned, images to torment and torture. *Where* had he loved Kath? In the barn, where they had loved? *How*? *Why*? Till Meg felt insanity threaten and prayed for exhaustion to bring relief.

At first she had expected a letter from Kath, an enquiry about Melissa at least, or word that she had found a job. When summer had followed spring and still Meg heard nothing she put the thought from her mind. She wasn't ready to face Kath again, wasn't even able to think about the effect Kath's betrayal would have upon their friendship. And betrayal was the only word for it.

Their threesome had become dangerous, she could see that now. A mistake had been made, boundaries had been crossed from which there was no retreat.

But she continued, despite Tam's and Effie's protests, to write to Jack as if nothing had happened.

'He's gone to fight for his country, perhaps even die for it. I can't just abandon him.'

'I would,' declared the less complicated Effie, who had learned the whole sorry tale by this time.

Once, in the depth of her despair, Meg had written to Jack, based now in Southampton, to say that perhaps it would be best if they called off their engagement, in view of the war, and go their own way. It was a coward's way out but she felt short on strength.

He replied almost by return, saying he needed to be able to think of her, waiting for him at home, and whatever was bothering her could wait until Christmas when the war would surely be over and they could sort it out. The rest of the letter was about how hard life in training was and how he was expecting to be sailing any week now, so that might liven things up a bit.

'Wish I could get up to see you, but it's so far I might not manage it. Thinking of you, Jack.'

Ashamed that she was fussing over a spoiled love affair when he might lose his life in this terrible war, she never again suggested they break their engagement. It seemed only fair to wait, as he suggested, for the war to be over. So she never did tell him about Melissa. That was for Kath to do, after all, when the time was right. Nothing to do with her.

'You're a fool,' Tam told her. 'Why concern yourself with those two, after what they've done to you?'

'I can't help it. Kath and I have been friends all our lives, it's hard to reject her even now. I'm sure she never meant it to happen. We were all too close, that's all.'

And Tam raised one eyebrow in disbelief. 'And Jack?'

Meg dipped her head, not wanting to answer or even consider the question, yet even that simple gesture seemed to annoy him.

'Don't do that, Meg. The shame is not yours.'

Deep down she knew that worrying over Kath and Jack was all tangled up with her own self-pity. So long as she centred her thoughts upon others, she didn't have to think of her own future, and what she would do with it, without Jack. Meg Turner had no future.

It was Rust, strangely enough, who turned the tide for her. By her side at all times, he was her comfort and her joy.

The dog had made a good recovery, thanks to the services of the veterinary and the care he received at home afterwards. He lolloped about on three legs, rarely putting down the fourth, which poked out at an odd angle, not entirely under control. But this in no way hindered him. And he couldn't seem to take to retirement at all.

'Don't let him out for an hour, till I'm well gone,' Meg would instruct Effie, as she set off up the fells to check the sheep. But no matter how long Effie kept him fastened up, the moment she let him go, he was off, a streak of black and tan up the hillside, running in his own peculiar way. He always reached Meg long before she had done any really serious work. But then how could she possibly manage without him?

'Would you look at that dog? Never say die, eh, lad?' And she would pat him and rub her cheek against his, glad of his courage for she needed his solid friendship by her

If a dog could bravely put injury behind him and soldier on, surely she could? No matter what it cost, Meg decided, she would find the strength to build her life again and put the past behind her. Easier said than done, but she would try.

She would concentrate entirely upon turning Broombank into the best sheep farm in the district. And she would do it too. On her own if necessary. Without help from anyone, particularly her father.

This decision brought such a blinding delight, such a joy to her heart, that Meg knew, in that moment, she would survive. On a beautiful morning like this, puffs of white cloud marching over Striding Edge, she knew this was the best place in the world. She did have a future, here at Broombank. No matter what pain and hurt Jack and Kath had caused her in their youthful carelessness, she could overcome it. She must.

'Were you wanting a permanent job?' Meg asked Tam and waited, stomach muscles clenched, for his response.

Tam stopped scraping grass from the mower long enough to glance up at Meg. The harvest was in; not as good as it might have been because of the drought at just the wrong time, but at least there would be oats and hay for the stock this winter. It had crossed his mind that it was time to move on, but he hadn't fixed on it yet. He continued steadily with his task. 'I don't generally make permanent arrangements. I come and go, when I choose.'

Meg sat on a stone wall, smoothing the yellow lichen with her fingers, trying to organise her thoughts so that she might find the most persuasive words. She needed Tam to stay. He was a good worker, and strong. There was no denying she needed some muscle about the place. She'd little hope of carrying out her plan without some form of male assistance, much as she might balk at the idea. And labour was hard to come by. Besides all of that, she trusted him and that didn't come easy to her these days.

And she liked him. He was cheerful, kind and friendly. Good for morale, as the government posters would say.

Meg cleared her throat. 'I wouldn't normally push you, only it's been such a hard year, one way and another. And I mean to survive.' Then in case this wasn't quite positive enough, she added, 'I mean to do well. And I believe I can. But I'm not so stupid that I don't know when I need help.'

And now the teasing laughter was back in his eyes and Meg felt her own sigh of relief. It was going to be all right, she knew it.

'That's something, for Meg Turner to admit she needs help.'

'I might even be able to pay you soon. Though not too much, I'm afraid.'

'Well, that'd make a welcome change, to be sure. This is to be your way of coping, is it, your battle?'

'Don't tease me. I'm serious. I can't bear to think about the war.' Meg blinked rapidly. 'I daren't think of Charlie up there, being taught to fight in the skies. I can't do anything to help him, or any of the others up there. But I can do my bit here. This is my place. My home.'

Meg dipped her head, not wanting him to see her vulnerability. 'I miss Lanky. He knew everything there was to know about sheep farming, about Broombank. His family has worked this land for generations. I owe it to him not to give up. I have to make a go of it because if I don't it will be as if I'd flung his generosity back in his face, and that would be terrible. I look at my Luckpenny every night and remember his faith in me.

'He couldn't go on because he was too ill but he thought that I could. He handed his good fortune on to me and I must believe in that.' Despite herself she lifted her face to his and Tam quite forgot he was supposed to be cleaning and oiling the mower, preparatory to putting it away for the winter. 'Lanky believed in me, you see. No one else ever has.'

'I believe in you.' Where had those words come from? Tam was astonished that they'd popped out of his mouth without even a thought. 'I believe you can do anything you want to do. But if you're serious about making a go of this place there'll be no room for sentiment.'

'I realise that.'

'Farming is a hard business. Are you tough enough?'

Her lips curved into a smile, tremulous, sensuous, beguiling, and a sudden need raged through him, leaving his hands shaking so much he felt obliged to put down the oil can he was holding and pay excessive attention to wiping them on an old rag.

'I don't know but I'm learning. How can anyone know if they are up to a job until they try? And I want to try. Besides how I feel about Lanky leaving me Broombank, I have Effie to think about, and now Melissa, but also I want – need – to do this for myself. I've always felt the desire to be independent, to prove myself. This is my opportunity and I mustn't give up, just because life is tough.'

'And no medals at the end of it.'

'I know that.' She smiled. 'Grinding hard work in all weathers with little cash in hand. What I want to know is, would it bother you?'

'Bother me?'

'My being a woman?'

Tam fought his thoughts back into order. He'd never worked for a woman before, let alone one as entrancing as this one. But if he was to stay, and there were worse places to spend the war, this relationship must be strictly business. Meg Turner might look homely enough at first glance, childlike almost, with her hair all tied up with string and dressed in scruffy overalls much of the time, but a second glance, a smile from those lovely lips, and a man could forget his manners in a moment. 'So long as you realise I'm as independent as yourself.'

'I realise that.'

A long pause, then, 'We could start by getting rid of these damn' rabbits, not to mention the foxes. Since all the hunt has been called up, the place is overrun with them.'

Meg laughed, her heart soaring. 'We could sell the rabbits for two or three shillings a brace on the Kendal market.'

'Three shillings?' Tam grinned at her. 'Then I'll clean the gun next. If we get enough it'll help pay next quarter's rent.'

Suddenly excited, Meg knelt on the grass beside him. It had been decided. He would stay. 'I mean to fatten more turkeys for this Christmas. I'm taking orders already. I've nearly paid Will Davies for those two cows and then I'll buy one or two more. The Co-op will take the extra milk off me, or I could get a hand-buggy and take it round myself. It'll give a regular income till I've time to build up the flock.'

Tam was watching her face, wondering how it was he hadn't noticed before how beautiful it was. He'd seen her as a young girl, playing at farming, content to ride out life in the quietness of her own home in an unquestionably safe area. But there was much more to Meg than that. She was exciting, ambitious, beguiling. And very likely passionate. He blanked that last thought at once from his mind.

Come on, man, pick up the oil can and get back to work. It wasn't proper to want to consider taking your employer to bed, and he'd see that the thought never entered his head again.

'So? Are you with me?'

'I'm with you,' he said, without even a pause. Meg smiled her thanks, openly, and with delight in her grey eyes. Tam knew it would take a good deal to set him against her. He would stay with Meg Turner for the entire war. Longer, were she to ask.

21

The small Austin car left the rough cart track and started along the lane. It drove past a cluster of whitewashed cottages around a former bobbin mill and on over a humped bridge. Ahead lay the wild grandeur of mountains and the rugged outline of Goat Scar and Raven Crag. 'I hear you have a baby staying with you?' Rosemary Ellis had stopped to offer Meg a lift into town and she put the question briskly, as if the answer were of no consequence. Meg felt her heart quicken.

'That is so.'

Mrs Ellis did not take her eyes from the road as she shifted the gear lever and eased the car forward. 'Is it Kath's baby?'

A slight pause while Meg thought over her line of approach. 'Everyone thinks she's mine,' she said, avoiding the issue.

'She?'

'Yes. Melissa. Effie has started calling her Lissa and I'm afraid we've all picked it up. But it seems to suit her.' Meg cast the other woman a sidelong glance, then stared out at the passing scenery, achingly beautiful on this September morning, the bracken aflame to a rich russet red. Here there was freedom and solitude. Space to breathe and feel. She could scarcely imagine Kath's despair, living in that dreadful home. How thin and desperate she had looked. And Rosemary Ellis, her own mother, had known where she was. 'Kath has gone. I don't know where.'

'I rather thought you might.'

'Isn't that what you wanted? For her to disappear?'

The question was very nearly impertinent and Meg heard the sharp intake of breath. 'I don't know what I wanted,' Rosemary admitted. 'For it not to have happened, I suppose. The scandal . . .'

Meg wanted to feel sorry for the other woman but somehow couldn't quite manage it. 'Did you send her money when she was in that place – Greenlawns?'

Mrs Ellis fell silent as they drove on beside the tumbling waters of the beck, a worked-out quarry and an old farmhouse with a medieval pele tower. She was quiet for so long Meg thought she had decided not to answer the question, which had been cheeky on Meg's part anyway.

'We were asked to provide what we could towards her keep though the girls were expected largely to work for it themselves. I felt lucky that Ruby had found somewhere to take her, somewhere the baby could be born and cared for.'

'And what did Mr Ellis think?'

The car swerved slightly and Meg grabbed the door strap, heart in mouth for a moment. But the road was empty as usual, so no harm was done. They came out of the narrow lane on to the main road.

'Jeffrey doesn't know anything about it. He mustn't. His heart, you know. He isn't as strong as he likes, to think.'

Meg had no trouble in feeling sorry for Mr Ellis. 'He seems to miss Kath. Doesn't he ever wonder why she doesn't write?'

The silence lasted so long this time, they had almost reached the bridge that led into Kendal before Rosemary answered. 'I pretended once that she had. I read him a letter that was supposed to have come from her, saying she was going to be away for a long time, somewhere secret, and she couldn't write again for ages. It seemed to satisfy him. He thinks she's doing her bit for the war.'

Meg gasped. To shuffle off one's pregnant daughter to avoid a scandal was bad enough; to lie to one's husband about her welfare was altogether more terrible. The words burst out of her before she could prevent them. 'How could you do such a thing? Kath loved you. She still loves you. Both of you. All right, so she made a mistake but she has paid for it. It's not a criminal offence, for God's sake. Lissa is just a baby and she's beautiful. She is very dark, and sitting up nice as ninepence. Kath's child. Aren't you going to see her? Aren't you even going to tell Mr Ellis that he has a granddaughter?'

'*No!*'

'Stop the car here, please.' Meg had to get away before she said something truly unforgivable.

'Just as well Lissa has me then,' she announced to the retreating vehicle as it sped away, Rosemary Ellis sitting stiffly at the wheel. 'Letters or no letters.'

Kath had, in fact, written several letters. Hardly a week had gone by without her writing to someone or other. Her father, mother, Meg, or Jack. The letters were all in her locker, stampless envelopes stuck down as if they had already been seen by the censor, neatly tied into bundles. She had no intention of posting any of them.

'Why do you bother?' Bella asked, as she watched Kath slip yet another into its appointed place. 'Either send the dratted thing or stop wasting time writing them.'

Kath only smiled. 'It's like a diary. Who knows? One day somebody may be glad to know what I was up to.' Her daughter perhaps?

Bella took the pen from her fingers. 'Stop, this moment. I won't have you tempt fate with such wild notions. My father thinks women in uniform are the lowest of the low, so let's brave the local hostelry and prove it, shall we? We have two whole hours before the ten-thirty curfew and we all have to drink our cocoa and go to bed.'

Kath laughed. 'Like good girls at school.'

Bella tucked Kath's arm into hers as they clattered past the row of beds and left the Nissen hut. 'You're lucky if you went to that sort of school. No one gave out cocoa at mine, only verses of Old Testament to be endlessly learned, and the cane every Friday.'

'I can just see you as a schoolgirl, all pigtails and short socks.'

Bella grinned. 'I was a terror. Bigger than most of the teachers. Come on, old sport, tonight we celebrate the end of the dreaded training, for tomorrow we face the horrors of carrying our kitbags half across country to the outer wilds of East Anglia.'

Kath had met Bella on Euston Station. Surrounded by more girls than she had ever seen in her life, all chattering twenty to the dozen, the noise had been deafening. Then one black-haired, black-eyed girl of Amazon proportions had turned to her with a wry smile.

'They'll soon shut up when reality sets in.'

It had set in alarmingly early. The moment they saw the train backing into platform one, in fact. It came home to them that this was the moment of no return. When they boarded, they'd be on their way to becoming a member of the Women's Auxillary Air Force. A Waaf.

To Kath it had seemed the only answer. She'd come straight to London on the money the home gave her, not quite knowing what she intended. She'd tried a series of temporary jobs – waitress, barmaid –

boring, mindless tasks and always with the problem of where to lay her head. She used the underground if she could get away with it, though it wasn't, strictly speaking, allowed. The government had decided it would be bad for morale to hide like rats in a hole. Or a women's hostel if she could find one, a park bench if necessary.

But then she had seen the poster and the answer seemed suddenly obvious. In the WAAF she would be provided with food, clothing, a bed to sleep in, work with pay at the end of it, and no questions asked. One of hundreds of girls, her indiscretions could be safely buried if not forgotten. Worn out and feeling far from clean, she'd gladly signed up.

She hadn't minded the weeks of hard training that followed. It hadn't troubled her in the least to stand for hours in the freezing cold, run up and down on the spot or do a half-day route march. She had been forced to do far worse in the yards of Greenlawns. And it was a blessed improvement upon working in the laundry.

Nor had she objected to the school-type lectures on mathematics, geography and morse code. She'd written her letters during some of the more boring ones, meaning at first to keep in touch. In the end her courage had failed her and the letters had stayed in her bag, then been consigned to the locker. For the moment.

'So long as they don't give us any more of those damned inoculations,' said Bella, 'I can take anything they throw at me.'

Bella had been ill with fever and the shakes after the typhoid, tetanus and smallpox injections. Kath was glad to be able to prove she'd already had them.

'And no more of those unspeakably awful FFI examinations,' Kath laughed. 'Cavorting about knickerless is not my idea of fun.'

Hadn't it been proved already that she was free from infection? And no WAAF Officer could make a worse job of it than Miss Blake had at Greenlawns. Not that she admitted to anyone that she'd suffered the dreaded test once already.

Bella looked at her in open admiration. 'Bloomin' hell, I'll never forget the way you walked in to that room. Cool as a cucumber you were. Everyone else was white-faced and trembling, or giggling and weeping from nerves, and you strip off your pink regulation panties as if it were common place. That isn't what you were, is it, in real life? A stripper?'

Kath giggled. 'No, but maybe I should have tried it. It might have paid better than a waitress job at the UCP.' The best of it was that Bella would have accepted her just the same if she had been.

'Undoubtedly, and with better tips. Only snag would be all those men, gawping at you. Give me the shivers, that would. I'm off 'em myself.'

Kath grinned. 'Right now I'm inclined to agree with you.'

Bella cast her a sideways glance as she handed over a half pint glass of cider. 'Got your fingers burned, did you?'

'You might say so.'

'Well, that's another thing we have in common. No romantic story of partings and promises to wait for ever for me either. My old man put five bob on the table, told me he was off to join the Army and ta ta, thanks very much. And that was the last I heard of him. No letters, no pay cheque every month, not even a so and so telegram. I can only assume that he's alive and well and keeping out of my way, which is fine by me. Not a marriage made in heaven, I can tell you, more like in Epping Forest.'

'Any children?'

'Nope. Nor do I ever intend having any, smelly, demanding creatures that they are. My mother had one a year for fourteen years then dropped dead. That ain't for me.'

A vision of a small crumpled face came into Kath's mind and she took a quick draught of her cider.

'Steady on, it's stronger than it looks.'

'When do you think we'll get our uniform?' Kath asked. 'When we get to our new posting?'

'Let's hope so. You look like you might be off to Ascot in that posh suit. Not to mention that hat of yours. Have you nothing else to wear?'

'I lost all my luggage,' Kath lied.

'Poor sod. Well, at least take off the hat in here or they'll double the price of the drinks.'

'Sorry, I didn't think.' Kath realised the outfit spoke of money and class but Aunt Ruby never had sent on her other clothes and it was all she possessed in the world.

Even if she'd been dressed in rags, her background would still have shown. It was all there in the way she held her head, the swing of her walk. Very nearly insolent arrogance. If she was unaware how her instinctive style, her air of confidence, were all signals that Katherine Ellis was sure of her place in society, it only showed how little she cared.

She did realise that those who took the trouble to look closer might find some surprising contradictions. A few calluses and blisters in unexpected places for one thing. But the arrogance hid her fears, something she'd never been troubled with before and didn't mean anyone to see now.

It would be a misinterpretation on their part, a travesty of the truth to assume her to be that same socialising, careless Katherine of long ago.

Let them look and see me as I really am, she thought. A woman who has been to the bottom and is clawing her way back up. Let them see courage, guts, and a warning to stand clear and not dare to bully me or I'll blast their socks off! Greenlawns had introduced her to physical pain but had failed to destroy the intrinsic strength she held inside. Not so reckless as she once was, nor so restless, but a whole lot tougher. So let the WAAF do its worst.

It was a dull, cloudy day in the early summer of 1940 when she and Bella arrived at Bledlow, together still thanks to some crafty swopping of postings on their part. A light drizzle had started and a thick mist was blowing in from the sea.

Italy had declared war on Britain and France. Housewives were stripping their kitchens of pans to make aeroplanes. Churchill was talking of Britain's finest hour, but depression was rife and the forces were pulling in new recruits as fast as they could, even women.

'You would think they'd be glad to see us, wouldn't you? Instead of leaving us standing here like lemons,' Bella said as they staggered off the bus with their kit bags to stand uncertain and abandoned on the cinder path, wondering where they should go next.

'At least we look like WAAF girls now.'

'This tie is strangling me already.'

They'd been issued with a basic uniform at last and for all it was either five sizes too big or fitted where it touched, most of them, particularly Kath, had been glad to get it. It made them seem more professional.

There'd been much complaining, of course, and desperate swopping to try to find a near match in size. But the blue jacket and skirt for all its coarse newness, even the stiff-collared shirt that chafed her neck, seemed an infinite improvement upon the shapeless overall of Greenlawns.

A voice loud enough to lift the dome off St Paul's sounded across the parade ground. 'You two Waafs! Cut along and get signed in and stop standing about like dummies. There's a war on, you know.'

They fled through the first door ahead of them. Unfortunately it was the wrong one. A sea of blue uniforms met their eyes all right, but there were men inside them and not women. And some of the bodies didn't have uniforms of any sort on them.

'Oh, dear lordy, let's get out of here.'

'Hey, look who's come calling, chaps. Two new little darlings. Lost your way, have you? Come over here. We'll explain the drill to you.' A riot of whistles and cat calls greeted this remark, and as one the girls turned and fled, giggling madly, straight into the Waaf Officer.

'Checking out stores already, Waafs?'

Kath choked. 'Sorry, we – um – made a mistake.'

'Ma'am.'

'Ma'am.'

'And you salute an officer, Waaf, every time you see one. Didn't they teach you that at training?'

'Yes, ma'am.' Kath dropped her bag and attempted a salute. She wasn't very good at it, and Bella was even worse, looking very like a lamp post gone wrong.

'I hope the Airforce hasn't made a bigger mistake in taking you two on. If you'd care to follow me you might give us the benefit of your name and number while I have the pleasure of directing you to your quarters.'

Kath trusted the officer's soft tones even less than her official one. Dragging her kit bag behind her, Kath gabbled out rank and number and followed Bella along the cinder path.

The Waaf Officer stopped. 'Do you have a problem with your kit, Airwoman?'

Kath shook her head, glancing beseechingly at Bella. Whenever she tried to swing it up on to her shoulder she very nearly decapitated herself or else flung herself off her feet. When there was no wall to prop it on first, Bella gave her a hand to lift it.

'I didn't quite catch your reply.'

'No, I don't have a problem.'

'I think you do. *Ma'am*.'

'Oh, sorry, ma'am.' And to Kath's great mortification, the Waaf Officer stood and smilingly waited while Kath manoeuvred, with considerable difficulty, the long heavy bag into place.

'You look in need of more training to me, Airwoman.'

'It's my narrow shoulders. The thing keeps slipping off. Ma'am.' Kath attempted to explain but saw by the frosty expression she was wasting her time.

At the Guard Room they booked in and were directed to their

billet. With thoughts of hot tea and a soft bed to lay their tired bodies they reached it at a smart pace.

Yet another Nissen hut lined with beds and heated, if that was the word, by an ancient coke stove that no doubt belched out more smoke, dust and fumes than warmth, Kath thought, dropping her bag with a weary sigh. Fortunately this was summer so that was a pleasure in store for later.

Waaf Officer Mullin, or Mule as she came to be known, attempted to show a more human side to her nature. 'Get yourself unpacked. There's hot water for a bath if you're quick. Be in the Mess Hall by six.'

'Oh, blimey, this is good,' said Bella, falling prone on to her bed. The springs creaked ominously, the mattress was as hard as the iron bedstead, but she didn't care. 'This is bliss.'

'Don't get too comfortable,' Kath warned, her own eyes half closed in almost instant sleep. 'We have to be quick, remember?'

But before the delectable promise of hot water and food dragged them from their beds, an air raid warning sounded and then they moved very quickly, blindly rushing out to follow a trickling mass of people who seemed far from pleased at being interrupted, and confusingly not all going in the same direction.

'Bloomin' Hitler. I'd just got my head down.'

'Where's the shelter?' Kath asked one passing Waaf.

'Shelter? Ditch more like. We call it a slit trench. Most people only bother when it's really necessary, and if it's dry, for obvious reasons. New, are you? I'm Liz Parry.'

'Ellis. And this is Kendrick.' Kath felt quite pleased with herself for picking up the correct style. 'Does it show very much that we're new?'

'Your tie is tied all wrong for a start. It'll come loose that way. And you'll need to spend every evening polishing those buttons to get a lovely mellow shine. Then you might not look such complete rookies.'

'This tie's near choking me.'

The girl called Parry laughed and her serious face lit up. She was pretty, Kath decided, with her golden curly hair and neat figure. Reminded her a bit of Meg.

The sound of the siren was overwhelming coupled with the awesome roar of aircraft overhead which would, Kath was sure, at any moment blast them out of existence. It was the nearest she had been to danger and she was not to know they were Stirlings taking off, rather than German bombers coming in. She flung herself into the trench and landed in a huge crop of nettles. Her shouts of agony brought forth no sympathy from anyone, only laughter and ribald offers to rub her down all over with Calomine.

The All Clear sounded and nobody took any notice of that, either. She and Bella seemed to be the only two in the entire camp who had shown any concern.

During an almost sleepless night of itching, despite Bella's ministrations with the said lotion, and the fear of a bomb being accidentally dropped by the noisy aircraft that seemed to be taking off every five minutes right over their hut, Kath spent the time worrying over how ill prepared she was. She thought of the lectures she hadn't properly listened to, the drills she'd skipped. Had she missed anything vital? What could one do to make a good life for oneself in the WAAF and avoid being ridiculed by the Mules of this world?

Someone gave her a mug of tea sometime before dawn because she happened to be still awake.

'Thanks.' Kath sipped gratefully at it then set it on the shelf above her bed while she started on yet another letter describing her arrival. It was about then that she fell asleep, to be awakened by something hard smacking her forehead and a trickle of warm liquid running down her face.

'Dear God, I've been *hit*.'

'Where, where?' Bella was by her side in an instant.

'My face. Oh no, my face. I can feel the blood all over it.'

A torch was brought, shone into her face. A moment's startled silence then laughter, pure and true, from a whole gaggle of interested girls.

'You're covered in tea,' giggled Bella. 'Decorated by a splendid pattern of tea leaves.'

'It's the vibration from the returning aircraft. Sometimes nearly shakes this place to bits,' chuckled Liz Parry. 'Oh, but the expression on your face! It's the funniest thing I've seen in weeks.'

It was the final humiliation.

Kath decided she didn't much care for being new. It made her feel gauche and uncomfortable and could clearly have disastrous consequences. Nor did she care to be laughed at. Whatever she needed to learn, she would learn it. Fast.

On their way to the Mess Hall, dreaming of hot tea and bacon butties, they came again upon Waaf Officer Mullin.

'Ah, Ellis and Kendrick, sleep well on your first night, did we?'

Beguiled by the officer's smile Kath answered quite naturally. 'Yes, thanks. Bit noisy but could have been worse I suppose.'

'Oh dear, oh dear. I must have a word with the pilots and try to get them to turn the engines down. Can't have them disturbing your beauty sleep.'

Kath flushed deeply, most unlike herself.

'You weren't the little Waaf who imagined herself shot with a pot of tea, were you?' And when the flush deepened, the officer smiled with pure delight. 'What a prize you are, Ellis. How did we amuse ourselves before you came?'

Kath ground her teeth together and said nothing. She had learned patience in a hard school, so if this dreadful woman expected, or wanted her to retaliate and humiliate herself further, she had mistaken her mark.

Bella was ordered to report to Signals after breakfast.

'And you can take yourself off to the drivers' unit.'

'But I was to be on the switchboard.'

Mullin looked at her as if she were something unpleasant upon the drawing-room carpet. 'Not questioning the service are you, Air-woman?'

'No, ma'am. It's only that I understood we could choose our own trades.'

'So you can, as a rule.' The tone was dangerously sweet. 'It happens that we find ourselves short of drivers at present and you, I see from your form, were one of the fortunate few civilians who could afford a motor. Now isn't that splendid? How useful you are going to be to us, Ellis.'

'Yes, ma'am.' Kath saluted and was at once reprimanded.

'*No saluting unless you are wearing a cap.*'

'No, ma'am.' Oh lordy, would she ever get used to this? Kath wondered, poignantly, how she could have come to mess up her life so thoroughly. She could be at home now, at Larkrigg, helping her mother do something suitable like holding fund-raising tea parties for the soldiers or perhaps a little light volunteer work at the local hospital. Except that her mother had disowned her because of her carelessness in daring to bring an unwanted, unsuitable child into the world.

'Have you done your morning chores?'

'Um.' Kath glanced at Bella despairingly, not knowing quite what chores Mullin referred to. 'Ma'am?'

Mullin sighed, looking delighted at finding this new recruit wanting yet again. 'Before you report in, you can sweep out your billet and give the floor a good scrub.'

'What, all of it?'

Mullin smiled. She'd had this type of girl foisted upon her before. A classy little madam who thought she was easing her social conscience by volunteering and then wasted all their time by asking too many questions, thinking herself above discipline. She probably didn't know one end of a sweeping brush from the other.

'Yes, Ellis, all of it. Think you can manage that, do you? Concentrates the mind wonderfully, scrubbing, don't you think?'

Kath bit hard upon her lower lip. 'Yes, ma'am.'

'Best get on with it then. A delightful new experience for you to try.'

'Oh, but . . .'

'But?'

Kath pushed the thought of breakfast regretfully from her mind. 'Yes, ma'am.'

'Certainly, ma'am. At once, ma'am,' cut in Bella, smartly.

And the two of them returned bleakly to the Nissen hut. Worse, Mullin followed, and while Bella swept, she watched with obvious pleasure as Kath filled a bucket with hot water and added a good handful of soda crystals.

'More, Ellis. We want the floor clean, don't we, not a murky mess?'

Kath added more, a vicious cocktail that would make any fair hand bleed. Except hands like hers, which were hard as leather after the Greenlawns' laundry.

She plunged them into the scalding water without a flinch, lifted out the brush and began to scrub. Her arms and shoulders moved with a long practised rhythm, and using a separate, well-wrung out cloth, Kath swiftly and efficiently mopped up the excess water leaving not a streak upon the polished floor.

It took no more than a moment or two watching this process for Mullin to frown in puzzled surprise. It was all too apparent, to her experienced eye, that Ellis had done this job before. Odd. She would never have thought it.

'Surprised your mama didn't have a housemaid to do this job for you, Ellis.'

Kath hid a smile. 'No, ma'am.'

Irritated, Mullin snapped her fingers. 'Jump to it then. Remember

Parade is at 8.45. Prompt. And since you are so skilled at the task, you can scrub out Picquet Post as well. And don't forget the outside lobby. Call me when you're done, then I can check it. Jump to it, Airwoman, jump to it.'

'Great,' said Bella with resignation when the Waaf Officer had gone. 'Next time you're asked to do something, make a bad job of it, will you? We can kiss goodbye to any breakfast after all this lot.'

'Sorry.'

'I'll forgive you, thousands wouldn't.'

Driving was a doddle after that, Kath decided. She was issued with a staff car and instructed to drive one of the Commanders to another station. The mist had lifted and the sun was shining. Liz Parry managed to sneak her out a bacon buttie, which quite perked her up.

Besides, she was young and filled with optimism at having escaped from Greenlawns, thanks to Meg. And a mug of tea would be waiting for her when she got back from this run, which would go down a treat.

So taking everything into account, life wasn't at all bad. Were it not for the awful guilt and loneliness she felt inside at betraying her best friend and abandoning her daughter.

1941

22

In a summer with a late spring, a dry June and an indifferent July, a few days' sunshine to dry up the land and the fleeces on the sheep were all the farmers had needed to set the clipping off. The early-morning mists had lifted like a fair woman's feather hat to reveal sunshine and beauty beneath. Satisfied the dry spell would continue for the two or three days necessary, the Turners of Ashlea, the Davieses and Meg, had gathered, ready to visit each farm in turn to shear the sheep.

The sheep had been brought down from the heaf, a jostling throng, growing ever larger as flocks joined on from neighbouring heafs. And Meg had counted every one of hers as they passed through her gate, to make sure they were all safe and well.

'Yan, tyan, tethera, methera, pimp,' she had chanted, enjoying the sound of the old celtic words as she'd sat on the gate, marking off each five on a slate in her hand. And as she counted, she felt as if they were bombers bringing Charlie safely home from a raid.

Whatever satisfaction it had given her to see how her flock had grown, near two hundred and fifty now, not for a moment did she underestimate her good fortune. While London had been battered, almost daily in recent months, here on the Westmorland hills the sun shone, the sheep bleated and all seemed to be perfectly normal. No blitz for them.

'You'd never think there was a war on, would you?' said Sally Ann, coming up beside her and uncannily catching her thoughts.

'We realise it when we listen to the drone of bombers in the sky and hear the vibration deep through the ground as some other poor soul is getting it,' said Will Davies, not pausing in his labours as he started on the next sheep. Sitting astride his special stool, in a row with the other clippers, he turned the ewe belly up, the head tucked beneath his arm while he cut the fleece, not too close and with no pulling of the flesh which might form ridges, till the wriggling sheep was released, looking oddly naked and highly affronted by the indignity of it all.

'Or when we have to queue an hour and a half for a paltry few ounces of margerine, or barter precious eggs for extra sugar to make jam. And I can't remember the last time I saw an orange or a tin of fruit,' Sally Ann mourned.

'Trying to get a can of paraffin for the lamp the other day was like asking for gold,' Meg agreed. 'I'd love to try that,' she said, her mind clearly still on the clipping.

'Aye, I dare say you would. The sheep mightn't be too keen,' laughed Will, and Meg conceded that although the farmers accepted her as one of their own, shearing was a skilled task. Their confidence in her had not quite reached that level. Watching Will peel the fleece from the neck down each side, then as the sheep was flipped over, off the back like a banana skin, she didn't wonder at it.

She stood ready with her stick with the rounded end to dab her mark on the back of the clipped sheep. Rust red for Broombank sheep, so that if one ever wandered too far another farmer could check it, together with the ear mark, in his Shepherd's Guide and know to which farm it belonged. Come the autumn meet, wanderers could be returned to their rightful owners.

Sally Ann moved out of the way while Meg deftly brought another ewe to the clipper, who never left his stool. Six or seven minutes for each sheep, though some could manage one in less if it didn't kick about.

'I heard the other day that Miss Shaw has had a telegram about her nephew.' All hands paused as eyes, bleak and questioning, were raised to Sally Ann's flushed face.

'Eeh, no. He was nobbut a lad.'

'Lost at sea. Missing, presumed dead, it said.'

After a long silent moment while hands were stilled and thoughts turned to that bright-faced boy who a few summers ago might have been chided by these same farmers for some youthful misdemeanour, shears started to clip again, long breaths exhaled. Life moved on.

A chill ran through Meg and she rubbed her hands together, sore from holding and turning the sheep, greasy with the lanolin from the wool. Think positive, that was the secret. Charlie said so.

'On Charlie's last leave he was like a dog with two tails. Talk, talk, talk about his dratted aeroplanes and how he'd been promoted to navigator. I told him that I wished they'd promote him safely home again. Call the whole war off as a terrible mistake.'

An impossible dream. It was just that she couldn't bear to think of him in those terrible raids over Germany and France, and prayed each night as she added a few lines to the regular letters she sent him, that he would survive the next, and the next.

And where was Jack? She hadn't heard from him in an age. His letters were becoming more and more rare.

'The war will run its course,' Will said, with a farmer's natural pragmatism. 'And nothing you can do will alter that. Work hard and keep faith.'

'I try to,' Meg agreed. It was easier to do the former than the latter. Charlie was no longer a boy and Tam often told her she worried too much over him.

But then she too was a different Meg to the young girl of four summers ago. This Meg was tougher, quieter and more thoughtful. If she didn't laugh or feel ready to give her love quite so recklessly as that other girl had done, then she at least felt more sure of herself, more certain of where she was going. At least now she had control over her own destiny, her own future. She had Broombank and her sheep, Effie, Tam and her family about her. She was happy in her work, doing her bit to produce good food for a war-torn country. This was the nearest she would probably ever get to peace of mind.

Meg wished that everyone could be so blessed.

Seeing the suspicion of tears in her eyes, Sally Ann stepped close. 'You look tired. I'll do that for a while.' She took the marker stick from Meg's hand. 'Go and rest. Effie says she's put the kettle on.'

She eased her back. 'I won't say no.'

'I reckon Will wouldn't mind a break either, would you, Will?'

'I'll do a few more, then your Dan can take over for a bit.'

Meg smiled at Sally Ann. 'You want me to watch the children at the same time?'

'No, you don't have to worry about them. Hetty has them all in hand. At least as far as they will allow her to. For such small bairns they're as wick as fleas. They run rings round her sometimes.'

Will laughed. 'And doesn't she just love it?'

Sally Ann's gaze drifted lovingly over to the far meadow where her two children sat with the kindly Mrs Davies in the long grass, a small

273

group of curious cows nosing about around them. Young Daniel, the baby, was lying on a blanket, kicking at the delicious joy and freedom of having sun on his chubby legs. Nicholas was curbing his more natural, boundless energy to studiously attempt to thread a daisy stem through the slit Hetty had made with her thumb nail, to form a daisy chain. At thirteen months old, he was a sturdy, well-formed little boy, round-faced and bright-eyed, golden hair shining in the sun. Sally Ann loved him so much in that moment, her heart ached.

And beside him, quieter and far more serious than her companions, Lissa attempted to do the same. Three months older than Nick, yet she copied his every action.

'Sometimes I worry over that child, she's too quiet by half.' Sally Ann spoke before she'd thought to guard her words.

Meg frowned, her eyes resting quietly on Melissa, pretty as a picture in the flower meadow. 'I hadn't really thought about it. I just take it for granted that she's not a chatterbox like your Nick, nor half so naughty. She's so small and delicate, like a little fairy, and no trouble at all.'

'Perhaps a bit too good, don't you think?'

Meg laughed. 'What would you have me do? Tell her to be noisy and rough?'

'I suppose it does sound a bit silly, but somehow it isn't quite natural for a child to be so – so obliging, so mature. I'm sure she understands every word I say. She's far more intelligent than our Nick.' Sally Ann laughed. 'Not that that would be difficult.'

It was a conversation that came to mind that evening as Meg asked Effie to put the child to bed.

'Will you see to her? I can't spare the time from the shearing,' she explained, eating a sandwich on the hoof to keep her going. There would be food for all later, though not eaten in the barn as they would have done before the war, with a fiddle and the lamps all burning.

Instead, all the workers would crowd into the kitchen, everyone having contributed something, due to the difficulties of rationing. Chicken soup thickened with potato flour, stewed apples sweetened with dried figs. But they were lucky here on the farm, having their own butter and eggs. And Ashlea had provided some ham.

Meg bent down and dropped a kiss on the child's soft curls. 'Sorry, darling, but Meg is busy tonight.' A shaft of guilt pierced her heart. How often she had said those words? Too often, perhaps, in recent months.

Lissa said nothing. She merely wrapped her arms about Meg's leg for a moment till she had won another kiss, then went, happily enough, Meg was sure of it, with Effie, up to bed.

She watched a moment longer as the child climbed the stairs on all fours, one step at a time. She did love her, oh, she did. However much she might try to deny it, it was there, a living presence in her breast. Sometimes it was hard to appreciate that Lissa wasn't her child at all. In all these long months, more than a year now, there had been no word from Kath. But Meg still remembered that last day, in every tiny detail.

There had been times when she'd thought the pain would never go away.

For months afterwards she'd been in a sort of panic, as if she wanted to run away but there was nowhere to run. Jack had cheated on her, and with her best friend. So she had turned her face away from the child which provided, all too clearly, the evidence of that betrayal. She had seen that Lissa was fed and well cared for, but mainly by Effie, while Meg had tortured her mind with questions. What had she done wrong? Why hadn't she been enough for him? Hadn't he loved her at all? Questions to which there were no answers.

In time, assisted by Tam, and Effie, and of course the unstoppable Rust, Meg had painstakingly put her life back together again. But deep inside, largely unacknowledged, there still burned a resentment, a fear. She still held herself back from Lissa, not touching her, scarcely speaking to the child sometimes, afraid to show love.

Tam came in, interrupting her thoughts for which she was thankful. She was busy scribbling on a sheet of paper at the table.

'Not writing him another letter?' There was a mocking tone to his voice that made her hackles rise.

'If you mean Jack, yes, I am as a matter of fact.' She tilted her chin at him, eyes flashing the message that it was none of his business what she did.

Tam snorted and went to pour himself tea. 'Must be months since he replied to any. Why do you bother?'

It had seemed too cruel to continue to hate Jack for some youthful misdemeanour carried out one hot, lazy summer when they had all been silly and young. She had done her best not to condemn, written to him every week, telling about the farm and Effie learning to read, Dan getting to be quite full of himself as a contented married man, working for the Government War Committee. Always happy things. 'A man deserves cheerful letters when he's fighting a war. This is not the time for recriminations.'

'Why you still feel this loyalty towards that eejit, I can't sort out.'

'Well, there it is, I do.' But what else could she feel? For whether Jack knew it or not, he was still Lissa's father. All their lives were still inextricably linked.

Tam sipped his tea quietly while he gazed at her with steady eyes, reading her thoughts with uncanny precision. From above came the sounds of a child's voice, objecting to being put to bed. 'Did you ever tell him about Lissa?'

'No.'

'You don't think he has a right? What if he were to be killed, or captured. He'd never know then, would he?'

Meg swallowed the hard lump of guilt that came to her throat. 'It's Kath's job to tell him, not mine.'

'But Kath isn't here. We've no notion where she is. And the child needs a parent. Isn't it a bit hard on her, not to be knowing who they are?'

'She has us. She's too young to understand.' Would Kath take Lissa back when the war was over? She would have the right to if she so wished. Kath was the child's mother after all. Meg's stomach clenched, as it always did, at this thought. How would she cope with losing Lissa? How did you prepare yourself for fresh pain? However much she tried to avoid it she knew it would be there. Work was her release, her protection, and she must keep her mind firmly upon her plans for Broombank.

She wanted to go to her now, soothe the tears away. But better not. Leave Lissa to Effie.

She set the letter behind the clock on the dresser. She would finish it later. 'I have to get back to the sheep.'

'Can't you hear her crying?' It was always Tam, if Effie was busy or failing to cope as now, who comforted Lissa and put her to bed. He'd seemed happy enough about that as he missed his own large family back in America. Now he was frowning, almost glaring at her, sounding fierce and uncharacteristically tough. 'She wants *you*.' Meg took no notice.

'Be quick with that tea,' she said. 'You know we can't work after dark with the black-out.'

The child's piercing cries caused her to flinch but she set her mouth firm as she pulled open the door and went back to the sheep, her heart beating twenty to the dozen. *Lissa was not her child.*

276

* * *

Kath decided quite early on that Parade was a horror she could live without. In those first few weeks at Bledlow, she soon discovered that you were excused Parade if on duty. After that she usually managed to avoid it by being hard at work polishing her vehicle so early that she was often picked out to drive the top brass somewhere or other.

Kath found that she loved her job and was almost grateful to Waaf Officer Mullin for denying her the opportunity to become a telephonist. Driving about the countryside was much more fun.

She and Bella became great friends, often cycling into Bledlow itself for a drink at the pub, or visiting the Flicks, as they called the local cinema. And then there were regular dances at the station with no shortage of partners.

There were days when no one could manage to be cheerful, when yet another crew of smiling faces had vanished, or a plane had crashed on landing. Or, as once happened, a whole ground crew were blown to smithereens while trying to unload unused bombs.

But one way or another, despite the awfulness of the war, the weeks and months slipped by.

Mule continued to watch Kath, as stubbornly determined as her name to find fault.

'What have I done to offend that woman?' Kath asked Bella. 'She never misses an opportunity to put me down.'

'That's what should have happened to her, when she was a pup,' grinned Bella. 'Aw, take no notice. It's all jealousy because you're eye-catching and come from a comfortable home, and she certainly can't lay claim to the former and possibly not the latter either.'

'Not everything is as it appears,' Kath said, a touch of asperity in her voice.

Bella's eyebrows lifted slightly but she said nothing. Aware that her new friend never spoke about her personal affairs, she had asked no questions, seen no reason to pry. 'Chin up. Don't let the bugger get to you.'

Kath's diligence became a habit and after a while she got promoted to Aircraftwoman 1st Class. She bought the drinks that night.

'Even Mule can't stop me now. Maybe I'll be giving her orders one day.' Kath had a determination never to be in a vulnerable state again. It was a new experience for her not to be in charge of her own destiny. But ever since she had left Larkrigg, that's the way her life had been. She meant one day to change it.

'Don't tempt fate,' Bella warned, being overly superstitious.

277

Then one morning Kath's efforts came to be noticed by a newcomer to the station – one keen-eyed Canadian, Ewan Wadeson, Wade to his friends, of whom there were many for he was known for his ready wit and generosity. He had groaned when first learning there were Waafs on this, his latest posting, but having seen the line up of drivers, was beginning to change his mind.

It was Kath's swinging walk that first attracted him. A certain swivel to the hip which he found most interesting. And when she hitched up her skirt to get into the driving seat, his blood pressure almost peaked.

'Boy, oh boy, what legs.'

Fraternising, or fratting as it was called, with other ranks was of course quite out of order. A hanging offence, almost. But Wade had always been one to take chances. The secret was not to get caught. He meant to get to know this new little sweetheart or his name wasn't Ewan Maximillian Wadeson III.

He made a point of being at the depot by eight o'clock prompt the following morning.

'Driver? Are you taken?'

Kath glanced up to find herself appraised by the most outrageously sensual blue eyes she had ever encountered. Several pips decorating the impressively broad shoulders brought her to attention. And her salute proved the value of hours of practice.

'I need a driver today. Got several meetings to attend.' It wasn't strictly true, but in the Airforce, he'd discovered, you could walk around all day with a clipboard in your hand and no one would bother you.

He climbed into the back seat of the car.

'Where to, sir?' Kath enquired when they had been checked out of the station and were bowling down the road.

Wing Commander Ewan Wadeson was engrossed with trying to decide the colour of her eyes through the driving mirror. Green? Brown? Or somewhere in between.

He cleared his throat. His day was largely free since he was not on duty till the evening. But if anyone ever discovered that he had pinched a staff car, complete with Waaf driver for his pleasure for the day he'd really be up for the high jump. Best to make it look genuine to stop any loose talk.

'Take me to Remlington-on-Sea. I have to speak to my opposite number there.'

Kath did so, and to the next airfield after that. She drove, in fact, from airfield to airfield all morning and well into the afternoon, getting in and out of the car so many times she was quite dizzy with it all, and light-headed from want of food. While Ewan Maximillian Wadeson had a smashing view of those lovely legs each and every time.

'I'll be about a half hour,' he told her on one occasion. And taking a chance, as soon as he had disappeared from view she locked up the car and went in search of food.

She was nibbling her way through a limp sandwich when she decided to step on to a weighing machine. It stood at the door of an amusement arcade and was the kind that told your fortune as well as your weight. Might as well know what she was in for. But before she had time to open her purse a hand had slipped a coin into the slot and a voice spoke in her ear.

'Ain't nothing wrong with your figure, ACW Ellis.'

Kath jumped, dropping the unfinished sandwich.

'Aw, gee, now see what I've made you do. Were you hungry? I didn't realise. Look, why don't I go and get us some real food? Er, you'd best wait in the car.'

'No, no, I'm fine. Are you done now? Do you want me to take you back, sir?' Kath knew only too well what trouble they'd be in if anyone saw them talking like this.

'You go to the car, Ellis. I'll be along shortly.'

'Yes, sir.' She didn't need telling again.

Kath had parked the car, as instructed, on a headland looking out to sea. Wing Commander Ewan Wadeson was sitting beside her in the front seat and the pair of them were eating fish and chips out of newspaper. Sinful, but nothing had ever tasted so good in all her life.

'Do you mind if I ask you a question, sir?' He seemed the approachable sort. Not like some of the stuffed shirts around. Probably because he was a Canadian, Kath decided.

'Sure, fire away.'

'If one wanted to find out what had happened to someone, a friend say, how would one go about it?'

'One would write to the Red Cross,' he teased, mimicking her accent. 'Boy friend, is it? Missing in action?' The tone was sympathetic and Kath warmed to him. He was also, she had not failed to notice, a very attractive man.

'N-no, not a boy friend exactly. And so far as I'm aware he isn't missing. He's in the navy but I don't know where he's stationed.'

279

Wade moved closer. She had offered him just the loophole he needed to get to know her better. Never miss an opportunity, that was old Wade's motto.

'Not got a boy friend then?'

Kath hid a smile. 'Not at the moment, no. And you?' she ventured, with a flash of her old recklessness.

Straight-faced he replied. 'No, I haven't got a boy friend either.'

Kath rolled her eyes. 'You know what I mean.'

He chuckled. 'The answer's still no. Tell me his name, this guy you're interested in. I'll find out for you.'

'You're very kind.' Kath rewarded him with the full warmth of her hazel eyes. The gaze held overlong as chemistry crackled between them, and after a stunned moment, Wade smiled an acknowledgement of it.

'You're some woman. You know that?'

She knew the dangers. She knew he was an officer. Out of bounds. Against King's Regulations. As were most things, Kath decided, that were anything like fun. But to Katherine Ellis he was just a man, a rather fine-looking man: light brown hair, blue eyes, good teeth and a smile to melt your heart. But she was finished with men, wasn't she? 'Some might disagree with you,' she said, very gravely.

'Then they must be blind. This guy, I hate him already, what is he to you?' Wade slipped one arm along the back of the car seat. Drat this war and the rules it created.

'I told you, he's a friend. Well, engaged to my best friend, in point of fact. Or was.'

'You sound doubtful. Is she about to chuck him?' He longed suddenly to stretch out his fingers and caress the bare neck just inches away. This Waaf's hairstyle might be as short as any man's, but she was all female, no doubt about that.

Kath was staring out to sea, wishing she'd never started this dangerous conversation. 'I'm not sure. It's all a bit confusing. He's called Jack Lawson, from Broombank in Westmorland. I'd be grateful for any information about him.' She turned her beautiful eyes back upon Wade. 'For the sake of my friend.'

'Sure,' he said, heart starting to thump with an excitement he hadn't felt in a long time. 'I'll look into it.'

A small silence fell between them while each seemed to study the other, assessing, considering, liking what they saw. 'I suppose we'd best be getting back,' Kath managed at last.

'I suppose.'

'I'll deal with these. Wouldn't do for your image to be seen with chip papers.'

'It would do my image wonders to be seen with you.'

Kath's breath caught in her throat. 'You don't mess about, do you?'

'Not as a rule, no.'

'It would get me lynched.'

'I know. Me too. That's the pity of it. Damn' war.'

Kath stared out to sea again. 'Best not to think of it then.'

'Reckon you're right.' His voice sounded far from convinced. 'Wouldn't do for folks to start thinking things.'

'No, sir.' Kath could feel the warmth and weight of his arm across her shoulder. It was pleasant. She'd forgotten how good a man could make you feel.

'You know it's as if I've known you for an age, not just one day. Tell me your first name, ACW Ellis.'

'Katherine. My friends call me Kath.'

'Aw, I like Katherine best. That's a beautiful name. May I call you Katherine?'

'My mother calls me that.'

'Would it bother you then?' He saw the shadow cross her face, fleeting but not imagined, he was sure of it. 'Okay, Kath it is.'

'Thanks. Are you ready to go back to camp now, sir?'

'Don't be so formal, okay?' Wade climbed reluctantly out of the car and got into the back seat. He adjusted his hat. 'Back to camp, Airwoman.'

And when she dropped him at the Officers' Mess he nodded briskly to her, the smile gone from his eyes, completely professional. 'I'll be in touch about that matter, Airwoman.' And he walked briskly away.

Kath stood holding the car door, at her very best salute. 'Yes, sir. Thank you, sir.'

'You drove *who*?' Bella's eyes were popping. 'Wow. He's a real dreamboat. Aren't you the lucky one. And here's me with my ears glued to signals all day. I'm ferociously jealous.'

Kath laughed. 'Don't be. He's an officer. A very grand officer, therefore untouchable. What are we doing tonight?'

Bella wrinkled her nose. 'Cedric has suggested a foursome.'

'You mean Jimmy is mine?'

Bella grinned. 'Thought you'd be pleased.'

'I suppose it's better than staying in.'

'Won't argue with that.'

They huddled over the tiny mirror to get ready, fluffing out hair, sharing out what bits of make-up they possessed. Certain items were becoming hard to find, lipstick for one.

'I'm sick of this uniform,' Kath said. 'Somehow it seems worse in summer.' And met Bella's enquiring gaze.

'So?'

Flagrantly breaking rules, they slipped summer frocks on under their skirts and jackets, and with non-issue shoes tucked in to their greatcoat pockets Kath and Bella set off for an evening out.

They walked to the local hostelry since none of the four possessed the transport to try out distant, more exciting places, despite the obvious risks involved. But Kath soon decided that dressing up had been a bad mistake for she spent the entire evening fending off Jimmy in a corner.

It grew hot in the pub and she suggested they all go outside. Which proved to be a yet worse mistake, she soon realised.

'Good evening, Katherine.'

Kath froze, turning slowly to find Wing Commander Ewan Wadeson gazing at her with open speculation. 'It sure is a hot night,' he said, eyes running over her figure in its silky dress, right down her bare tanned legs to her pretty summer shoes. 'Wouldn't you say?'

She was aware of the others standing fearfully behind her. If this man chose to, he could march them straight to the Guard House, forthwith, on a charge. 'Yes,' she said, smiling warmly, deliberately avoiding the use of the word 'sir'.

His smile tilted the wide mouth to a sensuous curl and Kath responded similarly. He wasn't going to report them, she could see it in his eyes. But he might want paying for the favour, later.

23

When they came off Parade Bella nudged Kath rather painfully in the ribs. 'There he is. Glamour Boy is waiting for you already. He'll complain about your being late. I can see why Jimmy doesn't come up to scratch these days.'

'If you want to survive this war, today even, you'd best watch your tongue, Bella Kendrick,' said Kath sweetly.

Bella grinned. 'He sounds pretty smitten to me. Why else would he have you drive him all over the countryside for no apparent reason?'

'Perhaps it's some sort of secret ops he's on, or a survey or something? Not my job to question why.'

'Only to do or die, I know.' Bella strode off, laughing.

Later that day when Bella came off shift, she went straight from the Signals Room to the vehicle depot to find Kath changing a wheel. Maintenance, Kath had discovered, was an essential part of the job if you weren't to spend your life begging favours from the sparks, armourers and ground crew.

'Kath, Kath!' Bella bent down and yanked her friend out from under the car. 'Listen to this. Mule fancies your officer.'

'What?'

'Old Mule. She's got the hots for Wing Commander Wadeson. I heard them talking in the Ops Room. She was telling him that she had two tickets for a symphony in Cambridge and was he fond of music?'

Kath knew she shouldn't ask but did anyway. 'And is he?'

Bella's grin stretched from ear to ear. 'I was pretending to be engrossed taking signals but really I was listening like mad. "Thanks for asking me", he says. "It was a kind thought. But really it would be wasted on me. I'm deaf as a post where classical music is concerned. Jazz is more my scene. Besides which my schedule's pretty full at the moment. Thanks for thinking of me." And smiling charmingly at her, he touched his cap and walked off. Boy, was she mad! She went turkey red.'

For no reason that she wished to examine, Kath felt suddenly light-hearted and anxious all at the same time. 'It's probably true, his schedule will be pretty full.'

'Not so full he hasn't time for women.'

Kath concentrated on tightening the wheel nuts. 'Admittedly, there isn't a soul on this camp wouldn't grab a date with him. But he's not *my* officer, so I'd appreciate it if you didn't say as much to anyone else.'

'Wouldn't dream of it, old sport. But I'd watch her if I were you, at least if I had any passing interest at all in the gentleman.' Bella stood up. 'Fortunately, as you say, you've given men up so it doesn't matter. See you later.'

Kath laid out her kit on the bed, ready for inspection. Next to Parade it was her pet hate to have her gear prodded and peered at. She felt that by nature she was not meant to be a tidy person, especially if she'd been up late the night before driving the top brass back from some meeting or other. Life was too short to waste in polishing and cleaning.

Nevertheless it was a boring but essential part of the daily routine.

The Waafery was rigorously guarded and inspected by Waaf Officer Mullin, General Duties, who loved to stalk the length of the Nissen hut, mule face grinning with ecstatic anticipation of discovering some minor misdemeanour.

Mullin insisted that quarters must be kept immaculately tidy at all times. Even shift workers sleeping during the day were frowned upon and liable to have their beds remade while they were still in them.

'Is this your clutter, Ellis?' she would ask, and Kath would smile and attempt to explain about being late which meant that she hadn't had a moment to clean her shoes or buttons or do a *thing*.

'That is no excuse,' was nearly always the reply.

For some reason she was never afterwards able to justify, this morning Kath decided to answer back. 'I had to drive the Wing Commander out to dinner last night. It was near two when I got in. How could I possibly clean my kit in time?'

The lips thinned dangerously. 'You must *make* the time. I suggest you miss breakfast for the rest of this week in order to rectify these deficiencies.'

'But, ma'am . . .'

'You wish to say something, Airwoman?'

'No, ma'am.' Drat her runaway tongue.

Against King's Regulations or not, Wing Commander Wadeson had taken every opportunity to deepen their friendship over these last weeks by constantly employing Kath's services as a driver. Their regular weekly jaunts into the countryside had become an important part of her life. And he no longer made any pretext of visiting other stations. Instead she would be instructed to drive straight to the headland or they'd walk by the dyke or drive to the woods and talk.

He was there, as usual on this his morning off, grin on his face, hat not quite at regulation angle.

'Hi.'

'Good morning, sir.' Kath saluted. She never risked slipping from formality while in camp. 'May I be of service?'

Ewan Wadeson rolled his eyes. 'Aw, don't tempt me, honey. I'm sure we can find somewhere I ought to be for all I'm off duty.' Then just as he was about to climb into the back of the car, Waaf Officer Mullin came up.

'Ah, I'm glad I caught you, Wing Commander.' She half glanced at Kath, saluting like mad as she stood holding open the car door for her passenger. Mule drew Wadeson some distance away while Kath kept her eyes firmly fixed on the distant hangars where the ground crew were busy at work checking over Stirlings in readiness for the next night's operation. But she longed to know what was being said. She also couldn't help wondering if it would likewise be out of bounds for a Waaf Officer and a Wing Commander to get too friendly. She didn't know, told herself she shouldn't care. And realised that she did.

'Okay, let's go.' He was beside her and with a start Kath saluted again and closed the door neatly behind him before briskly going round to climb into the driving seat. WAAF Officer Mullin watched her drive away.

'You can take a car whenever you like, sir?' she asked as they drove towards the coast. The question was very near to impertinent. Kath heard him chuckle.

'Damn' right, I can.' He leaned his elbows on the back of her seat. 'You know, if things were normal, I'd ask you out on a date, maybe take you to a movie.'

She caught his eyes in the driving mirror and for a moment became disorientated before forcing her attention back to the road. 'But things are far from normal. Sir.'

'Lot of old gossips round this camp, just love to massacre a guy. Your Waaf Officer, for one, seems concerned about my keeping you out too late. Seems to think I should spread my charms a bit more. Use other drivers.'

Kath's face remained impassive. 'The fault was mine, sir. I used the late night as an excuse, when really I'd simply forgotten to clean my kit.' She flickered her eyelashes outrageously at him. It was worth a try. This man could cause her a lot of trouble if he wished. 'I'm sorry, sir. It won't happen again.'

He stared at her for a moment then put back his head and roared with laughter.

'I bet you gals lead her a merry dance.'

'I'm sure that's true,' Kath agreed, with false demureness. She caught a glimpse of the eyes again, sparkling at her, challenging, and unable to help herself Kath found her own lips curving into a smile.

'That's better. I hate it when you look too serious. There's a sadness to your face, do you know that, Katherine? And there shouldn't be for it sure looks cute when you smile.'

Later, as they walked in a quiet spot of woodland, he told her that he had news of Jack.

'That friend of yours. She should write to Portsmouth. Jack Lawson is on *HMS Bramton*. Reckon it will be leaving port soon so she shouldn't waste too much time about it.'

'Oh, thank you. That was kind of you, sir.' Kath's eyes were stinging, though whether from pleasure or pain, she wasn't too sure.

'You're looking sad again.'

'Sorry.' She hadn't decided quite why she must contact Jack, or what she would say to him when she did, but was grateful for the opportunity. 'I do appreciate your help.'

He picked up her hand and kissed the finger tips. 'You're a real fine gal. I wouldn't mind getting to know you a whole lot better.'

Kath removed her hand and clasped it behind her back. 'What part of Canada do you come from, Wade?' Formality had no place when they were alone.

'My folks live in Montreal. What about yours? You've told me so little about yourself.'

'There's little to tell. My father is a retired doctor. Mummy looks after him when she can spare time from her garden and her good works.' There was a certain edge to her voice which Wade was not fool enough to miss.

'How does your family feel about your being in uniform, Katherine? Not prejudiced against it, I hope.'

She smiled. Not knowing how best to answer she decided not to. Best to keep the conversation away from herself. 'What did you do in civvy street? Before the war.'

'Would you believe a lawyer? My father has his own practice in Montreal. I went in with him. It was expected, you know?'

Kath nodded sympathetically. 'I can imagine.'

'But what I'd really like is to be a farmer, or a rancher. That would be great.'

'A farmer?' Kath laughed, a short, rather bitter laugh that this time Wade didn't pay proper attention to.

'I know. It's a crazy idea. But I just love the countryside. I like physical things, being outside. I'd just love it.'

'Farming is hard work, long hours and badly paid. Stick to the law.'

'You sound like you know something about it.'

'A little. We have a few acres of our own which are more trouble than they are worth. And my friends are all farmers.' She wrinkled her nose. 'Don't do it, Wade.'

He was watching her keenly. 'I know what I want to do right now.'

'Oh?' He took her by the elbow and drew her to him. 'Oh, I see. Um, look, I don't think this is a good idea, do you?'

'Best one I've had in a long while. I've held off pretty well, don't you think? I really like you, Katherine – Kath. You're a lovely gal. I'd love to see you again. Properly, I mean, not driving this damn' car.'

She relaxed slightly as she saw that he wasn't about to ravish her in the undergrowth. Ewan Wadeson was a gentleman, a real old-fashioned sort. But in a more comfortable setting it might be a different story. And then where would she be? 'That would have been good, if, as you say, things had been normal.'

His eyes were burning into hers and one thumb was smoothing the inside of her elbow. The sensation of it, even through her jacket sleeve was euphoric, making her feel slightly giddy. 'No one need know. What the eye don't see, the heart don't bleed over. Ain't that one of your sayings?'

'I believe so.'

'I can't keep hijacking you this way, but we could sneak off some place. If we're clever. It's done all the time. I really like you, Katherine, you're my sort of girl.'

'And if we got caught?' In more ways than one, she thought bleakly.

His arms were right about her now, caressing her spine, her hips, pressing her close to him, the hard strength of him intoxicating. He was very tempting. 'The secret is, not to,' he said. His lips came down gently to claim hers and Kath made no protest. One kiss surely didn't matter. Lifting her arms about his neck, she gave herself up to the ecstasy of it.

Kath stood at the dock gates, a letter in her hands. She'd been due a few days' leave and had written to Jack to tell him she was coming over to see him.

He'd replied at once, a cheerful Jack-type letter saying he'd be delighted to see her. Now she was actually here, she was riddled with a thousand doubts. What should she say to him? She hadn't even devised any plan of action. Should she mention Melissa?

And then there was the all important question of what she would feel when she saw him again.

Jack Lawson had been a dear friend and great fun, though not to be taken too seriously. But Kath had to admit that there had been a time when, if he'd asked her, she'd have married him like a shot. To hell with Meg and the obvious disapproval of her parents. And not just for the sake of the baby either. Jack Lawson had that certain something to attract any girl, call it charisma, sex appeal, whatever, but Kath was curious to know if he still had it, and if it would still affect her.

Would Jack be the answer to her long-term problems?

'Kath, there you are, I didn't recognise you in uniform. Hey, you look great.'

A sailor stood before her, bronzed, handsome, hair shorter than she remembered but the same violet eyes wickedly teasing, the same tilt to the wide mouth she'd once been so eager to kiss. Hands were stretched towards her and she grasped them. The next moment she was in his arms, laughing, crying, the smell and feel of him bringing a rush of sweet memories.

'How tall you are. Have you grown?' she laughed.

'It's the cut my tailor gives this outfit. Smart, don't you think?'

'Wonderful. Who presses those creases in all the wrong way?'

'Me, who else?'

He hugged her close. He smelled salty, and as if he spent a lot of time polishing and scrubbing. 'It's so good to see someone from home, you wouldn't believe how homesick I was at first. Stupid when you think how we longed to get away to new adventures, both of us. We were just kids though, eh?'

Kath laughed, feeling oddly numb inside. Her mind racing on, wondering what she should say, how much she should tell. He was a man now, not a boy, and so much more sure of himself. 'We did escape in the end though.' He had walked away, she had run.

They started to walk now, arms linked, along the dock road. 'You're not homesick now, I trust?' she asked.

'Hell, no. We're off to foreign parts again soon. All a bit hush hush but the word is it's Italy. We'll soon polish the Italians off. Looking forward to it as a matter of fact. I prefer it at sea. Come on, I'll buy you a G and T, or whatever your tipple is these days.'

'A half of cider will do fine.'

'A half it is then.'

Tucked into a corner of the local pub, Kath returned to the subject close to her heart. 'Will you get leave, before you go?'

'Probably.'

'And go home, do you think?'

He met her gaze. 'To see Meg, you mean?'

'I suppose I do.'

Jack frowned. 'I ought to but ... well, it's a long way, Westmorland, just for a few days.'

A shaft of sudden irritation pierced her. 'You're as selfish as ever, you rotten bastard!'

He jumped, startled by her choice of language, as well he might be. The old Katherine would not have used such a word. But then the old Katherine was gone.

'What's that supposed to mean?'

'Meg loves you and you don't deserve her. All you care about is yourself.'

His dark eyebrows lowered but he didn't deny it. After a moment Jack shrugged. 'Meg is lovely and great fun. She writes screeds of chatty letters all about the farm and what everyone's doing there. A real nice girl.'

Kath winced. 'That sounds rather damning.'

'I don't mean it that way. She means a lot to me, don't mistake that. It's a good feeling, to know she's there, you know? Waiting for me till the end of the war.'

'She loves you and apparently still believes, though God knows why, that you feel the same way about her.'

'I do, I do.' He shifted in his seat, looking uncomfortable. 'What the hell, I suppose I can tell you, Kath. I've been out with other girls. It's a year since I saw her, that's a long time. I would have liked to get home more but it's a long way, trains are terrible and I'm always short of funds.'

'Surprise, surprise,' she said dryly.

'Anyway, I'm not ready for all of that.' He downed most of his pint in one gulp and rubbed the froth from his lip with the back of his hand. 'All that marriage and babies and stuff. Want another?'

'Er . . .' Kath glanced at her scarcely touched glass. She felt empty inside, as drained suddenly as his glass. 'No thanks, I'm fine. You help yourself.'

Jack went off to do just that. There was a bounce to his step now, Kath noticed, as she watched him go up to the bar then return with a fresh, brimming glass. A real sailor's roll, chock full of arrogance. And as totally selfish as ever. What a fool she had been.

'We get special rations of rum and brandy on board ship. Good that. One of the perks of the job.'

'What do you do? What's your job?'

'Just another bloody sailor.' He laughed.

'Following the tradition of a girl in every port?' She wanted, very badly, to smack the self-satisfied smirk from the too handsome face.

'Let's say I'm working on it. Now have you seen the landlord's daughter?' And he burst out laughing.

She did not laugh with him. An awkwardness fell between them and she let it lie, sipping at her drink, wondering why she had come. Wanting suddenly, desperately, to be gone from this place and never to set eyes on him again. She stood up.

'I've got to go,' she lied. 'I only have a short pass.'

'Right. I'll walk you to the station.' Jack winked at her as he stood on the platform. 'We had some fun, eh? You and me, once?'

Another notch on his belt, she thought.

Her heart sank with shame at every word he spoke. She couldn't wait to get away. Had she really found this man exciting? Had her pulses truly raced with liquid fire whenever he touched her? How young and foolish she must have been. But the Katherine Ellis of those youthful adventures had had no one to compare Jack Lawson with. He was the best they'd got because he was all they'd got. Men were thin on the ground on the Westmorland fells.

She smiled briefly, coolly, before climbing on to her train. 'I suppose we did,' she said brightly, leaning out the window, trying not to look at him.

'I'll always remember that, you know. You were special to me, Kath. Always will be.'

'You sound as if you aren't going to see me ever again?' There was a sudden tightening in her breast as she looked into his face, regarding him more keenly.

Beneath the brazen banter, despite the swagger of his walk, there was panic in the violet eyes.

'Got to go and put Mussolini's lot in their place first,' he said, his tone cocky as if he meant to do it all by himself. 'Time enough to get serious about women when the show is over, eh?'

She nodded, unable to speak, unable to tell him that it was already too late, his responsibilities had begun. Perhaps she'd be best to put it in a letter. Some time. Later. When he got safely back perhaps.

Nothing could bring her to swallow her pride now and tell him, face to face, that she had borne him a child.

Train doors banged, a whistle blew, and Kath sighed with relief. It was over, she had seen him, and with that visit a ghost had been laid. He meant nothing to her. Not a thing. It'd all been sex, as she'd thought at the time. No more, no less.

When the train drew out of the station she did not look back. Whatever memories she had of that sun-kissed time before the war, Kath knew for certain now that it was over. She had a daughter to think about one day, once she had her life in order again, but for now at least life was shaping up pretty well at Bledlow.

She would enjoy her leave, take a few days' rest in the country somewhere, but not too long. Waiting for her back in camp was someone she was very much looking forward to seeing again.

'Hi, I've missed you,' were his first words to her.

They were sitting in a cinema in Cambridge, in the dark, far from the station, having come in separately hoping like mad that no one had seen them.

He took her hand in his. Kath's heart was thumping crazily. All thoughts of celibacy were quite gone from her head. She wanted this man, and if he still wanted her, as far as she was concerned, he could have her.

Ewan Maximillian Wadeson III, however, was a gentleman, and liked to do things properly.

He kissed her now, deep and lingering. 'You realise it is prejudicial to good order for me to be seen with you, as another rank?'

Kath ran her lips lightly over his jawline, such a lovely strong jaw. 'No one can see us in the dark, so that's all right.'

'Why don't you marry me?'

'What?' She couldn't see his face in the smoke-wreathed darkness but she could feel his smile. 'Very funny.'

He put his arm around her, pressed his lips close to her ear. 'I mean it, honey. You know how I feel about you. A quiet little ceremony with just you, me and a witness. Our secret.'

Kath couldn't believe what he was saying. Yet a part of her wanted to, she realised. 'Are you quite serious?'

'Never more so. I want you. I've never felt this way about a woman before. We'd be good for each other, Katherine.'

Her heart was racing. A million thoughts teemed through her head. On screen, Deanna Durbin was singing her heart out, and nothing seemed quite real. It would be too, too easy to get carried away on a tide of romance, and look where that got you.

Outside, after the show, reality struck with the cool night breeze and rain-polished pavements.

'Hurry now, before anyone sees you,' she told him as he lingered on, holding her hand. 'My bus is over here.'

'Let me give you a lift.'

'Who is your driver?'

'I drove myself here this evening. So you can take me back. Pretend you're on duty.'

'How very clever of you.' Laughing, against her better judgement, Kath agreed.

All the way back to camp he tried to persuade her.

'Don't rush me, Wade. It's too easy to make a mistake.'

They stopped on a quiet road so he could stroke her face, her throat, her thigh. 'Don't you want me?'

'That's not a good reason for getting married,' Kath protested, returning his kisses with an eagerness she could scarce control.

'It is in wartime. You know damn' well we could both be dead next week.'

It was a sobering thought. Still she hesitated. 'You know nothing about me.' Like for instance that I have a daughter, she wanted to say, but the words wouldn't come.

'I know enough.'

'Best to leave things as they are for a while. See how it goes.'

'You're not offended, are you?' Anxiety in his voice, in his face. 'I wouldn't hurt you for the world, Katherine. I hope you realise that.'

Her heart was filled with a rush of compassion for him and she put her lips to his softly. Desire flared like a torch between them and his mouth caught hers, deepening the kiss to something far more dangerous. Did she love him? She didn't know. How could she tell? But he was all male, and she was a healthy, normal woman. He had her jacket unfastened and was reaching for her tie when he broke away with an abruptness that hurt.

'Hellfire, I can't keep this up for much longer! I'm too old to play footsie in a car. Promise me you'll think about it? I'll buy us a lovely home in Canada after the war, anything you want. Just say yes, honey, and I'll buy you the world in gold paper.'

Somewhere inside, her heart melted. Kath could hardly drag open her eyes, so drugged was she with wanting, with loving. But was what she felt enough? Would it last? She had felt this terrible longing with Jack and look where that had got her.

But Wade wasn't like Jack. Surely he would keep his promises. What they felt for each other was different. Or was it?

How would Wade react if she told him about Melissa? Would he still want her, with an illegitimate daughter? And she certainly couldn't marry him without telling him. 'I'll think about it, I promise,' she said.

When she garaged the staff car and walked across to her hut she saw Mule, checking quarters at the end of her shift.

'Late in again, Airwoman?'

Kath glanced at her wristwatch. It said ten-fifteen. 'No, ma'am. Still fifteen minutes to go.'

'Driving Wing Commander Wadeson to yet another meeting?'

Kath half turned, glancing back over her shoulder as if expecting to see him standing there. Then she realised that since she'd dropped Wade by the gate, the woman couldn't possibly have known for certain she'd been out with him. It had been a guess, but by Kath's own guilty reaction, one that had been proved accurate.

'Just doing my duty, ma'am.'

'I've been told you were at the Ship the other night.'

Kath schooled herself not to overreact. 'It was our night off and we were back by ten, ma'am.' Worn out by Laddo Octopus, she thought.

'And the Wing Commander was there too. What a coincidence.'

'Yes. Wasn't it? If you'll excuse me, ma'am, I'll check in.' Kath saluted smartly and started to walk away. Mule kept pace.

'A little bird tells me you were seen wearing civvies the other day.'

Kath's heart jumped with shock. Surely not Wade? Would he tell on her? No, it could have been anyone.

'I'm afraid I don't understand,' Kath said, with blithe innocence.

'You understand me perfectly, ACW Ellis.'

'Couldn't say, ma'am, whether there were any Waafs in civvies or not. We would certainly never step off the station without uniform, as you well know.' It was not quite a lie for they had left in uniform, and changed in the Ladies at the pub, so Kath was able to meet Mule's gaze unflinchingly.

A long, silent appraisal. 'There's something not quite right about you, Ellis. You are not entirely what you seem.'

Kath raised enquiring brows. 'I'm a simple Waaf, doing my job. What more could I be?'

'Not quite so simple. Where did someone of your evident class acquire such skills with a scrubbing brush? And such rough hands to go with them. Why had you only one set of civvies? And why do we know no more about you than we did the day you arrived? You say nothing about your family, your background, your upbringing. Why is that, I wonder?'

'Didn't realise you were so interested. Ma'am.'

'Your remarks are close to insolence, Airwoman.'

Kath ground her teeth together and apologised. 'Is this a serious interrogation, ma'am?'

'Quite the mystery woman, aren't you?'

Kath had reached the door of her Nissen hut and turned to face her aggressor. 'I do my job. Mind my own business. I'd prefer everyone else to do the same. May I go now, ma'am?' She had pushed it too far. Kath could tell by the expression on Mule's face.

'Let me see you at Parade once in a while, Ellis.'

'Ma'am.'

And smiling to herself, Kath went in to Bella and the waiting cocoa. Nosy old troublemaker, she thought.

Three weeks later the smile was wiped from her face when Kath discovered that a new posting had come through for her. She'd been given her movement orders to go to another section of Group Command, far away from Wing Commander Ewan Wadeson. Mule, it seemed, had won.

24

Joe Turner enjoyed his ill temper as some people relish poor health. But then, as he so often told himself, he had a right to be upset. Nothing was going right at the moment.

By heck though, if he were in the government he'd stand no nonsense from this Hitler chap. And he was right glad they'd got that Hesse fellow locked up in the tower. Proper place for him an' all. Keep him out of mischief for the rest of the war, that would. Oh, aye, he made a point of keeping abreast of the news, and offering the wisdom of his opinion upon it. He'd followed with increasing dismay the German advancement on Malta, on Yugoslavia even, for all it'd proved a tricky country to take, and then Greece and Crete. Whatever way you looked at it, things were not good. Now they were after the Ruskies. By, but the Huns would find them a tougher meat to tackle, for all they'd taken Kiev, cheeky as you please.

'What we need is Lloyd George to tek this lot on,' he announced not for the first time to Sally Ann who patiently read him snippets from the newspaper each morning and tuned in the crackling nine o'clock news for him at night on the battery wireless.

'Don't talk soft, Dad. Lloyd George isn't running the country now, Churchill is.'

'Aye, well, Lloyd George'd do better.'

Sally Ann sighed and spooned cereal into little Daniel's mouth. 'You live in the past, that's your trouble, Dad. You'll have to come into the twentieth century one of these days so best start getting used to the idea.'

'You sound like our Meg.'

Sally Ann laughed. 'Sometimes I understand exactly how she feels about you, you old misery boots! Pour me out another cup of tea, my hands are full.'

Joe did as she asked. He was not displeased with this new daughter-in-law of his. She could cook, was easy to live with, and kept a smiling face about the place. And she had given him two grandsons. 'Meg's always wanting summat she can't have.'

Sally Ann wiped the baby's mouth and lifted him against her shoulder, rubbing his back gently. 'I know you miss Annie. It was sad she was taken so soon, but you can't expect Meg to step into her shoes.'

Joe glared into the fire. 'You can't turn back the clock, that's for sure, though there's things I'd put reet if I could.'

'We all feel that way when we've lost someone,' Sally Ann said softly. 'Don't blame Meg for not being more like her mother. She's like you. And she wants what it is perfectly reasonable for her to have, a farm. She's your daughter, all right.'

'She's nowt like me.'

Sally Ann actually laughed out loud at that. 'Isn't she just? More than either you or she realises, I reckon. She's tough as old boots, and soft as good leather. Just like you. Only difference is you won't show it. You'd go to any lengths to keep your feelings hidden, and Meg has been behaving exactly the same way with little Lissa.' Sally Ann frowned. 'It worries me, it does really.'

'That yan maintains that child i'nt hers.'

'No more it is, in my opinion,' said Sally Ann quietly. 'Though I don't lay claim to having the answer, I have my own idea on the subject.' She caught the gleam in Joe's eye and laughed again. 'No, I'm not going to tell you what it is, you old goat.'

'She should get herself wed and stop messing aboot wi' things she knows nowt about. Sheep farming is man's work. Bairns are for women. I've said so afore . . .'

'And you'll go on saying it, I know. Now, if you've nothing better to do than gossip, you can fold those nappies for me.'

And without demur, Joe pulled the nappies one by one from the rack and folded them into a soft white pile, not realising the incongruity of the task after his last words. He found he didn't mind having childer, as he called them, about the place. They kept a man feeling alive. Pity Meg didn't bring her youngster to visit him more often, though a girl was not to his taste. A man needed sons to follow him on. One day Joe would like Dan to have this place, as was only right and proper, for himself and his sons. Though what he'd make of it, God only knew.

And mebbe, if Joe played his cards right, Broombank an' all. Money was tight just now. Things weren't going well at all. Childer took a lot o' feeding, wanting clothes and such like. How Ashlea would manage to keep them all he didn't know. Now if Meg would only stop being so stubborn he and Dan would be right set up. There was plenty of time, though, to get his hands on the land he wanted. He hadn't given up hope yet, not by a long chalk.

But first he had to secure Ashlea.

'Haven't you done enough for today?' Tam said to Meg a few days later when she was pouring over the accounts one evening by the light of the lamp. 'Don't you know paraffin is in short supply?'

'I know, I know. But I must finish these figures.'

'It's rest you're needing.'

Tam knew everything there was to know about her and the business. He was always there for her when she needed a friend. Meg knew she was lucky to have him stay on since he was a man who claimed to have no roots, and might decide to leave at any moment. It was a good reason to keep him at a distance. He was simply an employee after all, and a man. Therefore not to be trusted absolutely.

'I must get these accounts done. I've an appointment to see the bank manager on Friday.'

Tam tightened his lips in that familiar way he had which spoke volumes without saying a word. Then he set the kettle on the new range they'd had fitted in the great kitchen inglenook. 'I'll make cocoa and you fetch some of those rice biscuits Effie made today.'

Meg tossed down her pen with a laugh. 'You aren't going to give up, are you?'

'I usually get my own way, in the end.' He looked at her gravely. 'You can have ten more minutes then bed, no matter what you say.'

The shutters were drawn, Effie and Lissa were in bed and there was a reassuring cosiness about being here, with Tam. A feeling that she was very safe, and protected from the world outside. Yet there was more to it than that, more than cosiness and homeliness, cocoa and biscuits. She'd had it before, this feeling that couldn't quite be defined and Meg chose to ignore.

The gaze held a moment longer and she smiled in order to break the tension growing between them. It disturbed her and she couldn't quite say why, not seeing him as he saw her, her mind already turning to the figures and why they wouldn't add up. Tam sighed and the sound said that it was just as well he was a patient man.

As they sat companionably enjoying Effie's biscuits, Tam nodded in the direction of the account books. 'Go on then, I'll listen. Why is it you must see the bank manager? Is it trouble we're in then?'

She liked it when he said 'we'. As if he was a part of the project, and meant to stay.

Meg flushed with excitement and pleasure. 'No, quite the opposite. We were lucky in having a good lambing season this year when for many people it was a disaster. Thanks, in no small part, to you and Effie.'

'Thanks duly accepted.' Tam regally bowed his head.

'Which means that our stock has increased, even accounting for some losses. Which is good, don't you think?'

'Splendid.' Tam reached for another biscuit. 'Perhaps then Effie could afford a bit more sugar in these?' He held one up, puckering his lips.

'Sugar? You'll be lucky. Be grateful you have biscuits at all, you oaf.'

Tam chuckled. 'Go on. What's your plan? I can see that you have one by the twinkle in your eye.'

Meg wrinkled her nose at him. 'You are far too knowing, Thomas O'Cleary.'

'Where you are concerned, maybe I am. Don't you know how transparent you are?' The biscuit airily instructed her to continue and Meg, feeling suddenly shy, did so. Her plans felt oddly precious, hard to share. She took a deep breath.

'I mean to buy a tractor.'

'Ah. A tractor. Hence your decision to see the bank manager.'

Meg's eyes glowed. 'Yes. Look.' She laid out the pages showing her reckoning on the table before them. 'I've paid what I owe to Will Davies for the cows and tups, and Lanky's debts are all settled. We've bought in two Tamworth pigs which are fattening up nicely. The ducks and turkeys are doing well. But these are largely ways of feeding ourselves, and of surviving from day to day. We should start looking to the future. We need to expand but more sheep means more land, more work, and more time needed to attend to them. And the War Committee are asking for still more land to be ploughed up. Mechanisation is the way forward. Don't you agree?'

Listening, chin in hand, to the excitement in her voice, watching the lamplight dance over the high cheek bones, Tam O'Cleary would have agreed if she'd said the moon was made of green cheese. Not that she recognised this in him for he had the sense to keep it well hidden. He had his pride.

'And how do you intend to get more land and more sheep?'

'The land idea will have to wait, but I mean to buy more Swaledales.'

'Why Swaledales when you've got a growing flock of Herdwicks?'

'Herdwicks are fine strong sheep, their meat is sweet, but the wool is only really suitable for carpets, and heavy army blankets. The days of hodden grey are long gone. Swaledales make bigger lambs and I can sell them on to be crossed with other sheep such as Leicesters to make better apparel wool. I might make more out of that than the meat. And I can even cross them myself with a Herdwick tup to keep them hardy if I want. They're much more economic, do you see, so why not?'

'How will you do it?'

'By selling half of my Herdwicks this backend and starting to buy in Swaledales.' She closed the book with a flourish, nearly knocking over the untouched mug of cocoa in her enthusiasm.

'For goodness' sake, drink it. You get so involved with your damn' sheep you almost forget to eat sometimes.'

Tam's fingers closed hers about the warm mug and Meg felt herself jerk, as if something had moved inside her. They were comforting, strong, reliable hands. That was all it was. No more than that. Safe. Tam was good to her. What would she do without him?

'Do you think it is a good idea?' It mattered, somehow, that he did.

Tam chuckled. 'Would you not carry out this wonderful plan if I disagreed?'

She pretended to consider. 'Nope. I'd still do it.'

'And will you have enough money to buy in your new Swaledales, pay your quarterly rent, and instalments on a tractor?'

Meg flushed. She hadn't quite got that far yet, but she was optimistic, broadly speaking. 'I don't see why not, if we work hard. But I need you to be with me on this.'

Tam gave a half laugh, almost at himself. 'I told you once before, I'm with you all the way.'

Meg finished the cocoa swiftly and set the mug on the sink.

'Good. I'm off to bed then. See you in the morning.'

'Goodnight to you.' Tam sat staring into the empty grate long after she had climbed the stairs. Was he a fool to stay, to want her so much? He couldn't quite make up his mind.

On Friday morning, Meg stood before the mirror, adjusting her small blue hat, her spirits high.

A small hand tugged at her skirt. 'Lissa come too.'

Meg did not glance down. 'No, darling. Meg has to go out alone today. See, I've got my best setting-out suit on. You stay here with Tam and Effie.'

Lissa stamped a foot. 'No. Want to come.'

Meg bent down with a sigh. 'Don't do this, Lissa, not today. I have an important meeting.' She picked up her bag and a brown paper packet in which were her carefully worked-out figures and plans. The small hands gripped the skirt, preventing her from taking one step. 'Effie,' Meg called.

'What is it?' Effie gazed at the child clinging to her skirts. 'You should take her out more. She needs you.'

Meg's eyes were pleading. 'Not today. I can't today. This is important, for all of us. Take her, Effie, please.'

Effie heaved an exaggerated sigh and reached for Lissa. The child at once stiffened her body, refusing to be picked up. 'Don't be naughty, there's a good girl,' Effie pleaded, prising the curled fingers from the blue fabric. 'By heck, she's wilful.'

'I hope her hands were clean,' Meg mourned. 'I can't go into the bank manager's office looking crumpled and covered with sticky finger marks.'

Effie was panting for breath. 'I wish you'd help a bit more with her, Meg. She's getting to be a right handful.' But Meg had taken her chance and slipped out of the door. With a cheery wave to Tam who was striding off up the fell, she hurried down the lane to the bus stop. A bright future beckoned, far more important at the moment than a wilful child.

It was the bank manager who brought Meg down to earth. 'Perhaps you are trying to run before you can walk, Miss Turner? Changing to Swaledales seems to be a sound proposition, but a tractor?' What do you know about tractors? his expression seemed to ask. Nasty, smelly, unreliable things.

Meg explained her belief in the future, the need for mechanisation. But she could tell by the bland politeness in the bank manager's eyes that he was not convinced.

'Farming is going to become far more competitive,' she persisted. 'And efficiency is essential. So much time, and land, is wasted by trying to do it all by hand.'

'The War Committee would do your ploughing and harvesting for you.'

Meg sighed. He simply wasn't listening to a word she was saying. Patiently she continued with her explanation. 'I know they will. My own brother works for them. They've given me grants to drain my low-lying land and helped me with the work. But I get two pound an acre for doing the ploughing myself and the War Committee will not always be with us, nor will the war, praise God.

'In farming you have to think long-term, plan ahead. And I now have a dozen more acres of well-drained, good land to deal with. For now most of it must be ploughed but later it will make winter pasture for my sheep. Even land that isn't to be ploughed needs tending, cleaning and harrowing. Feed has to be carried to those sheep that need it. Sick animals carried back. A tractor would more than pay its way in time alone.'

'Yes, but you are a woman, Miss Turner.'

'So?'

'So, when the war is over,' his lips curved into a condescending smile, 'you will no doubt be wishing to marry, have children?'

She wanted to tell him that she had a child already, which fact didn't at all prevent her from working. Common sense stopped her. There were those in the community who still believed that Lissa was her own daughter, she could see it in their eyes. Joe for one. There was little to gain by involving the bank in the mess.

'It doesn't mean to say, even if I were to marry, that I wouldn't still need a sound business behind me. On the contrary.'

'Oh, quite, quite,' agreed the bank manager, clearly not meaning it. 'But then you would have a husband to attend to such matters for you.'

'I have never found any prejudice in the farming community,' said Meg, very firmly. 'I have been accepted from the beginning, the moment they realised I was serious about making a go of the farm.'

'I do not doubt your determination. But taking on a loan, Miss Turner, demands a different kind of commitment.'

'You are afraid I won't be able to pay it back?'

The bank manager tutted. 'These are difficult times, Miss Turner. Money is in short supply. 'Do you have a guarantor for the loan? Your father perhaps?'

Meg knew then that she had lost. She picked up her portfolio of accounts and plans from the bank manager's desk. 'Thank you for listening to me. Will you tell me just one thing? I can see that I would have had no difficulty at all in getting the loan had I been a man. Will the same rules apply when I come to you for a mortgage?'

'Mortgage?'

'To buy Broombank. I have three years left, according to Lanky's will, to find the deposit. If I make a go of the farm in the meantime, will you look more favourably upon me?'

Fingers tapped thoughtfully together, the same bland smile. 'We shall have to see. Time, as they say, will tell.' Which meant no.

Disappointment was keen in her as she walked away. But she wasn't defeated. It took more than one bank manager to stop Meg Turner, she thought. There were other banks, after all.

Not a speck of cloud marred the blue heavens on this perfect, late-September day as Effie dragged her bike out of the lean-to and clattered it over the slate slabs of the farmyard, startling a family of sleek-coated weasels as they squabbled over a heap of chaff by the barn door. She was setting out early for school this morning since she wanted to post her latest letter to Mam. Effie was proud to be able to write a letter every week to her family, not that her mother could read it, of course, but she would take it to the parson and he would read it for her.

Effie liked to tell her what she was learning at school. Lissa's latest naughty tricks. Her happy life at Broombank and all about Meg and Tam, Sally Ann and the children. Her mam liked to hear about the children.

There had been times, recently, when she'd been able to send her a postal order, if Meg had sold enough milk or eggs. That made Effie feel proud, to be able to contribute a bit towards her younger brothers and sisters' care. And every now and again, when he had time, there would be a note back from the parson, to say how they all were.

All in all, Effie was very pleased with life. Except that this morning, Meg had been in another of her 'moods'. There'd been a few of those recently, most unlike her usual cheerful self she was. All to do with banks and money and being a woman. Effie didn't understand a bit of it but oh, even when Meg was at her most irritable, Effie would rather be here than anywhere else.

If the thought wasn't so wicked, she'd wish for the war to go on for ever. What she really meant, of course, was that she wanted to stay here at Broombank, for ever and ever, with Meg and Tam and her lovely Lissa. She wouldn't ever take to the cows but she'd come to terms with the crags and towering mountains.

She was twelve now, or so she supposed, and almost a woman. Clean, healthy and well fed, and though she'd never make a scholar, doing well enough at her lessons to get by. The thought of returning to Manchester made her want to throw up. This was her place now, as it was Meg's. She felt safe here, and exquisitely happy.

Effie was pedalling furiously, as she usually did, half her mind on the day ahead: helping Miss Shaw with the younger ones, doing a bit of work on her own account, though not too much. The other half was on the potato and onion patties she would fry up for their tea. Maybe she'd open a tin of that Spam she'd managed to get the other week. Meg needed a bit of cheering up.

She was getting up a good speed, pretending she was riding a horse, not a rusty old bicycle that squeaked because it was in need of a good oiling. Galloping across country on a fiery steed with the wind in her hair.

The best bit was when she reached the crest of Coppergill Pass. If she went really fast along the flat part of the hill, she could zoom down to Slater's Bottom with her feet stuck out at the sides and the pedals whirling free. It was almost worth the climb up for the exhilaration of that descent.

This morning when she reached the top of the hill she heard the sound. A great droning noise filling the heavens, frightening the birds into silence. The noise grew louder and when she half turned to see what it was, she almost fell off her bike with shock.

It was an aeroplane, flying alongside the hill. It was right over the dale and heading straight for Ashlea.

Sally Ann heard the plane just as she was pegging out the washing. She saw it bank once as it zoomed over the house, shaking all the windows with the vibration of its engines. She ran, frantic with fear, back into the house, desperate to find Nicky who, as usual, was not where he was supposed to be. Heart pounding, her screams frightening the little boy into hiding all the more securely she finally located him under the sideboard. By the time she had snatched up little Daniel from his crib, and got them safely out in the yard the plane was again overhead and she flung the children down beneath an old hawthorn bush with herself on top of them.

The plane rose up over the house, banked, tipped its wings in an impertinent salute and flew on. But it wasn't done, even then, for Sally Ann saw it turn and start to come back towards her.

Breathless with fear, mouth hanging open, Effie watched it swoop across the blue sky, trailing vapour behind it. 'Bloody hell, it's coming again.'

She jumped on her bike and started to pedal furiously, as fast, faster, than any horse could gallop. The plane came level with her and for a crazy instant it seemed that she and the aeroplane were travelling each at the same speed as the other, and Effie was in the unique position, from so high on the fell, of looking right down into the cockpit, at two faces grinning at her through the window.

The shock was too much. The bike went flying and Effie with it. If this was the end, dear God, let it come quick. Don't let it hit the house and Sally Ann and the children. She didn't think much of Joe, or Dan, so their safety did not cross her mind. She flung her hands around her head and waited for the explosion.

When nothing happened, only the continuation of the terrible droning noise, Effie dared to peep through her fingers.

There it was again, coming round for a fourth time.

'He's playing with me, the bugger,' she cried. This time she saw something fall. No bomb doors had opened, nor was it a bomb that drifted down on the morning breeze to land on the bottom field behind Ashlea. But whatever it was, Effie meant to find it.

With all thought of school gone from her mind, Effie pedalled back down the lane, flung herself through the gate and started to search the grass. It took some time as the bag lay in a clump of nettles.

Oh, very clever, she thought, getting stung for her trouble. But the moment she had examined her find, she was on her bike again, pedalling with the wind behind her, back to Broombank.

Effie ran into the house, panting for breath, her hand shaking as she gave the paper to Meg.

'Look! Look what I've got.'

Meg took it, frowning her puzzlement. 'What is it?'

The paper carried a few words, in bold black pen. 'Got married on Saturday. Letter and photo to follow. Love, Charlie.'

Meg gave a shout of laughter. 'Where did you find this?'

'The plane dropped it. From the sky. The plane . . .' Effie's knees finally buckled and she collapsed on to a chair, clutching her sides in agony.

It was some moments, and several glasses of water later, before the whole story came out.

'The mad crazy fool!' cried Meg, admiring her brother's guts all the same.

'He must have been miles off course,' Tam pointed out. 'Good job he didn't meet with any problems. Who would have known where to look for him?'

'Don't even think of it.' But Meg hugged the paper to her breast, thankful just to know that Charlie was safe and well, if cheekily flying where he shouldn't.

'And married. Oh dear me. I have a new sister-in-law. I wonder what she's like? I do hope we get on.'

'She'd be a fool, to be sure, if she didn't get on with you, Meg Turner.'

'Oh stop your blarney, it won't wash with me,' she laughed.

'I know,' said Tam mournfully. 'That's the trouble.'

What was going on? Sally Ann crawled out, scratched and dishevelled but surprised to find herself still alive, from beneath the hawthorn bush with her two children.

She got to her feet, cradling the weeping Daniel on one hip while trying to keep hold of the squirming Nicky with the other hand. Were her eyes deceiving her or was that Effie pedalling like fury down the lane? Watching the tail of the plane disappear, Sally Ann realised now that it was one of theirs, a Lancaster. So what was it doing playing games over Ashlea? She'd go up to Broombank later, when she had the children settled for their afternoon nap. Joe could take care of them for once and she and Meg would catch up on a bit of gossip. Perhaps she would understand. It would be good to go up anyway. Must be a week or more since she'd seen Meg. Right now though, she'd have a cup of tea. She felt in dire need of one.

'Married? I don't believe it. The sly boots. Oh, and we've missed out on all the fun.'

'That's war, isn't it? I don't blame him for doing the deed so quickly, though I would have loved to be there,' Meg agreed, grey eyes alight with joy as she told Sally Ann the news. 'Let's just be glad he's well.'

'I wonder if it's the same one? You know,' put in Effie, 'the one he danced with in the Tower ballroom that time.'

'Heavens, I've no idea. The letter doesn't say.' Meg clicked her tongue with disgust. 'Isn't that just like him? Tells us he's married, but doesn't say who to. Not that it matters. I'm sure she'll be lovely. We'll have to wait for his letter, if it ever comes.'

'I still think it's a pity,' Sally Ann mourned. 'We could have done with a good wedding to cheer us all up.' She slanted her eyes across at Tam who was sitting in the porch, cleaning tack with saddle soap and linseed oil. 'You weren't thinking of taking the plunge, were you?'

'Would you like me to call on Miss Shaw, and see if she's available?'

Sally Ann giggled. 'She's well past fifty. You can do better than that, I'm sure. There's a dance on Saturday as a matter of fact. Renton Ralph's Blue Rascals are playing at Kendal Town Hall. How about it?'

'Is that an offer?'

'I mean for us all to go. It's in aid of the War Appeal Fund and soldiers' comforts.'

'I can guess what sort of comforts the soldiers would like,' quipped Tam with a wink, earning himself a slapped wrist from Meg for his cheek.

'A lot of service people will be there and some of the VAD nurses. You never know, Tam, you might strike lucky.'

Meg laughed along with the rest of them as he brought out a comb and started to titivate his mahogany curls, but the thought of him dancing with some pretty little nurse did not greatly amuse her, oddly enough.

25

Meg had her head pushed into the side of the cow, working at the
teats with such fierce effort she had a wonderful head of froth in her
milk bucket. She loved the smell of the warm milk, the sense of
seclusion here in the cow shed. It was a good place to escape.

'Meg? Are you in there?'

She heard the door open, felt the draught of cool air flow in. Drat,
she'd been discovered. She heard him approach and stand beside her,
silently condemning. 'Are you going to be long?'

She did not pause for a fraction of a second. 'Why?'

'Dan is coming for us in the Ford at seven and Effie is asking if
you'll be wanting a bath before we go.'

'No.'

'Why not?'

'I'm not going.'

The silence grew ominous, then he kicked out at a bale of hay. He
was cross, even angry. 'Are you going to tell me why you aren't
coming?'

'Someone has to stay with Lissa, and Effie deserves a night out for
once.'

'Effie is too young to go to dances. They'll be fine here. It won't
hurt them to be alone for once.'

'What if something should happen? I'd never forgive myself.'

'Well, that's easily solved. We'll get Mrs Davies to come and sit
with them. Or better still, they can go and sleep at her house. I'm sure
she'd be delighted to have them.'

The cow lifted one foot and stamped it in protest as Meg's fingers dug in too hard. She eased off a little. She was almost dry now but Meg continued to pull on the teats, not wanting to get up and face Tam.

'You'll make her sore if you carry on at that rate. Meg, leave it.' He hunkered down beside her. 'What's the real reason?'

'I don't want to go, that's all. I don't like dancing.'

'Yes, you do.'

She shook her head, turning away, picking up the milk pail as if to use it as a shield between them. At dances people put their arms around you. They took you outside and kissed you. As Jack had once done. She couldn't face it, not again. Not with someone else. In spite of his betrayal, no matter how sensibly she tried to view her changed relationship with Jack, her body still ached for a man's arms about her.

She heard Tam sigh. It sounded rather like a growl.

'All right then. We won't go. I'll walk down and tell Dan not to bother coming for us.'

Meg was astounded. 'You must go. I don't mean to stop your pleasure.'

The leanness of his face looked almost boyish, and strangely vulnerable in the dim light of the cow shed. But he wasn't a boy, he was a man. He moved closer to her and Meg just managed to stop herself flinching away as he reached down and took the bucket from her. He set it safely on the slate floor. 'It's that damn' Jack, isn't it? You're still pining for him.' The words were grated out, mercilessly cruel, and now Meg did flinch, inwardly at least.

'Y-you don't understand.'

'I do. Oh, I understand very well. More than you might think.' He took hold of her shoulders and pulled her round to face him when she might have escaped, run from the shed, from his accusations. 'Are you never going to let him go? He's gone from your life, Meg, forget him. He rarely replies to those damn' letters you insist on sending him. He has no intention of committing himself to you, ever. He's a lout.'

The words were cruel, intentionally so, and she opened her mouth to protest but on seeing the implacable expression on the face so close to hers, she thought better of it and merely gave her a head a sad little shake.

'It's time you stopped mourning for him and started living again.'

'I'm not mourning. I'm too busy with the farm to mourn.'

'Ah, yes, the farm. Broombank, which you guiltily feel should still be his by right. Why? He wasn't interested in farming and his father chose to leave it to you. Stop looking backwards all the time, comparing, analysing, feeling guilty. And you hardly acknowledge Lissa's presence.' He half shook her in his irritation. 'You are only half a woman, do you know that? Your mind is so fully occupied with making plans for the future of your farm, that nowhere in those plans is there time for any personal happiness.' Meg wriggled furiously but his grip was unrelenting.

'I'll please myself what I do.'

'Maybe you will. But don't tell me that you don't want to spoil my pleasure. Because I'll have you know that you spoil it all the time! You don't give a thought to what I want, whether I might like to take you to this dratted jive. Just by living and breathing you ruin my life. Did you know that, Miss Turner?'

He kissed her then. Long and hard. Holding her fast in his arms so there was no hope of her breathing, but judging by the cataclysmic sensations surging through her body, she was still very much alive.

And when he had done he gathered her up in his arms and sat her, very firmly, in the cold water trough in the yard. 'Take your bath here then, in your precious farmyard. And when you've done, get dressed in your prettiest frock. You are going to a dance, Meg Turner. With me.'

Effie was giggling as she helped Meg button up her best dress. It was a blue print crepe with a slightly bloused bodice, padded shoulders and soft pleats falling to just below her knee.

'For a soft-hearted Irishman, he can make his wishes felt when he has a mind to.'

'It's simply the wickedness of an eccentric sense of humour,' said Meg, somewhat huffily. 'I could have caught double pneumonia.'

'Instead of which you just lost a bit of your pride.'

'And I'm still going to this dratted dance under protest.'

'You'll have a lovely time.' Effie hugged her. 'And no trouble at all keeping him away from the VAD nurses.'

Meg opened her eyes wide in surprise. 'As if I shall try! He can dance with them all night, for all I care.'

Effie giggled again. 'If I had the chance to dance with an attractive Irishman, I'd not complain.'

'Oh, Effie.' Meg clung to her young friend in a sudden gesture of affection and fear, as she might have done to her mother, or Kath, had they been here. 'I daren't go. I simply daren't.' The tremor in her voice was lifting it to something very close to panic. 'I do like Tam, I do. He's good and friendly and he makes me laugh. But you know he doesn't intend to stay for ever, don't you? One morning I'll wake up and find him gone, I know it.'

Effie smiled and tucked back a stray curl of Meg's hair. 'I wouldn't be too sure about that. Go on now, off you go and have a good time. We can't disappoint Hetty, can we? You know how she enjoys having Lissa. And she's even getting me into the bargain tonight. So be off with you and not another word.'

'Oh, Effie, I do love you.' Meg hugged the girl close, no longer a child but still much too thin, as she always would be, no doubt. 'I'm so glad you came to us.'

'Me too.' They held each other for a moment, as they had so often done, sharing their strength. Then Rust came and pushed his nose between them, giving a whimper of jealousy at this show of affection which did not include him. They both laughed, hugging him close and tickling his ears till he rolled over and waved his legs in the air with pleasure.

There was the sound of the van in the yard and Tam's voice, calling to her. 'Will you be coming, girl, if we're ever to get to this dance!'

Meg dabbed at her eyes, quickly powdered her nose and grinned at Effie. 'Yes,' she called. 'I'm ready.'

Meg enjoyed the dance. They all did. It had been crowded, packed with uniforms as well as hard-working civilians wanting to forget the war and their worries over loved ones for a few hours. On the way back they sang 'Green Eyes' and 'Chattanooga Choo-Choo', sitting on blankets in the back of the old van. Dan proved to have quite a good baritone and their praise brought a flush to the tips of his ears, making them all laugh.

Broombank was in darkness when Meg and Tam stumbled out, slightly the worse for the several glasses of beer they had drunk. They waved, giggling, as the old Ford bumped off back down the lane.

'It seems odd with the children not here,' said Meg into the sudden silence. 'As if the world were empty of everything but us. It always surprises me how big the sky is here, how wide and lonely the fells.'

With the same thought they turned to gaze at the fiery glow that flickered in the sky over the distant coast where the Royal Navy base was situated at Barrow-in-Furness. It brought a sick feeling to the pit of Meg's stomach to see this fire of death from their green and quiet world.

'It's hard to imagine that elsewhere homes are being destroyed, lives torn apart. Puts things into perspective, doesn't it?' Tam said. 'At least our plane was only a message from Charlie, not a package from Germany. What do bank managers matter?'

Meg nodded. 'I'm lucky, I know that. I have Effie, and Lissa, and Sally Ann. Even Dan speaks to me in a half-civilised way these days.'

'And there's always yours truly, don't forget,' said Tam softly.

She turned her face up to him. 'How could I? Where would I be without you, Tam?'

'Without my Irish brawn, you mean?'

'No, I don't. I could never have managed Broombank this well without you.'

'Ah, yes, the land. And what of me? Have *I* been of any use, for myself perhaps?'

'I hope that we are friends.'

Tam was silent, wanting to say that no, they were not friends. He could never think of her as simply a friend, but Meg was again talking of Barrow and how she could feel, rather than hear, a humming vibration through her feet.

'How do the German bombers know where they are? They might miss and drop their bombs in the wrong place.'

'I suspect even the Germans can find the sea,' said Tam, in his usual jokey fashion.

'Yes, but how can they *see* where to drop them? I mean, I've heard that our pilots eat carrots, to improve their sight in the dark. Do you think the Germans do too?'

Tam, obviously straining against laughter, considered her suggestion gravely. 'If carrots are so useful, perhaps you should become a vegetable farmer.'

She slapped at him, catching his mood. 'I'm serious. If it's cloudy and dark, how can they know where the target is? How do we know they won't make a mistake?'

'We don't. That's the problem with war. It is often the innocent who suffer.'

Meg stared at him with such earnestness in her expression he was hard put not to kiss her there and then and hang the consequences. 'I pray every day that Charlie will be safe.'

'You know that he is. He's proved it. Spectacularly so.'

'Yes. It's a good feeling.'

'You must tell him to eat more carrots.'

Meg started in astonishment and then burst out laughing. 'You're wicked.' And Tam grinned.

'You've got the black dog on your shoulders, that's all. Just because of that stupid bank manager. Stop worrying. Charlie is fine and you're doing your bit here, quietly, without heroics. Just plain hard work. But growing food is important. Never forget that.'

And he wiped a tear from her cheek, his fingers lingering over the silk of her cheek bones, wondering how she would react if he kissed it away instead.

Meg looked up into his eyes for a long moment then brushed past him to walk into the kitchen and light the lamp. 'I'll put the kettle on. Tea or cocoa?' She was trembling, he could hear it in her voice.

Tam sat in the rocking chair by the fire, saying nothing, watching with a smile in his eyes as Meg busied herself with the kettle. She said not a word while she waited for it to boil.

The tantalising aroma of tea filled her nostrils and she risked a half glance at him. The light from the Tilly lamp highlighted the planes of his face and set a gloss on the mahogany curls but Meg could not see his eyes which were in deep shadow. She would have given a good deal, right then, to read their expression. She set a mug by his hand upon the table. He did not move to pick it up.

When his voice came to break the silence, Meg started as if she'd been stung.

'You don't seriously expect for one minute that I am going to sit here meekly and drink tea with you in an empty house?'

Her own mug half raised to her lips, she found her fingers setting it down again, quite of their own volition. 'Wh-what do you mean?'

'Do you know how lovely you look in that pretty frock? Like a bluebell in spring, you are.'

Meg got to her feet. 'I think you're drunk.'

Tam caught at her hand as she would have passed him and held her still. He leaned forward slightly and she could see his eyes now. The expression in them set a pulse beating deep in her stomach. 'I think I might be, Meg Turner, but not with beer. Do you know what I want to do?'

When she didn't answer, not because she didn't want to, but because she couldn't, he pulled her down on to his lap. His arms came about her so firm and warm and hard with his desire that a spiral of shock, mingled with delicious pleasure, surged through her. She could have touched his face now had she wanted to, it was so close. And quite unable to prevent herself, she did so, with the softest brush of her lips.

'Why didn't you tell me?' she softly asked. She felt as if her insides were burning and her head was somewhere close to the ceiling.

'Tell you what?' The voice was oddly gruff.

'How you felt.'

'Would you have believed me? Would you have listened, or even cared?'

'I'm listening now.' He considered her for such a long time that the ache inside threatened to devour her. Then slowly, desperately slowly, he lowered his mouth to hers and she drank in the sweetness of his lips as a thirsty woman might take her first drink after a lifetime in a desert.

Why hadn't she realised how much she wanted him? *Why could she never see what was right in front of her?*

His hold upon her tightened convulsively and she felt him shudder against her.

'It's not a child I am, Meg Turner, to be content with kisses. Don't kiss me back like that if you don't want more.'

'Oh, I want more. Much more.'

His face was quiet and intensely serious as his eyes moved lovingly over every inch of her face, as if memorising it for all time. 'Let us be absolutely clear about this. I want to take you to bed and take off all your clothes and make love to you as you have never been loved in your life before.' The lips curved upwards into a crooked smile and the lamplight glinted upon the whiteness of his teeth. 'Would you have any objection to that, I wonder, Miss Meg Turner?'

'Oh, no objection at all, Thomas O'Cleary. Except . . .' She dipped her head in a moment's embarrassment. 'I'd want you to keep me safe.'

'You will be.'

'And it's wicked.'

His lips touched her brow, her nose. 'No, not wicked. And doesn't everyone think we've been doing this for months already? So why not? If you do want me, that is.'

A gurgle of happiness bubbled up inside, setting light to the excitement. Oh, she wanted him all right. How she wanted him.

And the loving was every bit as wonderful as he had promised. He took off her garments with exquisite care as if he was afraid to startle her, afraid she was a fragile bird who might fly away if he moved too quickly. He laid her on the bed and traced the line of her breasts with the tips of his fingers, exploring, learning her till she was pulsating with need of him, crying out for him to take her.

But just to make sure he had the picture right in his head, he followed along with his lips. Meg clutched at him, pulling him closer, offering herself to him, a willing, joyous partner in this loving.

'Tam?'

'I won't hurt you, my lovely.' Nor did he, making sure she was moist and ready before taking her with a love and passion that made her cry out with joy in her climax. Their lovemaking was fierce, and all too short. Later, when he took her again, it was slower, more sensual, their first flush of passion sated so that he was able to pleasure her till every nerve throbbed.

Afterwards Meg lay with her face a rosy glow from their loving, an after-love lethargy making her limbs heavy as they lay still entwined with his. They talked softly, punctuating the words with frequent kisses, as lovers do.

'To think you were here, all the time, and I never noticed.'

'A year or more wasted. We've some time to make up.'

Meg burst out laughing. 'You are a wicked Irishman, Tam O'Cleary, and...'

His eyes teased her in the shaft of moonlight that traced its ghostly light over their naked bodies. 'And?'

Meg was glad he could not see her blushes. She had very nearly said it. Nearly said that she loved him. Yet that would never do. It was too soon. Even if she could ever allow herself to risk such a thing again. Love was dangerous, painful. No, she would take a leaf out of Kath's book, and stick with sex. That was fun, and far less complicated. Safe from pain.

'Stop your teasing, you dreadful man. Do you know that in all this time you've been at Broombank, you've told me nothing at all about yourself.'

'There's nothing at all to tell.'

Meg snuggled down into the curve of his side. 'Nevertheless, I want to know everything about you.'

Tam drew in a long breath and told her his life story swiftly, being far more interested in studying the line of her shoulder blades and the small hollows in between.

'How many brothers and sisters have you?'

'Seven. At the last count.'

'No wonder you are so good with Lissa.'

'Families are important.'

'Then why are you here, in England, if they are in America? Sorry, I shouldn't ask.' What she really wanted to ask was, how long are you staying? But she did not.

'Didn't I want to see the world? I've worked and lived in as many places as I could find. I'll go home and see them all one day. For now I am here.'

For now, she thought.

His hand was looped about her thigh, stroking the soft inner flesh with the heel of his thumb, and Meg began to lose track of her thoughts. 'What was that you said about time to make up?'

'You are insatiable, Miss Turner.'

'Yes, yes, yes, Thomas O'Cleary, I am.' She moved against him to kiss him, rubbing herself enticingly against him while holding his hands away so that he was frustrated in his efforts to touch her. His breathing quickened and Meg felt her own resolution to hold him back rapidly slip away. 'Perhaps you don't want me, is that it?' she asked, her voice thick with need.

'Since you are my employer and I have no wish to find myself out of a job by morning, I dare say I'd best obey. Not that I want you for my own sake, you understand?'

'I understand perfectly.'

His words were coming out jagged and raw with his efforts to keep control. 'Shall I be about what you ask of me then, Meg Turner?'

'If you think you're up to it, Thomas O'Cleary.'

'Dear God in heaven, will you listen to the woman? I should have known better than to have got myself a woman boss. 'Tis time you learned that in bed the man is master.' Thrusting aside her staying hands he spread her beneath him, pinning her down with his own body. Meg laughed softly and arched herself to him, winding her legs about his thighs. 'It's shameless you are, woman.'

'Whatever you say, oh, master. Only make it quick, for God's sake, Tam. I need you.'

'Did you enjoy the dance?' Effie stared at the two untouched mugs of tea, still sitting on the kitchen table the next morning, then removed them quietly to the sink. Meg, avoiding Effie's gaze as she considered her answer, did not notice.

'Yes. It was fun. The band was excellent and there were loads of people there. I think it did me good to get out.'

She was busy mixing Lissa's breakfast cereal very carefully with milk in her teddy bear bowl as she talked. Then she set it down upon the kitchen floor for Rust to eat.

'I can see that it did,' Effie replied, very seriously, staring at the bowl.

The child gurgled and laughed delightedly as Rust swiftly devoured the luscious treat. Meg rolled her eyes in self-disgust. 'Would you look at that? What must I be thinking of?'

'What indeed?' said Effie, and got on with the washing up.

Meg was in a fever of excitement all day, just longing for the evening when the children would be in bed and she and Tam could be on their own. She had to admit, even to herself, that she had known nothing like this feeling in her entire life before.

Losing her virginity to Jack in the barn had been a painful, clumsy affair by comparison. She could see now that only Jack had experienced pleasure from it. With Tam she felt needed, cared for, nurtured, as if she mattered to him more than any pleasure he might get from their loving. It was a wonderful feeling.

She supposed he was her lover. Even the word sent shivers down her spine. She had a lover.

Changes would have to be made. Though they each had their own bed, Effie was still a physical presence in Meg's big, high-ceilinged bedroom. How could she explain the situation to her? Was it fair to think of carrying on such a relationship with a child in the house? All day she agonised over how she was to approach the subject.

'I was thinking,' Effie said, as she served Meg soup at dinner time, 'that maybe I should move in with Lissa, or take the room next-door. What do you think? Would you mind very much, Meg, being on your own?' She waited for her answer, wide-eyed and mildly enquiring.

Dear, darling Effie, so sensitive to other people's needs. Right from those early days when she had helped Meg over Lanky's death, her one concern had been to think of others and not be a bother. As if she ever could be. Meg heard Tam smother a spurt of laughter. She cleared her throat and smiled at her friend. 'I think that would be an excellent idea. Lissa would enjoy having you near, wouldn't you, darling?'

'Yes, yes. Want Effie next to me,' cried Lissa excitedly, and Meg refused to catch Tam's glance.

It was a simple matter to dust out the bedroom next to Lissa's, set up the bed and make it up with clean sheets. Meg set a lamp on the chest of drawers and a nightlight by the bed.

'There you are, Effie. Leave the candle lit till you sleep, if you like. Just make sure the shutters are closed and no light shows out the window.'

'I will.' Effie put her arms about Meg's waist and laid her cheek against hers. 'Didn't I say it would be all right? I'm so happy for you.'

Meg very nearly protested innocence of her meaning but then thought, no, this is Effie, my dear friend, so she hugged her close and didn't pretend.

'Yes, I am happy for myself.'

And then it was Effie's turn to look anxious. 'You won't be wanting me to leave, will you?'

'Leave? Heavens no, why should we? We love you.'

'And Tam loves you,' Effie said quietly. 'I've known for ages but you were too blind to see.'

'As always.' And then with some curiosity: 'What made you think so?'

Effie laughed. 'Oh, it was in his face every time he looked at you. In the way he moved close to you whenever you passed by. And once I saw him capture the scent of you from your scarf by holding it against his lips. Then he brought it out to you in the yard as if it were any plain old thing, of no account.'

Meg was stunned by these disclosures, afraid suddenly of what she had unleashed. 'I can't love him. I mustn't love him.'

'Whyever not?'

'I just can't, that's all. It's too soon. How will I know if I can ever trust him?' There was the hint of a sob in her voice and Meg quickly swallowed it. 'See how weak I'm getting already? It won't do.' She snatched up the pillow. 'Maybe it's a mistake to move you. Come back.'

'No.' Effie took the pillow and placed it on the bed. 'It's time I grew up and slept alone. It's time for us all to grow up. I know you loved Jack, and he let you down. So what? It happens. Now he's gone, you have his home and you feel guilty. Well, I say you've nothing to feel guilty about. It was him who did the dirty on you. Him and that so-called friend of yours. And when I meet that little madam . . .'

'Kath is still my friend. If she came here in trouble, I would still welcome her.'

'Maybe you would, because that's the way you are, Meg. But what you have to ask yourself is, would she do the same for you? Would she? Would Jack, if he were here?'

'I can't say.'

'Yes, you can, you know very well, neither one of them would give you a second thought. No, perhaps that's a bit hard on them. They'd think about you right enough, and probably be nice as pie to your face, but they'd still reckon that their own needs and wishes were of greater importance.'

Meg gazed at Effie, transfixed. There was an awful logic in her words. How was it some children were born with wisdom? And others, herself included, remained vulnerable and naive, seemingly throughout life?

'And I thought I was getting stronger, a tough woman running a farm practically single-handed.'

'So you are. But that doesn't mean you don't have a heart. Let it love, Meg Turner. Let it love.'

26

'It crossed my mind,' said Joe, 'that you might not be averse to letting me buy me own land off you. Well, what I think of as me own land.'

Jeffrey Ellis frowned. 'I didn't realise owning land was so important to you.'

'Well, I hev sons to think of, and grandsons now. I happen to have some money saved and, begging your pardon, since I'd heard you weren't too well, I thought you wouldn't mind being rid of the worry of it, like.' Cheap, he meant.

Jeffrey Ellis thought he didn't care one way or the other about land. The income from the rental that Joe Turner paid for Ashlea was useful but the capital, properly invested, would do almost as well. But he was surprised by the offer. 'I thought money was tight. Things haven't been good in farming these last years.'

'Aye, well. We make do. Just.'

'I had hoped, one day, to leave it to – my daughter.'

Joe shuffled his feet. 'If you want my opinion on that score, women shouldn't be trusted, not when it comes to land. They can't cope with it. It's a living thing is land and needs a man's hand to control it.'

'Your own daughter seems to be managing well enough.'

'She isn't on her own though, is she?' Joe blustered. 'She's got that great Irish lout staying with her.'

Jeffrey Ellis smiled. 'But the responsibility and the decisions are hers.'

'Happen.'

'It's funny how we fathers never take to the men our daughters choose.' Not that I know whether Katherine has a man, he thought bleakly, or where she is or why she left. If he knew she was well and happy, he'd have some reason to get up in a morning. He could fight off any illness then. As it was . . .

'You've not heard where she's at?' Joe, as ever, was blunt.

Mr Ellis turned away to fiddle unnecessarily with papers upon his desk. 'Not recently, no.' Not at all, in fact. 'But I'm sure we will hear soon.'

'Aye, aye. They come roond in the end. Allus do.' Joe cleared his throat. This conversation was wandering a bit far off track for his liking. Nevertheless he sympathised with this man. Jeffrey Ellis had been a good landlord, leaving Ashlea very much to Joe's care, not like some who were always poking and prying where they'd no business to. 'We all hev our troubles wi' family,' Joe confided, thinking it would do no harm to butter him up a bit. 'Our Meg took it upon herself to fetch a child home, says it's an orphan from Liverpool.'

Jeffrey Ellis listened with half his attention. 'Yes, I'd heard something of the case. Must be plenty about at this time. That was kind of her.'

'There's some as say it in't an orphan at all but her own brat.'

'Do you think it is?'

'Don't know what to think. She tells me nowt. I'm only her father, aren't I? But I can put two and two together and it looks very like that lad o' Lanky's.'

'Jack?'

'Aye, that's him. Black curly hair just the same it has. And eyes you wouldn't believe.' Joe's tone had softened slightly. 'Not that it's any fault of the child's, but if Meg was going to have a bairn, better if it'd been a son to follow on.'

Jeffrey Ellis laughed. 'You have to take what you're given and be thankful where babies are concerned.'

'Aye, mebbe. But now she has another man living with her. No morals that girl, no morals. I'm ashamed to call her me own daughter.'

'How old is this child?'

'Oh, eighteen months by now. Born last March after that hard winter.'

Jeffrey Ellis was looking oddly thoughtful. 'I saw Meg once or twice around that time. She didn't say she was having a baby, nor look it. Certainly didn't mention it or ask for my advice. How surprising.' It would be easy enough to check. The local midwife would know.

'You never can tell what daughters are at, can you?' Joe was regretting ever mentioning the subject, impatient as he was to get back to the question of his land. As a sitting tenant he might get Ashlea for a few hundred and save himself the rent every quarter. And he was of the opinion that land would rise in price, after the war. Things always seemed to, and then he'd never get it.

'I knew she and Jack were very friendly. Katherine too,' Jeffrey was saying. 'The three of them went everywhere together.' He lapsed into silence, seeming to forget for a moment that Joe was there.

Joe gave a polite cough just to remind him. 'So then, aboot Ashlea. Would you consider selling it to me, as sitting tenant? At a reduced price like.'

Jeffrey Ellis studied Joe with new interest. He didn't like the man, but he'd always paid his rent each quarter, never a day late. And Katherine probably wouldn't be interested in Ashlea, anyway. She'd get his savings and investments and Larkrigg of course, which should be enough for anyone. All the same, he didn't want to give it away. He was a careful man and Jeffrey felt surprisingly optimistic all of a sudden, after talking to Joe Turner. If what he suspected was correct, he might find another purpose for Ashlea.

'I'll speak to my lawyers about it, first thing in the morning,' he said, and named a price that made Joe blench.

'Here! I weren't thinking in those terms at all.'

'Ashlea is a fine farm.'

'Aye, because I've made it so.'

'We'll see what my lawyers have to say, shall we?'

And Joe was forced to doff his cap with unusual deference and leave Jeffrey Ellis to his thoughts.

Nobody would have known, looking at Meg beside Tam in the saleroom, that she was nervous. Dressed in a soft green tweed jacket and cord slacks, she looked relaxed and confident, a woman who knew what she was about.

They had walked her flock of Herdwicks the nine miles or so from Broombank down into Kendal, a long cold trek with all three dogs working hard the length of it. She'd seen each and every one of them booked in and penned. It had taken hours of effort and she felt tired and flustered and very far from confident.

'What if nobody wants to buy them?' she whispered, and felt Tam's body shift beside her as if he were smiling, though she dare not, for the life of her, look up into his face. 'What if I don't get a good price?'

His hand closed very briefly but firmly over hers. Held it by his side long enough to reassure, telling her to stop worrying and have faith.

Meg drew in a great gulp of air, not that it was particularly fresh in the confines of the auction ring but it got her lungs working again.

'I'll leave you to it then,' he said briskly, turning away, and she instantly panicked, almost snatching at his sleeve till she realised people were looking at her, smiling and nodding. She thrust her hands in her pockets, and smiled and nodded back.

'*Why*? Where are you going?' she hissed. She was appalled. She needed to know he was there, feel him beside her.

Tam's eyebrows raised very slightly. 'I suppose a man might enjoy his day off without interrogation from his boss?'

'Don't play games with me, Tam O'Cleary. You said you would be here with me. Morning, Will.' She nodded at Will Davies as he took his place by the ring.

'And so I am. But you don't need me to hang around all morning and hold your hand, now do you? You're the farmer.'

Doubts beset her. 'Do you think I'm doing the right thing? It's not too late to withdraw them. Even if I do get a good price that isn't the end of our worries. There's always the danger that the new flock won't settle. They might simply walk away. It has been known for sheep to walk forty miles or more, with lambs at foot, back to the heaf where they were born.'

'Then we'll just have to make them feel at home, won't we? You have other Swaledales, that'll surely help. And you mean to buy them in young, don't you?'

'Yes. Gimmers, first-year sheep.'

'So there shouldn't be too much of a problem. And as soon as they have lambed in their turn, the new stock will know no other place.'

But she wasn't to be reassured. 'Then again, with no natural immunity to the bugs on my land, they might sicken and die. Then I'll be bankrupt, finished, and have to go home, tail between my legs, and listen to my father gloat over how a woman can never make a farmer.'

Tam leaned back to consider her rump carefully. 'Then I'd say your father must have docked your tail when you were young. I can't see one for you to bring home, and I'm sure I would have noticed. It's a very nice rear.'

'Oh, Tam. Stop joking with me,' she hissed in a fierce whisper, even as the corners of her mouth twitched into a smile.

'Then stop fussing, woman. I'm just the hired help, remember?

You've bought and sold sheep before and managed perfectly well enough on your own.'

'*But not my whole flock.*'

'Don't exaggerate.' Tam winked at her with his usual outrageously wicked grin. 'It's more than half of it, I'll admit, but nowhere near the whole. And it's no fainting female that you are, Meg Turner, so don't pretend to be. Not with me who knows you so well. Haven't I told you that I like my women strong?' And, hands in pockets, he strolled away, whistling.

Damn him!

Meg gazed in desperation at the first lot of sheep already jostling into the ring. How long would she have to wait before her own came up? Every moment would seem a lifetime, more than enough to wonder at her sanity in taking this risk.

If she didn't get a good price for her Herdwicks, then all her plans would fall flat. There was admittedly no hurry for the tractor, but she needed to buy in enough Swaledales to start her off well. And she needed to leave some money over to put in the bank towards the deposit she was saving for Broombank. She had some saved already, but nowhere near enough. And then there was next quarter's rent. She groaned. What had she done? Today's sale was vital.

At last Meg went to join her flock in an agony of suspense. She was doing all right with the Herdwicks. Why was she never satisfied? Why make changes?

They came into the ring at last, dark and lively, their hoar frost faces looking faintly bewildered, white ears perked. As Tam had rightly pointed out, there was no room for sentiment in farming, nevertheless she was woman enough to hope they went to a good farm where they would be well cared for.

'A handsome crew we have here,' said the auctioneer. 'Good stock. Miss Turner tells me she is only parting with these splendid animals because she is making some changes at Broombank. Now, who'll give me the first bid?'

Silence for a moment while a hundred faces turned upon her. Pipes were sucked, eyes of every hue considered her but not a soul moved. Meg strove to keep her face impassive. It wouldn't do for them to think her weak or anxious. Not that she was, Meg thought stubbornly. These were good sheep, fit and healthy stock, animals to be proud of, and here she was in the ring with them to prove it. Sometimes you had to take a risk in life, in order to make progress. Her land was clean, her plan sound. She lifted her chin with fresh resolve and waited. All she needed was a good price to get her started.

'I did it, I did it!' Meg was almost bouncing with delight as she met up with Tam for a quick bite of lunch at the Duke of Cumberland. There was a fire in the inn's hearth for which she was grateful as there was a bite to the air this autumn day. 'They've gone to Blencary, a good farm in the Langdales. Perfect spot for them. Didn't I do well?'

'Yes,' said Tam, quietly. 'You did.'

'I mean we. We did well. I couldn't have got this far without you.' She hugged his arm close and smiled up at him, finally getting a like response.

'So now you can buy in your new stock.'

'Yes. I've been thinking about that. I shall buy half now, and half later. Perhaps next spring, just before they lamb. Then I can keep an eye on them easier. I'll need to gather the new sheep in every day, shepherd them well to make sure they stay. Once they've had lambs the progeny won't know any other heaf so it will get easier. I can do it, I know I can.'

'Whatever you say.'

'Then in a year or two I can sell on the progeny that I don't need. Probably make me more money than selling for meat.'

'You seem to have it all worked out.'

She glanced up at him, eyes shining. 'Oh, I have, I have. Everything is going right at last. The tractor will have to wait, but never mind. You can't have everything.' She took a sip of her beer then frowned. 'What is it? Why are you looking at me like that?'

'I'm pleased for you, that's all.'

She glanced at him again, finding herself catching the excitement that seemed to emanate from him. 'Tell me. Is it something I've said?'

Tam shook his head. 'Not that I'm aware of. Eat your sandwich. Then I'll show you what I've been up to this morning. I've a surprise of me own for you.'

It was a pony and trap. The fell pony stood, its grey coat already developing a winter fluffiness, patiently waiting in the yard behind the inn.

Meg could hardly believe her eyes. She walked up to it, then reached out to rub its nose with tentative fingers, constantly glancing at Tam.

'Is this ours?'

'If we can't afford a tractor we'll have to stick with the old ways for a bit longer. Petrol's hard to come by anyway. But I thought it was time Broombank had its own transport. We can't keep relying on other people.'

'But how did you find the money?'

'Don't worry about the money, I got it cheap from a bloke I know, complete with the old trap. It should make life easier. And horses I do know about. She's a grand mare, don't you think? We can get her covered and sell on the foals. Make a bit that way.'

Meg's eyes were shining. 'Oh, Tam, you are clever.' She hugged him. He was so thoughtful and kind and strong, a gentle, quiet man, just like this grand horse. Maybe she would let herself love him, just a little, though nothing in any way serious. 'What progress we're making. Come on, let's go home then I can really thank you.'

'We can go home in style today. Climb aboard, madam.'

And so they rode the long miles back up to Broombank with no trouble at all. Which was a relief, since it was all uphill with the wind in their faces, and Meg was far too excited to find her breath.

The mare was called Carrie, which seemed appropriate as she did a good deal of that. Winter was coming on and the ground was iron hard. Meg and Tam were collecting the last harvest of the year. Together they scythed the tawny bracken, packing it on to the sled which Carrie would pull down to the farm so they could use the fronds as winter bedding for the cows. The late sun was warm on her bare head and Meg could hear the drone of bees, busy with their own harvest in the heather blossom. It made her think of another harvest, another time when she had lain in the bracken with Jack and he had given her a ring.

The tiny sapphire and diamond ring was now tucked away in a dressing-table drawer. She supposed she should write to Connie about it one day, for it had belonged to her mother, and let her have it back. But she couldn't do that until she'd spoken to Jack. It wouldn't be right.

Why should she think of him now, when she had her lovely Tam and things were going so well? She lay with her lover nightly in the great bed and never thought of Jack then.

She wondered sometimes if she still held some love in her heart for him, or whether it was simply nostalgia and the tug of old loyalties. He'd been so much a part of her life for so long it was hard to put him from her. If there hadn't been the war it would have been easier to hate him for what he'd done to her. It was hard to be angry with a man far away, who might die at any moment.

Where was he? Had he gone overseas yet? Why hadn't he come home on leave? Had he been captured perhaps? Made a prisoner-of-war?

If he had come home, as promised, they could have talked things over, as old friends perhaps. They could have discussed in reasonable fashion what was best for Lissa, and whether Jack objected to Meg's still planning to buy Broombank. They could have come to terms and agreed to go their separate ways. Instead, her life and future was left undecided with nothing settled between them.

'Penny for them?' Tam was easing his back, resting from the arduous task of scything, and Meg went to him at once, slipping her hands about his waist, pressing her cheek against his back.

'They're worth much much more and I've no intention of flattering you by revealing them,' she said, crossing her fingers against the white lie.

He turned and crunched her in his arms, making her squeal, then kissed her till she was beating him with her fists, appealing for him to let her draw breath, just a little.

'Then I can start over again?'

'Hm, please.'

He handed her the scythe. 'Back to work, shameless hussy. The days are too short to waste in play.'

And so they were, all too short. The swallows had left already for warmer climes though Meg could still hear the chack-chack of fieldfares and the clear-throated tones of the robin to cheer her days.

Close by her feet, harvest mice and voles gobbled up the insects disturbed by the scything, filling their stomachs with as much food as they could find in readiness for the long hard winter ahead. Not for them the endless queueing.

Watching them, taking care not to disturb a vole's lunch, Meg prayed this winter would be kinder than the last. Never had she known such hard winters as they had experienced since the onset of the war. It was as if the weather wished to echo everyone's gloom.

'I think I'd better go and round up the new Swaledales.' Rust was at her feet in a second, understanding every word. 'Come on, Tess, Ben.'

'Right,' Tam agreed, frowning slightly but accepting her sudden need to be alone.

'I won't be long. You know I have to do it regularly.'

'I know.'

Meg thankfully set down her scythe and strode off, up to the heaf. Would the new sheep stay? Would they thrive? Or would they up and leave her as Jack had done, and Kath? As Tam might do, one day.

High up on the fells could be heard the deeper-throated carrion crow, and the funereal black raven. These birds brought a shiver to any farmer for the damage they could do to stock trapped or injured on a crag. Nothing of the sort must happen to her new flock.

She reached down a hand, feeling the wetness of Rust's nose nudge against it. At least her lovely dog stayed with her always, for all his three-legged gait. Even horrific injuries had not kept him from her side. He'd been saved from the crows and from her brother's jealousy. And Dan had learned his lesson and not bothered her since.

She hadn't given in to his bullying then, nor would she.

As she looked over her land and gathered her sheep, finding only one or two had strayed and would need fetching back from their old heaf, Meg knew she was as ambitious as ever, if not more so. Life might be hard with the worry of the war, the grinding work, bad weather, little ready money and a whole list of shortages, not to mention her anxieties over Charlie and Kath, but despite all of that, her world was about as perfect as it could be.

Lanky had wanted her to have Broombank, not his son. She should remember that and honour his belief in her. Her new sheep were doing well. She had Effie and Tam. And she had her Luckpenny, didn't she? Everyone was happy. So what could go wrong?

As she sat at supper that evening, almost too exhausted to eat, it seemed she had made her judgement too soon. One person was not happy. Upstairs in her cot, handmade from finest birchwood by Tam, Lissa began to cry.

'Go to her, Effie, will you?' Meg asked, pulling the string from her hair with a tired hand, and shaking out her curls.

'I've been up six times already,' Effie complained. 'The little bugger is playing me up something shocking.'

'Effie.'

Her cheeks flushed pink as they once would never have done at use of such a word. 'I love her like anything, but it's true, she is. She won't do anything I say these days.'

Meg sighed. 'Well, what's wrong with her? Is she hungry?'

'No, course she ain't hungry.' Effie was affronted. 'Would I send a hungry child to bed?'

'What is it then?'

'Don't you realise that Lissa has needs too? She's crying for you,' Tam said, not looking up from his mutton hot pot. More potato than mutton in it, but it tasted good after a hard day's work all the same.

'I can hear she's crying.' Meg's own appetite had quite deserted her. Why did she fail to make Lissa happy? The child was well fed and nurtured. What was wrong? Even Effie was implying that the fault was hers.

'Then go to her.'

Meg glanced up in surprise at the tone of Tam's voice but did not move. She could feel a headache starting and all she wanted to do was fall into bed and sleep. 'Scything bracken is a hell of a job. And I have to do this extra shepherding every day. I'm tired.'

'Damn you, woman, can't you think of someone else besides yourself and your sheep? Lissa *needs* you.'

She turned on him then, furious as a spitting cat, ready to scratch his eyes out. 'Don't you tell me what to do! Or imply that I don't care, because it's not true. I do care, I *do*!'

'Then prove it. Show it.' Throwing down his fork, he caught her flailing hand in his own. Sensual lips curled into a harsh line upon the disturbingly handsome face.

Meg longed to smack it, hard, but this was their first real argument and it terrified her.

Then the soft, Irish tones melted her anger to butter. 'Don't take it out on me, Meg, or that child, for what Jack did to you. Lissa needs your *love*. It's unworthy of you to deny it.' The words cut deep into the heart of her and when he gently let her hand go, Meg hesitated for a long moment, then pushed back her chair and went upstairs.

She stood and gazed upon Lissa. The child sat in her cot, fat tears rolling down her chubby cheeks, small hiccuping sobs filling the room with heartbreaking sadness.

She looked so alone, so desperately unhappy.

Kath's child? Or her own?

'What is it, sweetheart?' Unable to prevent herself, Meg reached over and picked up Jack's child, of her own accord, for the very first time.

Lissa's sobs quieted instantly and violet-blue eyes swimming with tears gazed up into Meg's in a silent plea for loving. And as her small arms curled, warm and damp, about Meg's neck, she closed her eyes against the agony of it, unaware of Tam and Effie watching with smiles on their faces from the door.

Soft fingers curled about her ear, baby lips pressed against her cheek and a tiny, snuffling sigh was expelled on a hiccup of relief.

Only then did her own tears come. Whether she was crying for the baby's father, whose silence seemed deafening in this dreadful war, or washing away the last of the pain for a man she had once loved, Meg did not rightly know or care. The relief was wondrous.

Only then did she realise that self-pity and bitterness was destructive, not only to herself but to those about her. It was true that Lissa was too often watchful and silent, as if she were not entirely sure if she were a part of things and was trying to work it all out. As if she did not quite belong. Meg hugged her closer, breathing in the sweet baby scent of her.

'If only Kath had written,' she said now, looking at her two friends with pleading in her eyes, begging them to understand. 'I was so afraid. Still am. If I only knew what the future holds. If I knew I could keep her.'

Tam came and put his arms about them both. 'We can none of us know that. Life is a risk for us all.'

'And what will I tell Lissa, when she asks?' A day Meg dreaded. 'I can only explain about the Liverpool orphanage, about Greenlawns and how her mother couldn't keep her there.'

'Then that is what you must say. But it does no good for her to think you don't love her either.'

'Oh, but I do, I do!' Meg cradled the child close, tears bursting out afresh. The tiny eyelids fluttered, closed, grew heavy. As transculent as porcelain, blue-veined and beautiful. A small contented sigh banished the last of the heartbreaking sobs.

Though it troubled Meg that Lissa would not be told the truth, what else could she do, in the circumstances?

'Once I told my father that I would never put the land before those I loved. Yet look at me, I've done exactly that.

'When Kath needed me, where was I? Did I hurry to get her out of that dreadful place? No. I stayed home to see to the lambing. Have I given any time or thought to Lissa's needs? No. I've left her to you, Effie, and Tam. Yet it is people who are really important, not land. We can only borrow land, for the length of our lifetime. After that it belongs to someone else. But people live on in your heart even after death, don't they?'

Tan smiled. 'It's never too late to learn a lesson.'

Meg dried her eyes. 'Do you truly think so? Will she ever forgive me?'

Effie, anxious as always to be a part of the scene, came into the room. 'Course she will. Lissa loves you. She always has.'

Meg smiled down at the now sleeping child curled contentedly in her arms, belonging at last. 'I'm all right now. You go and finish your supper. I'll sit with Lissa for a while, make sure she's all right.'

She laid the baby down in the cot and drew the covers up to her chin. So much time she had wasted. Yet if she hadn't worked hard, where would they be now? But she must always remember that however important her farm and her sheep, Lissa was more so. As were Effie and Tam. She must remember that.

Never must she make this mistake again.

27

Charlie came that autumn, seeming bigger and more mature than the young boy of memory who'd liked to avoid chores and play with cigarette cards. And with him came his new bride, a shy and smiling fair-haired girl whom he called Sue with such affection in his voice, and so rarely released her hand, that Meg felt quite choked with emotion just watching them together.

They stayed for three days and it was such fun, just like old times with Charlie eating them out of house and home, and talking twenty to the dozen about his plans for the future.

'I'll have finished my thirty missions as navigator soon. Then I could do a second tour or go on and learn more about engineering. Once the war is over that will be the way forward, I'm sure of it.'

'Meg wants to know if you eat carrots,' Tam said, and as they all laughed, a blushing Meg was forced to explain.

'Actually, many pilots did at first, thinking it might help. But now we have pathfinders. They drop markers so we know where to drop the bomb. Makes it much easier and there's less likelihood of hitting civilian targets by mistake.'

Meg shivered. 'Does it bother you, dropping bombs?'

Charlie's jaw tightened and she knew she'd asked the wrong question. 'I've nothing against the German people. Many of them want rid of Hitler just as much as we do. So I'd rather not hit them.'

'Of course. I didn't think. I'm sorry. But you'll be glad of a quiet job for a change.'

'Maybe. But all jobs are important. We'd be nothing without the ground crew. Anyway, I might change my mind yet. I might do another tour.'

He looked like a flyer. He had about him that casual, devil-may-care appearance that all flyers had. It declared him a veteran of many missions and promised he would win this war, no matter what.

Tam, noticing that the new young bride was looking less than happy at this talk of a second tour, changed the subject and they talked about farming for a while, telling how Meg had tried and failed to buy a tractor.

'Are you anywhere near buying Broombank?' asked Charlie, and she shook her head.

'Not yet.' The bank manager would give you anything, she thought. A man, so young and handsome, and with such an air of determination about him.

'I have absolute faith in you, Meg. Whatever you make up your mind to do, you'll do it. You're right, mechanisation is the way to go. You never know, you might even get electricity up on these fells one day. Never say die.'

Never say die. No, thought Meg. Nor you either, my lovely boy. She was forced to flee to the kitchen and fuss over the huge pie she'd baked to hide her sudden flood of emotion. It was cooked to perfection, crust lightly browned with a bubble of gravy coming from the steaming hole in its centre. It consisted chiefly of vegetables but with just a flavour of rabbit. And the pastry was good, made with their own pork dripping. It would go down a treat.

But as she set out the warmed plates and called for everyone to come and eat, she couldn't help but think how unfair it was, that their youth and love should be threatened by this awful war. Would it never end? And did she have the courage to see it through?

It was late on a November afternoon when Mr Ellis finally plucked up the courage to call and see Meg. He had walked all the way from Larkrigg, glad of the exercise, smiling at the thrushes feasting on the bright rowanberries. He hoped the thick flush of scarlet berries did not betoken a harsh winter ahead. He was tired, as the whole country was. Beginning to realise that they were in for a long haul and there would be no quick solution to Hitler's threat.

He found Meg busily engaged in layering a hedge. The energy and skill she displayed in the task gave the lie to her slender youthful frame. It made him feel ashamed of his own inactive lifestyle.

'You look busy. I hope I'm not interrupting?'

'Not at all. I'll just finish this bit.' She'd cut a long slit down the side of the slender trunk; now she bent it over and wove the pliant frond into position with the others to form a living, unbreakable windbreak against which the sheep could shelter but not escape. Then she set *down the* small billhook she was using in a safe place, pulled off her leather mitts, and wiped her brow. 'I'm glad of the excuse to stop, to be honest. Tea? I was just about to have one.'

They sat at the big deal table in the kitchen, enjoying the scalding tea, weak though it was, not speaking for some time. Meg could almost feel him thinking.

From the bedroom upstairs came the sounds of Lissa playing with her dolls. Effie had made them for her out of clothes pegs and she loved to line them up and pretend to teach them, as if they were in school. Meg could tell that Mr Ellis had his ears cocked, for every time Lissa's little sing-song voice rose in pitch, he half turned his head towards it.

'Would you like to see her?' Meg asked at last, finally finding the courage.

Eager eyes met hers. 'I would.'

She went to the door and called up the stairs. 'Lissa, it's time for your cod liver oil and orange juice. Come down, there's a good girl.'

A moan of protest followed by running feet, and Jeffrey Ellis found himself holding his breath. Too late now to wonder if he should have come at all. A pair of chubby legs appeared on the stairs, followed by the prettiest little girl he had ever seen. At least, since Katherine had been about that age. He was instantly disappointed that Lissa bore little resemblance to that long-ago child. But why should he have expected her to? Yet there was something about her. Something in the way she walked, the toss of her head. Or else he was a foolish old man with an over-ripe imagination.

He smiled reassuringly as the child hesitated but it was Meg who spoke. He could not have found his voice if he'd been strung up by the heels.

She held out the cod liver oil spoon. 'Come on, Lissa, open wide.'

Lissa screwed up her nose. 'Don't like it.'

'Cod liver oil is good for you. Isn't that right, Mr Ellis?'

'It must be, that's why it tastes so nasty. Hold your nose, Lissa, then you won't notice. I think I have a mint in my pocket somewhere when you've finished.'

The mixture went in a trice and the mint was accepted with one of Lissa's most entrancing smiles.

'She is a lovely child,' Jeffrey said, eyes never leaving the small figure.

'Yes.'

'Your father thinks she's yours.'

'I know.'

'She isn't though, is she?'

'She is now.'

'I mean...'

'I know what you mean. We ought to be careful, she's like British Gaumont News.'

'I beg your pardon?'

Meg chuckled. 'The eyes and ears of the world.'

'Oh.' Jeffrey Ellis laughed while Meg turned to the watchful violet eyes. 'Go on, you can take your orange juice upstairs, but see that you drink it all.'

'I will, Meg.'

When the child had gone, Meg turned to Mr Ellis. 'Was there something particular you wanted to say? I don't mean to be rude, only it's rare for you to call. In fact in all the years I have known you, this is the first time.' She smiled to try to soften the import of her words.

Jeffrey Ellis returned her frank gaze with an equal frankness in his own. 'You're right. I did have a purpose in calling. I'm glad to have found you on your own because it's connected with Lissa. She's Kath's child, isn't she?'

Startled by his abruptness, Meg didn't answer immediately. 'What if she was?' she hedged, sudden fear clutching the pit of her stomach. 'How would you feel about that?'

'It's all right. I wouldn't dream of trying to take her from you. Seems to me you are doing an excellent job of bringing her up. Besides...' He paused and sipped his tea for a moment.

'Mrs Ellis would not approve?'

Jeffrey met her clear-eyed gaze. 'Rosemary means well, but she is bounded by convention. She has lived a sheltered life, too sheltered perhaps. Never had to rough it in the real world as most of us do. It is very important to her that her respectable, rose-tinted life is not besmirched in any way.'

'She pretty well said the same about you, though not quite in such picturesque language.'

Jeffrey set down his cup sharply and some of the tea spilled out. 'She is far too protective for her own good – for *my* own good I should

334

say.' He drew in a long steadying breath. 'Why didn't you tell me that you knew where Kath was? You know how I have longed to know.'

'Because I have no idea where she is.' Meg found herself setting aside pretence, deciding there had been too much secrecy already. 'Oh, I did find her once, by bullying the address out of your wife if you want to know. But Kath refused to come home with me. She left me with the baby on Lime Street Station, said I would make a better mother, and disappeared into the crowd. There was nothing I could do but return home without her.'

'I see.' Or did he? It hurt to think that Rosemary had known where she was all along. And why hadn't Kath written to him direct? 'Where was she when you found her?'

'In a home for unmarried mothers.' Meg did not wish to reveal the stark horror of the place. She could leave him with some illusions at least.

'And the father? Do you know who he is?'

She looked him full in the face, summoning every vestige of courage she possessed. 'Yes, I know who he is.'

'It was Jack, wasn't it?'

Meg felt choked suddenly, grateful she didn't have to say his name out loud. 'You only have to look at Lissa to know that.'

Jeffrey Ellis nodded, compassion strong in him. 'I guessed as much. And you loved Jack, whereas my daughter, bless her careless heart, merely wanted to play with him.'

Meg swallowed the sudden lump that came into her throat and stood up, taking the empty cups to the sink. 'It doesn't matter now. That's all in the past. I have Effie and Tam, and I have Lissa. I don't need anyone else.' Coming back to the table, she took Mr Ellis's hand. 'But I still miss Kath. I want you to know that I bear her no grudge. She is still, despite everything, my very dear friend. How could she be otherwise when she left me her child to care for?'

He blinked. 'I hope one day she might appreciate that fact. I wish only for her to come home.'

After Mr Ellis had gone, accepting gratefully Meg's invitation to call and see Lissa at any time, Meg laid her head upon her hands and cried her heart out.

Bad news arrived on the heels of the bitter east wind that scoured the fells before Christmas.

'The Japanese have attacked Pearl Harbour,' Sally Ann read, ashen-faced. 'Even while their special envoy was making peace talks with Washington, Japan's fleets were attacking Hawaii and Manila. Oh, dear God, there were more than two thousand Americans killed.'

'That'll fetch them in,' said Dan, with satisfaction.

Sally Ann frowned at her husband. 'Don't be so brutal. They'd have come in anyway. What a price to pay. All those young men and women.' Tears ran down her plump cheeks. 'What if they were your sons? How would you feel then?'

Dan looked at his two boys, pride evident in his round face, and pain at such a dreadful prospect. 'We're fighting this war for them. Then they won't ever have to fight another. Mark my words, we'll win it. Right always triumphs in the end.'

'By heck,' said Joe. 'You've learned some long words. Been swallowing a dictionary?'

Sally Ann held her breath, wondering fearfully what Dan would answer. Many secret hours had been spent improving her husband's reading skills, teaching him simple addition and subtraction. She had hoped it might give him the courage to stand up to his father. Was this the moment?

Dan got to his feet, crimson to the tips of his ears. 'It was only an opinion, that's all.'

'You great daft oaf. Thoo, hev an opinion? In that rattle head o' thine. Pigs might fly!'

Knocking over his chair, Dan blundered from the room.

Sally Ann was on her feet in an instant, red in the face herself, livid with her father-in-law. 'How can you talk to him like that, your own son? He's working flat out driving tractors for the Government Committee all day, as well as trying to run this place with you.'

'I don't hold wi' tractors. Nothing better than a good horse.' Joe was in a particularly sour mood this day. His hopes of buying Ashlea had died a death. Jeffrey Ellis's lawyer had increased the price he'd first suggested, not reduced it. Anyone would think Ellis didn't need the money, which couldn't be right. What did he want with Ashlea, anyroad? Joe hated failure, it made his bitterness against life yet more acute. And he was feeling his age today. Full of aches and pains he was, and a cough coming on. Annie would have made him a paper of goose fat for his chest.

'Not to mention working in the Home Guard at night,' Sally Ann was saying. 'Sometimes dangerous work, conducting prisoners to the POW camp, fire fighting, as well as drilling and training in case of invasion or bombing.'

'There are no bombs here. He's safe enough.'

'He doesn't feel safe, or wanted. Can't you ever give him credit for trying, offer a kind word, just once in a while?'

'Kindness makes a man soft.'

'It makes a man feel he's appreciated.' She steadied her breath. It did no good to shout at him. That way he was bound to win. 'You were glad enough to see Charlie here, yet you never showed him that you were. Why not?'

'I don't approve of my son's choice of career.'

'He's fighting a war, that's hardly a career.'

'All this talk of engineering when it's over. He should be a farmer.'

'You already have two farmers in the family, Dan and Meg. Isn't that enough?'

'Only yan.'

Sally Ann sighed. 'Not that again. Won't you ever acknowledge her efforts?'

'She'll get fed up. Women hev no staying power.'

Sally Ann decided not to pursue this fruitless argument. 'Anyway, how do we know what the future will bring for any of us in the years ahead? The war is a long way from over. It seems to be getting worse in point of fact. There might not be work for any of us by then, or not here at least. We might not manage to hang on to Ashlea. I know it's a hard struggle now to make ends meet.' She reached for his hand. 'Why don't you put Dan properly into the picture? Tell him what state the farm really is in. Perhaps then he'd work on it more. He'd feel wanted.'

Joe got up from the table and flicked on his cap, adjusting the neb to its right position over his eyes. 'There's no danger of us losing Ashlea. I'll see it's there for my grandsons when they need it. You leave the worrying to me. I'll let you know when I can't manage.'

When he had gone Sally Ann sat alone by the fire. There was no getting round Joe's stubbornness. Oh, but he worried her. He really did. He insisted on doing everything himself. Wouldn't share a thing with them, not a thing. She reached for her two boys and pulled them on to her knee. They always soothed her after an argument.

'Joe's in a temper. He's been up to something, I can tell.'

Sally Ann stood watching Meg split logs. She stood by the old yew chopping block, chips of wood all about her, a fine figure of a woman, there was no denying it. Taller and slimmer than the young girl she had once been, her fair skin tanned by the weather though hair as raggy and unkempt as ever. Its beauty came from its colour, as bright as a polished penny. She was looking more than usually attractive today, Sally Ann had to admit, for all she was dressed in work overalls and a checked shirt that could have belonged to Dan or Charlie.

'So what else is new?' Meg had neither the time nor the inclination to worry over her father. She hummed as she swung the axe, more interested in the satisfaction of seeing a growing pile of logs for the winter evenings ahead.

Sally Ann propped herself against the edge of the saw-horse. 'I think there's something wrong.'

Meg stopped working, pushed back her hair and set down the axe carefully. 'What can be wrong?'

'There isn't much money coming into the house, you know. We've had two bad lambing seasons. And Joe and Dan hardly speak, let alone work together. Dan would rather be off working with the tractors than on his own farm. But then he has to. We need the wages he brings in.'

Meg sat on the chopping block and propped her elbows on her knees. 'I'm sure you're worrying unduly. Ashlea will be all right. It's a good farm.'

'It *was* a good farm.'

'You must make Dan talk to Father. Get everything out into the open.'

'Huh.' Sally Ann gave a bitter little laugh. 'Easier said than done. The tension between them is something terrible. And he still wants Broombank, you know. More than ever now Ashlea isn't doing so well.'

Meg smiled and squeezed her sister-in-law's hand. 'Ashlea will do all right. Every farm has its bad years. It'll pull back next season, you'll see. As for Broombank, well, he'll get over it. Let him want.'

'You don't seem too bothered.'

'My father can do his worst for all I care, Sal. We are doing fine, thanks very much. He can't hurt us now. Nothing can.' Brave words, but she believed them to be true.

Sally Ann examined her sister-in-law with new interest. 'You've fallen in love.'

'What?'

'You have. There's a glow about you. I can see it in the way you can hardly stop smiling, and I could hear you singing from right down the lane. You look like a woman in love. Why, you're positively blooming. You're not . . .'

'No, I'm not.'

Sally Ann laughed. 'It's Tam, isn't it? Oh, I'm so glad. He's a lovely man. When's the happy day?'

Meg tried to look shocked. But deep down she knew that in spite of all her efforts to the contrary, she could not deny it was true. She was falling in love. And she wasn't even sorry. 'Who said anything about marriage?'

It was Sally Ann's turn now to look disapproving. 'My word, we have changed, haven't we? There was a time when you couldn't wait to get down that aisle. Now you're presumably content to give the gossipmongers a run for their money.'

'Things change. I've changed.'

'Are you saying you don't trust him?' Sally Ann asked quietly.

'I didn't say that.'

'Why don't you marry him then?'

'I don't want to make a mistake, that's all. There's no hurry.'

'And there's always a chance Jack might come back, is that it?'

'That's not it at all.'

'I should hope not. Because you'd be a fool if you let some kind of misguided loyalty spoil things for you and Tam. If he were mine, I'd marry him like a shot, before he had time to think twice.'

'I'm not you, Sally Ann. I like to think things through properly.'

'You think too much sometimes. Follow your heart, that's what I say.'

'I did that once before and look where it got me. Anyway, he hasn't asked me, so there.'

'Aw, Meg.' Sally Ann's soft heart filled with remorse. 'I'm that sorry. I didn't think.' And she put her arms about her sister-in-law and hugged her. 'Men,' she said, with feeling.

Meg pulled on her clean white nightdress and climbed in between the sheets, sighing with contentment as she stretched out, a knot of anticipation in the pit of her stomach as there always was when she waited for Tam to come to her.

I don't need Sally Ann's pity, she told herself. And I don't care about marriage. But conviction was hard to find.

They were like a real family already, she and Tam living together with Effie a sister to Meg and Lissa their own little girl. Except that they were not a married couple, and Lissa was not the child of either of them. It was a game of pretend that could all end at any moment.

Only Effie was really a constant. Meg reminded herself of that fact now. One day she could lose both Tam and Lissa. Kath would come, or Jack, and take Lissa away. Or maybe even Mr Ellis might decide to exercise his right as a grandparent. She had seen the love and longing in his eyes whenever he looked at Lissa.

And Tam had never claimed to be anything but rootless, a man who liked to be free to move on when he chose. Marriage had not been mentioned by either of them and Meg understood that, for their different reasons, neither of them wanted it. How could she even consider it while she was still engaged to Jack, theoretically at least? She would need to see him and give him back his ring.

How she had changed. And some might say not for the better. Proper little Miss Meg Turner with a lover. She hugged herself with pleasure, determined not to feel guilty. Well, why should she? There was a war on. Things were different.

Count your blessings.

Effie was happily settled in the bedroom next to Lissa's while she and Tam shared this lovely big double bed.

Her new flock of Swaledales, which she checked almost hourly, were well and healthy, standing on all four feet.

And the purchase of the horse must be a good sign. Perhaps Tam meant to stay for a long, long time. At least until the end of the war. Meg dared think no further than that. She wanted him to stay for ever. So badly, it hurt. Snuggling down between the sheets, her body started tingling with anticipation.

These were the best times, when they could shut the door on worries over the war and the daily grind of endless chores and lie together between the covers.

He came to her now and she flung back the sheets, opening her arms to welcome him.

'You've got my favourite nightdress on,' he said.

Meg looked surprised, then laughed. 'The one you like to take off, you mean?'

His body sank on to the mattress beside her. 'I enjoy unfastening all the buttons down the front. Naughtily Victorian.'

'It was my mother's, and the warmest I could find. This house is freezing.'

'She must have been as lovely as you.' He ran his eyes over her face, then followed his gaze with his hands and while he cupped her cheeks he kissed her with a delicate tenderness. Meg nestled her face into the warmth of his palms, the familiar excitement mounting within. It seemed wicked to be here with him, like this, but she couldn't have stopped it, not for the world.

'I want you, Thomas O'Cleary.'

He chuckled. 'And shall ı let you have me, I ask myself?'

She loved the touch of his hands upon her naked flesh, the loving warmth of him beside her, the thrust of him inside her. He was her man, and protest how she might, she loved him. What did it matter about the local gossips?

Life, Meg thought as he started the ritual of undoing buttons and kissing each freshly exposed inch of flesh as he did so, was deliciously sweet. She was so lucky, with no room for complaint at all. Despite the rationing and the endless queueing, despite her worries over Charlie which knotted her stomach at night when she heard the drone of faraway aeroplanes, despite even her fears for the future, she was coping. She was happy.

Tam laid her back upon the pillows as he drew the garment from her. 'There, didn't I do that nicely?'

Oh, yes, things were going fine.

And there was no reason that she could think of why they shouldn't continue to do so.

They had an unexpected visitor just in time for Christmas. All at Broombank were enjoying breakfast when they heard the sound of a vehicle turning in the yard and Meg opened the door to find Connie standing on the doorstep, several ominous-looking suitcases about her feet.

'I've left Grange,' she announced peremptorily. 'Peter's gone and volunteered before he's even been called up and I won't stop there on my own. Anyway, they're using the lovely estuary to fire anti-aircraft guns and I've had enough. Even when there are no enemy aircraft overhead they practise all the time, using old biplanes to tow targets about. It's too much, it really is. I can't stand any more, I simply can't.'

Meg bowed to the inevitable. 'You'd best come in, Connie. Have you had breakfast?'

'Oh, I couldn't eat a thing.' She surveyed the breakfast table. 'Well, perhaps just a slice of toast, plenty of butter. I dare say you've no shortages here. My word, that porridge smells good, Effie. Perhaps I might manage a spoonful. I've eaten hardly a scrap for days. My nerves, you know. They can take no more.'

Can we take you? came the uncharitable thought which Meg quickly banished. She felt a wave of sympathy for the absent Peter who would rather face the Germans than his own wife.

Yet how could she turn Connie away? Not only was there a war on, but she was Lanky's daughter and Jack's sister and as such Lissa's aunt. Oh, it was all so complicated.

'I'm very worried about Jack.'

Meg lowered herself into her chair, at once sensing bad news. 'What is it? What's happened?'

'I don't know. That's the annoying part. He's not the greatest letter writer in the world, as you know, but he generally sends me one a month. And I send him little treats. Knitted socks and such like. But I've heard nothing from him for weeks. I'm very concerned.'

Tam pushed back his chair. 'I'll be up mending walls on the Knott if you need me.' Meg could tell by the way he strode from the room that he was not pleased by this new development, or by her reaction to it.

'I'm sure there's nothing to worry about,' Meg consoled the older woman. 'Letters often get delayed. You'll probably get half a dozen all at once.'

Connie dabbed at her nose, but her other hand was already reaching for a fresh slice of bread. 'You're probably right, dear. We'll not start to worry till we hear something definite, shall we?'

Meg excused herself, assured Connie she could stay for a few days, for Christmas at least, and went after Tam.

28

Meg had to run to catch up with him, slipping on the rain-slicked stones in her haste as his long legs made short work of the distance, striding over the coarse grass at such a cracking pace he was halfway up the fell and she was out of breath by the time she reached him.

'You ought to go in for fell running,' she gasped. 'What is it? Why are you angry?'

Tam began to sort stones on the ground, rather as Lanky had once done, only in short, jerky movements. 'Who said I was angry?'

'I know you well enough by now. It's in the way you walk, the tilt of your head. What was I supposed to do, tell her no, she couldn't stay here? When she knows we have bedrooms to spare?'

'Finding bedrooms is not the problem.'

'She'll have brought her ration book.'

Tam threw down the stone he had just carefully selected and met Meg's pleading gaze with the closest to fury she had ever seen in him, barring the time he had dropped her in the water trough when she wouldn't go to the dance with him. 'I'm not talking about rations, and you know it. The woman is a bore, but worse than that, she's a trouble-maker.'

'She's Jack's sister. And he might be the one in trouble, Tam.' Meg spoke quietly, her skin parchment cold. 'Why does Jack always have to come between us? I feel nothing for him.'

'And there's me thinking that you're riddled with guilt and some foolish kind of loyalty. Why has she come? If she never came before, to see this lovely Lanky of yours, her own father, why is this the perfect place to come to now?'

'Because it's safe. She's frightened, can't you see? She needs sanctuary for a while, as we all do. She's worried.'

Tam sighed. 'I see that you are a difficult woman to teach a lesson. You see no bad in anyone, do you? Hell's teeth, what am I to do with you?'

Meg, sensing a softening in him, a light sparking in the green eyes, moved closer. 'I can think of something.'

'What, here? On a fellside, in December? Do you think I'm made of stone?'

A stiff breeze wrapped itself about them, reminding Meg of reality. 'Perhaps you're right.' She leaned against him, loving the warm closeness, the sense of being cherished. 'Later then?'

He pulled her roughly into his arms and kissed her savagely. When he had done, leaving her gasping, he thrust her from him. 'Didn't I say I wasn't made of stone, you witch?' He gave a playful slap to her bottom. 'Go and see to those fine sheep of yours and give a man some peace.'

Listening to Connie's endless complaints later that day, Meg couldn't help but admit that Tam might have a point.

'Of course, I've always liked this house. Were anything to happen to Peter, I might well come back to live here.'

'Come back? How can you come back? I have a lease on the place,' Meg gently reminded her.

'Ah, yes, but only for five years and three of those are very nearly up. Let's face it, Meg, you have little hope of finding the purchase price. Your stay here is only temporary.' Connie folded her hands and her lips, well satisfied with the start of fear she had produced in Meg's grey eyes.

'I'm doing rather well, actually.'

'I'm sure you are, dear,' Connie simpered. 'But it's a fair sum of money to find, and who would give you a mortgage? A woman alone. It isn't really the thing, is it?'

'Perhaps you should leave me to worry about that.'

No indeed. Life was not going to be easy with Jack's sister around.

That night as Meg and Tam lay, untouching, in the great bed, she fiercely regretted their quarrel and ventured to resolve it.

'I think you might be right, about Connie wanting to cause trouble,' Meg admitted at last. 'She's got it into her head that one day she might come back here.'

'Not she,' said a soft voice in the darkness.

'She might, just so's she can sell it for a higher price than I would pay her for it. Is that why you were angry, because you guessed that's what she'd say?'

And when he didn't answer, Meg rolled over and nuzzled into his neck. 'Or is this all about Jack?' she whispered. 'That's the real reason why you didn't want Connie here, isn't it? Because she reminds you of Jack.'

'Because she reminds *you* of Jack.'

'You're jealous.'

'Rubbish.'

'You are.' Very gently she bit his ear. 'You think that since I've let Lanky's daughter live here, I might do the same for his son.'

She felt Tam twist round in the bed then found he was on top of her, wrapping her body in his own. She wasn't complaining, but from what she could see of his face he still didn't look too happy. 'Would you?' he asked, very quietly.

'Would I what?'

'Don't play games with me, Meg Turner. Would you let Jack come and live here?'

'Not live exactly.'

'But you'd let him stay?'

'Only for a little while. If necessary. I could hardly throw him out now, could I?' she pleaded, seeing that this was not at all the reply he wanted.

'Why not? I would have thought that was exactly what you should do, after the way he treated you.'

She supposed that he was probably right. 'I find it hard to hate people.'

Tam made a sound of exasperation in his throat and flounced away from her to sit on the side of the bed. Meg felt the loss so acutely she was stunned for a moment. Then she crept up behind him and slid her arms about his waist. When he didn't protest, she leaned her cheek against his back. 'I find loving harder though.'

He made as if he wanted to turn round but she held him firm, not letting him. 'No, listen to me for a minute. Hating is easy, wanting revenge may seem a good idea at first, but bitterness only makes the hurt worse. I've learned that much.

'Healing the wounds, rubbing away the scars, that's the hard part. And learning to love again. It's not that I don't want to trust you, Tam, or that you've given me any cause not to, it's just that I can't believe you'll ever love me as I love you. I expect any day for you to pack your bag and go off on your travels again, or find someone you like just as much, or better. You'll leave me. As Jack did. As Kath did.'

Tam did move then, to gather her in his arms and hold her close against him. 'How can you think that? I love you, Meg. I'll never leave you, not of my own free will. For as long as you want me, I'm yours. For a day, a year or a lifetime. You must be the one to decide.'

He cupped her face in his hands and his lips were seeking hers while Meg clung to him, loving, wanting. 'Then I shan't ever let you go. Not ever.'

Their lovemaking was the fiercest and most passionate yet. Held fast in the security of Tam's arms, Meg felt completely fulfilled. For the first time in her life she really believed herself cherished and loved. What did it matter if he'd made no mention of marriage?

On Christmas Eve, Meg and Effie worked a twelve-hour day but sold all their poultry, and such butter and cheese as they were allowed. The streets of Kendal were packed with people seeking bargains at the street stalls run by farmers' wives. But everyone was in good spirits even if some greedy stallholders were forced to lower their prices as the day wore on.

Meg and Effie, however, went home content, if exhausted.

They arrived home to find that Connie had done very little towards preparing for the Christmas Day festivities. Restrained they may be, due to the shortages and the war, yet the Turner family meant to celebrate, as was only right and proper.

They exchanged longsuffering glances and set to work stuffing the bird and making mince pies with more than a fair helping of apple, carrot and bread crumbs amongst the dried figs and fruit they'd managed to scrape together. But they'd saved enough dripping to make a delicious pastry. And it was Christmas, so what did it matter if they used all their ration?

Connie sat with her feet up on a stool, a damp cloth across her forehead and declared herself, 'Quite worn out from looking after that child all day. What a handful she is. Kept wanting me to play with her.'

Effie giggled and cast a sideways glance at Meg who attempted to remain impassive.

'Endless imaginary tea parties can get a touch trying, I suppose, if you're not used to children. But you should be pleased by her attention, Connie. She doesn't take to everyone.'

Connie looked unimpressed by this piece of flattery. 'The Victorians, in my opinion had the right idea about children.'

It remained a mystery to Meg how it was that Connie could find nothing appealing about Lissa. Nor had she ever remarked upon the child's resemblance to her own brother. Either she was short-sighted, or else blind to Jack's faults. Possibly both. In her eyes, Lissa was Meg's problem nothing at all to do with Jack or herself. And Meg didn't tell her otherwise.

'I expect it seems rather dull for you in this remote spot after Grange-over-Sands?' Effie suggested, thrusting her short arm up to the elbow in the huge turkey. Connie took one glance and shuddered.

'Not at all. Grange will never be quite the same again in my estimation. The young women seem to spend half their time searching for parachute silk to make into, well, undergarments.'

'And the other half showing 'em off?' whispered Effie, earning herself a dig with Meg's elbow as a result.

'Perfectly immoral,' finished Connie. 'And most unsafe with all that shooting going on. Who'd have thought it? In Grange. I am glad to be out of it.'

Meg and Effie exchanged glances again. 'You'll be wanting to return soon though, to see Peter?' Meg suggested.

Connie pinched her lips. 'He seems to be enjoying the army, would you believe? I'm sure he can find me, when he can spare the time to come and look.'

'Probably thinks he's escaped the old bugger at last,' Effie hissed, and this time Meg slapped her.

'I'm sure he will,' she said to Connie with just the right amount of sympathy. By the sound of it, she intended a long stay. If that was the case then she'd best learn to make herself useful. 'I wonder, Connie, since we're so busy and you are thinking of returning to country life, if you wouldn't mind going to shut the hens up for me?'

'Oh.'

Meg smiled brightly. 'I'd hate to dirty my hands when I'm making pastry and Effie is still stuffing the bird. We don't want to lose them. The hens, I mean.'

'But it's dark outside.'

'There's a torch in the lean-to, with a hood to shield it. You can use that.'

'And you'll know the way even in the dark, won't you?' Effie cheerfully suggested. 'None better. You having been born here.'

'I'll have the kettle on by the time you come back,' Meg promised. 'Now where's my rolling pin?'

With obvious reluctance, Connie put on her galoshes and raincoat as if she were travelling a mile instead of half a field. But then it might start raining or she could step into something unspeakable. She added her thick scarf and bonnet for it was sure to be bitterly cold out, and collected the torch.

It was black as coal outside, a blanket of thick cloud obscuring the moon and stars and a brisk wind whining hollowly about the farm buildings.

She had never enjoyed this task, even as a child. Connie had always been quite certain that ghosts and ghoulies lurked behind creaking barn doors, and the black mountains seemed to move in on her. No, indeed, she would talk Meg Turner into giving up her preposterous idea of buying the freehold of Broombank, then it could be sold for a proper price and Connie could enjoy some comfort for a change, once the war was over.

With these pleasant thoughts in mind she stepped out across the yard. Pulling on the string, she released the door and let it drop down over the pop hole. She turned to hurry back indoors, anxious to get out of the cloying darkness that blurred the edges of her narrow torch beam, and have a soothing cup of tea. She had hardly taken two steps when the faint light from her torch caught the reflection of a pair of glinting amber eyes.

'Oh, dear God.' In her terror she dropped the torch and heard it smash as it rolled away. Then the sound of stealthy footsteps and something not quite human brushed against her legs.

Connie screamed, and fell to the ground in a hysterical faint. Meg and Effie came hurrying to her aid.

'What is it, Connie? What's happened?'

'It's the devil, or a German. They've invaded. Or dear Lord, they've invaded.'

It took several cups of tea, a tot of medicinal brandy, a sound sniff of sal volatile and a soothing hot water bottle in her bed to calm her. But investigation proved it was neither Hitler nor the supernatural which had come to claim her.

By the state of the hen ark next morning it was all too evident that it had been a fox that Connie had disturbed. Not one live hen remained.

'It's my fault,' Meg mourned, desolate at her loss. 'I was so busy with Christmas, I forgot them.'

'Never mind,' Tam soothed her. 'We can get some more.'

But it seemed a bad omen somehow, to lose her hens just at Christmas, and Meg spent some time that evening before going to bed, polishing her Luckpenny and setting it in pride of place on her bedside table.

The day after Boxing Day, Connie took the first train home. Grange-over-Sands was less terrifying than vermin running wild in your back yard.

When bedtime came the next night Meg refused Tam's appeal to retire early, despite the silent accusation in his eyes, and sat up for hours with her account books, adding up, making notes, drawing plans and thinking, thinking, thinking.

It seemed more important than ever that she make her future at Broombank secure. She couldn't give it up now, not with success so near. Not to Connie, or her father, not to anyone.

Perhaps she should slow down her programme of growth and not buy any more Swaledales in the spring, as she had planned. It would be a disappointment and mean the lamb crop would be less than she'd hoped for. And it would make it worse the next year too. But she could then use the money saved towards the deposit. Could they tighten their belts still further? Could they manage with fewer sheep for the moment?

'Will you come now?' Tam asked, seeing her put down her pen.

'No.'

He said no more. Merely tightened his lips and left her.

Her eyes were pricking for want of sleep but she couldn't bring herself to go to bed, even with Tam waiting for her. Her thoughts were whirling too much.

She'd bought in a couple more cows, neither perfect, but the regular milk cheque from the Co-op helped. Small but essential. Their foodstocks for the winter were already stored. And they'd done well with the Christmas Eve market.

Only when the figures started doing a jig before her eyes did she crawl off to bed and snuggle up to Tam's broad back to fall instantly asleep. She wasn't much nearer finding a solution but tomorrow she would go in search of a mortgage.

Meg had been awake before it was light. Quickly she milked the cows, apologising for her haste, accepted a cup of tea from Effie but declined anything else.

'You must eat.'

'I'm too nervous. I'm going in to town. I have some business to do.'
Tam offered to drive her but Meg opted for the bus.

'We can't both afford to take the time off. I'll take the bus.'

'Something special?' She saw the questions in his eyes but Meg refused to answer them, smiling to herself.

'I'll tell you later.'

'Secrets, is it?' He looked almost hurt, like a small boy, and she laughed at him.

'Have patience. You'll find out all in good time.'

'When you're ready to tell me, eh?' He stood up and went to the door. 'Of course, I forgot. I'm only the hired man round here.'

'Tam!' Damn his pride. But he had gone and Meg sighed with exasperation. Never mind. He would forgive her for deserting him when she brought back some good news tonight.

Meg trailed about town all day trying every bank she could find. None was interested.

'You don't have an account with us, Miss Turner.'

'Farming is a risky business.'

'There is a war on.'

'Were you perhaps be considering marriage? Children?'

Meg's patience ran dangerously short but no mortgage was forthcoming.

In the end she was forced to return to her own bank manager who had declined to loan her money even for a tractor. She sat on a hard chair in his wood-panelled office, her knees placed neatly together and her hat on straight. He scarcely looked at her. He shuffled her carefully drawn out plans on his desk and adopted an anxious expression.

'I don't see how I can help you, Miss Turner.'

'I have raised one hundred pounds towards the purchase price as you can see, Mr Bricknell,' she carefully explained.

'That is a very small deposit.'

'It's the best I can manage at the moment.' She'd put her blood, sweat and tears into raising it. 'I was hoping that you would grant me a mortgage on the balance, at five percent interest.'

'Were you indeed, Miss Turner?'

'That is the usual rate, I believe?'

'For farmers, and for men of good character.'

She raised her eyebrows at him. 'I am a farmer. Are you questioning my character, Mr Bricknell?'

The bank manager cleared his throat. 'Hm, well um. May I speak frankly, Miss Turner?'

'If you wish.' She could feel the thump of her heart against her rib cage. Why did people always ask your permission when they meant to insult you?

'You are very young still, I appreciate that. And as such perhaps not aware of the – um – correct way of going about things.'

'I am ready to learn,' she said, thinking he meant her farming.

He looked at her with a pained expression. 'It has come to my notice that you have a hired man living in.'

'Indeed that is so. As do most farmers.'

The bank manager actually blushed. The red stain started at his neck and spread upwards to his jowly cheeks. Meg was fascinated by it. 'But you are not, if you will forgive me, Miss Turner, quite the same as most farmers. You, my dear, are a woman, and as such it is not proper. Not at all proper. And you have a child, I believe. Tch, tch. Not proper at all. You do see that?'

She was so shocked that for a moment all breath left her body. Then she was standing, her knees knocking so much she felt certain he must hear them. 'No, Mr Bricknell, I do *not* understand. Lissa is an orphan, if it's any business of yours. A war orphan you might say. And Tam is a good worker, and a friend. I have come here today for a mortgage, not comments upon my – my personal life.' She had very nearly said 'my lover', right in the sanctum of the bank, thereby setting proof on the tittle-tattle.

Mr Bricknell flapped a hand at her, waving her to be seated again. 'Pray do not take offence, Miss Turner. You permitted me to speak frankly and there has been talk, you see. Which does you no good, nor your growing business, no good at all, to get the reputation of a . . .' The red stain had passed his moustache now and was heading for his spectacles. He took them off and wiped them on a large handkerchief.

'I take your meaning, Mr Bricknell. There is no need to go on.'

The bank manager cleared his throat. 'If you were considering marriage, of course . . .'

Meg swallowed. 'No, I am not considering marriage, as I think I have already said, until this war is over. I have a fiancé overseas.'

'Of course, of course. But this man, he is Irish, I believe? An itinerant worker, no doubt. Will he be moving on soon, do you think?'

Meg was surprised her voice sounded so calm when all she wanted

351

to do was shout that of course Tam wasn't leaving. He loved her, didn't he? 'I wouldn't know. I hope not. He is a good worker and I trust him. Even if he did, I would still need a man about the place, for the heavy work. So I do not see the problem.'

'Oh, quite so, quite so, but one of respectable character, Miss Turner. A local man, do you see? And he should live in the barn.'

'The barn is falling down, Mr Bricknell. Would you care to give me a loan for the repairs?'

The bank manager laughed as if she had made a joke. It turned into a fit of coughing. 'All in good time, my dear, all in good time.'

She wanted to tell him that she was not *his dear*, but she held on to her dignity, what little she had left. 'Do I take all this to mean that you will not consider a mortgage. Ever? Unless you are permitted to vet the people who live in my house?'

The bank manager had the grace to look embarrassed. 'As I think I mentioned once before when you expressed a fancy for a tractor, if you could perhaps persuade your father, in lieu of a husband, to act as guarantor, there would be no difficulty, no difficulty at all.'

Meg ground her teeth together in silent fury, all the while smiling serenely. At all costs, even to her pride, she must get a mortgage. But to allow her father to have any say in her affairs was out of the question. Joe would take control and win Broombank, as he had always intended. Then he would have his revenge against poor Lanky, and against her, for being a girl and for being so determined to beat him in spite of that. He would give it to Dan and she would have nothing.

A thought occurred to her. 'What about my brother Dan? Would he do?'

The bank manager pondered.

'He is respectable.' She emphasised the word slightly. 'A married man with two children, and a farmer.'

The bank manager stood up and extended a hand.

'Bring your brother in to see me and I will give the matter my serious consideration.'

Meg swallowed her pride and shook the outstretched hand. But at the door she turned and faced him again, her expression resolute. 'I will agree to your request, Mr Bricknell, only because I must. But I assure you my brother will have no say in the running of Broombank, nor will the bank. And whom I employ and have living on the farm is my affair, and mine alone.

'No matter what problems may come in the future, I will succeed, woman or no. Believe it.'

'I'll not do it.' Dan stood stubbornly in the farm yard, a too familiar pugnaciousness to his face.

'Whyever not? It's only your signature I'm asking for, nothing more. You'll have no say in Broombank, no work, no involvement at all.'

But he was far from mollified. 'You think I'm daft? Well, I'm not. A guarantor means that if you can't pay the mortgage, then I would have to, and I've no money. You know damn well that Father pays me a pittance, or nothing, which is more likely the case these days.'

Meg sighed. 'I'm not asking for you to pay anything. There's no danger of my not being able to pay the mortgage.'

'That's easy said but things can go wrong in farming very easy. Disease, a bad winter, and you're up the creek without a paddle. Be content with what you've got for once, Meg. Pay rent and have done with dreams. I'd like to help but I daren't take the risk. Not with Sally Ann and the bairns to keep. You must see that?'

She sighed, conceding that he did have a point. 'Yes, I do understand.'

'Besides which, Sally Ann is expecting again.'

'Oh, Dan, congratulations. I didn't know. When is it to be?'

'Not till the summer,' he said gruffly, sounding pleased for all his previous moans and groans. 'So you see, I daren't risk it. I don't want her worried about money. She has enough with the children, and Dad.'

'Yes, I can see that. And I do understand, about the guarantor business. Forget I asked. I'll think of some other way.'

Then she surprised him by kissing him on the cheek. Never close as she and Charlie were, yet he was her brother and marriage seemed to be softening him. 'Sometimes, you know, you're very nearly human,' she teased him, and laughed at his blushes. Perhaps she could find some other solution.

Meg marked out the area to be ploughed with sticks. March had come in with a bluster. There was still the bite of winter in the air, a crispness to the soil, and that clarity of light peculiar to the north. A perfect day for the last of the ploughing. A few seagulls whirled overhead, blown in on the bitter winds from the coast, seeking food.

She and Tam were set to work it themselves, taking turns with Carrie, teamed with Will's old horse, Arlott, pulling Lanky's rusty old plough cleaned off and brought back into service. It was back-breaking work but more cost effective than bringing in the War Committee to do it for them. Besides, she needed to prove that she could cope without help from anyone.

She flicked at the reins, hoping the two horses wouldn't prove too mettlesome.

'Don't pull too hard on one side,' Tam called after her as she set the pair in motion. 'Keep them well balanced.'

Meg attempted to fix her eyes on the stick planted at the end of the field and drove the horses towards it. The rough fell ponies, taking no notice of the stick, and finding an amateur driver at the end of their reins, started to veer off at an angle to where more tempting vegetation beckoned.

'Damnation.' She could hear Tam's laughter as she struggled to keep them on an even course, without giving them their head and losing control altogether. Not an easy task. What had made her think she could do it herself?

The draining work had successfully given her more usable land and after decades of rest was proving to be surprisingly fertile. But the War Committee kept on putting up her quota to be ploughed. The wheat and oats she grew would be taken by the government but Broombank would be allowed to keep the kale for the milk cows and some turnips for the sheep.

'An acre a day,' Tam said.

After two agonising hours she judged his reckoning to be out by a half, certainly so far as she was concerned. Her longing for a tractor had never been so strong. But she wouldn't give in, oh no. She'd plough her acres or die in the attempt. She'd show her father and brother, and the bank manager, and everyone else who cared to watch, that a woman could farm.

Meg was nevertheless profoundly thankful when midday came at last and she could let Tam take over for an hour or two.

'Are you all right?'

'My knees feel like jelly and my back and arms will never move again. I'm going to find Effie and some embrocation.' And turning her nose in the air, refusing to rise to his great guffaws of laughter, she staggered away.

Later she lay on the bed, unmoving, flat on her stomach, too exhausted even to think while he rubbed her aching limbs with lavender oil, smiling at her groans which were a combination of agony and ecstacy at his touch.

'Why aren't you in agony too?'

'I've worked with horses most of my life. My muscles are attuned. It's partly a knack.' He kissed her ear. 'You'll learn, given time.'

Meg groaned. 'When the ploughing is all done, we're still nowhere near the end, are we? Every grain of seed will have to be sown by hand, broadcast in time-honoured fashion.'

'Then chains attached to the horses and the whole lot harrowed in.'

'And every rootcrop planted by hand?'

Tam nodded, eyes brimming with laughter. 'Regretting the extra land now?'

'I shall die, Tam, I know I shall. This land isn't meant to be ploughed. And what has it all to do with sheep?'

He kissed her neck and slid the towel from her, so he could admire her back. 'It has to do with feed for sheep, and for cows.' His hand was sliding beneath her now, seeking her breast. 'It has to do with feed for people. With war. With being a farmer.'

'I hope you weren't thinking of making love to me this night? I couldn't move a muscle,' she mourned.

'You don't have to,' he whispered. 'I'll move them for you.'

To her surprise she managed to turn over and respond without any difficulty at all.

The next morning she was back at the plough before eight.

And by now she was determined to stand no nonsense from the two horses. Gritting her teeth, she drove them straight as a die. She'd show them who was in charge.

1942

29

It was a soft spring day with the kind of settled warmth rarely found in Lakeland, the crags looking blacker than ever against the sharp green of new grass. The kind of day a raven might fly upside down for the sheer joy of living. Meg felt a similar joy as she checked her flock. All her efforts seemed to be working, for the Swaledales were settling well. Lambing had started and she hoped for a good crop.

She and Effie laughed now when they remembered that first lambing season.

'How green we were,' Effie said. 'I even remember trying to put each hen to bed at night. Didn't realise they all lined up in proper pecking order and did it all by themselves.'

'I made plenty of mistakes too.'

'We did it though, didn't we? We managed to keep the farm, Meg. We succeeded.'

'Yes,' she said with a smile. 'We did, didn't we? We can thank the Luckpenny for that.'

'And your hard work.'

Jeffrey Ellis came striding up the hill towards her and Meg tried to ignore the flutter of fear in her stomach that she always felt when she saw him these days. Foolish, she knew, for though he came once every few weeks under some pretext or other to see Lissa, he never suggested that he should remove her from Meg's care. But she still worried that one day he might. That's what people did. Got up and walked away one day. At least you could rely upon land to stay put.

'Run and put the kettle on, Effie. We'll be down in a minute.'

His conversation was not about Lissa today.

'You know that we have about sixty acres of land with Larkrigg? Pasture for Kath's horse, some woodland, the rest too stony and steep to be of any use for anything but grazing.'

Meg knew Larkrigg land and said so, curious at what he had in mind.

'Well, I've sold Bonnie.'

Meg was astounded. She didn't know what to say. If he had sold the old pony then he had obviously given up hope of his daughter's ever returning home. It was a bleak moment. She took a hesitant step forward then put her arms about his neck and hugged him.

'I'm so sorry.' Meg felt close to tears. How could Kath be so cruel? Why didn't she at least write?

He patted her shoulder but did not answer for a moment. Probably could not. His brisk self again, he turned the conversation. 'We ploughed up the two-acre paddock, according to instruction, at the beginning of the war. The rest is too stony for the plough and too much work for me to deal with. I wondered if you would be interested?

'What I'm suggesting is that you take over responsibility for all my sixty acres and my few sheep. I'm a hobby farmer, always have been. Supposed to be good for my health, once. Now my own doctor tells me it's too much for me to manage. What do you say?'

She dipped her head and blinked hard. She felt choked inside by his generosity. 'I don't know what to say.'

'I've depended upon a few POWs. They come every day but need more supervision. Much of the grazing is going to waste for I've hardly any sheep on it these days. A dozen at most. It seems a shame, and we're not supposed to waste anything, are we, these days?' Jeffrey Ellis thrust his hands in his pockets, not looking at her. 'We're almost family, in a funny sort of way. I'd like you to make use of it, Meg.'

'What about Rosemary? How does she feel about the idea?'

'Haven't told her yet. But she'd have no objection. She isn't at all interested in the land, only her garden.'

'I'm not sure that I could . . .'

'Oh, there would be no charge. No rent or anything. In fact, quite the opposite. I'd pay you, my dear.'

'Pay me?'

'Oh, yes. I'm sure we could work something out that was beneficial to us both.'

Meg smiled. 'Without my losing face, you mean? Mr Ellis, you are a very kind man, but even if I agreed to work your land, and I'm not saying I could, I certainly would not accept wages for using your grass for my sheep. It wouldn't be right.'

'All right then. Rent-free grazing for your sheep and you keep us provided with lamb or mutton.'

'We are only allowed to kill one lamb or sheep for ourselves each year. The government checks up, you know. The same would apply to you.'

'I understand. But if you take over the care of my sheep in lieu of payment for the use of the land, and provide me with fresh food, then I'd be quite happy. Do we have a deal?'

She'd be a fool to refuse. 'It's a deal.'

Jeffrey Ellis grinned. 'I also understand you've been trying to get a mortgage, so you can buy Broombank?'

'I won't borrow the money from you, so please don't offer it.'

'I am aware of your desire for independence and applaud it. No, I've been having a word with my bank manager. I have told him how much you have achieved here already in such a short time. He sees no reason why he shouldn't be able to offer you one.'

'Oh, Mr Ellis!'

'You would need to provide a deposit. Can you manage that?'

Her eyes were alight. 'I have it all saved up ready. Oh, but it's in another bank.'

Jeffrey Ellis smiled. 'My manager will be happy to open a new account for you and offer you very favourable terms.'

'I won't need a guarantor?'

'Not at all. You are your own woman. This is a business proposition between you and the bank. You must go and see him, of course, explain your plans for the future, impress him with your ability and creditworthiness, which I feel sure you can do. Is that not so?'

Meg was grinning now. 'Absolutely. Mr Ellis, you must be Santa Claus.' And she flung her arms about his neck and kissed him, making him blush furiously.

'No, Meg. I won't have that,' he protested, embarrassed by this show of affection. 'It's your own hard work that has brought this about. I feel it deserves recognition. I've only offered the right word in the right ear to help you on your way, that's all.'

'I appreciate it.'

They shook hands. Tea was poured and Lissa was brought down to climb upon Mr Ellis's knee and demand a story that he had promised to tell her, if she was a good girl.

Meg sat and sipped her tea and listened too, with pleasure and joy in her eyes.

A day or two later she was working with Tam out on the fell when suddenly he turned to her with a defiant twist of his body and said, 'I'm going to join up.'

She stared, speechless with horror. 'Join up? Why? When?'

'You're going to get your mortgage to buy Broombank. You have Mr Ellis's land as well as your own and you can use POW labour. You can manage without me now.'

'That's a damn' fool thing to say and you know it. I don't want you to go. I need you here, with me.'

He looked at her levelly. 'You managed well enough before I came.'

'That was different.'

'How so?'

'I didn't know you then.' As I know and need you now. In every sense. She took a step towards him, laid her hands flat against his chest. He smelled of sunshine and fresh earth and she drew in those scents to be a part of her, for ever. 'You said you didn't ever intend to join up. Didn't need to fight.'

'The Americans are seriously in the war now. Everyone is. I feel I ought to be too.'

'But you are Irish, not American. And Ireland is still a neutral country.'

Tam didn't smile at her, or joke as he once might have done. He gently removed her hands, looking serious. Far too serious. 'I still think I should go.'

Meg became very still. 'Are you saying that when the war is over you'll go back there, to America?' A pain was starting somewhere around the region of her heart. But he shook his head.

'That's up to you. I rather thought I might ask you to marry me. Probably should have asked you already.' He attempted a smile. 'Make an honest woman of you.'

'I did rather wonder.'

'I love you, Meg.'

'And I love you, Tam.'

'So what do you say? We could marry now. Before I go.'

She met his gaze. Open, loving, with anxiety in it as if he were not quite sure of her.

'You want me to marry you and then you intend to go off and fight in the war?'

'I have to.'

She swallowed, but it did nothing to ease the ache in her throat. She had longed for these words, now she hated them. 'I can't.'

The silence was appalling.

'Why can't you?'

'Because.'

'Because of Jack?'

'I still have his ring. I'm still engaged to him. Officially, that is. At least, I've never managed, never had the opportunity, to end it.'

'Perhaps you didn't try hard enough.'

'Don't be bitter, Tam.' She put out a hand, wanting to say she would marry him, wanting to have him gather her in his arms, say he wouldn't go. But he ignored it and the hand fell to her side, untouched.

'He betrayed you. You owe him nothing.'

'It was a youthful madness. It could happen to anyone. But he needs me. I can't just abandon him. You know that I was waiting for him to come home on leave. I didn't want to go into all the recriminations by post. I never intended to fall in love again. Only I did. And then I couldn't bring myself to send him a "Dear John" letter.'

'Lots of other people manage it.'

'Well, I'm not other people. I'm me, and I thought it best to wait till I saw him. Only, I never did. He went overseas and disappeared.' As you might do, her heart said, and fear shot through her, hot and piercing. Oh, why did I ever let myself love again? she thought.

'So the answer is still no?'

She licked her lips. 'It would seem so – so cruel for Jack to think he still had a girl at home and come back to find me married. Can't we stay as we are, for now? Once the war is over I can tell him, explain about Lissa, decide what's best for her. And then there's Broombank, which I only accepted because I thought Jack and I . . .' She ran out of words, a sob on her breath, but Tam was too hurt to respond to it.

'Ah yes, of course, the land. It's fine for me to work it so long as I don't claim any rights to it. I'm just the hired man.'

Meg flushed angrily. 'That's not what I said.'

'Isn't it?'

'No.'

'What's best for the land. What's best for Lissa. What's best for Jack. What about what's best for you? And me? My needs don't count, is that it?'

Meg searched desperately for the right words to explain how she felt. How by rights both Lissa and the land belonged to Jack and how she couldn't bear to part with either of them. But she couldn't say all of that without hurting Tam further. 'I can't do anything about Jack, not yet. Why won't you understand?'

'Suit yourself,' he said and strode away.

And as she had always feared would one day happen, it was all over. He packed his few belongings and that night as they lay in the great bed made no move to touch her until she whispered his name, a painful sob coming from deep in her heart.

Then he reached for her and loved her with such a sweet fierceness it was as if he could not get enough of her, as if it were the last time.

And when she woke the next morning, the bed was empty. Tam had gone.

'I reckon that Lord Haw Haw chap should be horsewhipped, prating on every night.'

'Yes, Dad. Write to the BBC and suggest it.'

'It's not the BBC who's at fault, you daft woman, it's that Hitler. I'll not hev a jumped-up little dictator telling me what's what. "Jairmany calling. Jairmany calling." Makes my blood boil.'

'Why do you listen to him then? Go to bed.'

'No, I want thee to read me that news again. I want to understand what's going on.'

Sally Ann laid down the paper with a weary sigh. 'Sorry, Dad. I'm licked. Little Daniel will have me awake by five and I can't take any more.'

She came to stand by his chair and rested a gentle hand on his arm. 'Don't sit up too long. You're tired too and it could be a long while before Dan gets home. You know he's often late after a training exercise.' She glanced about the muddled room, children's toys and clothes scattered about. There hardly seemed a spare minute in the day to do all that had to be done. And she didn't feel up to trying. This pregnancy seemed more wearisome than the last two, somehow.

'I need more help,' she said now, surprising herself by the suddenness of her request.

Joe glanced up at her, then at the homely clutter. 'Aye,' he said, after a moment. 'Happen you do, since you're carrying again. I'll find a girl to help you, next time I go down town.'

Impulsively she kissed him on the forehead. He had never returned her signs of affection but she knew they did not displease him. 'I'm lucky to have you to keep me cheerful, do you know that?' she gently teased. 'Meg's on her own again now that Tam has joined up. Apart from little Effie, that is. I feel for her.'

'Perhaps she'll see sense noo then, and give up. Get yourself to bed,' he said gruffly. 'Thoo needs rest. I'm all right for a bit.'

Smiling, Sally Ann went wearily up the stairs. It had been a good day for her when she'd come to Ashlea to borrow money. She had no complaints, none at all. Dan had proved to be a good husband for all his insecurities and Joe wasn't a bad old stick, once you got used to him. More bark than bite these days.

Down in the kitchen Joe got up and turned off the wireless in disgust. He'd had enough of that propaganda rubbish. But he would wait up for his son and find out just what he was up to. Training exercise indeed! The last time Dan had come home late, there had been the unmistakable smell of beer on his breath, if Joe wasn't mistaken. And he meant to check it out tonight. If he was right, he'd have a few words to say on the subject.

Despite his best efforts, Joe's eyes soon began to droop. Jerking awake again, he went to brew a pot of tea, to keep himself alert.

But when Dan crept quietly through the door at half-past midnight, his father was snoring gently by the ashes of a dead fire. Grinning to himself, he made sure not to disturb Joe as he lurched past the old carver chair towards the stairs.

He might have made it too, had it not been for Nicky's pile of wooden bricks. Dan put his foot on one and skidded from one to the other like a cat on marbles.

'Bloody hell,' he yelled, crashing to the ground with such force that not only did he wake his father, but his wife and two sons as well. The baby's screams burst forth like ack-ack fire.

Joe was on his feet in a second. 'I knew it! Drunk. And swearing too. What hev we come to?'

Dan groaned in agony. 'I think I've broken my ankle.'

'Get up and don't talk soft. What have thee been up to, eh? No good, I'll be bound.'

Sally Ann came hurrying downstairs, dressing gown pulled hastily about her swollen stomach, eyes blinking with sleep. 'What is it? What's going on?'

'This lout is drunk,' Joe announced. 'Just look at him, great lump that he is.'

'Don't call me a lump.' Dan had had enough of being reviled and criticised. All his life his father had told him how useless he was. Charlie and Meg had been petted by his mother, but nobody had given a toss about him. He'd had enough. Pulling back his arm, he swung his fist with all the power of his awesome muscle.

Had it not been for the several pints he had consumed with his mates earlier that evening, some of it home brewed at Mike Lanyon's house, he might well have done considerable damage. As it was, the very act of swinging the arm sent him clean off balance and before he could stop himself he'd banged his head against the kitchen cupboard, tipped sideways, and landed with one foot in the coal scuttle, a look of comical surprise upon his face.

'Huh,' scoffed Joe, a curl of contempt at the corner of his mouth. 'Can't even do that reet. I'm off to bed.'

Dan waved the fist at him, determined to prove his point. 'If I want a drink, I shall have one. I'm near thirty years old and I'll please meself.'

'Thoo'll do as I say while you live in my house.'

Flushed with fury, Dan shook off the clinging coal scuttle, fortunately empty of coal since it was so hard to come by, and lurched to his feet. 'You're a bloody bully, that's what you are!'

'Dan, don't.' Sally Ann stepped hastily forward. She'd never seen him like this before, never. She feared what he might do next. 'Come to bed, love. It's the drink talking, Father, take no notice.'

Dan shook her arm impatiently away. With the skill peculiar only to the very drunk, he steadied himself and faced his father with narrowed eyes. 'You told me she wouldn't stick at it. You told me Meg would give up as soon as things got tough. You promised me that I could have Broombank, for me own.'

Joe regarded his son with something very close to pity. What a clod hopper he was. When things didn't quite go his way he got peevish, or turned to drink. Why had he ever imagined that this son might make a good farmer? But he was his eldest and the other one wasn't shaping to it at all, so he had to make the best of it.

For the first time in his life, Joe wished that Dan had some of Meg's skill and half her spunk and common sense. She was doing well at

Broombank, you had to face it. And despite his better judgement, Joe felt a grudging admiration for her. Why had the wrong one been born a boy?

'And so thee will hev it, one day. It's just taking longer than I thought.'

'It won't ever happen. She won't give up and you know it. Meg's as stubborn as you. She'll never let me have Broombank. And you won't let me run Ashlea. All I am is a bloody labourer. And you're too damn' mean to pay me a living wage for that. I can't even afford to keep me own wife and children, without food from your table.'

Sally Ann was crying now. 'Stop it, Dan. It doesn't matter.'

'Aye, it does matter. It bloody matters to me. I've had enough. I'm a man, aren't I?' The bloodshot eyes focused with surprising clarity and terrible ferocity upon Joe, 'I have my pride.' He took a step forward and laughed out loud when he saw his father flinch.

'Aye, you might well look nervous. Things is going to change round here. I'm taking no more orders from you.' He jabbed a wavering finger in his father's face. 'I'm going to see our Meg in the morning, and tip her out, once and for all. I want a place of me own, and mean to get it, one way or another. I'm not ending up bitter and dried up like you.' Swinging to Sally Ann, he clutched her about the shoulders, pulling her to him, turning maudlin now. 'You're a grand lass, Sal. I'll see you don't become his skivvy, like our Meg did. I won't have it, d'you hear?'

'I'm not. I won't,' she protested but Dan shook his head.

'Oh, aye, that's what he does to people, turns 'em into skivvies and labourers to do his bidding. It don't matter to him what you want, only what he wants.' Dan wiped the spittle from his lips with the back of his hand. His mind was starting to fog over again and he'd lost track of his thoughts. 'I've had enough,' he said, and slid senseless to the floor.

Which gave Joe the opportunity for the last word, as he liked to have. 'You can both be out first thing in't morning, if that's the way you feel aboot it.' And turning his back in disgust, he went upstairs to bed.

Sally Ann, crying bitter tears, not knowing whether to berate Dan for his folly in losing them a comfortable home, or admire him for finally standing up to his father, pulled off her husband's boots and covered him with the rug from the settle. There was no way she could get him upstairs, so she left him where he was and went to bed.

* * *

Meg could scarce believe the pain she felt. A great gaping hole was left where once joy had been. She lay sleepless at night, tossing and turning in the great empty bed, her mind and her body crying out for Tam. She thought she would never get over the pain of losing him.

Nothing she had ever felt before could possibly have prepared her for this. It was as if a part of her were missing.

She wrote to him every day and lived for his letters, which were never often enough for her liking. She tried to fill her days with work but she seemed to have lost interest and became listless, without her usual energy. Every morning she had to drag herself downstairs and couldn't face the breakfast Effie tried to make her eat.

'It'll be all right in the end,' Effie consoled her. 'He feels he has to do his bit, that's all. As you have to do yours. When this topsy-turvy world rights itself again, he'll be back.'

Meg's grey eyes turned upon her friend, begging for it to be true. 'I can't cope without him, Effie. There seems no point in anything any more without him here beside me. Was I wrong? Should I have married him, even though I couldn't tell Jack?'

Effie's face turned blank. 'Don't get me into that one. That's your decision. No one else's.'

'I was afraid too, Effie. Afraid that if I married Tam, committed myself to him, it would hurt more if he didn't come back.' She gave a hard little laugh with no humour in it. 'I can see now that that can't be true. With or without a piece of paper, I'm committed.'

'Course you are, and he is to you. Don't worry. He understands.'

'Does he?' She remembered the cruel words between them and wished she could feel as sure as Effie. She glanced about her breakfast table and wondered what right she had to complain. They were all safe and well. Lissa happily playing with the ever patient Rust. Effie healthy and fit, growing into a lovely young woman, reading the papers which recently had been full of what were being dubbed the Baedeker Raids.

From May through into June, while the foliage thickened, the cold earth softened and the spotted coats of the new deer calves could be sometimes glimpsed in Brockbarrow Wood, many of England's most famous historical cities were under attack. Meg wept to hear of the terrible consequences of these attacks. They were at least safe here.

And this morning there was the joy of a letter from Charlie. She held the crisp blue envelope in her hand now, savouring the anticipation of opening it.

'Families are trekking out of the cities each night and sleeping in the fields to keep safe,' read Effie. 'I don't blame them. They won't get bombed there.'

Meg glanced at the picture Effie showed her. A weary group of people with smiles on their faces, carrying their entire belongings in parcels, trying to make the best of life. But if you looked closely, you could see their agony all too clearly behind the bravery. Plymouth, Bath, York, so many towns had suffered devastating damage. Whole areas of ancient buildings wiped out.

'Those cities weren't as prepared as London,' Effie said. 'And anyway, they thought the raids were all finished by the end of the blitz. Now it's starting all over again. Do you think we'll bomb Germany again?'

Meg ripped open the envelope, anxious suddenly to read how her brother was.

Charlie's handwriting. She held a part of him in her hand. She smiled at Effie. 'He's all right. We should remember that however terrible it is to bomb cities, the real tragedy of war is its effect on each and every individual. War is a personal tragedy and we should never forget that. What matters is Charlie and all the other Charlies. Every single family like that one in the paper, not just bricks and mortar, stone and slate, however precious.'

There was no address at the top of the single sheet of paper, but Charlie's happy voice came over loud and clear.

'Is he still flying?' Effie quietly asked.

Meg nodded. 'Says he's fine. Doing a second tour, as he said he might. She started to read aloud.

'"Feeling fine. Sue OK but don't get to see her as much as I'd like now she is in the ATS. Well into Second Tour of Ops. The big one is coming up soon. Don't want to miss it."'

The big one?

'What does he mean?' Effie looked as troubled as Meg felt.

'I don't know. We must pray for him, Effie. Every night.'

She nodded, blinking furiously. 'Oh, I do, Meg. I do. And Lissa does too, don't you, sweetheart?'

Lissa happily nodded, not understanding, and went back to feeding Rust with toast crusts.

'He'll be all right. Eat your breakfast while it's hot, there's a hard day's work ahead, and I mean to churn some butter this morning.'

Meg folded the letter and tucked it into her overall pocket. One day at a time, that's all you could hope for in this war. Today, Charlie was fine. And Tam hadn't got anywhere near the fighting yet.

Meg was busily engaged in checking the feet of one of her sheep later that morning when Jeffrey Ellis called.

'Got foot rot, has she?'

'I don't think so but I'm giving her a dab in the foot-bath, just in case. I think she's only sprained it though.'

Rust lay close by, nose to his toes, a wary eye on the sheep, just in case it should take any daft notion of escape into its silly head.

Meg finished her task and opened the gate to let the sheep go. It hobbled off at a cracking pace to rejoin a very noisy, anxious lamb. Jeffrey Ellis laughed.

'Someone's been missing Mum.'

She chuckled. 'Lively as bairns they are. I love to watch them. Can I get you a cup of tea?'

She was always ready to spend time with him these days. He'd been good to her, and to Lissa. Jeffrey Ellis had once seemed a lonely, careworn man. Now he was alert, alive again. All due to Lissa, no doubt about it. The child had given him a reason for living. He looked particularly fit and well this morning, showing signs of the handsome man he had once been in spite of the greying hair.

'No thanks, I mustn't stay. I know you're busy.'

'I'm thrang, as my father would say, but all the more ready for a break. Particularly on a lovely bright morning like this.' And it was, the June sun shining fat and yellow as if it were high summer. Somewhere in the distance a cuckoo made its two-note song and wood pigeons hooted. A day for lovers, Meg thought, for cherry blossom and weddings. And for a moment the keenness of Tam's going pierced her heart so fiercely she had trouble catching her breath. But she must be bright too. Keep her heart and hopes high. He would be back, Effie had said so.

Jeffrey Ellis grinned at her. 'The searches have been done and your mortgage prepared. You only have to go in and sign the papers and it's yours.'

'Oh, it's an omen! This lovely day, a letter from Charlie, and now my mortgage. I shall go right away, this very minute.' She turned to run, then remembering Mr Ellis, leaped up and gave him a swift kiss upon his cheek. 'Bless you,' she said.

Jeffrey Ellis stood and laughed at her excitement. 'Now who's acting like a bairn?' he teased.

Meg dashed into the house to find Effie, tell her she was off into town to see her new bank manager. Then she changed into clean slacks and pulled on a light sweater.

Moments later she was out in the yard again. Rust came straight to her heels. 'No, Rust. Stay here, there's a good boy,' she instructed the dog, who looked most put out, as he always did, at being so abandoned. He lay down by the gate so that he could watch her go along the lane, and see her the moment she returned. He could also keep a guard on the house from this position, so no one would leave that he didn't know about.

Meg watched this with amusement as she pulled out her bike. 'Effie is inside making butter, aided and hindered by Lissa of course. She'll gladly put the kettle on, if you want that tea.'

'Don't worry about me. I won't stop the good work. But I might pop in and just say hallo.'

A stocky figure loomed into sight on the lane. 'Oh no, what does Dan want? I really have no time this morning for my brother's moans and groans.' Meg grabbed her bicycle and dusted off the seat. 'Tell him I was in a hurry, will you? Apologise for me,' she begged.

'I'll tell him this is the best day of your life.'

Meg grinned and was off, pedalling furiously along the lane. Oh, he was right. It was the best, by far. Not counting the times with Tam of course.

Dan called to her 'Here, Meg, I want to talk to you.'

'Later, Dan. Go and see Effie. She'll make you a mug of tea if you ask nicely. I won't be long.'

As she reached the corner of the lane she turned to wave. Dan was glowering with fury but Jeffrey Ellis was still where she had left him, laughing, his hair glinting like silver in the sunshine. But most of all she saw Broombank, its white walls almost beaming with pleasure, windows blinking with delight at the promise of this new future.

When she returned later that day, the paperwork all done, her mortgage secured, and a precious bottle of wine in her cycle basket to celebrate, she found the roof of her lovely home had been lifted off as if by some giant hand and placed, very neatly, in the next field. Half the walls, the ones that had taken the worst of the blast from the bomb carelessly dropped by a passing bomber, had fallen in. Just as Effie was stirring her butter with a rowan twig, to make it turn quickly and protect it from witches.

30

It had all begun as a great lark so far as Jack Lawson was concerned. Chasing Italian warships off Italy and sinking the ships which carried enemy troops and supplies, without too many British losses, was right up his street.

But that had been back in March 1941. The feeling that it was some sort of game had ended by summer of 1942.

By the autumn, enemy submarines and shore-based aircraft started picking off British ships, one by one, like fish in a pond. In no time at all the Med was not a safe place to be and longer routes had to be taken around the Cape and through the Suez Canal to supply reinforcements for the men fighting in the Western desert. Rommel decided Suez was a place he coveted, and as far as Jack was concerned, he could have it.

At the first sign of the enemy it was Jack's task to man the anti-aircraft guns while Len, his best mate, fed in the ammunition. They did their best, gave it all they had, firing in what sometimes seemed the forlorn hope of hitting one of those black shapes that swooped and dived, high in the heavens. Sometimes they'd be wet with fear, but mostly they kept their minds safely blank. Do the job and leave the thinking to those in fancy hats, that was the best way.

And then a shower of shells lifted Len from his feet and nailed him to the deck. Jack grabbed the gun, rage burning so fiercely behind his eyes it took three men to wrench him free as he swung it round and round, firing indiscriminately, in more danger of killing someone on the ship than hitting an enemy plane.

And so Jack Lawson, for one, had lost his taste for war.

Was it any wonder, he told himself, that by the end of that year he was less than thrilled to learn he'd been assigned to Special Boat Ops? His task was to row a small rubber boat under cover of darkness, carrying a select group of men whose target was a munitions dump on mainland Italy. That mission changed his entire war, perhaps even his life.

He'd certainly been fleeing for his life ever since.

He never learned what went wrong. The four men didn't come back, simple as that. And when Jack attempted to return to his ship, the pathetic little boat had been shelled out of the water, fortunately before Jack had climbed into it. He'd been blown backwards on to the shore and supposed he should feel lucky to escape with only a broken shoulder even though the pain of it in those first few days had made him almost wish he was dead.

But now he had Lina.

The days that he had spent crawling and dragging himself through rough country were a blur in his mind. He'd probably spent Christmas on his belly somewhere though he had no recollection of it. Only of the bitter cold, and the ceaseless pain.

He remembered being thankful to find an area of peace and quiet, nursing his injured arm across the stony ground till he came to lush farmland on the edge of a small village. Somewhere in the distance could be heard the roar of guns, the skies lit with red every night to remind him of it, but here all was quiet.

He saw a row of houses, a few shops, one of them giving off a most enticing aroma of fresh bread. It reminded him how hungry he was and he had made his way round the back of them, hoping for a chance to find some of the delectable stuff. Most of all he recalled his first sight of the barn, huddled in a ramshackle group of wooden buildings. He chose it because it reminded him so much of the one at Broombank, and when he'd seen Meg he'd been sure of it.

Only it wasn't her, for this girl did not have Meg's golden curls or her bright smile. This girl was dark, olive-skinned, and her lips were wider than Meg's and a paler pink. She did smile occasionally but mostly she looked anxious and hurried.

Most of all he remembered her hands. Soft and comforting, he had wanted to fold himself into those hands and cry like a baby. He hadn't done so, of course. He was a man, wounded but still Able Seaman Lawson. And grown men don't cry, however much they might hurt and feel the need to.

'You are Breetish?' she had said to him that first day when she'd found him, and the relief of hearing his own language spoken to him so gently by this delectable creature turned his innards to water. Jack recalled with shame how he had emptied the contents of his stomach into the clean hay which she had packed about his battered body for comfort.

But she hadn't seemed to mind. 'Do not fret, you are safe here. Stay quiet.'

And for all she was clearly Italian and the enemy, he had believed her. She had brought her brother, Giovanni, and together over the following weeks they had tended to his wounds, strapped the shoulder up and fed him as if he were a child when moving was too painful to contemplate.

Now, at last, he was beginning to feel half human again. The strappings were off the arm and he was learning to use it again, anxious to repay her kindness and get out of this hot, musty barn. The snows had long gone, spring was turning into summer and the sun looked enticing. He wanted to be out in it, to feel the baking heat on his face.

'Let me do some chores,' he begged her now. And when she pulled a face he grasped her hand and pulled her down beside him. She was bewitching when she pouted at him in just that way, one shoulder lifted beguilingly. No man could resist her. 'I'm fit now, and bored silly with staying in this loft. I owe your family some labour if nothing else.'

'My family are happy to help you. We are not fascist, you understand?'

'I understand.'

'All Italians are not in favour of the new regime but we have to be careful, yes?'

'You think I will endanger their lives? I wouldn't dream of it.'

'I know you would not intentionally do so. But it ees so very dangerous. You must stay here, where you are safe. I would have nothing happen to you.'

And when he would protest she set soft fingertips against his lips and Jack wanted to crush her to him, and take her then and there in the straw. Instead he smiled at her and kissed the fingers.

He loved the way she wore her long, glossy black hair in a tumble of curls down her back, and the brightly coloured frocks. They looked as if she'd made them herself out of a selection of others that had been cut up for the purpose, as perhaps they had. Nothing matched, not the sleeves, nor the bodice with the skirt, but the patchwork effect was delightful and the flowing style clung to her body and rippled about her brown legs.

And when she leaned over him to refill his water pitcher he had a clear view of her breasts and nipples, enticingly dark.

As if aware of him for the first time she looked directly into his eyes. It was a moment to savour, a moment when words were not needed. An understanding was reached and would, in the fullness of time, be acted upon.

'You may come into the house thees evening for supper,' Lina told him. 'My father, he ees very strict. You will have to be the gentleman. *Si*?'

Jack gave her a lop-sided smile, one side of his face still bruised and swollen from his abrupt landing on the rocky shore. 'Scout's honour.'

She did not understand him and he had to explain but then she offered one of her rare, shy smiles and as he sat watching the dust motes settle after she had gone he began to appreciate the extent of his good fortune.

Jack spent the long hot summer doing odd jobs for Lina's father. He told himself that he wasn't really a deserter. He would willingly go back, only how could he when his ship had left long since? And to wander about an enemy country on his own, looking for more British, would be madness.

And he enjoyed working at the bakery. Mr Ruggierri was teaching him how to mix and knead the bread dough.

'You make good baker,' he said in Italian, and Lina laughed as she translated for Jack.

'And he looks so Italian, does he not, Papa? With his black curly hair and charming smile.'

At this, Papa frowned and started to scold, sending Lina away.

'Good girl,' he said sternly to Jack, in perfect English, wagging a finger. And Jack smiled and agreed, anxious to keep the old man happy.

Every moment they could, they spent together, and Lina started to teach him a little Italian. She was so beautiful, so delightful to watch, the lessons were a joy and the summer passed speedily and pleasantly enough.

Kath strode down the street, a trail of GIs in her wake.

'Aw, come on, hon. Have a cigarette.'

'Sorry. Don't smoke.'

374

'How about chocolate? Everybody likes chocolate. Or I could put my hands on some real purty silk stockings if you like.'

'So long as my legs aren't inside them, that's fine by me.'

She smiled to herself. Verbal and sometimes very nearly physical combat with the American military had become a daily hazard since her posting to HQ three months ago. She'd been in many stations since Bledlow, but this was proving to be the worst in many ways.

Group Headquarters was a large, redbrick house situated on the edge of a small market town in Cambridgeshire. Whenever Kath walked through the ancient streets she felt a jolt of surprise that people still carried their baskets to market, wheeled babies in prams or rode their bicycle to college in the next town, just as if life was normal.

But step through the blue-painted door and she became a Waaf again with a job to do, swallowed up in a sea of blue and brown uniforms. The latter, of course, worn by the American airmen who, to Kath's way of thinking, were far too full of their own importance.

She ducked now into a tea shop to avoid her latest pursuer and with difficulty found a seat in a corner farthest from the door. She ordered tea and a scone and pulled out her newspaper, hoping that here at least a rather new Corporal might find a few moments' peace.

There was certainly none in HQ. The place buzzed with activity. Teleprinters spewed out their news from the many out-stations in the Group, Waafs operated switchboards, plotted weather charts and peered short-sightedly at strange-looking instruments. Middle-aged men seemed to be absorbed with pins and flags and sheaves of paper which they wrote upon endlessly and carried back and forth for no apparent purpose.

'Is this seat taken?' Kath looked up to find that today she had happened upon one of the more stubborn type. Not only had this airman miraculously found a seat in an otherwise packed-to-the-door teashop, but it was at her own table. The cheek of the man!

She offered what was meant to be a frosty rebuff. 'I really wouldn't know.'

'Great. Then I'll take it till I'm kicked off of it.' He sat down, ordered tea, and started to pull out a pack of cigarettes.

'I'd rather you didn't smoke, if you don't mind?'

'Oh, sure. No problem.' He slipped them back in his breast pocket.

Kath was lonely. She missed the cheery faces of the aircrew coming and going all the time, and their lively banter, though admittedly she did not at all miss having her sleep interrupted by the roar of Merlin engines and aircraft taking off at all hours of the night.

She missed the many friends she'd made on all of the stations. Olive, Rosie, Alice, but most of all she remembered blunt, cheerful, open-hearted Bella who'd started the war with her way back in 1940, three years ago. But most of all she missed Wade, still, after all this time. She'd heard of him from time to time on various postings but they'd never been given the same one, and he had made no effort to contact her. Not that there was any reason why he should.

But she had no wish to be reminded of him now by this cheeky-faced GI, looking for a woman, any woman with two arms, two legs, and everything in the right place in between.

Much to the amusement of the other customers he smilingly continued his conversational battery as if they were old buddies.

'Hey, how about you and me taking in the dance on Saturday night, honey, up at the station? You'll just love it. I bet you're a real sharp little mover.'

'I don't think so.' Kath offered him her best drop-dead-Corporal stare. It didn't work.

'Why not, for heaven's sake? What else is there to do around here? Unless you're fixed up already? I've no wish to tread on anyone else's toes.'

But I'd just love to step on yours, Kath thought. She drank her tea, rather more quickly than she'd intended, and stood up.

'Thanks, but no thanks, if you get my drift.'

And left. Maybe it's the loneliness that makes me feel so sour and hard, she thought. Or all the neglected things that she'd meant to do one day but had constantly pushed from her mind. Like write to Meg. There were some things best not thought about at all. What she had done to her friend was one of them. Nothing could ever be the same between them again, deep in her heart she knew that, and regretted it more than she could say. Perhaps that's why she hadn't written.

And then there were her parents. I suppose they don't even know if I'm still alive, she thought. Odd feeling that, and another source of guilt.

Somehow it was as if the optimum moment had passed. As each week, month and year had slid by, sometimes whirled by in a welter of work and sleepless nights, the unresolved decisions seemed harder to make. And now, in the summer of 1943, a simple letter to her family would prove to be a major incident. One she could well do without.

What was the point, anyway? Getting to know and like people was waste of time. You only lost them in the end. Meg, even her arents, must have grown used to her absence by now. So what did it atter?

Except that she had a daughter somewhere, whom she burned to ee.

There is a war on, you know.'

Kath arrived back at HQ to be told to pack a bag and drive a ommander Thompson to Lincoln, and would she get a move on? 'I wish I had a pound for every time I'd heard that remark,' she uttered. 'It is my day off. I was planning on going to a matinee this fternoon.'

'Not now it isn't. Get a move on, Corporal.' And having delivered is bombshell, the jumped-up little sergeant went to harass someone se while Kath stumped off to her room with every sign of ill grace ough secretly pleased to be on the move again. She hated having othing to do. Nevertheless a moan was expected, the point needed be made.

'It's a madhouse. Thank heaven I don't have to stay in HQ longer an it takes to collect my passengers,' she wrote that night in her gular letter to Bella.

'I spend most of my time driving the top brass to some meeting or ther in camps all over East Anglia. I've slept in more strange beds an any decent woman should in one lifetime.'

Though Kath decided not to risk mentioning it in the letter, it as hard not to be aware of an air of expectancy about the place. veryone had the feeling that there was to be some great push on to finish off the war. Tension was high and tempers often ort. No one quite liked to talk about it too much, in case they oke out of line. But the Second Front was definitely being anned. All these meetings she'd driven to must have some urpose, for goodness' sake. Everyone knew it. But then Bella uld read between the lines.

At the end of the letter, Kath chewed on the end of her pen for me time then added a postscript. 'Have you heard anything of ommander Wadeson lately?' She didn't know why she felt the mpulsion to ask. He too had moved on long since, but every now d again Kath couldn't resist putting it in her letter. Bella would ply that no, she hadn't seen him in an age, and that would be that. When her friend's reply came a couple of weeks later, Kath ripped it open at once, eager for news, for the imagined sound of a friendly voice.

She flicked through the usual jokey stories and mishaps of WAAF life and then was brought to a stunning halt. 'Hey, what do you think, old sport? I'm getting married. Yep, got the divorce from old po-face easy as pie and am doing "The Deed" on Saturday. He's called Alan and he's a dear. Wish me luck.'

Doing '*The Deed*'. Getting married? Kath could hardly believe it. And I won't be there. Damn. It hurt her, more than she cared to admit, not to be invited. But weddings were often in a rush these days. And transport was always difficult. Would Bella leave the WAAF now, or carry on?

And then she turned the paper over and saw the postscript.

'Funny you should ask about old Wadeson. He called in to see me once when he was visiting Bledlow. Asked after you. Where you were stationed and so on. Did he contact you? Glad to hear you are enjoying your work. Will write again when more time. Love Bella.'

Somehow, to her shame, the letter made Kath feel more lonely than ever. Bella, frustratingly, hadn't said when Wade had called. But no, he had not contacted her, not in all of the last three years. Why she even expected him to was beyond reason. No doubt he flirted with all the new young Waafs. But try as she might, it was hard to put him out of her mind.

On Saturday morning Kath was bargaining over the price of a pair of new shoes at a market stall when the same GI turned up again, persistent as a bug in bed. Which is where he'd like to be, Kath thought, unable to quench a smile at his cheek.

'Hallo again. How ya doin?'

Kath very nearly told him to go and take a very long walk off a very short pier but the memory of Bella's letter was still strong in her mind. Great big cheerful Bella, who had once sworn that she had given up men for good, was getting married.

And when she stopped to think about it, several of the other girls she'd come to know in recent months had also done 'The Deed'. Not only was there no likelihood of herself following suit but, Kath thought morosely, at very nearly twenty-four years of age she was ashamed to say she didn't even have a fella, let alone a whiff of orange blossom. Drat the war. Drat Ewan Wadeson.

'Is that offer still on?' she asked suddenly, laughing at the shocked surprise on the GI's face.

'Sure thing.'

'See you there about eight?'

'*Wow!* Okay, lady, you're on.'

Kath was aware of his eyes following her all the way down the Market Street. Oh lordy, what had she done now?

The five-piece band was really not at all bad, but the dancing was something else again. Lots of girls in bright red lipstick and curled hair dancing cheek to cheek with the American airmen and soldiers.

'It's called smooching.'

'Really?' Kath had no wish to try it. In fact she was beginning to regret accepting this GI's offer of a date at all. She longed suddenly to be back in her room at HQ with a good book.

'And the other is the jitterbug. Have you ever tried it?'

'Don't even consider rolling me across your shoulders in that way,' Kath warned, and he moved his gum from his mouth, stuck it on the door post, and grinned at her.

'Why not? It's fun.'

'In a tight blue WAAF skirt it could be hysterical.' Not to mention the regulation knickers.

'What did you expect? The waltz?'

Kath gave a thin smile. Maybe she had, but nothing on earth would have her admit as much. 'Is there a way to do this jive without quite going overboard?'

'Sure thing. Come on, I'll show you.'

And he did. Brad, as he introduced himself, was an expert. And to be fair Kath soon found she was enjoying herself. The music quite chased the blues away. But Brad wasn't Wade. She'd make this the first and last date. And by the way he clung to her, she'd best find a crowd to go home with.

At the interval, when the band took a rest, Brad went in search of ice cream while Kath sat and fanned herself in a corner.

She was so busily engaged in trying to overhear a most interesting argument going on between a GI and an ATS girl right behind her that she didn't see the man approach until he was standing right in front of her.

'Kath Ellis, isn't it?'

And then she gave a loud squeal, bringing everyone's head swivelling in her direction.

'Dear lordy, *Charlie*! I don't believe it. How are you? What are you doing here? Where have you been? Oh, Charlie let me look at you?'

He was laughing and hugging her and swinging her round and

trying to answer her questions, all at the same time. Breathless with laughter, they both fell back on to the chair, Kath on his lap, since there was only the one.

'I'm stationed near here,' he told her. 'What about you?'

'HQ. Driving the top brass to hush-hush talks.'

'A Waaf?' He held out her arms to examine her properly. 'Who'd have thought? This is a far cry from haytiming in Westmorland. Wait till I tell Meg.'

And the smile died from Kath's eyes.

'Oh. I haven't told her or anyone about my being a Waaf. Where I am, or anything.'

Charlie regarded her with Meg's look-alike eyes then ran a hand through the pale gold hair that still fell forward on to his brow. 'I knew there was some sort of problem, and that she's been anxious about you. But I didn't know what.'

'It isn't important.'

Charlie gave a disbelieving smile. 'It must be for you two to fall out. Are you going to tell me about it?'

She shrugged her shoulders with airy indifference. 'Meg is better off without me. Let's leave it at that, shall we?'

'About Meg . . .'

They were interrupted by Brad returning with two dishes of ice cream and the usual broad grin. The latter swiftly faded when he found 'his girl' sitting on another guy's lap, particularly since he hadn't even reached first base.

'Hey, what gives?'

Kath scarcely glanced at him. 'Sorry, Brad, this is Charlie, a very old and dear friend of mine.'

'So I see.'

Charlie set Kath on her feet and put a hand on Brad's beefy shoulder. 'What Kath says is right. We go back a long way.'

'And I bought the goddam' tickets.' A stubborn unpleasantness was now coming into the other man's eyes and Charlie held up a placating hand.

'Hey. Look, mate, I don't want any trouble.'

'Well, you sure as hell got it.' And Brad flung the ice cream aside and hit Charlie smack in the jaw. He went sprawling across the dance floor, sending couples flying, girls screaming.

In a frighteningly short space of time a pair of MPs appeared, fighting their way through the mêlée of arms and legs to march both Charlie and Brad away.

'I'll call you later,' Charlie shouted as Kath stood, dazed and helpless, watching them go. 'I need to talk to you.'

'Forget it, airman. You won't be calling anyone for a long time.'

A few days later Kath found a note from him in her pigeon hole. 'Survived the glasshouse. Want to see you. Can you get away Friday? Fourish. The Bluebell Caff?'

Kath was at a table by three-forty-five. She'd always liked Charlie. He'd seemed chockful of enthusiasm and plans as a boy, and just the same now by all appearances. But she was also anxious suddenly to hear all the news of Broombank and Meg. To know that her parents were well. She allowed her thoughts to go no further than that.

The tiny doorbell tinkled and in he walked, broad-shouldered and cheerful as ever, with the kind of easy swagger she'd grown used to seeing on aircrew. But as he came towards her she recognised that some of the cheeriness was no more than bravado. She'd seen that too, in any number of faces going off on ops. A certain stillness, a haunting quality in the eyes, the skin tight and the mouth drawn in. Later, when the crew returned after a successful mission, they would be relaxed and noisy, laughing and boisterous.

He took the seat opposite her. She'd no intention of fussing him, that wouldn't do at all. If he wanted to talk about it, he would.

They ordered tea and two sticky buns, which were an improvement on the 'wads' they got at HQ.

'Where are you stationed?'

He told her. An out-station no more than a mile or two down the road. 'You'll come and see me? I have a bit of time free sometimes, in the late-afternoon and evenings.'

'No ops these days?'

Charlie shook his head. 'I've done two tours, one with Stirlings, one with Lancasters. That's enough.' His face lit up for a moment. 'W for Whisky. We were the cream.'

Kath laughed. 'And don't you know it!'

He grinned. 'Why not? It was a good feeling. We were the survivors after all.'

Silence for a moment as they both thought of the less lucky ones who did not survive, so many young friends lost.

'When the invasion starts, will you be with them?'

'Who knows? The Americans are having a terrible time of it. Finding daylight raids not such a good idea. But I've done my bit. Time to stand down.'

'And you're flying a desk now?'

'No chance. I'm no paper shoveller.' The enthusiasm was back in his face and Kath saw with a start how young he was. No more than twenty-two, after all. 'They've got me on a course in aeronautical engineering, which is great. There'll be a good future in aviation after the war and I mean to be involved in it.'

'Building aircraft?'

'Why not?'

'Good for you.'

Silence fell again, awkward and strained, and a terrible fear was born inside of her. If he wasn't worried about ops, then what was it that tightened his jaw in that dreadful fashion?

'What is it, Charlie?' she asked, suddenly afraid. 'Tell me what's wrong.'

31

'We'll be closing soon, dear. Will you wanting any tea?'

'What? Oh, sorry.' Kath's cup stood cold and untouched while she sat stunned, unable to take in all that Charlie was telling her.

'Meg's all right, you say?'

'Oh, yes. And your father. He didn't go in the house apparently, though he was about to, for a cup of tea. Then when Dan arrived he changed his mind and took Lissa for a walk instead.'

Kath held her breath. 'Lissa?'

Charlie met her gaze evenly. 'Meg got a little girl from an orphanage in Liverpool. Lovely little thing called Melissa, but we all call her Lissa for short. Seems to suit better.'

He didn't know.

Kath cleared her throat, her mouth having gone suddenly dry. She raised her hand to the waitress. 'Perhaps I do need a fresh pot after all. This one is cold.'

'That's all right, dear. I'll fetch you one.' The waitress hurried off. She'd seen that white-faced look a lot lately. Why folk always chose to tell their bad news over a pot of tea was quite beyond her. Waste of a good brew, it was.

'So Meg is back home with Father and it's not going down too well,' Charlie continued. 'It's knocked her flat. Feels she's right back where she started. Not quite true, of course, because she still has the land. Though she lost a lot of the stock she'd built up.'

'And Dan . . . was he killed?'

Charlie nodded. 'Outright. And Effie too.' He blinked and swallowed a mouthful of cold tea. 'Everyone loved Effie. She was an evacuee. Came up to Westmorland because it was a safe area. Loads came at the beginning of the war but most went right back home again within days. Effie found she loved it. Meant to stay for life. And she loved Meg. Like a mother to her, Meg was.'

'How sad.'

There seemed nothing else to say for a long time after that. The waitress brought a fresh pot and cups, whisking away the old ones with comforting clucks of her tongue. Charlie and Kath sat and sipped the soothing liquid, deep in their own thoughts for some time.

'You'll go and see her?' Charlie said, anxiety in his voice. 'She could do with a friend right now.'

Kath kept her eyes down. 'I'm not sure she'd want to see me.'

'I don't believe that. You two were the best of friends, inseparable.'

'So we were. Once. Things change.' And seeing the questions in his eyes, she shook her head. 'Don't ask, Charlie. It's complicated.'

'And none of my business?'

'I didn't say that.'

He smiled. 'You didn't need to. OK, I'm not one for pushing my nose in where it's not wanted, but don't let this thing, whatever it is, go on too long. Soonest healed, soonest mended. Isn't that what they say?'

Kath tried to smile but it came out wrong, twisted somehow. Her head teamed with questions. All about what Meg was doing, living at Broombank. Perhaps Lanky had died. He was an old man. But how did Tam O'Cleary come to be there? Most of all she wanted to ask about Lissa. What did she look like? What colour were her eyes? Was she well? Did she seem happy? Did she laugh a lot? So many questions they all scrambled together in her throat and not one came out.

She stood up. 'I have to go.'

Charlie walked with her up the street. At the corner where their ways parted he put a hand on hers. 'I know this has been a shock to you. But maybe we can talk again later, about ordinary things?'

Kath nodded, and turned a bright smile upon him. 'That would be lovely. What about the farm? Ashlea? Now Dan isn't there to . . .'

Charlie shuffled his feet, looking uncomfortable for a moment. 'I can't live Dan's life for him. He's gone. Father will have to find some other answer for Ashlea. I don't want it, never have. I'm an uncle now, did you know?'

Kath punched him playfully in the chest. 'Good for you. How many?'

'Two boys, so that should keep Father happy.'

'Not thought about it yourself then?' he asked, and as she saw the bright young face darken a shade, wished the words unsaid.

'I'm married.'

Kath gasped and hugged him. 'Why didn't you say? Congratulations.'

He shrugged, giving a half laugh. 'She's called Sue, and in the ATS. We kept it secret because we didn't want her moved. Only they did move her. To Scotland, would you believe? Haven't seen her in six months. There's talk her lot might go overseas. God knows where. In the thick of it she'd be then.'

'Oh. I'm so sorry. Still, it might never happen. She might be lucky and get another posting. It happens all the time.'

'Bloody war.'

He left her soon after that, swinging up the street whistling, determined to be strong, as they all were. But sometimes she wondered. What was the point? What was the bloody point?

One evening that September Jack heard that Italy had surrendered. Never with any real heart for the war, Lina's neighbours celebrated as if they had won it.

'Eet is good. Now you will be safe,' she murmured, flinging her arms about Jack's neck in the excitement of the moment.

Mama Ruggierri advised caution. The country was still overrun with soldiers, she said. 'The Germans will not give up. The Germans have not surrendered.'

At the end of September they heard that the American Fifth Army had broken through the German lines on the Salerno Mountains, and entered the Plain of Naples but there would be no speedy end to the war in Italy. Winter was coming on again and German patrols were holding their own.

Papa Ruggierri liked to explain to his guest what he learned from his customers as they bought their bread in his shop. And Lina quickly translated, her dark eyes wide with fear.

'The Germans are quickly taking over some of the Italian prisoner-of-war camps. And they are searching houses and barns, picking people up and taking them to Moosburg in Bavaria, and to camps in Czechoslovakia and Germany. We should make plans to get Jack away.'

'Soon,' she protested. 'Not yet, Papa, Mama. Soon.'

And the old couple sighed together, looking anxious.

It became even more important after that to keep Jack well hidden, and he began to worry about the danger he put these good people in. But the thought of leaving filled him with dismay.

He had come to love this area, the cypress trees, the warm musky scents of oleander and pine, the sight of a lizard basking in the hot sunshine. He didn't want to leave. Not ever.

One evening Lina came to where he was sleeping in the loft, begging him to hurry, to wake up, dragging him to his feet. Jack's heart jumped with terror. Was this the end? Had they discovered him?

'*Tedeschi, tedeschi*, Germans, Germans. It is a patrol of soldiers, wanting food, I think. Quick, quick.' She pushed him, loudly protesting, out into the yard and under a dung heap, piling the fortunately dry material over his head.

'You must make no sound. If they hear you they will kill you.' She kissed him briefly, and left him to his fate.

And while the Germans tucked into a delicious supper and laughed and joked with the Ruggierri family, Jack lay like stone beneath the straw-caked manure, thinking of England and Broombank, Meg and Kath. And of Lina and her family,

'*Buongiorno, Jack*.'

Impossible as it seemed he must have fallen asleep for here it was morning and Lina and Giovanni were laughingly tossing aside the stinking straw.

'I think perhaps a bath, *si*?'

And now Jack was laughing. He was still alive and a beautiful girl was smiling at him. The German soldiers had moved on and he had survived. Life at this time consisted of such sweet pleasures. And Britain must be winning if Italy had surrendered. He only had to keep quiet a short while longer and he would be safe.

Jack sat naked in the stingingly cold river while Giovanni helped him scrub himself clean. Little more than sixteen, he nevertheless was not short of the famous Latin charm and Jack supposed the village girls fell at his feet for a smile or a kiss. He said as much and the boy blushed and laughed.

'And you like my sister, yes?'

Jack gave a non-committal shrug but something in his expression must have given him away for the boy continued in a hoarse whisper:

'Then you must get her away from here. Take her with you when you leave. My family, they are kind to you, but they mean to marry her to the butcher. He has had two wives already and is fat as a sow.'

'Pig.'

'*Si.*'

This information troubled Jack more than he would have expected. He had put all thought of leaving from his mind. Why should he consider it when he was content here? He had no wish at all to return to the killing. Whenever he gazed upon the surrounding blue-grey mountains, daunting and alien, a chill would settle about his heart at the prospect of crossing them, into the unknown.

'Why do you marry this butcher if you don't love him?' Jack asked one morning when Lina brought him breakfast. The fresh scent of coffee and rolls made the juices run in his mouth but his appetite for good food paled beside his delight at seeing Lina each day. He waited always in anguish until she came, worrying that something might have happened to her in the night.

'He has asked for me and young men are in short supply in thees village. They have all gone to the war. And Carlo, he has money, and a kind heart.'

'But you don't love him.' Jack broke off a piece of bread and held it out to her. Lina pursed her lips and caught the bread between her pretty white teeth.

'No, but I think he will not let me go hungry.' She laughed but Jack did not. He looked into those velvet dark eyes and recognised the glaze of sadness in them.

'You haven't thought it through properly,' he told her. 'No woman can marry a man she doesn't love. If I were Italian I'd offer for you myself.'

Startled eyes opened wide.

'What you say, Jack?'

His head was soaring. He knew well enough what he was saying and he didn't care. He took Lina in his arms and cradled her, as if she were made of some precious material and he was afraid to tarnish her. 'You know what I'm saying. You feel it too.' His voice was gruff with emotion.

'Oh, Jack. You are so preetty.'

Her lips were warm, trusting, and Jack was hard put to control his need. 'I want you, Lina. How I want you. I will speak with your family. Ask them if I might come into supper tonight.'

'Oh, but . . .'

'You *must* ask them, Lina.' And he kissed her again, his hand smoothing the length of her silky thigh, wanting to remove the pretty patchwork dress.

But when she came to him that evening it was all too evident that she had been crying.

'I am sorry, but my family, they do not want you in the house again.'

'Why? What did they say?'

Lina sat down upon the straw, her skirt sagging between her knees, the heart-shaped face a picture of disaster and despair. 'They wish for you to leave. They mean you no harm, you understand? You can stay no longer. It is too dangerous, they say. They have others to theenk of, my grandmother, my brothers, my sisters...'

Jack interrupted before she felt duty bound to recite the entire family to him. 'I get the picture. I do understand.' The thought of losing her brought an odd tightness to his chest. He didn't want to leave Lina. The thought of never seeing her again appalled him. Dear God, was this what he had spent a lifetime avoiding? *Was this love?*

She was talking again, giving him instructions. 'I will bring you food, and a map that I will draw for you, to point the way.'

A map? Point the way to where? 'Through the mountains, do you mean?'

'*Si*. It is the only way to go.' She was crying again, turning from him, scrambling to her feet in the straw.

'Lina.' He grasped her hand, pulled her down beside him. She was warm and fluid in his arms, smelling of sunshine and sweet hay. The patched dress slipping easily from her shoulders, the breasts almost leaping to be caressed. No more words were spoken. None were necessary. They clung to each other, biting, tasting, loving, needing. And knowing that death might come at any moment made the coupling doubly sweet.

He plunged his fingers into the mass of her glossy curls and held her to him while he kissed her throat, her arms, her lips, her breast, as if he could not get enough of her. Only when he had spent himself, shuddering inside her, did he lie unmoving, unwilling to end this amazing moment of fulfilment and love.

It was then that he heard the sound outside. 'The soldiers, they are back!' Lina cried, scrambling to her feet, adjusting her dress.

The loft doors burst open and Jack knew that this time there would be no escape. Surprisingly, his last thought, before they took him, was of Meg. If he'd stayed at Broombank to marry her, he wouldn't now be in this mess.

1943

32

Meg sat in her chair by the empty hearth. It where she always sat. From the moment she finished milking the cows and doing her few morning chores, to the moment when she could thankfully return to her bed, she sat in this chair.

What else was there to do?

She'd moved back into Ashlea because there was nowhere else to go. And there seemed little point in anything. She could still smell the acrid smoke, the scorched air, still hear the terrible silence. Still see the flames devouring her home, clinging to the walls and running over the grass towards Effie's garden. Meg flinched, as she always did at this point.

A hand touched her shoulder and she jumped. 'Would you like a cup of tea?' Sally Ann. Dear Sally Ann had lost her husband and then her baby and all she ever thought about was whether Meg wanted a cup of tea or a bite of something to eat. She was constantly complaining about the weight that had dropped off her. 'You must eat,' she was always saying.

Why? What would it matter if she didn't?

There was nothing for her at Broombank now. In the long year since it had happened Meg had never been back but she could imagine how it looked. A brokendown building with tarpaulin where once the roof had been. The great inglenook fireplace with its shining andirons that Lanky had so loved still flanking the living room but giving off no warmth now. Grass would already be starting to grow between the cracks. The new kitchen stove she'd bought with such pride a twisted lump of rusted metal. And the old scullery and dairy flattened beneath a pile of rubble. It had taken near a day to find Effie and pull her out.

She still had the rowan twig and butter churn in her hand.

Not even the sheep remained. The bomb blast had sent them running, crazy with fear, probably back to the safety of their old heaf. Meg didn't know and didn't greatly care. She had done nothing about getting them back. What was the point? It was people who mattered, not land nor sheep. Who was there left to work for, or with?

'Come on,' said Sally Ann, urging Meg from her chair. 'Come up to the table. I've got a nice bit of fish to tempt you today. Here, take Daniel while I carry a tray up to Father.'

Father. Still suffering from the stroke he'd had when he heard that his son had died in the blast. Nevertheless Joe Turner was a survivor. He sat in his bed at the top of the house, half his body paralysed but issuing orders as ferociously as ever. Still a bully. Why did only the good die?

Tears filled Meg's eyes. She hadn't the energy to hate him any more. She felt only pity for this half existence that drove him to the abyss of despair. To be dependent upon two women for his every need was, for Joe Turner, worse than death.

But this was war. They had to accept terrible things in wartime. Oh, but it was hard. So very hard.

'It's Will Davies.'

Meg, eyes closed, pretended not to have heard.

'Will Davies,' Sally Ann said. 'He's at the door. He'd like a quick word.'

She opened her eyes and brought them into focus. Lissa was busy setting out her tea things, pouring out imaginary cups of tea for Nick and Daniel to sip politely. She was telling them, in her bossy way, how to hold the cup with the saucer neatly poised beneath. Effie had taught Lissa her own hard won etiquette, and the child had never forgotten. There was a lot that she hadn't forgotten. Things that woke her screaming in the middle of the night. And she still asked for Effie, wanting to know where she was and when they were going home. It broke Meg's heart every time.

But at least Lissa was alive. Every day Meg thanked the good Lord, and Jeffrey Ellis, for saving her lovely child. Nowadays Meg never left her side, not even for a moment. It wasn't safe.

'Tell him to come in.'

Will Davies stood before her, cap in hand, fidgeting his booted feet, clearing his throat.

'Sit down, Will,' said Sally Ann cheerily. 'I've got the kettle on. And I've a carrot cake made we can cut into.'

'Don't bother about me, lass. What I have to say won't take more than a minute.'

'Take the weight off your feet while you do it then,' Sally Ann smiled. 'Go on with you.'

Will cleared his throat again. 'I was wondering, Meg, what you wanted doing about your gimmers.'

She stared at him, uncomprehending.

'You'll recall as how your sheep – well – they were a bit startled like that time and . . .'

'I know,' she cut in, sparing him, and herself, the agony of reminiscence.

Will took a deep breath of relief at her response. Worried him it did, to see her so blank and shut off from the world. Did no good at all. Like it or not, life had to go on. He only wished they could stir some life into Meg. 'You'll know that most of those new Swaledales you bought went back where they come from, to their old heaf? When we had our Autumn Meet . . . not that it were a merry one I should add, as it usually is. Wouldn't have been proper, that, in the circumstances . . . we found out where they were. So we took the chance to deal with yours, along with the other lost sheep, even though you weren't there.'

'That's very kind of you, Will, but . . .'

'Oh, it's no trouble. What are neighbours for after all? I'm sure you'd do the same for me if the boot were on the other foot, as it were. I spoke to Joe about it. I hope that was right, since you were, well, not quite yourself.'

Meg nodded and smiled, trying to be polite but not really listening to what he was saying. Her head was aching again and she felt so unutterably weary she wished only for him to say what he had come to say and leave her in peace.

'Nobody wanted to trouble you last backend. What with one thing and another, we thought happen you had enough on your plate. And you've been ill for so long . . . Anyroad, Joe said as how you wouldn't be wanting them back.'

Something seemed to penetrate then. 'Joe? He said what?'

Will tucked his cap in his pocket and sat down at last, relieved by her response. 'Aye. Said as how you'd had enough of farming and wouldn't want to start all over again. We agreed a price, a fair one, mind, and took your sheep off your hands.'

Meg held up a hand, wanting to stop him, but not able to find the words for a moment or two.

'You took my sheep?'

Will looked perplexed. Perhaps she hadn't quite taken it in. 'We didn't pinch 'em,' he stressed. 'Paid a fair price. Joe took care of all that like.' He half glanced across at Sally Ann, his old eyes begging for support.

Sally Ann at once stepped forward to rest a hand upon Meg's arm. 'You couldn't expect folk to look after them for ever, Meg, and you weren't up to it. And then there were the mortgage payments to find.'

She blinked, struggling to unfog her mind. Mortgage. Of course. Why hadn't she thought of that before? Who had found the monthly payments to the bank? She asked Sally Ann now.

'Joe, of course. Who else?'

Joe. Meg was struggling to her feet. 'Are you telling me that my father has been paying the mortgage on Broombank, my farm, for the last year? And that *he has sold my sheep*?'

'For a good price,' Will cut in, worried now by her response. 'We thought that was what you wanted.'

Meg found that she was trembling. What had she been thinking of to sit here and do nothing for months on end while Joe Turner took over? 'Who is looking after my land?' she asked.

'I've kept me eye on Broombank. You don't have to worry about that.'

'But the ewes are gone?'

'Aye,' Will agreed, nodding and shaking his head sadly all at the same time. 'Those that Joe sold have all lambed again, done well this spring they have. Course, they'll have taken to another heaf now. Wouldn't be worth your while to buy 'em back, even if you wanted to. Not now.'

Meg slumped into her chair again. Will was right. A lamb gave its loyalty to the land on which it was born and spent its first formative year. It was of vital importance on these high fells where a sheep could roam for miles if it chose, with little to stop it. Its homing instinct was its means of survival.

'So I must start again,' she said bleakly, wondering if she had the energy.

'Oh, no, not exactly. That's what I'm trying to tell you, Meg. The lambs born that spring on your own heaf, before the bomb – before – well, they all came back. Well, they would, wouldn't they? Those gimmers didn't know any place else to go. Question is, do you want to keep them or do you want me to sell them on for you this backend?' He waited for her decision.

For a long time it seemed that she would never speak and then Meg blinked and focused properly upon Will. 'They're not all lost then?'

'Dear me, no. You still have the progeny from your Swaledales, and money for the ones that went back home.'

Meg was staring at him now with the first glimmer of hope in her eyes. It would be almost like starting again, but not quite. She still had a good young flock, Will said so. Then she turned to Sally Ann. 'I owe my father money for the mortgage?'

Sally Ann nodded. 'You can pay him back. When you get on your feet.'

The thought sickened her and yet increased the new determination that was starting to flow through her veins. To many these empty fells must seem hostile and inaccessible, yet if you studied them, lived on them, you learned there was order and sense to the rhythm of life in these remote parts. You learned where the old drover roads and tracks led to, the passes you could cross and those best left alone. You learned from nature. Her new Swaledale lambs had returned to her, as the unexplained instinct bred in them compelled them to do. She had been given something back.

'Our Hetty says if you do decide to carry on like, she'll be glad to help out, look after little Lissa any time. That's if you want her to. Course, Tam said as how you might not want to.'

'*Tam?*' She was alert in an instant. 'When did you see Tam?'

'Oh, not since he was here on his last leave.'

She'd rather not be reminded. It had been too terrible for words. Joe being as difficult as he could be about Tam's turning up here, as if he had no right. Taking his ill temper out on them all when Meg had quietly insisted that Tam did indeed have that right, as a friend. Connie had arrived in the middle of it all, complaining nobody had told her about the accident and that she hadn't heard a word from Jack in months. As if Meg had time to worry about him now.

Everyone's patience had been stretched, tempers shortened, and she and Tam had had their worst row yet. He'd accused her of wallowing in self-pity, of not having the guts to carry on.

'Can't you see there's no point in carrying on now?' she had screamed at him. 'Broombank is gone. It cost Effie her life when she came here to be safe. Dan was killed too. It isn't worth it. No land is worth such sacrifice. No house should matter more than people. If Mr Ellis, thanks to fate or the hand of God or whatever you believe in, hadn't taken it into his head to take Lissa for a walk that morning, and not let her help with the butter making, she might have been dead too. How could I have borne that?'

'It's not your fault that they're dead,' Tam had said, and Sally Ann had said it too.

But Meg wouldn't listen. She knew better. She'd been obsessed with owning Broombank for years. And because of that had failed to go to Kath when she'd needed her, had neglected Lissa and robbed Effie of her childhood. And as soon as she held her mortgage papers in her hands, the fates had taken it from her, together with the one person who had loved and trusted her most in all the world. What was that if not a punishment?

How could she live with such a terrible tragedy?

'Father can have it,' she had said then. 'And good riddance to it.'

Now that it was perhaps too late she was changing her mind.

Lissa came to lean against her knee.

'Are we going home, Meg?' she asked, reacting with that uncanny instinct children have to the sensitivity in the atmosphere.

Meg swallowed, and slipping an arm about the child, pulled the sturdy little body close. Three years old and starting to ask questions. Life went on, whether you wanted it to or not. She had Lissa to think about, entirely dependent upon her now.

'Broombank could be put right, given time,' Will said, carefully watching the thought processes in her eyes.

Meg met his shrewd gaze. Then she looked at Sally Ann. Paler, thinner, a deep sadness about her, but still determined to keep going day after day, for the sake of her children.

And her lovely Tam. How she missed him. He got home on leave when he could but it wasn't enough. Meg needed his warmth, his strength with her always. Though they might do nothing but argue these days, she still needed him. When this war was over, what sort of woman did she want him to find? He always said he loved a woman with spirit.

Putting down a hand Meg stroked Rust's floppy ear. He was lying against her foot as usual. She heard him breathe little gusts of pleasure.

'The other two dogs, Tess and Ben, where are they?'

'They're with me,' Will said. 'We thought it best to sell Dan's trailhounds, but knowing your land and sheep as they do, I kept yours. They've been working hard. Good dogs both of 'em. But with nowhere near enough to do to keep them happy. Tess and Ben need you, Meg.'

Rust had sat up at sound of these familiar names, one ear cocked so comically that Meg actually laughed out loud, for the first time in months, for all there were tears in her eyes. 'Look at him. Never say die, lad, eh?' The tongue lolled as he grinned at her, alert, expectant, reading her mind, knowing her decision almost before she knew it herself.

'I reckon it's time we all got to work. First thing in the morning, eh, lad?'

Rust gave one joyful bark, understanding exactly and replying in the only way he knew.

When autumn comes to the high fells there often seems to be a final celebration of colour and long hours of sunshine, like a last waltz before the close of a glorious dance. The wetness of summer has dissolved into a rare brilliance but this year Meg took no heed of the beauty around her. Her mind was entirely on work.

Two POWs had been appointed to Ashlea after the accident, both quite amenable. Brought each day in a truck, they got on with what had to be done without bothering anyone. Karl had lived on a farm in Germany so the work had gone on surprisingly well, and Sally Ann had been glad to have someone else to think about and feed. The War Committee had done Meg's ploughing and every neighbour in the dale had come in to help with the harvest. Now Meg felt as if she had been away for a long time and was glad to be home and working again.

The autumn dip took place and somehow the familiarity of the daily routine began to soothe and heal her wounds. Though there would be no forgetting, Meg was learning to live with the pain. Effie no longer haunted her days and at night she slept the healthy sleep of a tired body after a satisfyingly hard day's work. The relief was profound.

And it was a relief, too, to get out of the house, away from the sound of her father's voice calling down the stairs, demanding something or other every five minutes of the day.

'Tell him to wait,' Meg warned Sally Ann as her sister-in-law sat a complaining Daniel in his chair and started up the stairs for the fourth time in as many minutes to do his bidding.

'What else does he have, all on his own up there, not able to move properly? I can't just ignore him.'

Meg watched this performance day after day until she came to a decision.

With the help of Will and Hetty Davies, they cleared space in her mother's parlour and brought down Joe's bed and personal belongings. And then the four of them carried the protesting, grumbling old man and placed him in it.

'There you are,' said Meg, pleased with the result. 'Now Sally Ann won't have to run up and down stairs all the time.'

'It's come to summat when you're a bother to your own family,' mourned Joe.

Meg lifted a warning finger to him. 'Don't try anything on with Sally Ann. She'll up and leave you in two shakes of a lamb's tail if you don't treat her right. She has a family of her own, remember. She doesn't have to stay here and take your bullying. So mind your manners for a change.'

'And thoo mind thine, you young madam. I suppose you think you can take over the running of Ashlea now that Dan has gone?'

Strangely enough Meg had not got so far in her thinking. She was aware the work of Ashlea would be added to her own, but control of it had not crossed her mind.

'Ashlea is yours, Father,' she said quietly. 'And always will be. And after that Dan's two boys', as he would have wanted. But if there's something particular you want doing, you only have to tell me.'

'And how will I know if thee's done it?'

Meg laughed, though not unkindly. It lit up her face, reminding Joe of the old spunky Meg and for a moment he was glad they were into a battle of words again. He'd missed them. 'You'll just have to trust me, won't you?' she said.

'Tch. I'll be oot o' this bed in nae time, just you see if I'm not.' There was resolution in the faded eyes, and a new expression: fear. Meg saw it and felt her heart stir with pity. Though how could she feel pity for a man whom she did not love? Yet how could she hate him? He was her father and he had lost everything, just as she had.

'Course you will,' she said softly. 'And Sally Ann and I will help you do it. I'll talk to the doctor about it, get some advice. In the meantime you've no need to worry about the farm.'

'Humph, that's all thoo knows. I never thought the day would come when I depended upon a woman to run my farm for me.'

'You never know what life will throw up next, do you, Father?' she said, and went away smiling.

She had often walked on her beloved fells this last year, needing the peace to soak into her heart. She had watched the blaze of broom come and die away, followed by the bright patchwork of summer flowers, and now the white caps of mushrooms sprouting all over the fields. But she'd never come this close to Broombank before.

Its emptiness echoed in her heart, the solitude of the place more marked than ever before. The only sound was of a rustle of dry leaves where a quarrelling shrew warned insects in its high-pitched squeak that it was hunting and they'd best watch out.

But Will Davies was right. Broombank could be saved. The dairy and old scullery built up again and the roof restored. But how much would it all cost, and did she have the heart to do it? Wouldn't it always remind her of Effie?

The door was not locked and a rush of memories met her as she walked into the living room. Of Effie making cabbage soup or drinking cocoa by the fire, soaking in all of Meg's stories. Charlie pounding out tunes on the old piano in the parlour next-door. She could hear it all as clearly as if it were real.

Anything worth saving had been removed. The lofts and spare rooms at Ashlea were full of boxes and pieces of furniture, stored for safe keeping. Broombank stood a shell, empty of the life and love it had known throughout its long existence. Meg's dreams and plans for it too must surely be dead.

She went to the bedroom she and Tam had shared. All she could hope for now was to get through each day. Do what had to be done, for the sake of her sheep. She couldn't look any further than that.

Unable to bear it she turned away, but something bright caught her eye and she looked down. At her feet, half buried in the dust, was the Luckpenny that Lanky had given her with the sale of his land. Bending down, she picked it up and held it in the palm of her hand. She could hardly see it for the tears swimming in her eyes.

'You didn't bring Effie much luck, did you?' she said, but there was no bitterness in the words. Death was part of life, part of war. It had to be accepted. She had come to terms with that now. Her grieving was done.

Her fingers tightened over the penny. It was meant to bring good fortune to the land, and the farm. And they were both still there, weren't they? The house was badly damaged but not as badly as she had feared. The young sheep had returned, and her friends and neighbours had stood by her, as they always did. She tucked the penny into her pocket. It would be needed if she really did start again.

Meg left the house, Rust at her heels without needing to be told, and climbed Dundale Knott.

Angry slashes of red cut through a grey, lowering sky as she gazed down upon her former home from high upon the fell. She had felt just that sort of red hot anger within herself this last year. The feeling that she wanted to slash at everything, strike out at the tranquil beauty of the place. Feeling so much pain, it had seemed impossible to go on living. But that was fading now.

'Life is stirring in me again, Effie. I can feel it. Try to understand. I have to go on, for Lissa's sake. For Tam. Are you pleased for me?'

Behind her came the sound of the quiet cropping of the grass by her sheep. Above her head, the lonely mew of a curlew, like a sad echo of happier times.

She remembered the day that Charlie's plane had flown over and Effie and Sally Ann had been scared out of their wits. Then they'd celebrated Charlie's engagement with some of Effie's awful wine, joking and giggling, teasing Tam about going to the dance. The stinging of tears came to her eyes at the memory.

Yet despite their fright, they had imagined themselves in no real danger of being bombed. Not here, amongst all this beauty and tranquillity.

Meg brushed the tears angrily from her eyes and got to her feet. Time for tears was done. Best not to dwell on it, that's what Sally Ann said.

As Meg turned to climb higher up the fell, she saw a flicker of movement below. A dark figure broke through the hedge from the lane. Someone was crossing the field, walking towards Broombank. Curious, she stopped to watch. Not looters she hoped. Who dared trespass on her land? What should she do? Send the dogs down to chase whoever it was away, or ... Meg stopped, and her eyes fastened disbelievingly on the figure. It couldn't be. It couldn't. It *was*.

'Tam!'

Then she was running, falling, slipping and tumbling down the fellside at such a rate it was a wonder she didn't go head over heels right to the bottom, Rust bounding excitedly beside her. She was laughing and crying all at the same time and she could hear Tam laughing too. How she loved that sound.

Seconds later she was in his arms, smothering his face with kisses.

'Oh, my darling, my darling.' When she could draw breath she ran her hands over his beloved face, across his shoulders and down his strong arms and back to his face again. 'Let me look at you. Oh, you look so good.' He was a soldier in an American uniform. A stranger. But not a stranger. He was her love.

'You look pretty good yourself,' he said, moss green eyes devouring her as she had so loved them to do in the past. 'I thought never to see you smile again.' His lips were seeking hers , devouring her, needing her, and Meg felt the first shaft of desire like the stirring of new life within her.

'How long have you got?' She wished the words unsaid almost as soon as they were uttered for she didn't want to hear the answer.

'Long enough,' he said, holding her from him so that he could study her.

'It's never long enough,' she mourned. 'Why don't they give you a decent leave?'

'I'm lucky to be here at all. Isn't it nearly always cancelled? And would you know it, I've dreamt of nothing else but taking you to bed, Meg Turner, and I mean to do so. I mean to make love to you all night long, till you beg for mercy.'

'Oh, I want you too. I've needed you so much, Tam, so very much. But not at Ashlea. I couldn't bear it, not with Father listening and making acid comments. And Sally Ann all hollow-eyed, remembering.'

Tam smoothed a hand over her cheeks, her chin, down her throat, making her shiver with fresh longing. 'You're looking a bit hollow-eyed yourself, me darlin'.' The beauty of the cheek bones was still there though, for all the skin looked pale, stretched tight with tension, the eyes like dark bruises.

'I'm mending, slowly.'

He kissed her again, with poignant tenderness. 'Then where?' he whispered. 'When? I must have you before I go mad.' The touch of his lips on hers, the remembered maleness of him, set her senses whirling, her pulses quickening.

'Is it too cold today?' she asked, teasing him wantonly with her eyes, remembering past days of loving in the bracken.

'For the fells? In October? And aren't you as shameless as ever, Meg Turner?'

'Oh, I am Tam O'Cleary. With you, I am indeed.'

As one they looked towards Broombank, and she shivered. 'I wish I had a home to offer you,' he said.

'You have yourself, love, and that is all that matters.' She felt his sigh and clung to him, wanting so much to prove with every part of her being, how much she loved him. 'There are always the barns.'

And so the barn it was. Warm and dusty, fragrant with hay and old apples, and because of the perversity of fate, untouched by German bombs. And as they loved and touched, kissed and became one again, many ghosts were laid. Meg gave no thought to another time, another loving in this very same barn, in another man's arms. Tam was all that mattered now.

Connie came again that Christmas of 1943. There seemed something about the festive season that caused her to visit. Even last year, despite their being in mourning and not wanting to celebrate at all, Meg thought.

And then was filled with guilt when Connie announced she'd had official word that Jack was missing.

'Does that mean...?' It was no good, Meg could not speak the words. She had lost too many people already. Surely not Jack as well.

'No, it means nothing of the sort,' said Connie stoutly, setting down her great tapestry bag and her hat box with a thankful sigh that sounded very much as if she meant to stay for the duration, as perhaps she did. 'A cup of tea would go down a treat. And I'll have a piece of carrot cake, Sally Ann, if there's one going.'

Sally Ann went smilingly to put the kettle on.

'It means, so say the powers-that-be, that he's been taken prisoner. Went on some special boat operation and never returned. Well, he would, wouldn't he? Very special, my Jack. They must have appreciated his worth, mustn't they?'

'I suppose so,' Meg said. Somehow she didn't feel up to more bad news. She didn't love Jack any more, but she would always think of him as a friend. Despite what he had done to her, he was still Lissa's father.

Sally Ann put a comforting arm about the older woman's shoulder. 'I'm so sorry. It's dreadful to lose someone you love.'

Connie scarcely blinked an eyelid as she eased herself away from the embrace. 'A dab of milk and two saccharine for me. Couldn't get a sniff of a cup all the way here.'

Sally Ann obeyed, avoiding Meg's amused glance. 'Go in and see Father, he's in the parlour since his stroke.'

'Is he not up and about yet? Do him no good to sit about feeling sorry for himself.'

Meg shook her head. 'He has got some movement back, but it's limited.'

Connie sniffed her disapproval. 'Self-pity is the killer, not the stroke. Never indulge in it myself. Get on and do what you have to do in life, that's my motto. And see you make a proper job of it. We'll have to get him going.'

'Connie, you are probably exactly the tonic he needs,' said Meg, laughing. 'We'll leave him in your capable hands.'

She actually smiled. 'You do that.'

'How's Peter?' Meg asked later as they all sat down to a meal.

'Pork, eh?' Connie's eyes blazed with interest as the plate was set before her. 'Haven't tasted meat for months.'

Not since last Christmas probably, thought Meg.

Connie jabbed in her fork and carried a sizeable piece straight to her mouth. Moments later she thought to answer the question. 'Didn't I tell you? He was killed in action in '42. I felt sure I must have mentioned it. I could manage another potato, if you've got one going spare.'

And so a husband was disposed of, between the meat and the veg.

Kath arranged to visit Charlie's station a few weeks after their first meeting and was given the full conducted tour. Not that she really needed one. Same long low Nissen huts, same coke stove belching out evil fumes.

'Nothing changes,' she laughed as they stood in a long queue for the privilege of eating an unidentifiable stew and two slices of dry bread in the Airmen's Mess.

And as if to set the seal on those words Kath walked right into the solid presence of an officer and tipped the awful mess of it right down his uniform.

'Oh, I'm so sorry. I wasn't looking where I was going.'

'Katherine Ellis, as I live and breathe.'

She stared dumbfounded, her throat closing so tight she could hardly squeeze the words out. 'Wade. What are you doing here?'

'I could ask the same of you.' He glanced behind her at Charlie and sketched a salute to them both in response to Charlie's smartly clicked heels. 'Only I can probably guess. How are you these days?'

Kath was frantically trying to clean the mess with a cloth she had grabbed from the table.

She'd forgotten how blue his eyes were. Could he hear her heart beating? He must, it almost drowned their conversation. She kept her head down, her eyes fixed upon her task. 'I'm fine. Thanks. And you? But this jacket is ruined, I'm afraid.'

'That's okay, it'll clean. If I go and change it, you won't run away again, will you?'

'Er, we are in rather a hurry, I think. Charlie is showing me over...' Wanting to say so much, and daring to say nothing.

'Sure. That's okay. Well, good to see you again. Carry on, airman.'

After he had gone, Charlie brought her another plate of stew, though she had quite lost her appetite.

How cool he had sounded, how matter-of-fact. Giving no indication about how he felt. Kath couldn't even tell whether he was pleased to see her or not. Drat those pips on his shoulder.

Charlie was, of course, agog. 'You know old Wadeson?'

'I used to drive him places, that's all.' To a quiet patch of woodland where he could kiss me, she might have said, but did not.

'He's well liked around here. Decent sort of bloke. Don't you think?'

'Hm.'

'His wife is lovely too.'

Something inside Kath crumpled and died.

'Wife?'

'She came here once, on a visit. Didn't stay long though. She was a real smart lady.'

'I see.' No, she didn't. She didn't see at all. Wade had made no mention to her of a wife. The rotten cheat! Red hot fury gushed through her veins. What else should she have expected? Men didn't change, did they? The world was full of Jacks. 'Are you going to show me where you are going to be working?' she asked, with brittle brightness.

'Sure thing.' Charlie pushed aside his empty plate and led her outside, along the cinder path to the airfield. 'You've gone quite white, sure you're up to it? You should have eaten the stew, it wasn't that bad.'

'Don't worry about me. I'm up to whatever life can throw at me, Charlie. Lead the way.'

She might have guessed that he would be at her car, waiting for her. Charlie saw him first, leaning against the vehicle, arms folded, as if he'd wait all day if necessary. Charlie stopped.

'I'll say goodbye here, shall I? Don't want to get another sock in the jaw, or another spell in the glasshouse. He's out of my league.'

Charlie's eyes told her he thought Wing Commander Wadeson out of her league as well, but he was too polite to say so. Kath wondered why she had the knack of latching on to other women's men. She needn't let it happen. Not again. The next guy she went out with, would be all her own. She wanted exclusive rights. Katherine Ellis was done with sharing.

Reaching up she put her cheek against Charlie's and kissed him. 'Take care.'

'You too.'

'Let me see you again before they post you off to some other Godforsaken place.'

'Yeah. That would be fun.'

'And do me a favour, will you? When you write to Meg, don't tell her that you saw me.'

'For God's sake . . .'

Kath put a hand to his lips. 'I'll try to explain some time, just a little. And I promise I will contact her myself, when the time is right. I do need to, for lots of reasons. But these very special reasons mean it must be me who does it, not you or anyone else. Promise?'

Charlie looked far from happy. 'I suppose I'll have to. Can't I even say that you're alive and well? Meg deserves a bit of good news. And your parents too. What about them?'

Kath blinked away a sudden rush of tears. After a long silence she nodded. 'All right, you can say that you've seen me, that I'm in the WAAF. But don't say where. No details, not even a hint. I'll take it from there when I've worked some things out in my mind. When I'm ready. All right?'

'I don't know what's going on and maybe it's none of my business but so long as you play fair with Meg, that's all right by me.'

'I owe Meg a lot. No one knows that better than me. But our relationship is somewhat confused at present.'

Charlie glanced across at the Jeep. 'I think your commander is getting a bit impatient.'

Kath smiled and wrinkled her nose with a hint of the old mischief. 'Do him good to cool his heels for a bit.' She tugged her jacket into place and straightened her tie. 'Wife indeed.' And turning smartly on her heel, she strolled towards her vehicle, hearing Charlie's soft chuckle as she went.

* * *

'So, Wing Commander, this is a surprise.'

Kath stood before him, attempting nonchalance while her heartbeat pounded in her ears. She knew she looked good. A neat trim figure in her blue uniform. Hair smartly brushed up beneath her cap, tie knotted in the correct fashion, the buttons on her tunic palely glowing from many hours of polishing.

'Katherine. Life seems to have treated you well.' His eyes moved to the two stripes halfway down her arm.

'Yes,' she said coolly. 'Hard work brings its own rewards they say.' Meg would love me for that, she thought, smiling at the thought.

'Seems to have made you happy.'

Why did he look so uncomfortable? Probably embarrassed by the recollection of their little flirtation, hardly worthy of the title affair. Kath sat on the driver's seat and swung her legs inside, the skirt ricking up slightly as she did so. To her great astonishment Wade groaned.

'That was what did for me in the first place,' he said.

'What?'

'The sight of those lovely long legs swinging in and out of that staff car. Oh boy, Katherine, you're even more beautiful than I remember.'

Unable to help herself, Kath burst out laughing. Wade leaned on the windscreen and grinned at her.

'Did you forget me?' he asked.

'As a matter of fact, I didn't.' She glanced at him from beneath her lashes. 'Why did you never tell me you were married?'

'Who's been talking?'

Kath started the engine.

'Okay, I won't ask. My marriage with Donna was over long since. I should have told you, only I'd every intention of getting a divorce.'

'But she came over here to see you, to try to win you back?'

Wade gave a sceptical smile. 'She's a wily gal. Didn't like the thought of losing all that lovely real estate we own. She came to do a deal personally, where her lawyers had failed.'

'And she succeeded?'

'Sure. I gave her most of what she wanted. After she'd come all that way, how could I refuse? I'd fallen for and lost you by that time and was pretty mixed up. What did property matter? I thought.'

'You're still married to her?'

'Only temporarily. The divorce is going through this time.'

Kath met his gaze coolly. 'It seems to be a slow business.'

'You can say that again.'

'Perhaps she may think of other delaying tactics.'

'What's that supposed to mean?'

'That could be her aim, couldn't it? If she keeps the discussions going long enough, the war will be over and you'll be home.' Kath hated the sour note in her own voice but somehow she couldn't seem to help herself. Jack had promised to finish with Meg, but he hadn't, had he? 'Maybe then she can change your mind.'

'She means nothing to me. It's you I want. You know that, honey.'

Kath's lips moved into a smile but it didn't reach her eyes. 'Now where have I heard that before? Goodbye, Wade. It was nice knowing you.'

And she drove off, leaving him standing alone on the parade ground.

Meg was clearing out Joe's room when the letter from Charlie came. She'd tucked it into her overall pocket at breakfast, thankful just to see his handwriting, proving he was well. She meant to bottom this room properly. Then she'd read the letter over her morning tea. Soon it would be Hogg Day again and then the lambing, and she wouldn't have a minute.

'What are you doing?' Sally Ann asked as she discovered Meg, broom in hand, rolling up the bedroom carpet.

She giggled. 'Not like me is it? To be so domestic. Partly therapeutic. I need to establish in my mind that I'm staying here, that Ashlea is again my home. For the time being anyway.'

Sally Ann offered a sympathetic smile. 'I can understand it must be difficult for you. Make your mark then. Put some of your own things in here, if it makes you feel better.'

'It seems wrong. This house is yours now. Yours and your children's. I'm the outsider, the interloper. And I've no wish to take it from you, I want you to know that.'

'I do. But you know very well that I couldn't manage Ashlea without you. What would I do with a farm?'

Meg gave a wry smile. 'At least you like cows, which was more than Effie did, and she managed.'

Dear Effie.

'So I thought if I stopped living in that cramped little loft bedroom, I might feel as if I belonged.'

'And Tam can share it with you. Good idea.'

Meg flushed. 'Was it so obvious?'

Sally Ann hugged her close. 'You love him. Why don't you marry him? You can't go on feeling guilty about Jack. He might never come home.'

'Don't ask, Sal. It's too complicated. I've got so used to waiting I don't think I'm capable of making a decision any more. When the war is over, we'll sort it all out. For now I would like Tam with me, and to hell with what Father says.'

Sally Ann shrugged. 'He thinks you're immoral anyway. Come on and read your letter. Tea's brewed.'

Meg read it in stunned silence, her whole body tightening into rigid tension. It was not at all what she had been expecting.

Sally Ann, seeing her reaction, paled visibly. 'What is it? What's happened? Not Charlie. Oh no, please, not Charlie.' She pulled Daniel on to her lap as if for protection.

'No, no. Don't panic,' Meg hastily reassured her. 'This isn't bad news.' At least she hoped not. 'This is news about Kath.'

'Kath?'

'Yes. She's all right. In fact, she's more than all right.' Meg started to relax. There was nothing in the letter about Lissa. Not a word to ask how she was even. Perversely, that irritated her for all it brought relief. 'She's a corporal in the WAAF, would you believe? Says he met her in East Anglia, and she's fine and well, though he's not sure exactly where she's stationed.'

Sally Ann clapped her hands in delight and Daniel joined in, gurgling with pleasure, thinking it a new game. Lissa and Nicky came rushing into the kitchen to see what all the commotion was about and Lissa, catching sight of the letter, reached out to grab it.

'Me look,' she demanded, and flushing with confusion as if guilty of some crime, as if the child could actually read her life story in it, Meg folded it quickly and tucked it into her pocket. 'No, darling. It's a letter for me, not you.'

'Would you credit it?' Sally Ann was saying. 'After all this time. Why has she never contacted us?'

Meg shook her head, lifting the protesting Lissa on to her knee to hide her own flushed face. 'Who can say?' She had told Sally Ann nothing about Lissa's parentage and did not feel that now was the right moment. It had been a secret shared only with Tam and Effie. And Jeffrey Ellis had guessed, of course. Meg felt numb inside, any pleasure she might have felt at her friend's well-being overshadowed by old doubts and new fears.

'With that girl I could believe anything,' Sally Ann said. 'But a Waaf? That doesn't sound like Kath's sort of thing at all.'

'No, it doesn't. Not the Kath I knew. But I suppose everyone comes to terms with reality and responsibilities some time in life, even Katherine Ellis.'

'Oh, but it is good news,' Sally Ann repeated. 'You must hurry round to see Jeffrey and Rosemary Ellis. They'll want to know right away. I'll finish the room for you.'

'Yes,' said Meg slowly. 'I suppose I'd better.'

'You don't sound too excited about it?' Sally Ann asked, a frown marring her own delight.

Meg swallowed. 'Oh, I am. I'm pleased that she's safe and well. Just a bit startled that's all, hearing about her out of the blue.'

'Maybe she'll write herself now.'

'I dare say she will.' And ask for Lissa? Oh, dear Lord, please don't let her do that.

1944

33

'Have I got a daddy?' Lissa's great pansy eyes gazed up trustingly into Meg's.

She shook out the tea cloth she was holding and hung it carefully on the line to dry, while she gave herself time to think.

'Of course you have a daddy. Everybody has a daddy, sweetheart.'

'Where is *my* daddy then?'

Today was Lissa's fourth birthday and she had already amply demonstrated she was an individual, with a mind of her own. And judging by the firm set of her small, pointed chin, she did not intend to be fobbed off with platitudes on this occasion either.

Lissa's birthdays were growing easier. There had been a time when Meg hadn't wanted to remember that day when she had gone to find Kath in Liverpool and found a web of deceit instead. Betrayal, where she had looked for friendship and love.

In time she had come to accept it. But since the arrival of Charlie's letter she had hardly known a moment's peace. Inside she felt cold with this new fear. It was impossible to wish that she had never let herself come to love Lissa. She was a child after all, needing love, and Meg hadn't been able to help herself in the end. Only it made the thought of losing her all the more painful. How would she bear it?

'Well,' she said. 'The thing is, it's the war, do you see?' She hunkered down to the child's level and gathered her in her arms. Lissa smelled sweet, of soap from her morning bath and fresh spring air.

'During a war, men must go away to fight. They do this because they feel it is the right way to protect their loved ones. And so your

411

daddy has gone to fight for his King and country, along with all the other daddies.'

'And to fight for me?'

Meg swallowed. 'Yes, darling. And for you.'

'Will he come back?'

There seemed little point in lying. Everyone had to be grown up in wartime, even children. 'We hope that he will, one day. But we haven't heard from him in a long while. If he doesn't, it won't be his fault, or yours. Not all the men who go away to fight manage to get back home. Something might stop them – another soldier from another army, another country, or an accident at sea.'

Was it right to be so blunt with her? Meg didn't know. But Lissa was bright and intelligent and it didn't seem right to let her go on in ignorance. As if there would be a fairytale ending.

'And will my mummy come back when the war is finished?'

'She might. You remember how I explained, Lissa, that we aren't too sure where your mummy is right now?'

'Is she looking for me?'

'No. She knows you are safe with me. That's what she wanted. For me to look after you until . . .' Meg swallowed and blinked very hard. 'Until she is able to do it herself.'

Lissa considered this very gravely. 'You're not my mummy, are you?'

'No,' Meg answered quietly. 'But I feel as if I am. I'm your second mummy. Not every little girl has two. See how lucky you are.'

'What does my daddy look like?'

This was easy. 'He looks just like you, sweetheart. The same heart-shaped face, the same curly black hair, the same naughty eyes.'

Lissa giggled and became a child again. 'Can I go and play with Hetty this afternoon? She promised I could help her make dough babies.'

Meg hugged the child to her breast in an impulse of love as strong and natural as if Lissa really were her very own. She wished, in the intensity of that moment, more than anything, that she was. Then she could keep her safe, for all time. 'Of course you can. I'll take you after your nap. Don't be a nuisance now.'

'I won't.' Warm hands wrapped tight about Meg's neck. Hot, sticky lips pressed firmly against her cheek. 'I wish you were my first mummy, Meg.'

Her heart throbbed in agony but she could find no words to answer. After a moment Lissa stroked back Meg's hair, very gently, and cocking her little face on one side, she smiled at her. 'I do love you best, you see.'

'Do you?'

A fierce nod.

'How much?'

'More than all the world.'

'That's good.'

'I won't have to go if I don't want to, will I?'

'Where?'

'With my other mummy?'

'No, of course not.'

'That's all right then.'

And as she skipped happily away, Meg bit down hard on her bottom lip, fighting back the tears. Oh, but she didn't want Kath or Jack to come back for Lissa, not ever.

'Why won't you marry me?' Wing Commander Wadeson glared despairingly at Kath.

'You've been asking me that question for months now, Wade, and my answer has not changed. I can't marry you and I can't tell you why, not just yet.' It had been easy enough to say goodbye to him that day on Charlie's station, quite another to mean it. In no time at all they were right back where they'd started.

'Katherine, honey, I want to understand, really I do. This will be our last day out together for heaven alone knows how long. All leave is cancelled until further notice, you know that. As from Monday.'

'I know.' A prickle of worry touched her spine. 'You aren't going on a mission, are you?'

'Now, honey, you know better than to ask. I do what I have to do. The invasion is coming. No doubt about it.'

'Let's not waste time arguing then.'

And for a time they didn't. They were in their favourite spot, deep in a wood some miles from the station. The times they could escape to it were rare and therefore all the more precious. Kath found it astonishing that Wade didn't push her into more than she was ready to give. Their lovemaking was exciting but carefully controlled. And though Wade was becoming more and more irresistible, Kath had no wish for it to be otherwise, not just yet.

The Kath of old was quite gone. Not for this Katherine the careless rapture of a moment followed by months of pain and guilt.

So why didn't she marry him, she thought, when it was what she wanted most in all the world? Wade had got his divorce, yet still she held back. Lissa. Why else? She had not yet plucked up the courage to tell him about her. Bad enough to abandon a daughter, Kath thought. To deny her existence would be abominable.

'I thought we said no more secrets. Sounds like a goddamned excuse to me.'

She sighed. 'Some secrets are hard to reveal. Look,' said Kath, 'I'm not a girl to be pushed around, Wade, so don't try it. I'm my own person and I'll tell you when I'm good and ready and not before.' She trailed a hand over his chest and nipped at his lips with her teeth. 'Anyway, as you would say, what's the big deal? You managed to ignore me for this last three years, so why the rush now? And you had a few secrets of your own, remember.'

'I didn't ignore you. I thought it best not to pursue the relationship because of our rank. I got you in trouble once before, honey, I didn't want to risk messing up your life. Hell, but it was hard. I kept asking that friend about you – Bella. I didn't dare ask exactly where you were posted in case I forgot myself and came after you.'

'So what changed your mind?' she asked, guessing the answer.

'It was seeing you again with that guy.'

'Charlie?'

'Yeah. Charlie.' He pulled her into his arms. 'You'd never believe how jealous I felt. It shocked me, I don't mind telling you.'

Kath chuckled. 'That's good. I was wondering what would bring you out of the paintwork?'

'Out of the what?'

'Never mind.'

'I need you, Katherine. I guess I've been pretty patient but hand holding and kisses won't do for me much longer, however passionate. We have something special going for us. Be generous. I adore you, I love you, I want to make you happy. I want you to be my wife. I know it's breaking regulations but no one need know, not till the war's over, which it soon will be.'

Kath softened, kissing him gently. 'I think we have something special too, Wade. But I can't give in to you. Maybe one day I'll be able to tell you about my problem. When I've sorted a few things out. Will that satisfy you?'

Wade put his arms about her and gathered her close, as if she were very precious. 'What is it, honey? Tell me. You ain't got a husband tucked away somewheres?'

'No, of course not.' Only a daughter, she wanted to say. A

daughter I had in a seedy institution for wayward girls. A daughter I never held, didn't love, and gave away to the woman I betrayed.

For a moment his eyes, his touch, were so gentle and reassuring the words almost poured out. Almost. Would she ever be able to tell him? she wondered. He might leave her, once he knew the truth about her. Then it would all be over, and Kath knew that she couldn't bear the thought of losing him. Oh, what a mess she had made of her life.

'Whatever it is, we can sort it out,' he was saying. 'No crime you may have done in your murky past can be so terrible as to put me off. Aw, Katherine. Come on. Trust me. We can get rid of the problem, whatever it is, honey.'

Get rid of the problem. Was that what Lissa was? A problem to be disposed of? Kath's guilt at ignoring her child during these first precious years of her life was bad enough. Could she abandon her own daughter for ever or was that one sacrifice she wasn't prepared to make?

Connie's matter-of-fact attitude to life and death gave Meg the courage to approach her with her own problem.

'When will we hear for sure, about Jack?' she asked.

Connie's keen eyes regarded her shrewdly. 'Why do you want to know? You don't seem to have been too bothered about where he's been for a long while.'

'I've been thinking of little else, these last months.'

Connie's eyes moved to the third finger of Meg's left hand. 'I've noticed that you no longer wear his ring. Haven't worn it for years, have you?'

'It gets in the way of my work.'

'A ring from the man you love? Funny way of showing you care.'

'I do. At least . . .' Meg stopped to correct herself. 'I did love him. Once.'

'I thought that was the way the land lay.'

Meg fell into shamed silence. After a moment she said, 'I'm not sure that we – that we could carry on, anyway. Things had changed.'

'It's that Irishman, isn't it?'

Meg smiled. 'I can't – I won't deny it. I never meant to love Tam but I do. But Jack and I, our relationship was over before – before Tam and I became friendly.'

'Became lovers, you mean,' said Connie sourly. 'Don't think I'm stupid. And I've seen you making up that big bed that was your mother's. Should be ashamed of yourself, you should.'

'Don't say that. I've done my best, really I have. It didn't seem right to tell Jack, to end our engagement when he was so far away, fighting in the war. It seemed heartless and cruel to...'

'Send him a "Dear John" letter?'

'Yes.'

'So you had an affair with someone else instead?'

Meg's cheeks flooded with heat. 'That's not fair. Jack was...' She stopped. Why couldn't she say it? Why didn't she tell this narrow-minded, silly woman what her brother had done to her? Meg got up and walked to the door. 'I can't talk about it.'

'I know what you want to say. Why don't you go ahead and say it? That Jack was the father of Katherine Ellis's child.'

Meg stopped and stared at Connie 'You knew? You knew all along?'

'Let's say I made an intelligent guess. I thought she was yours at first, but then by the way you were behaving, so cold towards her, I realised who the real culprit was. Jack had talked about Katherine quite a bit. About both of you as a matter of fact. I put two and two together.'

Meg was astonished. 'But you never said. Why did you never say?'

'Nothing to do with me. Men will be men, after all. That's the way they are. It's up to the girl to stop them. If she doesn't, then she only has herself to blame.'

'Oh, my God. I don't believe I'm hearing this. And you think Jack is innocent?'

'I don't see why he should pay for someone else's lack of morals.'

'You don't believe he's responsible for the child he has created?'

'Why? Don't tell me you would have wanted him to marry Katherine Ellis, make an honest woman of her. I thought you wanted him for yourself, so you could get your hands on Broombank. But then you managed it anyway, didn't you?'

Meg was stunned into silence by this totally selfish attitude, this warped view of the facts.

'There must have been something wrong, something lacking on your part, for him to go looking for another woman in the first place.'

'I don't believe I'm hearing this.'

'I'm only saying God's truth. A man doesn't stray unless he feels unwanted.'

'That simply isn't true.'

Connie sniffed disapprovingly, then dabbed at her eyes with her hanky. 'That's easy to say now. Now that's he's missing. Possibly even dead.'

Meg could think of nothing to say in the face of this show of uncharacteristic grief. It was as if she were the guilty one, not Jack, or Kath.

It certainly helped to ease her own sense of guilt for not having told either Jack or Connie that Melissa was a part of their own family. Connie had known all along and blamed everyone but her own selfish, foolish brother.

'The ring he gave me is upstairs, in my room,' Meg said coolly. 'I'll go and fetch it for you. When Jack comes back, as I'm sure he will, I'll explain to him about Tam and me. I agree that I should have told him before. I wish I had now. Before it was too late.'

'Too late?'

'Now it seems that my own life is on hold. I can do nothing. So long as Jack is missing, for whatever reason, I feel tied to him, trapped by my own soft heart. If I couldn't tell him when he seemed far away, stationed down south, how can I marry Tam, as he wants me to, while Jack is a prisoner somewhere? That would be even worse.'

Connie gave a little grunt of satisfaction as if pleased that Meg found herself in this dilemma.

'Things don't always go as you would like in this world,' she said sanctimoniously. 'And if you do finish with our Jack, what about Lissa? His daughter, mind? And what about your precious Broombank then? Have you thought about that? You'd leave him homeless too, would you?'

The invasion of Europe began in early June 1944. The weather was far from perfect with rough seas and too much wind. The Turner family, as did everyone else, listened constantly to the BBC for any scrap of news, good or bad. Bulletins were frustratingly brief. But everyone grew skilled at reading between the lines. No news was very definitely good news in time of war.

'The bridgeheads are being held,' Joe announced. 'It's going to succeed. This is what we've been waiting for. We'll push them back, see if we don't.'

'There's no question,' Connie agreed stoutly. 'It mustn't fail. I never tolerate failure. Come on now, Joe, time for your exercises.'

'What a woman,' he said, gratification evident in his voice. 'Worse than a little Hitler she is. Get up. Do this. Do that. Stretch, pull, lift. Never stops going on at me, she doesn't.'

'And look at the good it's doing you. You can get out of bed on your own now,' she said.

'Aye,' Joe agreed. 'I'll be giving that daughter of mine the run aroond yet.'

As summer continued, the combined armies managed to make real progress on French soil, winning more and more territory into allied hands.

At the end of August Paris was liberated, shortly followed by Brussels. But the jubilation was soon dulled with the failure to seize the last of a series of bridges at Arnhem, by which the Allies were to advance into Germany and finish off the war.

A wet and windy summer had turned into a depressing autumn where the allies seemed bogged down either by bad weather or German resistance. The thought of a sixth year of war turned Kath's earlier exhilaration into fear and despair.

Fear that even in these closing days of war, she could lose Wade, just when she'd realised how much she needed him.

She knew that he was itching to be up there, in the skies, taking part in it all. Being grounded had never quite appealed, however vital his role in operations.

But she had one piece of good news. In September she heard that she'd been posted back to Bledlow. She couldn't wait to see Bella again who'd been lucky enough to spend her entire war in the same place.

Nothing had changed. She found her old friend huddled over the belching stove, writing letters.

'Kath, you old layabout. Let you out of HQ to come and do some real work, have they?'

When the joyful reunion was over, cocoa was made and they settled down to a long catching up of news.

A buoyant feeling of hope prevailed, that soon they would see an end to the agony of it all. 'At least we are making progress now,' Kath said. 'Pushing the Germans back where they belong.'

'Aircrew always seem to be ready for off or coming back exhausted,' Bella said. 'Every night to Berlin and Nuremburg. Scared rigid most of the time, they are. It's a long way across France and Germany to Berlin.'

'It's plain enough what they're after. Not that we can say. Careless talk costs lives and all that. So long as they help our invading armies to advance unhindered, that's what counts.'

'Losses are heavy though,' Bella said quietly. 'You can see desperation in their eyes sometimes. Makes my heart bleed. I hope it's all worth it.'

'It will be.'

'It'd help if the weather would be a bit kinder. If it isn't the rain or the wind, it's the fog. Thank God my man is reasonably safe. Works on the ground crew at the next air field. Handy, you know.' She grinned. 'Though it can get a bit dangerous when a plane comes back with its bombs still on board. Unsung hero, I tell him he is,' said Bella, with her usual dry smile. 'And what about your commander? And don't say he isn't, because it stands out a mile what's going on between you two.'

'Nothing is going on.'

Bella looked shocked. 'Then it's time it was.'

'He wants to marry me, that's all.'

'*All*? Then why don't you, girl? Jump to it, straight into bed.'

Kath laughed. 'You make it sound so simple.'

'It is. You pull back the sheets and . . .'

'Stop it, Bella. There are complications.'

'Tell me.'

'Thanks, but no thanks. I'd best tell him first.'

'Fair enough. Get on with it then. Live for today. Who knows what tomorrow will bring? Everyone knows he's crazy about you. Asked after every letter you ever wrote me, till he got posted too, so get on with it.'

'Oh, Bella. I wish it were that easy. Maybe I'll tell him tonight. What about old Mule, is she still here?'

As if on cue, Waaf Officer Mullin walked in. Face as sour as ever, she ran a swift eye over Kath's neatly dressed figure. Not a sign of untidiness. No scarlet lipstick on the sculpted lines of her wide lips. Hair grown longer but pinned up, well off the collar. Nothing at all to find fault with. Kath could almost feel her disappointment.

'I see we are to have the pleasure of your company again.' The eyes fastened upon the two stripes. 'Corporal.'

'Nice to see you too, Officer Mullin.'

And then, as if it pained her to have to say it, 'There's a telephone call for you. The Wing Commander, I believe. Asked for you to ring him back.'

'Oh, thanks.' Kath waited until the woman had gone then looked askance at Bella.

'What's with her? Why didn't she come down on me like a ton of the proverbial bricks?'

'There's more to worry about now than whether two different ranks get together. Go and talk to lover boy. Get that ring on your finger.'

Kath had butterflies in her stomach long before she got through to him. It was often like that these days.

'Sorry, hon,' he said. 'Can't see you tonight. We have some Mosquitoes ready to go out here and we're one experienced flier short. It's a bit foggy so I can't ask just anyone.'

'A bit foggy? It's like a pea souper out there. No one should be going out, let alone you.'

'Sure, the weather is too bad for the Lancasters to take off but Mosquitoes are smaller, lighter. And our boys need whatever air cover they can get right now, at whatever cost.'

'But not you, Wade! It's months, *years*, since you flew.'

'It's okay. Like riding a bicycle. You never forget.'

Suddenly Kath wanted to tell him, wanted to pour it all out, there and then. 'Wade, I need to talk to you.'

'Sure, honey. I'd love to talk to you too. But tomorrow, when I get back. Take care.' A click on the line told her he had gone. Dear God, let it not be for good.

Joe stood by Meg's side, leaning on the rail by the auction ring. It was the first time he had been out since his stroke and his presence had caused a stir. Even so he'd been surprised by the obvious respect shown by the farmers to his daughter. Not simply a doffing of caps or inclining of the head towards a pretty young woman but they stopped to talk to her about farming matters. One or two even asked her advice. Joe could hardly believe it.

Only last week he'd offered to deal with the buying for her when she'd gone looking for some new gimmer lambs to replace her lost Swaledales, but she'd only laughed and told him to stay at home.

But he'd insisted on coming to today's auction. He wanted to see what she was up to. So here he was watching his own daughter come into the ring with her own sheep. Broombank sheep.

'Why do you still call 'em that?' Joe had wanted to know. 'Broombank has gone.'

'Because that's what they are, and always will be. Only the house has been damaged, not the land, nor the sheep. I know I owe you money for paying my mortgage all those months, for which I am truly grateful.'

Joe had thought for a moment that she was going to embarrass him by kissing him before all his colleagues, but she'd contented herself with a smile. 'I'll pay you back. You'll get every penny, don't worry.'

'I'm not worried,' he told her.

'And we'll get the agreed interest in writing, shall we? So there's no doubt what the final sum will be.'

Joe looked thoughtful now as he listened to the auctioneer singing the praises of her stock. She'd learned a thing or two, this lass of his. 'Right enough,' he'd said, too bemused to argue. What else could he do? She'd rumbled him.

'You couldn't find a finer bunch of Swaledales anywhere in the district,' chanted the auctioneer, and Joe listened to the rapid bidding in open astonishment.

When Meg returned she was exultant, unable to keep the pride from her voice. 'They're fine sheep, aren't they? See that speckled-faced one? She's had twins two years running. And the greyer one beside her is so greedy you hardly need a dog to fetch her in. Rattle a bucket and she'll follow you right into your own kitchen.' Meg chuckled, not noticing how Joe stared at her, wide-eyed.

'You sound as if you know them all?'

She looked at him then, a smile of embarrassment on her lovely lips that showed she was a woman still. 'Wicked, isn't it? Don't be sentimental, that's what you told me, so I've tried not to be. I was sad to see the Herdwicks go but the Swales have a broader frame, and bigger lambs. Make more money in the long run. Don't you agree?'

Joe had never considered anything so risky as a radical change of stock in all his life, but he didn't say so. He was too bemused by what was happening before his eyes. He could not deny what he had seen. Meg had done it, for all she was a girl. Broombank sheep had sold for a good price, the top price achieved at this auction mart all day. Should have won a prize, the auctioneer said. Perhaps Miss Turner had best try entering her stock for the County Show next time it was on.

Flushed with pleasure at her achievement, Meg went home that day with a fat pocket. And Joe with a pocketful of thoughts.

That night was the longest of Kath's life. She had ample time to wish many things different. To wish she had never played dangerous games with Jack. It had seemed so unimportant at the time, a way of proving how close they were, that they could get away with the fun of sex without worrying about the love that should go with it.

And it was time to question her own motives at abandoning Melissa. How young she had been, how selfish. So wrapped up in her own needs she hadn't given a thought to the child. And then there had been the awful feeling of inadequacy. Greenlawns had been good at nourishing that feeling in everyone. They hadn't even let her hold her own baby at birth. No wonder she had felt nothing for her.

And now that she had found love it looked as if she might lose it. Was that to be her punishment?

Oh, dear God, let Wade come back this night, then I can spend my life loving him. If he still wants me, that is, when he learns what a cold-hearted, selfish young woman I really am.

Oh, Melissa. Can you ever forgive me? Is it too late for us to try again?

Kath and Bella sat with the other girls not on duty by the window, waiting for dawn, for the sound of six aircraft overhead.

'How could they take off when visibility was practically nil? And to carry a bomb of that size slung underneath the fuselage has got to be some madman's idea of a joke.' Kath's mind had relayed every possible catastrophe. The tiny Mosquitoes had been shot out of the sky a dozen times in her dreams as she struggled to sleep. Now that she was awake the pictures in her head were even more dramatic. 'And if anyone says there's a war on, I'll hit them.'

Not a soul spoke. Everyone knew that these kind of missions were common. They took place nightly, nearly always in less than ideal weather conditions, and to undisclosed destinations. What made it different was the fact that Kath knew one of the pilots intimately. There wasn't a girl present who hadn't gone through the same torment.

And then they heard them.

'There's one,' Bella said, jumping up. 'And another, and another.'

They counted them in. 'They're all there!' Whoops of joy and hugs and kisses all round.

Kath didn't hesitate even to grab her heavy coat. She sped out of the door and headed for the spot she knew Wade must pass when he returned to his quarters.

Waiting for him seemed to take an age. Oh, do come, my darling. I have so much to tell you. That I love you for one thing.

Then she saw the flames on the airfield, flaring up into the sky, offering a beacon of light for any enemy aircraft to follow. She started to run towards it. Hands held her back and she was screaming his name. 'Don't let it be Wade. Please don't let it him.'

'We don't want it to be anyone,' a hard voice said, and Kath sank to her knees in shame, for it was true. Why did anyone else have to die in this terrible war? Hadn't the fates had enough? She fastened her hand to her mouth to stop the sobs, watching as dark figures ran, calling instructions, desperately trying to put out the blaze as one Mosquito burned to the ground.

'Hey, what's this?' He was there. Unbelievably, beside her, holding out his arms for her to run into them.

'Oh, my darling, darling Wade. I do love you, I do. And I will marry you. There's so much I want to tell you.'

1945

34

Lissa wriggled her hand free from Meg's as they walked across the school yard. She did not wish to look like a baby. Her new shoes clip-clopped very satisfactorily and over her coat she carried a Dorothy bag with two wrapped biscuits inside, for her morning break. Hetty had knitted the bag for her out of some old blue wool.

She would be five less than three months away and this was to be Lissa's first day at school. Deep in her tummy was a knot of excitement. Apprehension too, had she been able to put a name to such an emotion, but not for a moment would she show it.

'I'll be all right now,' she told Meg as they both watched Miss Shaw come out into the playground and clang the school bell.

'I think I'm more nervous than you, sweetheart,' Meg said, bending down to kiss her. 'How will I get through the day without you? How will I manage all the chores?'

Lissa giggled, secure in her knowledge of being loved, she could afford to be generous. 'I can help you after I finish this afternoon. You will come to fetch me, won't you, Meg?'

She nodded, very seriously. 'I will be here on the dot of three-thirty. Now you be a good girl and do what the teacher tells you.'

Miss Shaw came up. 'Hallo, Melissa. Are you ready to come in?'

Lissa agreed that she was. 'You're not going to call me by that silly name, are you?' she asked, liking things to be straight from the start.

Miss Shaw hid a smile. 'Lissa then, if you prefer. Say bye bye to Meg. Then we'll go inside and sing some songs, shall we?'

Lissa was given a peg with the picture of a cat above it, but she could already read her name so thought that a bit babyish. Someone, she couldn't quite remember who, had told her that it was very important to know such things before you started school, so she'd made a point of learning it. Lissa didn't like surprises. Or big bangs. And she was glad it was a cat on her hook, and not an aeroplane. She didn't like aeroplanes either.

She needed no help to unlace her shoes and put on her pumps. Meg had taught her how to do that, and made her a pretty pump bag with her name in daisy stitch. She was ready for school and meant to enjoy it. She smiled at everyone, brisk with new importance, as she went into the warm classroom, secure in the knowledge that she was welcome here. And half the children present were already her friends from Sunday School. If they liked school and could do the work, then so could she.

How different from dear Effie's first day, Meg couldn't help but remember, as she walked back down the lane. The thorn hedges were heavy with snow and beneath a stand of beech a small flock of bramblings were foraging. She took no notice of their antics today but thrust her hands deep in her pockets and walked on, printing fresh tracks in the snow as her mind turned inwards. If Lissa was more ready for school than Effie had been, then the thanks, in no small part, were due to Effie herself.

I should have taken Effie right to the door that day, she mourned. Instead of being so concerned with the land and the sheep. Meg acknowledged the reason now. She'd been so determined to prove to her father that she was capable of running a farm of her own that for a time nothing else had mattered. People had seemed unimportant besides the overpowering nature of her obsession. And some had even represented a threat. Her father for one, and Dan. After Kath and Jack, she hadn't been able to trust or care about anyone for a while.

As a result she had almost lost Lissa's love.

Now she knew different. Now she knew that people were every bit as important as her ambitions, if not more so. People mattered most in life. Tam and Lissa were her life. What use was Broombank without them?

She felt pride in her heart taking Lissa to school today, and an odd sort of loneliness. She supposed every mother felt the same way on her child's first day at school. Her day now seemed suddenly empty, stretching ahead of her, though there was plenty of work to be done. Most mothers of course, were real mothers, and often had other children at home. Meg wondered if she would ever have a child of her own, one that wasn't borrowed. The question had never troubled her before. Now, for some reason, it did. She wanted a child, Tam's child, so badly in that moment, it was a physical pain.

Everything that is mine is borrowed. The land, which I can only guard for future generations. Broombank, which was destroyed before it became truly mine to keep. And Lissa. Even Tam might not stay. But Lanky's Luckpenny had kept most of her sheep safe, she should be thankful for that.

She mustn't grow morbid. It was a crisp, January day. The sun was shining on lavender mountains and the snow squeaked cleanly beneath her booted feet. The kind of day that made you feel good to be alive. And she wasn't the naive young girl she had once been. She was a woman, strong and independent. She could cope with anything now. Almost anything.

Best of all, Tam was home on leave. She could at least be glad of that. She'd left him deep in conversation at the breakfast table with Joe. It was odd that they talked so much these days. They even once took a walk together up to Brockbarrow wood. Could Joe be softening in his old age? He still missed Dan, perhaps that was it.

'Whatever is it you talk about so keenly?' Meg asked Tam as they lay together in the big bed that night.

'He's worried over Ashlea. Can't persuade Mr Ellis to sell it to him at a fair price. Joe wants it for the two youngsters one day and Jeffrey Ellis seems to have plans of his own.'

'Lissa?'

'That's what I'm thinking too.'

'Oh, dear God. You haven't told Father you suspect that, have you?'

'Is it daft I am? Do you want me to ruin the child's life? No, indeed. But I wish Jeffrey wouldn't do it. It will only cause trouble in the future.'

Meg snuggled down beside him. 'Then let's leave it till the future to worry over it. Who knows what might happen by then?'

Whatever her differences with her father in the past, it was good to see him making such a good recovery. He still walked with a stick and slurred his words a little but he got out and about most days, visiting friends or the auction mart. He'd even taken up his moneylending business again. Almost like old times. Except that he wasn't permitted yet to work on the farm.

She had to hand it to Connie for achieving such miracles. He'd even made no protest when Sally Ann started inviting the POWs into the kitchen to eat. It was a changing world, that was for certain. But then they'd all been moved by the upsetting stories of lines of refugees seen moving through France and Italy this winter. So perhaps even Joe had seen the cruelty in objecting to the presence of a pair of young men whose own war was over.

'The war will end soon,' they all kept saying. But even if the Germans were being pushed back, there was still the war in the east, still that awful uncertainty, for all it only seemed a matter of time.

Joe cheered when they heard of Hitler's suicide at the end of April and finally, on 8 May, came the announcement they had been waiting for. Victory in Europe Day.

Sally Ann and Meg went wild, cheering so much that Rust started barking and couldn't stop, the two older children looked bewildered, and little Daniel burst into tears.

That evening they left the children with Joe and Connie and went down into Kendal with the Davieses to join in with the celebrations. The streets were crowded with people, flags and bunting hung from every building, and with no blackout lights blazed from every window.

'It's like Christmas and birthdays and Fair days all rolled into one. Isn't it marvellous?' Meg cried.

There was dancing in the Abbot Hall Park and at midnight hordes of people collected outside Kendal Town Hall, laughing and singing. The celebrations were quiet and orderly, tempered by the knowledge of those who had died and weren't here to share in the victory.

It was well into the early hours by the time they arrived back at Ashlea but Sally Ann had made a decision. 'Tomorrow we shall declare a holiday and have the best party ever. We'll invite our dearest friends and neighbours, empty our cupboards and eat till we burst.'

Hetty and Will Davies came, always delighted to fuss over the children, particularly Lissa.

'I've bought her a clockwork clown that bangs a drum. I hope you don't mind? Only, she's the grandchild I never had,' Hetty whispered, flushing brightly with embarrassment. And Meg hugged her.

'And you are the grandmother she loves as her own. I don't know how I would have managed to bring her up without you.'

Jeffrey and Rosemary Ellis came too, because they were invited and Mr Ellis would not permit his wife to be so rude as to decline. Not on this special day.

'We've only popped in for a moment,' said Rosemary. 'We can't stop long as we are due at the Taylors for dinner at eight.'

They sat and sipped tea on the sofa and Rosemary studiously refused to glance in Lissa's direction.

'Uncle Jeffrey,' she cried, climbing up on to his knee and almost knocking the china cup out of his hands in her demand for attention. 'See what Hetty has brought me.'

'You are a very spoiled little girl,' said Rosemary in her most starchy voice.

'I seem to remember another little girl, equally spoiled,' said Jeffrey drily.

Meg withdrew to the kitchen, not wishing to be involved in this little drama. If Rosemary wasn't interested in Lissa, it didn't matter one bit. Lissa had more than enough people to love and care for her.

'Oh, but it is lovely to think the war is over,' she burst out, seeing Sally Ann recklessly slicing carrot cake and doling out tinned peaches she'd hoarded for over six long years. Would they be fit to eat? Meg wondered, and didn't care, she'd eat them anyway. Rust sat and watched the operation, just in case she should make a mess of it and drop a piece inadvertently on the floor.

'I shall be glad when we find some currants again. I'm sick of carrot cake. You pour the punch,' Sally Ann instructed. 'It's homemade and pretty tame stuff but all we have.'

Meg grinned. 'It can't be nearly so bad as Effie's beetroot wine. Do you remember that? And Charlie's first leave when we all sang songs and got very drunk?' Tears sprang to her eyes. Effie. If only she had lived to share this precious day with them. But that was the way of war. It took no note of its victims. At least I had the privilege of knowing you, Effie, she thought.

'We can start planning our future now,' Sally Ann said gently. 'Where will we all be a year from now, do you think? Five years.'

In Meg's skirt pocket was a letter. It had come that morning. She could tell from the handwriting that it was from Kath, and it didn't take a genius to guess it would be concerning Lissa. This was the first news she'd had from Kath since Charlie's letter two years back. She remembered telling Mr and Mrs Ellis about it at the time, seeing the light of excitement in Jeffrey's eyes, the tightening of Rosemary's lips.

'We might hear from her soon then?' Jeffrey had said. But they hadn't. Until now.

Where would Lissa be a year from now? Meg thought. Five years? Her heart shrivelled a little inside. Before the day was over she had to find the courage to open the letter. To read Kath's decision.

'Some of us hev planned our futures already,' Joe announced, puffing out his chest. And then to Meg's great astonishment, he turned and winked outrageously at Connie, who stood patiently by his side.

'What is this then?' Jeffrey Ellis jovially teased. 'Secrets?'

'Not any more. Connie has done me the honour of agreeing to become my wife,' Joe announced, very properly, and there was a small shocked silence, then everyone started to talk at once, and laugh and slap him on the back.

'Good for you.'

'Congratulations.'

'Well done.'

Meg found herself hugging Joe and wishing him every happiness. And to her own surprise realised that she meant it. 'I hope you will be very happy, both of you,' she said, dutifully kissing Connie on the cheek.

If only Tam was here, she thought suddenly, the aching need for him so strong that she had to turn away and pretend to busy herself with pouring more punch so that she didn't make a complete fool of herself. But he would be home soon, they all would. Charlie and his young bride. Kath. And Jack?

Mr Ellis made a toast. 'To absent friends, and loved ones. May they return to us soon.' He half glanced at his wife but Rosemary only sipped at the bland punch with pursed lips, almost as if it might poison her.

Nevertheless it was a day of complete happiness. Songs were sung, jokes told, reminiscences exchanged. Nothing was permitted to spoil it. After the Ellises left, the other ladies sat and drank tea while the men swopped old war stories and the children stayed up far too late.

After a while Meg crept up to her room to read her letter.

'Darling Meg,' it began, and she gave a grunt of disbelief. How could Kath address her as if nothing had happened, nothing had changed between them? She smoothed out the paper and prepared herself for the worst. The words spun and blurred before her eyes so that she was forced to close them for a moment to bring herself back under control.

I know you will be delighted for me when I tell you that Wade and I got married last Saturday. We still have some months to do before we are demobbed but hope to be out late next year. It is our plan to go to Canada since Wade has a home and family there. I'll write again with a date.

I would like to see Melissa. How is she? I know it must have been difficult for you but we can talk about what I owe you later. Perhaps it would be best if we took her out occasionally, when we are finally demobbed, to let her get to know us a bit first. Look forward to seeing you again.

All my love, as ever,
Kath

Meg sat rigid on her bed and read the letter again. She read the letter three times before the contents had finally been assimilated into her brain.

Kath was coming for Lissa. And for the first time a small knot of burning anger lit deep within. Owe? *What I owe you.* How dare she suggest that Meg should be paid for loving Lissa? The insult of it was humiliating, as if you could buy love. And the calm assumption that Kath could call and collect Lissa, like a doll. Well, Lissa wasn't a doll, Meg thought rebelliously. She was a living, breathing person with a mind of her own.

But Kath was the child's mother. She had the right to take her if she wanted.

Folding the letter with trembling fingers, she put it into her handkerchief box. She didn't want Lissa to find it. Not until she had had time to prepare her.

But how did you prepare a five year old to meet a mummy she has never seen? A stranger who is coming to take her to a faraway country?

And how did Meg prepare herself for the shock of losing this beloved child? She lay down upon the bed, every muscle, every limb

431

shaking. She mustn't cry. She mustn't let anyone, Lissa most of all, see that she had been crying.

'Oh, Tam. Please come home soon. I need you.'

A day or two later Meg called upon Kath's parents. Rosemary received her in the kitchen. No cosy fireside chairs in the drawing room on this occasion. There was a coolness between them these days, all signs of their original friendship quite gone.

Meg laid the letter out on the table. 'I thought you might wish to see this.'

Rosemary glanced fiercely at the letter, without touching it, then turned away to reach for the kettle. Jeffrey walked in at that moment, picked it up and took it to his chair at the head of the table to read it in silence.

'I wondered if you would want to see her, when she comes?' Meg said.

'Why would we?' Rosemary said, filling the kettle with a fast jet of water. 'She hasn't troubled to keep in touch all these years.'

Meg swallowed. Whatever her personal quarrel with Kath, this she knew to be unfair. 'Did you give her reason to think such contact would be welcomed?'

Rosemary sniffed disdainfully. 'She made her choice years ago. And she chose not to come home. Best to leave it at that.'

Meg met Jeffrey's bleak gaze. 'You could make things change, if you wanted to. Put the past behind you, as we all must with many things that have happened during this war. You could welcome your daughter home soon.' She made no mention of Lissa. Meg could not have borne to hear Lissa criticised simply for living.

Rosemary set the kettle carefully on the solid fuel cooker and started to set out blue and white kitchen cups and saucers. 'Katherine brought shame upon us all with her dreadful behaviour. For a time I could not bear to go out, to look my friends in the face. I have no wish to go through all of that again.'

'Have you heard from her?'

Rosemary looked uncomfortable and Jeffrey glanced at her in surprise. 'You have, haven't you?' he asked.

'There was a letter, last year. And another a day or two ago. I burned them both unread. It's for the best,' she cried, when she saw her husband's devastated expression.

'Oh, Rosemary. How could you do such a thing?'

'But she intends to go overseas, to Canada,' Meg said. 'You might never see her again. Don't you care?'

Rosemary tightened her lips in the familiar way and began to pleat and unpleat her fingers. 'It's best not to open up old wounds.'

'Perhaps so,' said Jeffrey anxiously, seeing how agitated his wife was becoming. 'Let things lie, for the moment.'

'She says she wants Lissa,' Meg said, unable to hold back her fears any longer.

They both stared at her then, the one with compassion, the other uncomprehending of her distress.

Jeffrey Ellis reached out and patted Meg's hand. 'She is the child's mother. I suppose she has that right.'

'*No!* It isn't right. Lissa is my child now. I have brought her up. I was the one who nursed her when she was sick. I was the one she came to for love and understanding, the one who taught her to read, fed her, bathed her, took her to school that first day. She is *mine.*'

Only the sound of the humming kettle coming to the boil could be heard in the small kitchen.

Jeffrey Ellis clasped his hands and stared down at them in misery. 'There's nothing I can do, Meg. Much as I would like to, I can't help you with this one.'

She ran from the room.

The following months were the longest in Meg's life. Waiting for another letter from Kath. Waiting for Tam to come home. Waiting to hear if Jack was alive. Always waiting.

Fortunately they were busy with the clipping and harvesting and her tired body made sure that she slept. The war with Japan ended in August 1945, but then a long winter crawled by before Tam came home on his last leave in March of the following year. Meg fell into his arms with relief. The joy of having him with her was enough to banish all other concerns from her mind, at least for a while.

'When will you be demobbed?'

'In just a few weeks,' he promised, kissing her.

'Then I shan't ever let you go away again.'

'I shan't ever want to.' They lay together in the big bed in her parents old panelled room and if they slept at all that night, Meg had no recollection of it. It felt so good to be held in his arms again. She loved to taste the sweetness of his lips and relish the scent of his skin against hers. All their past quarrels seemed silly now. She couldn't think of anything that she would let come between them. Not ever again.

Joe and Connie waited too, eager for their wedding which took place at the little dale church on a perfect spring day.

The sun shone, bees droned and the song thrush sang its heart out. The woodlands that enfolded the tiny church flowed with gentian and silver pools of bluebells and garlic flower.

They should by rights be working of course. But for today all was celebration. A respite of much needed joy.

Charlie had come home on leave with his own young wife, Sue, looking flushed and excited over the discovery that she was pregnant.

Meg held Charlie tight in her arms till the tears rolled over her cheeks and dampened the collar on her new dress. 'There were times when I never thought we'd see this day,' she said, rummaging for her handkerchief up her sleeve.

'Oh, fickle-hearted woman. I never doubted it,' boasted Charlie, but his eyes and the strength of his hug told a different story. 'I'll be demobbed soon,' he said, but then, casting a glance at the keenly attentive Joe, drew in a deep breath.

'Might as well own up to it now, Father. I won't be coming home to Ashlea. I've got a job lined up in the aircraft industry. A good one too.'

Meg held her breath as she waited for Joe's response.

'Aye, well, it's just as well. I don't reckon your sister would welcome you back here. Place is crowded enough already and you know how she likes to be in charge.'

They all laughed then, releasing the tension. Perhaps the war had taught Joe something too. Or Sally Ann had asserted a greater influence upon him over the years than even he realised.

His daughter-in-law came to him and kissed him, the only one who dared do so without fear of being rebuffed.

The wedding went off smoothly. The bride and groom looked suitably happy. Lissa, prettily dressed as a flower girl in lemon seersucker, carried a basket of buttercups and daisies made up by Hetty, as was the bride's posy of yellow iris and sweet-scented orchids. Nick and little Daniel were page boys, though not without some protest at the bow ties.

The happy couple were planning a prolonged stay in Connie's house at Grange-Over-Sands, by way of honeymoon and convalescence for Joe. They were being taken by taxi to the station, at Charlie's expense, as a treat.

'We've got our minds set on a nice little bungalow by the sea,' Joe said.

'Bungalow?' Meg's eyes widened. 'You're not thinking of retiring, are you, Father?'

'Aye, I thought happen I might. And Doc MacClaren seems to think it a good idea. It's a touch warmer down Grange way and it suits Connie better.'

She folded her hands possessively upon his arm. 'Your father isn't as young as he was, Meg, and that stroke was a bit of a shock to him.'

'Yes, I can see that it was,' Meg agreed, finding the thought of Joe Turner retired hard to assimilate.

'I thowt we'd tek a place wi a bit o' ground. Joost enough for a dozen sheep,' he explained, and everyone laughed at Connie's shocked expression.

'Sheep?'

'Aye. To keep lively like.'

'That's more like it, lad,' said Will Davies. 'Farmers never retire. Not properly.'

'Well,' said Connie, but in a tone that meant she was prepared to concede defeat on that one.

'And thoo can manage the farm wi'out me, I suppose?' Joe said drily to Meg. 'I seem to remember you wanted me oot o' the way all along.'

'That's not true. I just wanted my own bit of independence. A place in life of my own,' she protested.

'Aye, weel, I reckon you've got it.'

Had she? Right now it didn't seem as if she had anything of her own. The home that she'd struggled so hard to buy had been bombed. Old loyalties and ties with the past prevented her from marrying the man she loved. And her lovely Lissa was to be taken from her by the end of the year. Not exactly what she'd had in mind when she'd pleaded for an independent life all those years ago.

Everyone stood and cheered as Connie climbed into the taxi, tossing scraps of confetti into the wind.

Joe came to Meg where she stood quietly, in the porch of Ashlea, before going to join his bride.

'We'll be off then,' he said.

'Bye, Father. Be happy.'

Joe cleared his throat. 'We've had our differences in the past, you and I.'

Meg couldn't help but smile. 'You could say so.'

'Aye, weel, sometimes a lass hes to be kept in place. It's joost tha
you were harder to keep to it than most.'

'A chip off the old block maybe?'

'Aye, happen so.' He turned to go then seemed to hesitate
'Broombank is yours and always will be. I'll acknowledge I didn't wi
that one.'

Meg tried to look happy about that.

'But Ashlea is for Dan's boys. I haven't persuaded Jeffrey Ellis to
sell me the freehold yet, but he will when I've had time to work on
him. You hev to appreciate that.'

Meg met his gaze steadily. 'I've already said as much, haven't I?

'I joost wanted it understood.'

'It is.'

'That chap o'thine wanted me to lend you the money, for the
rebuilding. I told him no. I need it for me own retirement. I'm no
made o' brass.'

Meg froze. 'Tam had no right to do that.'

'Aye, weel, he happen thowt you wouldn't have the guts to ask me
theeself.'

'It's not a question of guts. I don't need your money, Father. You
helped me with the mortgage payments when I was ill, for which I am
truly grateful. But I've nearly paid you all that back now, so I'
manage on my own, thanks very much. As for Broombank, I intend
to take the problem to the War Committee. It's not my fault a
German plane unloaded its bombs on my house by accident. So it's
not my place to put the roof back. The Government can do it.'

'Pigs might fly!'

Meg straightened her back and a light came into her eyes, one tha
Joe couldn't help but admire. 'Oh, they'll do it all right.'

He gave a shout of laughter. 'Mebbe they'll have to when they
come face to face with your stubbornness. Happen I were wrong, al
them years ago. Happen you're the best son I've ever had.'

Meg gasped and took an instinctive step towards him but he turned
quickly and climbed into the taxi, waving to his family and friends as i
drove away.

'Did you hear what he said?' Meg asked Sally Ann. 'Did you hear?'

Sally Ann laughed as she linked an arm in Meg's. 'Perhaps he's
seen the truth at last.'

1946

35

Meg and Tam had separated the lambs from their mothers and the ewes were now being pushed through the dipping trough. The clean warm water was well laced with the necessary chemicals to kill the keds and mites that would damage and possibly kill the sheep if left to fester and grow undisturbed.

It was an unpleasant operation, disliked by shepherd and sheep alike, particularly on a hot August day like this.

Tam pushed them through one at a time while Meg held each head under water with a bristleless brush for a few moments, whilst trying to keep the sheep's mouth closed to stop it swallowing the stuff.

'What a way to spend my leave. How many sheep do you have now?' Tam asked as they stopped for a breather and Meg grinned.

'Not counting Ashlea sheep which I'm also taking care of at the moment, near five hundred.'

Tam gaped at her. 'And I thought you were a poor woman.'

'I would be without you,' she said. 'It's been hard building up the flock but I never thought for a moment that I wouldn't do it. One day, sooner than you think, I mean to have twice that. That will be a day to celebrate, eh?'

'Looks like everything is going right for you at last.'

'In some respects,' she murmured.

'I'm proud of you, Meg. You have done what you set out to do. To own the finest flock in the district. It humbles a mere man to see your success.'

She looked at him in surprise then gave a shout of laughter and struck at him with the brush in playful disbelief. 'You were never humbled in your life, Tam O'Cleary, and certainly not by a woman. What blarney you do talk.' And grinning broadly he pulled her to him.

'Sure and I'd take you here and now on this damn' hillside were it not for the fact that you stink to high heaven.'

'Get off with you.' And content with each other, catching glances and smiles as they worked, they put the next sheep through the deep pool and chuckled with sympathy as it stood on the side afterwards, miserably dripping and shaking itself while the surplus dip ran back into the trough.

'You'd think yourself too grand to wed a poor Irishman now, I suppose?' Tam called across to her.

Meg lost her grip on the poor sheep she was holding so that it very nearly escaped a proper ducking, until she realised and recaptured it.

'You choose your moments to ask,' she said. 'How romantic, to be proposed to over a sheep-dipping trough.'

'And when are you not with the sheep?'

'There have been other times when you've had my undivided attention. Perhaps you would care to repeat your offer then.'

'Huh. Take it or leave it now, Meg Turner. I'm not a man to beg.'

'I never thought you would ask me again,' she said quietly, suddenly nervous in case he didn't mean it. 'After me refusing you once already.'

'If you don't know a good thing when it's offered, the more fool you. But then, as I said, you'll be thinking yourself too grand perhaps, for the likes of me.'

'Do you want to be dipped in this pool, Thomas O'Cleary?'

Tam backed away. 'Indeed I don't.'

Meg put back her head and called out in a clear, ringing voice: 'Carry my words, wind, to anyone who cares to listen. I love this man, Tam O'Cleary, and he is to be my man for all time.' She looked at him then, at the broad strength of his shoulders as he casually lifted a sheep and tossed it into the water, at the warmth in his soft green eyes, the curl of his smiling mouth. Oh, how she loved him. 'All mine. To have and to hold from this day forth. Is that right, Tam?'

'That's right, my lovely.'

The following Saturday, when Meg went out to do the morning

milking she found Jack sitting on the doorstep, his head in his hand.

A wind was gathering the black clouds over Bowfell to Fairfield, like an impatient farmer with his flock. The chill feel of a storm in the air was echoed in the beating of Meg's heart.

'Jack?'

He raised his head, blinked, and focused sleep-dulled eyes upon her. 'Where have you been?' he complained. 'I've been waiting here for hours.'

She was taken aback for the moment. 'It's only six o'clock. Why didn't you come in? The door was unlocked.'

'I didn't want to risk a blasting from that father of yours.'

Meg held open the door. 'He isn't here as a matter of fact. Come in, Jack. I'll make you a mug of tea, you look half frozen.'

He was dressed in an ill-fitting suit, a soft trilby hat on his head. It sat oddly with the way he picked up a battered suitcase and rolled, sailor fashion, into the house. Meg could feel her heart pumping as she moved between kettle and teapot, mugs and milk. Her mind felt frozen, unable to focus upon a single sensible thought. What could she say to him?

When she had settled him in a chair by the fire with a hot mug of tea cradled in his hands, she stood back and smiled at him, in what she hoped was a welcoming manner. 'It's good to see you looking so well.' It wasn't true. He looked pinched and thin, skin pale almost to the point of yellowness. The once handsome features had slipped downwards somehow, and sunk inwards to a gaunt mockery of their former beauty. The glossy black curls had lost their shine and even the violet eyes looked paler, without their usual lustre. 'Did you have a hard war, Jack?'

His glance seared her, condemned her as a well-meaning, silly female who knew nothing at all about it. Meg cringed at the bitterness in that gaze. 'What happened to Broombank?' he asked. 'I went up there first.'

She sat on the edge of her seat, aware that the cows needed to be milked and the hens let out. She could hear their noisy cackle already, yet did not like to desert him the moment he'd arrived. 'It was bombed. A stray bomb some German pilot let drop, probably on his return home from the west coast.'

'Anyone killed?'

She told him about Dan and Effie. He looked at her blankly and made no comment, offered no condolences. 'So that put paid to the idea of your owning Broombank.'

Meg stood up. She had a desperate need for fresh air. 'Will you excuse me a moment? I have to do the milking. Sally Ann will be down shortly and she'll start on breakfast. But I must...'

His smile was more of a smirk. 'It's all right. I well remember how you always put the animals first.'

'That's the way it has to be,' she said, with commendable serenity, and left him.

She found she was shaking when she got outside and had to lean against the dry stone wall, pulling in deep breaths before she could bring herself to walk a step.

After she had let out the hens it was a relief to hide herself in the byre and feel at one with the lowing warmth of the cows. He'd clearly had a hard time of it and she must be patient. It was no good thrusting all her own problems upon him the moment he walked through the door. She must tread with care.

It proved to be easier said than done. Jack was not in the mood to make concessions, and he had little time for anyone else's war but his own.

'You don't know what it was like, being shot at, bombed, taken prisoner. Safe as houses you were, up here,' he said, choosing to ignore the inappropriate choice of phrase in view of their tragic loss.

Meg agreed that they had had an easy war, apart from the loss of Effie and Dan, and Broombank.

'We've worked hard though,' she said, feeling irritated by his high-handedness, as if they'd been enjoying themselves on some long party all these years. 'But then women have had to pull their weight with all the men away fighting. Some even built tanks and aeroplanes. That's good, isn't it, to see women taking a full part? If this war does nothing else, I hope it will win us equal pay and health welfare for ourselves and our children. Education for all. These things are important to fight for too. As for us, well, we ran a farm. Produced food for people to eat. And proud to do it.'

'You can stop all of that, now I'm home. You can sell Broombank, give up Ashlea too if there's no one to take it on, and go back to being a proper woman.'

Meg felt her hackles rise. This was not the time for a political argument yet she could not resist standing up for herself. 'I never stopped being a proper woman and I've no intention of throwing away everything I've built up. What would I do?'

Jack glared at her. 'So Broombank is still more important to you than me?'

She sighed and got up to go. 'We have to talk, Jack. But perhaps now is not the time. Later, when you are well enough.'

But somehow the right moment never seemed to come. He made one visit to Kendal to look for work, at Meg's suggestion. But when he failed to find employment, he said it wasn't worth trying again because of all the other returning soldiers.

'This town is too small. We need to get away. All I want is a quiet life. A bit of peace, and a wife to look after me. Is that too much to ask?'

Meg said nothing. Perhaps when Tam came home she would find it easier to broach the subject.

But the moment Tam walked into the kitchen, the air positively crackled with tension.

'Glory be,' he said, in his quiet, lilting voice. 'And this must be Jack.'

'And you must be an Irish conchie.'

Tam's ready smile froze. 'It's not how I'm normally thought of, as a matter of fact.'

Sally Ann, setting out the warmed plates for breakfast, clucked her tongue at Jack as if he were a naughty child. 'Tam fought on the side of the Americans, Jack, you've no call to make such accusations.'

The once handsome lips curled into a sneer. 'The Americans? Then he's had a pretty short war, and an easy one.'

Meg, coming through the door in time to capture the taut atmosphere, took off her coat and shook the raindrops from it. 'Would you believe it's raining again? When does it ever stop? Oh, scrambled eggs, lovely.' She smiled brightly at everyone as though there were nothing untoward in the two men standing facing each other as if about to embark upon mortal combat. Sally Ann fussed the children into place at the table, hoping they wouldn't notice.

The meal was a sample of the climate they were to endure over the coming days. Whatever was said to Jack he disagreed with it. Whatever opinion you offered, it was the wrong one.

The children irritated him by standing and staring at him, as children will, and every day he asked if there were any letters for him. When he was told there was nothing, he slumped in the chair and sulked for the rest of the day. Perhaps he's hoping for the offer of a job, Meg thought sadly.

They tried to be understanding but it was difficult. If Sally Ann mentioned a friend or neighbour whose son or nephew had not returned, he quickly capped it with a story of an entire household being lost.

Mostly he said nothing, only sat and stared into the fire, his legs thrust out, one side of his mouth lifted into a sour curl of displeasure. After a few days of this Tam took Meg for a walk.

'We have to talk,' he said, marching her off before she had time to protest.

They walked up towards Whinstone Gill. The beck gushed beside them, as it had done on that day six years ago when Kath had tried to warn Meg to leave Jack well alone, and she had refused to listen. An icy froth of water was racing down from the mountain tarns above, which were no more than melted glaciers from a past age and about as cold, Meg thought, as her own feelings towards Jack.

'Why can't I feel sorry for him?' she asked. 'Why don't I feel compassion for what he has obviously endured?'

'He fills me with rage, just sitting slumped in that chair, swamped in his own self-pity, expecting you to wait on him hand and foot. Can he not see how hard you have worked? Can't he see that you have suffered losses too?'

And might yet lose Lissa, Meg added to herself. She had received no more letters from Kath on the subject so had tried to put it from her mind, not even mentioning it to Tam. But the thought had set off another worry.

'I should tell him, I suppose, about Lissa. But how? What do you think his reaction will be?'

Tam gave a snort of derision. 'If you want the truth, entirely selfish. The pity of it is, he doesn't give a toss for anything or anyone but himself. Probably never has. The sooner you ask him to leave the better.'

Meg stopped and grasped Tam's arm. 'He's hurting, can't you see? So much he can't even bear to talk about it. We should try to get him to unload the pain then he'll start to heal. It does no good to bottle it up inside. It certainly will do no good at all to throw him out. Where would he go? He has no home now that Broombank has gone.'

Tam growled with exasperation. 'He wouldn't have had a home even if Broombank was still standing. Lanky left it to you, not to Jack. And you and Jack are finished, old history. Aren't you?' Tam's face became suddenly very still. 'You have told him about us? You have given him back his ring?'

She stared at the stones on the path at her feet, kicked one and watched as it rolled along the path to fall with a plop into the beck and be swallowed up by the gushing water. 'Not yet. There hasn't quite been the right moment.' She shivered.

Tam whirled about, putting his hand to his head in despair. 'Right moment? For God's sake, so that's why you creep to my bed like a guilty creature? Don't you see that you make it worse the longer you leave it? You must tell him. Explain that things have changed.'

'I will, I will, Tam. As soon as he seems well enough to take it in. Can't you see how ill he looks? And he barely touches his food.'

'He's been a prisoner of war, his stomach has shrunk. But he hasn't been a prisoner all that long, and not in the worst type of concentration camp. He'll survive. Tell him. About us at least. I'm not sure about Lissa.' He grasped Meg's shoulders and gently shook her. 'You have to be fair with the man and with us.'

Tears stood proud in her grey eyes. 'I know you're right. It's just so difficult to face a man with the fact that he has nothing left. Leave me alone with him this evening and I'll do the deed then. Now kiss me, Tam, please, to make me feel better.'

The moment supper was finished Jack got up and announced he was going out for a walk.

'Oh, where are you going? Up to the tarn? I'll come with you,' Meg said. 'I need to talk to you.'

'No.' He glanced desperately about him, like a ferret caught in a trap. 'Not now, Meg. Not yet.' And he was gone. Much later, she heard him come in. It was about two o'clock in the morning and judging by the noise he made, he was drunk.

'Who is that man, Meg?' Lissa asked one morning as they walked to school. 'Why has he come to live with us?'

She swallowed. She couldn't tell the child the truth, she couldn't say, 'He's your father.' Not just like that. Jack looked so awful. Nothing like the handsome, swaggering rogue he had once been.

He had taken to going out every evening and coming home rolling drunk. Where he got the drink from she did not know, nor care to ask. His mornings were spent in bed and his afternoons in a sullen sprawl by the fire so Meg had still not had the much needed talk with him. And Tam was right. As each day slipped by, the decision to do so became harder to make. So she said nothing to Lissa. No child deserved to have a drunkard foisted upon her as a father.

'He was a sailor in the war. He's staying with us because he has nowhere else to go just at present and he needs time to rest.' He could go to Connie, Meg's inner voice said. She had suggested it at breakfast only this morning and Jack had turned on her in a spitting rage.

'Want to be rid of me, do you?' he'd shouted, making Rust growl and Lissa flinch at his harsh tone. 'My own girl wants me out of the house. The woman who has promised to wait for me for ever. Only you can never trust a woman, can you?'

That had been the moment she should have seized, should have told him that she was no longer his girl, could no longer wait for a man she didn't love. But he had dropped back on to the chair, put his head into his hands and sobbed like a child. How could she, after that?

'And get that dog out of here. I can't stand the way it glares at me.'

So Meg had despatched Rust to the barn and given Lissa a reassuring cuddle before getting her ready for school.

'Will the sailor go when he's found a house of his own?' she persisted. She liked to have things tidily sorted in her mind. 'He isn't very happy, is he?' She wondered why Meg let him stay. It was all very puzzling.

'He's hurting inside. We must try to be kind to him, try to understand. We don't know what he may have suffered.' Meg smiled at Lissa. 'Here we are. Is it country dancing today?'

Lissa's small face lit up. 'No, Miss Shaw is going to teach us how to make potato prints. Won't that be good?'

Meg laughed. 'Oh, I remember enjoying that. So lovely and messy.' They had reached the playground and she leaned down to kiss Lissa. Two small arms clung about her neck and soft lips returned the kiss.

'I love you, Meg.'

'I love you too, darling.'

'How much?'

'More than all the world.'

'That's all right then,' Lissa said, and as Meg watched her skip away, small bottom wriggling importantly, an almost unbearable tightness stretched across her heart.

'Jack, we have to talk. I know things are not quite what you expected. Will you walk on the fells with me so we can be private?'

He sat moodily staring into the fire, not answering, the square jaw showing a four-day stubble and the violet eyes shot with red.

'You can't keep all this pain inside you. We need to talk it out.'

A short grunt of impatience was his only response but Meg was determined. Something had to be done and she might never find the courage again. She glanced across at Sally Ann who made encouraging signs. On the pegged rug at Jack's feet, Daniel zoomed up and down with an empty packet of soap flakes cut and stuck into the shape of a car. He was making loud noises in his piping, toddler's voice.

'We'll get no peace here,' she laughed, and tugged gently at his sleeve.

It took some persuasion but at last she got Jack to put on his coat. Out in the yard Rust got up to follow, as he usually did.

'No, boy. You stay here.' He looked affronted but obeyed, lying down again with a sigh of hurt resignation.

They walked up to Brockbarrow Wood. It was here that she had first let him kiss her. How young she had been then, how foolish. It seemed like a lifetime ago. She still remembered the satin smooth bark against her skin, the sound of lapping water, the scent of spring in the air. Such an innocent she had been. Naive. She had thought the signs of sexual desire on his part were the evidence of love. Now that she had Tam's love, she knew better. She had learned many things over the years. How to survive was one of them.

Jack sat beneath the same tree and leaned back against it while she sat on the grass some distance away. He was silent. How to begin?

'We can't go on like this, Jack.'

'Too much of a nuisance to you, I suppose.'

'It's not that. You know you are welcome to stay as long as you like, at least ... until you find your feet.'

'And how do I do that? Where do I start?' Tears suddenly filled his eyes and a wash of sympathy flooded through her.

'Why don't you tell me about whatever is paining you? I'm sure you'll feel better for it.'

And so, very slowly, the story began. She heard how his best friend, Len, had been killed. How Jack had to row a small boat to the mainland of Italy and how he was the only one to survive the operation.

At first she made a few sympathetic noises but then lapsed into silence as he told her about finding the village, and the bakery. Of Lina saving his life and how they became lovers.

'I never meant it to happen,' he said, staring bleakly out over the hump of the fells, tracing the lines of dry stone wall that traversed them while he thought of Italian mountains, biting hunger and soft, pouting lips. 'It was the war. Where she is now I've no idea. Probably married to the damn' butcher. Or dead. The Germans would find her as they found me.'

He said very little about the camp the German soldiers took him to, except to say that they were fed scanty rations and their captors took every pleasure in making life difficult for them. He obviously didn't want to talk about it and Meg didn't ask.

'Even after the war ended it seemed to take ages for us to get home.'

'Have you tried to contact her?'

'I wrote once or twice while I was in the camp and then again when I was in hospital in England. She's never replied.'

Meg couldn't find a word of comfort to offer. All these years she had suffered agonies of guilt for finding she had come to love Tam. She had backed away from ending their engagement by means of a heartless letter and all the time Jack had been making love to another girl. Probably not the first one he had enjoyed during the six years away.

'I suppose you want me to go now?' He gazed at her out of those terrible eyes, the bruises beneath black and awesome. 'Though God knows where. Certainly not to Connie. She would only lecture me all day long.'

'I suppose we're related now in an odd sort of way.'

Jack gave a bitter laugh. 'Nothing on earth would induce me to go and live with your father.' The eyes lit up for a moment with a touch of their old wicked humour. 'Life plays funny tricks, eh? Who would have believed it? My sister and your father.'

Meg smiled too and looking at her, Jack saw that the young girl with her hair tied up with string was quite gone. In her place was a lovely young woman, her curly hair framing a face so enchanting that for a moment he was seized with regret at what he had lost.

He leaned across and tilted her chin with sensitive fingers. 'Can you forgive me? You know what I thought about as the Germans dragged me over those Italian mountains? You. You and these mountains here. You wouldn't believe how I longed for them, the wind in my face, the sound of the rushing beck. All I want now, Meg, is a quiet life. I've lost my taste for adventuring, and for other women. I want a fresh start. How about it? Is it too late, do you think?'

There was an eagerness, a desperate pleading in his voice. As if she were his last hope, his only hope for the future. Meg swallowed. 'It's not that easy. I've changed too, Jack. Everything has changed.'

He stared at her. 'It's that Irishman, isn't it?'

She closed her eyes for a moment then plunged into her explanation. 'Tam has asked me to marry him. And I have said yes.' There, she had told him. She opened her eyes and smiled sadly at Jack. 'I'm sorry, but I can't marry you now. There's nothing left between us. I love Tam.'

Jack's face clenched with tight anger. The thought of some Yank moving in on his girl while he was sweating in a miserable POW camp was enough to wipe all the guilt from his own mind. 'Didn't take him long, did it? He's been living here nearly six years, Sally Ann told me.'

'There were circumstances which made it necessary. I was on my own after your father – after Lanky died. I couldn't manage a big farm like Broombank without help.'

'Very cosy.'

'Don't, Jack. The war is over. It's too late for recriminations.' All Meg's courage to deal with the other, more delicate matter of Lissa and how she came to be here, seemed to have deserted her.

'And what am I supposed to do now?' Jack coldly asked. 'You have my house, my land. And another man is sleeping with my girl. What do I get? A few crumbs from your table? A crust to see me on my way?'

'Oh, Jack, that isn't fair. You have no reason to be so bitter. I

447

could have written to you long since and confessed about Tam but . . .'

'Why didn't you?'

'It didn't seem right, not while you were away fighting. I kept hoping you'd come home on leave. But you never did. That wasn't my fault. I tried to be fair. Which is more than you were with me.' She had to say it. She had to get it out, now or never. 'I know about you and Kath.'

There was a long, awful silence then Jack scrambled to his feet, a snarl of disgust on his face. 'I see. You're going to fling that at me too, are you? I know what you're at. You're wanting to switch all the blame on to me.' He prodded his own chest. 'I'm the one who went away to fight the bloody war. And I'm the one left with nothing. No home, no job, one demob suit and a few quid in my pocket.

'All right, so Kath and me had a bit of a fling. What of it? We were young. And you were far too serious too soon, and too damned naive. So I sought a bit of comfort. Is that a crime? While you, Miss Goody-Two Shoes, live the life of Riley with a man you're not married to. I remember when you were begging for me to marry you. So don't try to put the blame on me.'

Meg got to her feet to face him properly. 'I don't blame either of us. I loved you once, Jack, you know I did. But things have changed, that's all I'm saying.'

He pushed his face close to hers and flecks of his spittle hit her face. 'They've changed all right. You've got exactly what you've been angling for all along. Every damn' thing that I own. You're just like your father. You're Joe Turner all over again.'

Meg was trembling with dismay and anguish. This wasn't how she'd meant the conversation to go. 'That's not true. That's not fair. I didn't set out to steal Broombank from you. It was Lanky's idea, not mine. You're only talking like this because you're angry and upset.'

'I've good cause to be.'

She drew in a deep, shaking breath, determined to finish the task, now she had started. 'I've paid a fair price for Broombank. The bank gave me a mortgage and your share has been put into an account in your name. You're all right financially.'

'A few hundred quid?'

'It'll set you up in business somewhere. Buy you a house, whatever you want. I can see that I've hurt you and I'm sorry for that. You're welcome to stay, just as long as it takes for you to feel well again. But that's all. I have my own life to lead now, Jack.'

'And it doesn't include me.'

'No. I'm afraid it doesn't.'

He had not taken his eyes from her face through all of this. 'Damned if I don't still want you! You're a fine woman, Meg. I'd forgotten just how lovely you are when your dander is up.' One hand snaked around her back and he pulled her to him, holding her fast in his arms when she tried to resist. His kiss was brutal, unforgiving, possessive and cruelly demanding. When it was done he grinned at her. 'I wouldn't mind trying to light your spark again.'

Meg pushed him away and started to run back down to the house to find Tam standing just below them on the path. He had obviously seen everything.

She ran down to him and grasped his arms to look up into his face. 'It's all right. I've told him.'

Tam didn't speak for a moment, nor look at her. His eyes were fixed on Jack. 'Good,' he said. 'Let's hope he was listening.'

36

As winter approached and the weather turned cold the tensions in Ashlea mounted.

Jack made no further effort to look for employment, though he continued to waste his demob money on drink.

'Be careful or you'll have none left,' Meg warned.

'There's plenty in the bank, or so you tell me.'

'But that's for your future. It's time you found a job, Jack, and a place of your own.

'What sort of a future can I hope for now? I feel too ill to work. And I need the drink to help me sleep.' Outside, a bitter, north-east wind howled, the windows rattling and whining behind the shutters. How could she throw him out?

And Tam kept on asking about their wedding. 'Are you going to fix a date?'

'Soon,' she would say. 'Soon.'

'And what is that supposed to mean?'

'What I say,' said Meg in exasperation. There was nothing she would have liked better than to buy a pretty frock and marry Tam. But she daren't relax yet, not for a minute. She felt close to breaking point. Her loyalties to the two men, who avoided each other like the plague, were stretched beyond endurance.

'Maybe it'll be me that leaves,' growled Tam, and slammed out of the house, as he so often did these days.

And still she kept the worry about Lissa to herself, not wanting to discuss it with anyone, even Tam. As if by not talking about it she could pretend that the problem did not exist. Yet every day she dreaded the postman bringing a letter from Kath. It would come soon, Meg knew it. And then she must make a choice. Either she must let Lissa go with her mother, or she would fight to keep her with everything she had.

One day Meg escaped down into Kendal to see the bank manager and check on her finances. She'd go mad if she didn't think of something else besides Jack's problems, she decided. Whatever happened over Lissa, it was important that she make every effort to restore their home.

She checked that Jack's money was safely waiting for him, then she paid visits to the War Committee, the Town Council and her accountant. She even treated herself to tea and scones in a little shop in the Shambles. When she arrived back home later that afternoon she was tired from her exertions but elated.

'The Government have agreed to put back my roof and repair the kitchen and dairy,' she announced, and Sally Ann cheered while Tam lifted her off her feet and swung her round in a hug of delight.

'Well done.'

'No listen, there's more.' Meg was bubbling over with excitement. 'I saw my accountant and he was very impressed with us. We've actually gone into profit this year. Father is paid off. So we are free of debt. What do you think of that?'

Now even the three children caught her excitement and started to dance about and yell, though they couldn't have said quite why. Rust bounded lop-sidedly with them, barking delightedly, while the three adults looked on, laughing.

'And would you believe it? He's arranged for all decisions about Ashlea to be made by me until such time as he returns from Grange-Over-Sands, or Sally Ann marries again and the boys get a new father.'

Sally Ann flushed dark red. 'Who said anything about marriage? I couldn't. I haven't even given it a thought.'

'One day you will. As Father says, you're too young to live life all on your own, Sal.' Meg kissed her plump cheek. 'And too pretty. But until Broombank is restored, and it won't be a quick job, perhaps we can carry on as we are? It's a bit of a squash, but would you mind?'

'Would I mind? I'd mind if you walked out and left me. How could I run this farm on me own? Anyway, I need your company. It'd be wicked lonely without you. I'll do the cooking and look after the children, and gladly take on the Saturday market which I know you're not too keen on.'

'That's settled then. And Tam and me can look after the animals and the land.'

'A perfect partnership.'

'We'll still need more labour,' Tam said. 'The POWs will be going home soon. Next March, I heard.'

'Broombank will be nowhere near finished by then. We'll worry about it later. Oh, and the bank manager is very happy to make us a loan, if we need it, to do any interior repairs when the building work is done.'

Tam folded his arms and regarded her with open admiration. 'There's no stopping you when you get going, is there?'

Jack, listening to all of this from the corner, smiled sourly. 'Broombank is everything. Sell her soul for it, she would.'

'It would be wiser, I'm thinking, for you to hold your tongue,' Tam said quietly.

'Didn't she tell you that she gave her virginity for that farm?' Jack smirked. 'To me.'

Meg gasped, all colour running from her face. 'How can you say such a thing?'

'You need that filthy tongue of yours clipped out. And I might just be the man to do it.' Tam leapt forward and Meg had to wrench at his arm, to stop him from planting a fist right in Jack's face.

'Leave it, Tam. It doesn't matter.'

But he grasped hold of Jack's collar and hauled him to his feet. 'Apologise for that remark. Don't think you can throw your weight about here. Meg has had to learn to fight for a lot of things these last five or six years. She's not the pushover she might once have been and she can certainly handle worms like you. And so can I.'

'You have some use then?'

'And what is that supposed to mean?'

Tam was turning white, then red, with his anger. Meg felt his whole body tense as again she held fast to his arm, trying to urge him into calm. 'Don't, Tam, don't let him get to you.'

Jack laughed unpleasantly. 'Seems to me you've got a cushy number here. You can sleep with Meg, live in her house and enjoy her success with no effort on your part whatsoever. Isn't that the way of it, Irish? There's a name for men like you, if I could only think what it is. Just as there's a name for women like her.'

'Damn you, Lawson. You can say what you like about me, but I'll not have you besmirch Meg's name in that way. If it weren't for the children having to watch, I'd tear you limb from limb and throw you out of the window to the dogs.'

Jack gave a sardonic laugh. 'You and whose army?'

'*No*, Tam,' when he jerked forward, fists clenched.

'Tell him to shut his mouth then or I'll do it for him.' And snatching himself free from her, he strode out of the house. The door rocked on its hinges behind him.

Two days later Tam came in and announced that he'd been offered a job.

'To them that hath,' muttered Jack, and Tam glared at him.

Meg paled visibly. 'What are you talking about? You've got a job already. Here with me.'

'I'm thinking mebbe it's time I did something on me own.'

'Where? What is this job?' She was trying to work out how it was her life was suddenly falling apart, just when she'd thought everything was going smoothly at last.

'Lord Carnsworth is looking for someone to look after his horses. He has a team he uses in the trotting races. It'd suit me down to the ground, don't you think?'

It would. There was no doubt that Tam was good with horses. Oh, but how could he desert her like this? Just when she was about to rebuild Broombank. And they could start to rebuild their own life, just as soon as they'd sorted Jack out. 'You're not going to do it though, are you? How would I manage without you?'

Tam gave her an odd look, most unlike himself. 'You managed when I was in the army.'

'That was different. I had no choice.'

'I wouldn't leave you in a mess. I'd give you what time I could until you found a replacement.'

Meg glanced at the interested faces all about her. 'Do you think we could discuss this somewhere else?'

She put on her coat and walked outside. Tam followed.

In the dimness of the dusty barn he faced her, and Meg shivered at the remoteness of his expression.

'Why are you not pleased for me?' he asked.

'How can I be? I can't grasp why you're doing it.'

'Maybe because I want to.'

'It's because of what Jack said, isn't it? You hate it because he accused you of living on me, of being a parasite.'

'I don't recall him using the word exactly, but yes, that was what he meant, I dare say. And mebbe he had a point. Broombank is yours. The sheep are yours. I help, but as I've said before, I'm only the hired man.'

'You are my future husband.'

'The emphasis being on the word future, it seems,' he said softly and Meg had the grace to blush. Then she moved to him and put her arms about him. 'Perhaps I was wrong about waiting for Jack to find a job. We could get married next week if you like. Isn't it possible to get a special licence?'

Tam's eyebrows rose. 'So what's brought this on?'

'I love you.' She leaned against him, put her arms about his neck. 'I have always loved you. And I don't want to lose you. It's just that things have been so confused, so difficult.'

'When are you going to send him away?'

'I beg your pardon?'

'You heard me.'

Meg swallowed. 'He's hurting. Jack feels he has fought a war for six years and come back to nothing. He needs time. Surely you can understand how he feels?'

'And that's important, is it? How Jack feels? Jack's sensitive nature. Jack's needs. Why do they always seem to come first? What about my needs? What about us?' Meg had never seen him so cold, so angry.

She put her hands to his face, smoothing his cheeks, his lips, his throat, but he twitched away from her. 'Will I tell you something, Meg Turner? You're a difficult woman to pin down. What time you don't spend on your sheep and planning the rebuilding of your farm, you spend worrying over Jack, all mixed up with your own guilt. Though why you should feel guilty is beyond me. Lanky left the farm to you, fair and square. Isn't it time you stopped crucifying yourself for that? What do you owe Jack? Nothing, I'm thinking, after the way he treated you.'

'I can't turn him out to walk the streets, can I?'

'He has a sister.'

'He won't go to her. Particularly now she's married to Joe. He never could cope with my father. I wondered if perhaps I could give him a bit of land. I could spare thirty or forty acres to give him a start. And he could get permission to build a house on it, in time.'

Tam had become very still. 'And where would he live in the meantime?'

'He could rent a cottage somewhere near, perhaps over at Garnett Bridge.'

'And he'd live on our doorstep? For ever?' Tam turned away from her in disgust and it cut straight to the heart of her that he seemed so against everything she suggested. 'It goes without saying, Meg, that I don't want that little toad living anywhere near us.'

A surge of anger went through her at Tam's reaction. 'You are so obstinate. Just as selfish as he is. Why will you not see anyone else's point of view?' She tossed back her curls with a defiant sweep of the hand. Why wouldn't he understand how she needed to do this? For Lanky. And for Lissa. She said as much now.

'Have you told him yet, about Lissa?'

'No. I keep thinking that it's Kath's responsibility, not mine. And I have to consider Lissa here, too.'

'Good,' said Tam crisply. 'At least you're thinking sensibly about that.' His expression softened slightly. 'And Kath. When is she coming? Has she written again?'

Meg swallowed. 'No, no firm date yet.'

'Why didn't you tell me? Why did I have to hear about her letter from Sally Ann?'

'Sally Ann knows nothing about Lissa.'

'I know that. She just told me how surprised you were to get a letter from Kath and how you went to her parents and they didn't want to know. Are secrets such a good idea, Meg? Isn't it time you stopped saving everyone's feelings and brought it all out into the open? Doesn't Lissa deserve that?'

'I don't want to think about it. I keep hoping Kath won't come.' She lifted her chin a notch. 'But if she does, I mean to put my case for keeping Lissa. She is six years old and should have some say in her life.'

'Good for you.'

'And I will tell her, I promise.'

'When?'

Meg glanced about her, as if cornered. 'Soon.'

Tam reached for her then, a smile in his eyes. 'See that you do.' But if he had been having second thoughts about taking this new job, Meg's next words soon stopped them.

'There's something else. I think it would be best, less embarrassing, while Jack is staying with us, if we occupied separate rooms. Would you mind?'

Tam's green eyes narrowed, sparkling like shards of ice. He

released her and his hands fell to his sides in a gesture of despair. 'You're telling me you no longer want me in your bed?'

Meg felt a stirring of disquiet but stubbornly kept to her request. 'I'm telling you that for the moment at least, our privacy is gone, and I can't cope with that. It won't be for long, just till we work out a way of getting him started some place else. I can't bear the thought of Jack at the other side of the wall, listening to us. You do understand, don't you?' Her cheeks were a hot pink but Tam's were frozen white.

'Yes, I understand. I understand perfectly. You'll fight for the land and Broombank. You'll fight for Lissa. But will you fight for me?' He shook his head, slowly, from side to side.

'Oh, damn you, Tam O'Cleary.' She was near to tears and hated herself for this show of weakness. 'That's not true and you know it.'

He made a disbelieving grunt deep in his throat. 'That's exactly the way it appears, Meg Turner. I hate to sound melodramatic, since you'll only accuse me of more Irish blarney, but it's long past time I said it. It's him or me. Plain and simple. Either he leaves or I do.'

'You're right. That would be melodramatic. Certainly very silly.' She turned to go. 'If you want your supper you'd best be quick about it. It'll be stone cold by now.'

'Have I not made myself clear?'

'Abundantly,' she said. 'But I don't answer to threats.'

'I'll not wed you while your former lover is living in your house. Is that plain enough for you?'

'*Tam!*'

'It's the truth, is it not? If you don't want me in your bed, then it seems to me that mebbe you don't want me in your life at all. It's as simple as that.'

'No, it's not.'

'It is to me.'

'Go then, if that's what you want,' she said, tears brimming. And she stalked off, head high, back to the house. Tam did not follow her. He did not come in for supper.

Meg moved his things into the small loft room she had used as a girl, and lay alone, unsleeping, in the big bed that night. In the morning, she found that he had indeed packed his bag and gone. As it turned out it was only to the lodge house on Lord Carnsworth's estate a few miles up the road, but it might as well have been a million miles.

Christmas 1946 was quiet and dull. Sally Ann, Meg and the children, still with Jack present, spent it alone. Joe was too ill to travel but, it seemed, had quite taken to life in Grange and for the time being at least meant to stay.

She'd seen little of Tam in recent months. Busy settling in to his new job, she caught tantalising glimpses of him taking the horses out as she walked Lissa to and from school. He would nod to her from a distance as if they were strangers. More and more she begged Sally Ann to take on the job, and, heavily disapproving, her sister-in-law agreed.

'I hate to say it but I would even welcome Connie right now,' Meg confessed as the two women sat together on New Year's Day alone by the fire. Jack was out, drinking as usual, and the children were tucked up in bed, hopefully asleep.

'The children enjoyed it. Did you see their faces when they found oranges in their stockings for the first time ever?'

'You perform miracles, Sal, you really do. Sometimes I wonder what we won the war for. Things have seemed to be tougher than ever this year. The rationing goes worse, even bread now.'

'It'll get better soon.'

'Look at us. What a pair we are. It seems ironic that Ashlea has become almost an all female household when once it was very much male, with women kept very firmly in their place. Sad in a way. Is this how we are doomed to spend our lives, Sal? As women with children and no men?'

Sally Ann gazed shrewdly at Meg. 'You could get Tam back tomorrow if you really wanted.'

'By turning Jack out in the snow? I couldn't be so heartless. I'm disappointed in Tam.' Her voice broke. 'I thought he had more patience, and more love for me.'

Sally Ann gazed morosely into her sherry glass and sighed. 'More patience? He's waited near six years for you. What can you expect? He's jealous.'

'He's behaving foolishly. How can that be love?'

'He still works on your land every day, after he's finished with the horses. What's that if not love?'

Meg shook her head, feeling bleak and empty inside, almost taking pleasure in hurting herself as much as possible. 'It won't last, I know it won't. Once the spring comes, before lambing starts, I'll have to find someone else, to replace him.'

'There's something else, I can tell. I've felt it all Christmas. It's not like you to be so gloomy. A part of you is somewhere else. Come on, Meg, what is it?'

She set her sherry glass carefully on the mantelpiece and drew in a shaky breath. 'Perfectly simple, actually. As well as losing Tam, I'm going to lose Lissa. There was a letter in Kath's Christmas card. She'll be here soon, in the New Year.'

'Kath? What has Kath to do with Lissa?'

And Meg told her, all of it. She emptied her heart while Sally Ann sat open-mouthed.

'Oh, my God.' Sally Ann was on her feet, wrapping her arms about Meg and despite a very decided determination not to cry, her tears were flowing fast. 'Why didn't you tell me before? Does Tam know?'

Meg nodded, struggling to find a handkerchief to stop the flow. 'Tam and Effie were both there when I brought Lissa home. He's always known. But Lissa doesn't and I still have to find the courage to tell her. And how can I, with Jack behaving the way he is? Oh, it's all too terrible for words. What am I to do, Sal? What am I to do?'

1947

37

Katherine Ellis drew up to Ashlea in a smart little Morris on the first day of February. She had given due notice of her arrival, asking to take Lissa out for the day, and Meg had been ready hours too soon, so tense was she about the forthcoming meeting. The bitterly cold morning had dragged by in an agony of suspense, Meg unable to settle to anything. How would she feel about facing Kath again? What would she say about Jack and the betrayal? What would Kath say? And how would Lissa react?

The night before, Meg had sat Lissa upon her lap and explained to her, as simply and honestly as she could, who Kath was. She decided to make no mention of Jack at this stage.

'Didn't I tell you that your mother would come for you one day?'

Lissa had said nothing for a long time. Almost seven years old now, her baby chubbiness was being replaced by a schoolgirl legginess that would one day blossom into beauty. Her black curls were kept cropped short and though these and the pansy eyes were all Jack, there was much in her that Kath would recognise as her own.

'Will she love me?' It was a most reasonable question and Meg answered it promptly.

'Of course she will love you. How could she fail to love you? You don't want me to tell her how naughty you really are, do you?' Meg teased but Lissa didn't giggle in response, as she usually did. She turned and looked at Meg with her direct gaze so like Kath's own.

'More than all the world?'

Meg swallowed. After a moment's panicking thought, she let her shoulders sag with resignation. 'That's not a fair question, Lissa, and you know it. Come on, let's go upstairs and choose which dress you are going to wear tomorrow. Shall it be the blue or the pink from your extensive wardrobe?'

Lissa had been unusually quiet as Meg tucked her into bed that night and was equally so now as they both stood, hand in hand, listening to the high heels clicking over the slate slabs of the yard. Suddenly making a decision, Meg turned to Sally Ann.

'Take Lissa and the other children upstairs. I'd like to speak to her first on my own.'

When Sally Ann had gone, Meg drew in a shaky breath and opened the door.

Had she not been so concerned for her own feelings, she might have seen evidence of Kath's own nervousness. In the way she picked at the tan kid gloves, or flicked unseen dust from her warm swagger coat with its smart fur collar. But Meg's head was filled with panic and her eyes saw only a beautiful, carefully composed woman standing on her doorstep, like a threat. True there was some evidence of change. The wide, smiling lips did not sport the usual scarlet lipstick. And the hair was mouse brown beneath a leaf green beret, though that was still tilted provocatively to one side.

The one-time friends stood and assessed one another and the long years between fell away. It seemed only yesterday that they had stood, awkward and unspeaking, on Lime Street Station, the baby left in Meg's arms as Kath had run from her life.

'Hallo, Meg. How are you?' And in the ensuing silence she answered her own question, as had always been her style. 'You look well.'

Meg held open the door for Kath to step inside.

She took a few steps into the room, glancing about her. 'It's just the same as I remember it. Where's Tam? I thought you said in your letter that he was working here.'

Meg cleared her throat, though emotion still blocked it. 'He is. He was. He's out at the moment.' Her voice tailed off into misery. I still pray nightly that he will return, her mind continued silently.

Kath turned on her in surprise, reading much more in to Meg's expression than she was intended to see but tactfully not commenting upon it. 'Have you seen Jack?'

'Yes. He arrived some months ago. Looking pretty sick.'

'And he's still here?'

'He has nowhere else to go.'

'And you, soft-hearted little fool that you are, let him in. Darling Meg, if I was too selfish, then you were far too generous. Mix us together and we might make one good one, two sides of one coin. Unfortunately it doesn't work that way. Let Jack go. He's no good.' She was shaking her head at Meg, her eyes sad but very certain. 'You know all that, deep in your heart. And it's not the first time I've said it.'

She felt a surge of resentment that Kath should walk in to her house and immediately start issuing advice. Perhaps she hadn't changed so much after all. 'Would you like a cup of tea?'

'I could murder a strong whisky but I'll settle for tea if that's all you've got.'

Meg looked startled for a moment, then let out a burst of laughter. 'My, you have changed. Gin and tonic was always your tipple.'

They sat together over the tea, not speaking for a long time. The log fire crackled and the grandfather clock ticked away the minutes, while both stayed locked in their own thoughts.

Meg couldn't quite frame the words that tumbled about in her brain. Why did you do it? What was it about our friendship that permitted you to hurt me so cruelly? She stayed silent.

It was Kath who finally spoke. 'Is she here?'

'Yes. She's upstairs, with Sal.'

'I heard about Dan, and your friend Effie. I'm sorry.'

'Thanks.'

'It was a sod, this war, wasn't it? Thank God it's over at last. I suppose I was lucky. Didn't lose anyone I loved. Though right at the end a Mosquito burned to a crisp on landing and Wade only just got out in time. One of the ground crew who helped him wasn't so lucky.'

She was talking for the sake of it. They both knew it. This wasn't the moment for swapping war stories.

'She doesn't like being called Melissa,' Meg said. 'I'm to tell you that. And she doesn't care for cheese. It brings her out in a rash.'

Kath stared at Meg, and her gaze was haunted but she made no comment.

Meg continued to speak now, very quietly and methodically, as if she had worked it all out. 'Sometimes, at night, she wakes up and cries. She has only a half memory of the bomb landing on Broombank but it has affected her. I still send prayers of thanks that she was out walking with your father at that time. But she still hears the sound of the plane sometimes, sees the bright light, the terrible flames that brought death. But then at other times when she wakes it might just be a tummy upset or worry over a mental arithmetic test at school.' Meg smiled. 'Sums aren't her strong point.'

'I understand what you're trying to tell me,' Kath said softly. 'I know that if I take her with me, I shall have a lot to learn.'

Meg swallowed. It had to be said, and now was as good a time as any. She straightened her spine and looked Kath straight in the eye. 'I have brought her up as if she were my own child. And I love her as if she were. But Lissa is six, very nearly seven, and she wants to have a say in her own destiny. If she goes with you to Canada, it has to be her decision, not yours. I'm aware of your rights as her natural mother, but if you try to force her, to exercise those rights, then I shall fight you to the highest court in the land if it costs me every penny I have.' Meg stopped to draw breath. There, she had said it. Tam would be proud of her. She was proud of herself, for all her heart was pumping like a traction engine.

Kath simply stared at her, unblinking. 'I would like to see her now.'

Meg sat all day in the same place. She chose a corner of the dry stone wall that ran from the back of the house to the barn. From here she would get the first glimpse of the car returning up the lane without being seen herself. It had been the longest day in her life so far. She couldn't eat, she couldn't talk, she couldn't even think. Nothingness seemed to fill her mind and she wanted to go on feeling nothing, being nothing. It was less painful that way. The alternative, to consider what her life would be like without Lissa, without Tam, was too terrible for words.

Now that she was faced with losing everything she wondered at her own lack of ability to make a decision. She was decisive enough with the land, with the sheep. Why so vulnerable when it came to her own personal life?

She looked at her beloved land, how it had been lifted and tipped sideways as if by some playful giant's hand, causing rocks bigger than a house to slide and roll and settle in dangerous heaps. Her life felt like that, as if it were slipping out of control.

In her hand she held Lanky's Luckpenny. Usually she kept it safe, on her table in her room. Today she had felt the need of it by her. It was all foolish superstition, of course. She knew it. But somehow it helped. As if Lanky were still here with her, wishing her well, when she needed a friend.

At long last the little car came into view, bumping up the stony track into the farmyard. It pulled to a halt at the door and Lissa was out in a second, scampering towards Meg, her small face alight with excitement. Meg's heart shot through with pain. Did this joy mean that the day had gone well?

'What do you think, Meg, we saw some horses.'

'Did you, darling? Where was that?' Meg pulled stiff lips into a smile.

'We went to Appleby, to watch the harness racing. It was so exciting. Kath says I could perhaps have a pony of my own one day, when I'm old enough to look after it properly.' The cheeks were flushed pink, aquiver with delight. 'Wouldn't that be lovely, to have a pony of my own? Wade has plenty of horses in Canada, Kath says. He's a lawyer but wants to have a whole farm of them. Wouldn't that be grand?'

Meg was unable to speak for fear of it coming out all croaky.

Kath came to join them. 'I wasn't trying to bribe her,' she said. 'She could keep the pony here, if she wanted to. It would simply be a gift.'

'Here?' If she stays, Meg thought. If she isn't enticed away to Canada by stories of riches, and horses in plenty. Meg responded to Kath's warmth with coolness. 'I'm sure Tam would find her a pony when the time was right.'

'I suppose he would.' Kath's face looked suddenly haunted and she turned away, to gaze out over the mountains, and there was a new rigidity to the figure, a stiffness about the mouth that hadn't been there before. Meg turned to Lissa. 'Go inside, sweetheart. I think Sally Ann has your tea ready. I'll be in later.'

''Bye, Kath,' said Lissa. 'Wait till I tell Nick where I've been today. He'll be *green* with jealousy. 'Bye.' And she ran off, filled with eagerness to tell her tale.

When the kitchen door clanged shut, Meg faced Kath. 'Well? How did it go? You seem to have made a good impression.'

'Very well. She is a delightful child, Meg. You must be proud of her.'

'I am.'

'Do you mind if we walk a bit, away from the kitchen window? Show me your sheep, or whatever you are doing with Broombank. I've heard enough about them today.'

Meg tried a chuckle but it came out sounding forced and unnatural. 'I can believe it. Lissa loves the farm and is proving to be a great help already.' Everything she said sounded as if she were trying to make a point. One that Kath did not fail to miss.

'She loves the lambs best, she told me.'

'Yes.'

They walked for a while and Meg started to tell Kath, hesitantly at first, of her efforts to make a go of the farm. She told of how she had struggled with her first lambing season, helped by Effie. And the loyalty of Rust, at this very moment with his nose at Meg's heel, as usual.

She spoke of the obstinacy of the bank in refusing at first to give her a mortgage. 'Your father put in a word for me there. You'll be going to see him before you leave?'

'I-I hadn't decided.'

'I think you should. Your mother is as intransigent as ever, but your father ... Well, he'd really like to see you, Kath. In all these years he's never said a word against you, not once. And treading a path between you and your mother has not been easy for him.'

Kath laughed. 'I can well believe it.' She stared down for a moment, at her smart shining town shoes, unsuitable for stony sheep trods. 'All right, I'll call in. I'd like to see how they are.'

They reached the bend in the road where a stile into the field led down to Whinstone Gill and Kath gave a sad little smile. 'Do you remember that day when you found me sunbathing? Jack was hiding in the bushes. Rust realised it but you didn't.'

'I didn't see because I didn't want to see. There are no shades over my eyes now. And I hope I'm not quite so easy to take advantage of these days.'

'And I hope that I am not so selfish. I've certainly been at the receiving end of some malice myself in recent years.' Kath glanced at Meg's face. 'I hope you don't bear me any. I would like us to remain friends.'

There was a small, strained silence before Meg spoke. 'You betrayed me. Both of you. But I've put the pain behind me. All that matters to me is Lissa. She is the one good thing that has come out of all this. Lissa comes first now.'

A figure loomed suddenly on the path as a man lurched around the corner towards them.

'Well, if it isn't Madam Ellis herself.'

'Jack.'

'Not in uniform? Pity. It suited you. Same old Katherine back again. Done up to the nines as usual.'